The Golden One

Catherine Bowman

Note for Librarians: a cataloguing record for this book that includes
Dewey Decimal Classification and US Library of Congress numbers is
available from the Library and Archives of Canada. The complete
cataloguing record can be obtained from their online database at:
www.collectionscanada.ca/amicus/index-e.html
ISBN 978-0-9783483-3-5

Published in Canada by Soul Asylum Poetry
79 De La Salle Blvd, Jackson's Point, ON L0E 1L0
www.soulasylumpoetry.com
Cover Design: by Charles Ross and Kenneth William Cowle

Soul Asylum
Poetry and Publishing

10 9 8 7 6 5 4 3 2 1

Project Editor: Kenneth William Cowle
Cover Design: Charles Ross & Kenneth Cowle

CONTENTS

Foreword

The warmth of this tale is a delight seldom found ...
With the depth of research into the time of the story; this will be a
superb read for many; plus an introduction to a lady author of much talent.
The delightful "word paintings" will bring much of the flavour into
crystalline clarity to be savoured through being read and re-read.

The finesse of this work is surely the hallmark of Ms. Bowman's talent.
This review of The Golden One is a great joy for this editor,
with highest commendation to the publisher.

Tristram – Tara News

Acknowledgement

Many thanks to Marilyn Jennison for her editing skills and
to Raouf and Adam for their continued support.

Chapter 1
Babylon

It was early dawn, a sacred time. The Temple workers, the entus, naditu and insharitu gathered in the courtyard to praise Ishtar's transformation of night into day. When the first blush of light appeared, the priestesses' arms extended to the heavens to invoke the Goddess.

"Goodbye to the dark, goodbye to the night,

Awake; awake oh sacred Mother of the Dawn

Mother of All Living, O Shining One.

Rise in beauty from Your divine sleep

Be with us ever as our guided light

To You we pray that Your illuminating ways

Be with us through all the days of our lives

You who are our morning star

Praise to You O Lady of Light

Bless this our humble earth with Your beauty

Awake, awake Daughter of Light."

When the Goddess had completely awoken from Her divine sleep, dawn streaked across the sky. The priestesses lowered their arms and gradually made their way into the inner sanctum chanting:

"Daughter of Light,
Accept this our earthly offering of refreshment.
Praise Ishtar, the Mother Goddess,
The Queen of women, the greatest of all deities
Hear our prayers for fruitfulness and blessings on this the last day of Nisan.
Hail Oh Mother Goddess that we might rejoice at Your presence."

Ceelyha mouthed the sacraments with a tinge of guilt, knowing full well that it went against Temple teachings not to be fully present in mind, body and spirit when praising Ishtar. But it was an impossibility right now to focus on the washing and anointing of the Goddess with her mind on an upcoming meeting with her father. Ceelyha had a strong premonition that this holy week would be a turning point in her life. She was at an age when something would need to be decided about her future. He could not marry her off since she was about to be ordained as an Entu,

1

neither could he couple with her during the Sacred Marriage ceremony. Her fate lay in his hands and in the hands of the Gods. In her mind, there were no choices. All of her training, up to this point in her life, was leading her to be an Entu. She must trust in the divine bidding of the Goddess.

This was the time when magic flowed in her beloved city. Nisan had started in a flourish of activity. All the citizens of The Land of Two Rivers, from the lowest slave to the King, were united in their mission to ensure that over the next eleven days, the Gods received due attention. A successful outcome was needed for the Sacred Marriage. Both women and men meticulously applied cosmetics, awakened their senses in baths filled with exotic spices, dosed their skin with heady fragrances, donned fancy clothing and adorned their necks and hands with jewels. In the streets, they danced with complete abandonment toasting Ishtar and Marduk at every opportunity.

While the general population indulged in hedonistic activities, it fell upon the religious orders to perform the essential sacred duties. Ceelyha, along with the priestesses of Ishtar and the priests of Marduk, reverently prayed for prosperity, danced to the Gods, sang hymns of thanks with the accompaniment of the lyre and fasted on behalf of all the citizens to prove to the Gods that the chosen ones were pure of mind and body. As further homage, the statues of all the Gods in the Temples were washed and anointed. If the deities were pleased, they would generously bestow another year of prosperity on The Land of Two Rivers. Not only was this an important time for the general population and the religious community, but also it was personally significant for Ceelyha. It was the annual date when she had an audience with her father, the King. It was as if Nisan was the only time of year that he remembered having conceived a daughter ten and four years ago. Ceelyha dreaded meeting with him. She could not help but think that if an Entu playing the role of Ishtar and he, being a mortal representative of Marduk, did not have a successful coupling not only would all of Babylon suffer but her position might as well!

Ceelyha felt a stab of annoyance as her arm was jabbed by one of the priestess' who was trying to alert her it was time to stand. She was shocked to discover that the morning ritual was over. She reprimanded herself, *It is time to begin my duties. This is not the time for daydreaming.* As a priestess in training, a naditu, an oracular priestess, it was her responsibility to invoke the Goddess' energy for advice and counsel. This gift, bestowed upon her from birth, enabled her to foresee certain events. Along with her priestess training, she was adept at reading the smoky vapors of incense for divination purposes. This holy week was especially busy for her as the citizens were anxious to know their personal future for the coming year. She could sense the crowd milling about in the outer courtyard waiting for the Temple to open. For the rest of the morning, Ceelyha would be called upon to predict pregnancies, marriages, business deals and crop growth for various petitioners.

Later in the day, Nintu, Ceelyha's personal servant, who was just a season or two younger than Ceelyha, summoned her. "Lady, your Mother, Shiroka, has sent me. Her message is that you come to watch the festivities of the King as he journeys to the Sacred Marriage. You are expected to go directly to her balcony before we prepare for your meeting with the King."

Ceelyha hurried up the steps, past columns painted in the golds and blues of the Goddess with their elaborate designs of serpents, stars, moons and lions, through the shining marble hallways, past the Goddess' chamber, up the shiny stone steps and into her mother's rooms. She usually paused to admire the High Priestess' quarters with its lavishly appointed soft red couches, cushions, low tables, braziers and rugs but today, there was no time. The shutters were open so Ceelyha stepped onto the balcony in the afternoon sun. In the distance stood the Temple of Marduk's ziggurat, its mighty presence dwarfing the rest of the dwellings.

"Hello, my daughter. Come quickly! The procession has just started," called Shiroka.

The entire twelve days had been building up to this moment, when the Sacred Marriage would take place within the highest, most consecrated chamber of the ziggurat, the Gateway to the Gods. It was the most solemn and magical of all religious sacraments. It was through this ritual that fecundity and the power of the Goddess was honored, released, and channeled to the land and Her people. Its success was dependent on the King. He would bed the goddess in the living form of a priestess. It was hoped that the Gods would decree him capable of ruling The Land of Two Rivers for another year.

Ceelyha and her mother watched the King walk towards the Temple of Marduk. Behind him were several carts bearing offerings of oil, precious spices and foods that would be offered to the Gods. The crowds, that surrounded the procession, chanted sacred erotic hymns to create a highly charged atmosphere of sexual anticipation. Amid cheers, the King disappeared into the highest chamber of the ziggurat. It was here that he would consummate the marriage and ensure the prosperity of the land. Ceelyha turned to her mother and sarcastically asked, "Who is the lucky priestess this year?"

Shiroka sent her a withering look. "It is Nanab. She has been chosen to represent the Goddess. Come, now let us start to get you ready."

The women hurried to the rooms housed beside Shiroka's chambers. As a daughter of the King, Ceelyha's royal status of princess, afforded her luxuries that the other novices did not have. Their simple cells were in the lower part of the Temple while hers was in the Temple proper. They slept on pallets while she had a comfortable divan with wall hangings and a personal servant to attend to her every need.

It seemed like the preparations were endless. Ceelyha felt powerless while Shiroka ordered the slaves and Nintu to bathe and anoint her body with the Goddess's scent of myrrh. Under the guidance of her mother, slaves braided her long black hair, which was then sparingly oiled with precious lotus oil that had been brought from Egypt. Flecks of gold scented with a special mixture of cassia and bergamot, that Shiroka personally supervised the making of, were applied to add effect. Cinnabar was dabbed on her cheeks to augment her delicate face before pomegranate juice was rubbed onto her lips to make them appear full. Her eyes were outlined in kohl to enhance their emerald depths before a malachite paste was applied to the lids.

While Shiroka motioned for Ceelyha to raise her arms for a slave to drop the long, scented diaphanous white shift over her head, Ceelyha said, "Mother, I have a feeling of dread about this meeting. It is not something that I look forward to."

The pungent smell of myrrh hovered in the air as the white sheath fell in a whisper, clinging sensuously to her budding figure.

"Have you consulted the oracles?" asked a distracted Shiroka as she expertly arranged the blood red belt, the symbol of the Goddess, around her daughter's slender waist.

While tiny gold anklelets with charms of snakes and goats were fastened on her slim ankles, Ceelyha replied, "The Goddess was not with me when I last tried. Do you think she has forsaken me?"

Shiroka stared with astonishment at her child. "Now, Ceelyha, you know that is not possible. You were chosen at the time of your conception to be Her servant. Have you not been given the gift of sight and healing?" Shiroka did not wait for an answer. "She has not forsaken you, it is just that She does not wish you to know your destiny yet."

While her mother fussed with the lines of her sheath, Ceelyha reflected on her life as a priestess. As a young child, she had asked why she needed to train to be the Goddess's servant when she could easily live a life of luxury and leisure as a princess in the Palace. Her mother had sternly replied that her life was not meant to take that direction! The Goddess had picked her out from all the others to be Her chosen daughter to channel the ways of the Immortals to the mortals. When Ceelyha had asked why 'her', Shiroka had retorted that only the Goddess could answer that. It was not up to mortals to question why. A priestess knows when she has been called. She had explained that it is the Gods who choose their servants and not mortals choosing them. Since that day, Ceelyha had channeled all her energy into perfecting the Goddess's bestowed gifts of healing and divination. She had particularly worked hard to hone her talents to predict others' futures through reading the smoky vapor of burning incense.

Ceelyha was brought back to the present when, as a finishing touch, Nintu placed around Ceelyha's upper arm, the sign of the Priestess – a pewter cobra bracelet with eyes of turquoise – a gift from her Egyptian Grandmother. Then, a white veil was draped over her head.

"Here," Ceelyha detected the astonishment in her mother's eyes as she critically viewed her daughter, "Put on these sandals and then off you go. The coupling of the King and Priestess should be finished by now."

Ceelyha anxiously held up a silver mirror only to gasp when she saw her transformation from a young girl to a woman. "Mother, I look more like a bride than a daughter!"

Shiroka had a wistful, sad look in her brown eyes. Ceelyha intuited that her mother was mourning the loss of her youth and appeal to the King. Over ten years ago, her mother had been the chosen one to represent the Goddess and couple with the King. She had magically conceived Ceelyha on that day. For many months, it appeared that the King considered himself quite Godlike and that she, Shiroka, was the living representative of Marduk's Goddess wife, Sarpanitu. The King had showered attention and gifts upon Shiroka until he realized that she could not conceive again. It had been several years since she had even had any direct contact with him. To Ceelyha, it seemed that he was much too busy with his young wives and concubines to bother with an aging priestess. This situation bothered Ceelyha probably more than it did her mother. At this moment, she longed to hold and comfort her mother but sensed that both of them would end up in tears if she made the attempt. Instead, she cleared her throat and asked, "Will the King be as I remembered him from last year?"

Shiroka sighed, "When I last saw him from afar, it looked as if he too had aged. Politics and wars have not been kind to him."

"Why must I go? I see no need to have an audience with him especially since I have been made up to look like one of the Temple quadishtu!" Her tone was one of defiance.

"You know quite well that he receives you at this time every year! His command must be adhered to." Shiroka's response was full of impatience. "And, both the Goddess and Marduk will it." She turned to her daughter's trusted servant and confident, " Now, Nintu escort my daughter to the Palace! See that no harm comes to her."

The two girls left the sanctuary of The Ishtar Temple on a brightly coloured palanquin carried by four strong slaves and entered the crowded winding streets full of revelers. The citizens appeared to be having great fun as they searched for Marduk who was held prisoner in the underworld. If he were not brought up to the earth, then the land would not prosper, so mock battles were reenacted between his detainees and rescuers. People pretended to kill one another, screaming and laughing with the sport of it. Delicious smells of baking breads and cakes for the God wafted through the open windows of humble brick houses. Further along in the marketplace, they detected the heady smell of burning frankincense, saw the slightly decaying fruits and colourful exotic spices. The smell of humans and animals mingled together to add to the magic of the city. The allure of honey, dates, fruits, cakes and other special holiday treats at the makeshift stalls were a temptation.

5

Ceelyha was about to call to the slaves to slow down so she could enjoy the festivities more, when the presence of the Goddess suddenly came upon her. Faces of
the clowns, dancers, musicians and merrymakers became blurred. Their songs and
shouts vibrated noisily in her head. The music of cymbals, lyres and drums flowed
around her.

The entire marketplace turned into a sea of colour as servants, slaves, masters
and royalty in all their finery became one with the sights, sounds and tastes of the
festivities. A high pitched buzzing resounded in her ears like the sound of angry
hornets, her body temperature dropped and the wings of the Goddess surrounded
her. She sensed her own energy field expanding upward and outward as the
Goddess moved into her consciousness. Then, as suddenly as the sensation had
come upon her, it receded, leaving her cold and feeling alone. Ceelyha clutched her
hands over her heart. This was a warning from the Goddess! Whenever she felt Her
wings surround her, it was a forewarning. Now she understood! She was seeing
everything for the last time! Nothing in her life would ever be the same again! A
sob caught in her throat and she bit her lip to prevent the tears that threatened to
fall. Her training overruled her personal feelings and she thanked the Goddess for
coming and took a few deep breaths before she was able to bring herself back to
the present. Ceelyha was about to tell Nintu, who was too mesmerized by the street
activities to be aware of what had just occurred, when she saw that they were
almost at the Sacred Passageway. The massive tall square towers of the Ishtar gate
were just ahead. Ceelyha's lips involuntarily formed a small smile of pleasure, her
earlier upset momentarily pushed aside. The view of the magnificently coloured
glazed tiles that depicted the sacred bulls of Adad and the dragons of Marduk on its
deep blue background momentarily overruled her upset.

But she was not yet fully skilled in the art of surrendering her emotions as her
mood quickly altered once more with the depressing realization, *I will never see
these magnificent gates!* The tears held earlier back, threatened to flow, but she
kept them in check with the possibility of how utterly humiliated she would feel at
the Palace with her face covered in smears.

Up ahead, the palace loomed with swarms of intimidating looking guards holding long, sharp spears against their shoulders to protect King Eulma-Shakin Shuki.
Ceelyha noted that the crowds of merrymakers disbursed as the palanquin came
abruptly to a stop.

The women were escorted to the throne room through the Palace with its rich
wood paneling inlaid with ivory and lapis. Its walls were more of the same deep
lapis blue tiles as the Ishtar gate but were decorated with lions, palm trees, dragons
and mountain goats. Ceelyha admired the opulence of the room's wall hangings of
gold threads interwoven with bright crimson scenes of dragons and snakes. Its
stucco ceiling was so high that it seemed to reach into the heavens. She quickly
glanced at her father as she was led into the Great Room.

He looks pleased with himself, she thought. *The coupling must have gone well. Perhaps my audience will be uneventful and all this foreboding was for nothing.* She mentally prayed to the Great Lady that no matter what the outcome, she might be given the grace and dignity to handle her emotions. The King sat on a high gold throne on top of a dais in the far corner while various courtiers and officials milled about. A bored overweight eunuch sat cross-legged to the King's left wearing yellow pantaloons. Her father was robed in a purple tunic embroidered with golden dragons, the symbol of Jupiter. It was fastened over one shoulder with a jeweled clip, which left the other shoulder showing aging muscles. The ruby studded belt did little to hide a protruding belly. He wore a simple gold tiara on a balding head. His long sharp nose reminded Ceelyha of a hawk. His bulky short neck was almost completed covered with a necklace emblazoned with glossy blue lapis stones. To Ceelyha, only his eyes were an attractive attribute – a bright sea green, like her own, that seemed to hold amusement at the sight of his daughter. As she prostrated herself, he fingered his tightly curled beard, releasing a spicy scent that Ceelyha did not particularly like. She tried to conceal her reaction to him as he spoke.

"Rise up my child." His deep voice was full of arrogance and authority. When he raised both his arms in a formal greeting, the gold bracelets surrounding his plump wrists clanged together. Ceelyha stood up and nervously adjusted her gown as he spoke with what seemed to her a touch of sarcasm.

"I see that since our last meeting, you have taken the slender rather sensuous build of your mother. I wonder if there is anything of me in you...." He seemed lost in the past as he motioned for Ceelyha to lift the thin veil from her head. He gasped, reached out to touch her face then withdrew as if he had forgotten himself. Ceelyha automatically lowered her eyes. Once more in control of himself, he continued. "Ah, you have her Egyptian black hair...yes; you have the Babylonian fairness of skin combined with her darkness to give you almost a honey colour." This observation seemed to please him.

"Now, look up child!" he demanded.

Ceelyha reluctantly raised her eyes. Tiny shivers surged through her body as her Priestess training took over. She felt his need for power, his thirst for blood and war, his craving for eroticism and excess.

"Ah, yes, the almond shaped eyes..." He peered closer. but yours are green with amber flecks"

This is my father; he cannot remember me from his other children. No wonder I do not feel a bond or commonality with him, she thought with disgust.

His thick lips curled up in a sneer as if he were reading her mind. "Well, let us hope that you have my ambition!"

Ceelyha nervously played with the ties on her red girdle and answered in almost a whisper. "Yes, your majesty, I have great ambitions. I wish to be an Entu like my mother, Shiroka."

"Ah, another Whore of Babylon! Well, well that is indeed an admirable ambition!" A loud sarcastic laugh escaped from his lips. The courtiers, within hearing distance, of the throne, duly laughed to humour their King before he dismissed their forced merriment with his bejeweled hand. His looks hardened and he dramatically whispered, "Well, we cannot have me coupling with you by mistake at the Sacred Marriage Ceremony, now can we?"

Temporarily Ceelyha lost her courage, repulsed at even the idea of lying with her father or any male for that matter. She took a deep breath hoping to restore her façade of indifference.

He motioned to his eunuch. "Arrange for the child to have the priests read her fortune. Have her mother present as well. Then give the child some gold and silver. See that she is taken care of." With that, the eunuch slowly rose then gestured to his Majesty's daughter. Ceelyha bowed as a sign of obeying while fighting back angry tears of humiliation. *How dare he treat me as if I were a commoner!* She could not get out of the palace quickly enough.

With a tray of dates and honey cakes, Shiroka sat beside Ceelyha in the privacy of her chambers. She pressed her daughter to take some nourishment for the time of fasting had ended. Ceelyha told her how formidably haughty her father had been and how he had little regard or emotion for her. She did not share with her mother the energy that she had picked up from him. She hoped that she not inherited any of his undesirable traits. She tried to appease herself that she had her mother's kindness and generosity rather than his ruthless disregard for anyone but himself.

Shiroka, as if she picked up on her daughter's thoughts, reached over, pulled her closer on the divan and gave her a warm hug.

"Never mind him; he played just a small part in the Goddess' plan. Look at how wonderful you have turned out!"

The tenderness and closeness of her mother, after the distant coldness of her father, was the catalyst that finally allowed the tears that had been threatening all day to flow. Shiroka held her until the sobs ceased. When she was once more in control of her emotions, Ceelyha begged her mother to tell her the story again of what happened between her father and mother. "How did you get chosen to be with him and were you ever attracted to him?" She seemed to require reassurance that her mother had not willingly gone to the King.

Shiroka sighed and with a far away look in her eyes began to tell her story.

"Ceelyha, as you know, my mother was not only a descendant of the Pharaoh Amenhotep but was also a priestess in Egypt at the Temple of Isis. When the soldiers from Mesopotamia ravaged her Temple, they brought her here to The Land of Two Rivers. She was to be sold into slavery, but one of the Ishtar priestesses had a vision from the Great Lady to go to the slave market to seek out your grandmother. Her regal air and powers were quickly recognized even though she was half starved and clothed in filthy rags. The priestess bought and freed her on the condition that she would become a priestess of Ishtar. I never knew who my father was as she was one of the Temple Priestess' that became a Holy Harlot, a qadishtu."

Ceelyha knew that as Ishtar priestesses, some of the women served as vehicles of the Goddess' creativity through the sexual union with men. Like the Goddess, her grandmother had enjoyed many lovers.

Shiroka continued, "When I was born, the omens decreed that I was to be brought up, as you have been, to be an Entu and I was to be coupled with the King because of my royal blood. The greatest honor an Entu could have is to be chosen to enact the Sacred Marriage. I was not much older than you." She paused, deep in thought before she continued.

"King Eulma-Shakin Shuki was not old, fat and repulsive at that time. He was quite handsome with fair hair and powerful muscles. And yes, to answer of your earlier question, I was attracted to him. It would not have mattered what our mortal feelings were for one another. He was Marduk the Great Father and I, Ishtar the Great Mother and together we gave birth to our God son Nabu, which was you! Not many priestesses conceive from that reenactment but the Goddess was generous and needed a vehicle for Her greatness here on earth, which happens to be you, my daughter Ceelyha. King Eulma-Shakin Shuki sent many generous gifts when you were born and we were lovers for a while. So you see, you are a very special gift from the Goddess. Her mark is upon you and that is why you are so skilled in Her arts. As long as you are true to Her, your talents will never leave you."

"Thank you mother for repeating that story for me. I needed to hear it one last time." Then her voice dropped to almost a whisper and she almost choked on her words.

"We have been ordered to the Temple to learn of my future. The King has decreed it."

"I was expecting this, answered her mother in earnest." "Has the Goddess contacted you yet?"

"What do you know about it? What has the Goddess told you?" demanded an anxious Ceelyha.

"It is not important now. What the Fates have cast cannot be undone. The Gods do as they please."

Chapter 2
The Prophecy

It was time. A Marduk messenger arrived to announce that the baru was ready to read the omens. The question of 'What is my daughter's destiny?' had already been written on a clay tablet by one of the King's scribes and had been set before Marduk's statue. A sheep, sacrificed under last night's full moon, had its entrails waiting on a golden tray.

The two women had carefully prepared themselves by fasting since sun up and by dressing in honour of their status as servants of Ishtar. Ceelyha wore a plain white linen shift of the naditu covered by a mantle in her favorite colour of cobalt blue. Her hair was plaited; her face scrubbed free of any cosmetics. Compared to her earlier outing to the Palace, she felt plain and innocent especially beside her mother who had taken great care to garb herself in the tradition of a High Priestess. Even the haughty messenger from the Marduk Temple had bowed in reverence seeming to sense her power. Shiroka looked timeless and immortal in a thin white gossamer gown with its interwoven delicate threads of gold which had been imported from the Land of Egypt. The dress was covered by an overcoat of a heavier material trimmed along the seams with the Goddess's symbols of iridescent silver snakes. A black plaited, straight- bang wig was crowned with a golden cobra circlet bejeweled with a colourful array of stones. Malachite paint and kohl heightened the brown of her eyes and around her neck hung the silver amulet of Ishtar, an eight pointed star encircled with the symbol of a snake with flashing lapis eyes.

The narrow stone passageway between the Temple of Ishtar and the shrine of Bel Marduk was empty at this hour. Most of the temple workers, along with the citizens of Babylon, were out in the market streets celebrating the last night of Nisan. As the two women, followed the torchlight of their guide, Ceelyha reached back and clutched Shiroka's hand.

"You don't need to be so afraid!" hissed Shiroka as she continued to walk.

Ceelyha released her grip to clutch her mantle closer to her shivering body then spoke in earnest with a weak voice, "I cannot seem to stop my unruly thoughts. I need your strength. I fear the Goddess has forsaken me."

Shiroka stopped to look at her daughter with astonishment. In a reprimanding tone she asked, "What are you talking about? The Lady never leaves! You of all people should know that."

Shiroka's features faded in the darkness as the guide left them behind. Ceelyha struggled to fully express her fears. "You don't understand, Mother. I have been plagued by visions from the Goddess that I am unable to understand. For many moons, I have dreamt of a man, a great large man of olive skin and black curly hair that has the eyes of a God but the soul of a man. He wears linens that are not from The Land of Two Rivers and has even spoken to me in a language that is of a foreign tongue! I know that my destiny is tied in with his, but the Goddess has not given me enough information to...."

Shiroka interrupted, "Perhaps you are not yet ready to know what fate She has in store for you. The Gods work in mysterious ways." In a softer tone she added, "And why did you not share this with me before? Perhaps I could have helped you uncover the meaning of all of this."

Ceelyha sensed the hurt in Shiroka's voice. "Mother, not even you can save me from what has already been decided. Until the day that I was on my way to meet the King, I had not given my visions much credibility; but while in the marketplace the Goddess descended. I believe She was trying to inform me that I was seeing my beloved city's festival for the last time!" She choked on these last words. Shiroka reached out and squeezed her daughter's hand in sympathy and support but did not speak.

The guide, realizing he had temporarily lost the women, retraced his steps. Then the three of them entered the sacred precincts of Lord Marduk's Temple. Sputtering flames from many lamplights cast shadows of palm trees on the high walls of the courtyard. A patrol of guards with their long spears held carelessly over their broad shoulders passed by, laughing and talking about the Festival. Up ahead loamed the entrance to the Shrine, flanked by a row of lion and dragon statues. Suddenly, Shiroka stopped walking, forcing her daughter and the now cautious guide to do the same. She closed her eyes, fingered the silver chain that held her amulet and began to invoke the presence of the Goddess. The guide immediately held his torch over the priestess. Ceelyha watched as her mother's face transformed into absolute serenity and youthfulness as she began to take on a luminescent glow. The Goddess had become one with her. Then, as quickly as the magic had come upon her, it left; and Shiroka nonchalantly resumed walking.

"Mother, what did the Goddess say to you? What happened?" cried an anxious Ceelyha.

"Not, now, my daughter," Shiroka motioned with her eyes that they were not alone and the disappointed guide carried on with his walking. They entered a low door and moved through a dim passage into an inner court. Ceelyha looked in awe at gigantic alabaster pillars decorated with the God's sacred animals, reaching up to a replica of the night sky with its simulated planets and stars glittering with quartz and other sparking stones. Painted dogs, dragons and mountain goats with red rubies for eyes, adorned the walls. Spewing water fountains and lush green plants added to the opulence of the sanctuary. But before she could get a good look at the bronze and silver statutes of the lesser Gods, their guide gestured for his charges to enter an arched doorway at the end of the courtyard.

The messenger retreated. The door slammed shut with a finality that startled an already nervous Ceelyha. It took a few moments before her eyes adjusted to the darkness of the cell. The smoking torches on the soot darkened walls, the brazier with the scent of burning hyssop and the stench of rotting meat added to her sense of foreboding. Her attention was drawn to a low murmuring like the sound of buzzing flies in front of her. Then she saw the King's own personal diviner, the baru, ominously cloaked in a dark hooded cape, whispering sacred spells over the remains of a dead sheep. She felt intimidated as he blatantly ignored their presence as they respectfully knelt before him. *He has no right to treat us in this manner. Our status is equal to his!* When Shiroka discreetly coughed, he curtly glanced up from his standing position in front of a high altar. Ceelyha thought she saw its faded tapestry of stars and moons faintly move. Before she could have a better look, the baru nodded his head to acknowledge their presence then turned back to the altar to further examine the entrails on a large golden platter. For a few seconds, not a sound was heard. As Ceelyha nervously reached down to clutch her mother's hand, she noted another stirring beneath the tapestry. Then the baru began his prophecy in a deep, monotone. The cell seemed to vibrate with a powerful energy that was foreign to Ceelyha.

"Oh Marduk, Lord of the Almighty, answer the matter into which our mighty ruler, Eulma-Shakin Shuki has enquired. From this day, the twelfth, of the Festival of Nisan, what is our lady Ceelyha's destiny?" He stood eyes closed, blood dripping down the sleeves of his robe as he raised parts of the sheep's organs high above his head.

"Allow me, as Your servant, to decipher Your answer on the entrails of this animal," he ordered.

For what seemed like an eternity, Ceelyha anxiously awaited her fate, feeling more than the cold from the stone floor wrack through her kneeling body. Finally the Baru spoke in a loud and peremptory voice that made the hairs on her arms stand up, "It is decreed that she shall leave The Land of Two Rivers and travel to the Land of the tribes of Israel. It is here that she shall fulfill her destiny as Priestess and advisor to the one that is making a great name for himself."

Her bowels turned into water; her knees weakened; panic rose. Her fate was cast. *No, this cannot be what is to happen to me! To go and live in a land I have never heard of? And who is this person that I am to advise?* It was all too much to deal with. She began a frantic silent prayer to Ishtar.

"Oh, Lady, Exalted Mother. Have you forsaken me? Have I erred against You? Please stop this madness and let me stay here in Your blessed Temple to do Your holy work!" In her confusion, she did not hear the soft nurturing reply of the Goddess. Instead, it was the voice of Marduk roughly speaking through her father's husky voice. "It is decreed my child. As soon as you become an Entu, you will depart to the Land of the foreigners. You will go and will fulfill that to which you agreed before coming into this lifetime. Both the God and Goddess have spoken. It shall be done."

King Eulma-Shakin Shuki had been hiding beneath the altar!

Her world went black.

Chapter 3
The Sacred Passage

Four full moons later, just before the blush of dawn, Ceelyha lay awake and reflected on how far she had come since fainting in the Shrine. After extensive conversations with her mother, intense praying and soul searching, Ceelyha embraced her destiny.

Initially Shiroka had empathized with her daughter's distress. Her advice was "Of course, it is only human to feel the emotions that you do now and you should take the time to honour those." But when Ceelyha was still unable to pull herself out of misery, that motherly concern was quickly replaced with reproach. With the authority of the High Priestess, Shiroka admonished Ceelyha. "When the sadness, self pity, pain and anger are spent, remember your mystical power lies in the knowingness that you are not of this world and therefore you need not surrender to its demands. This world is but an illusion and not your true reality. The only true reality for you is to align with the Goddess. Ask Her to take your pain away and to light the way for you."

Shiroka cautioned her daughter to be careful to never become powerless in times of adversity. She was to visualize such situations as being embraced by the Goddess's light. Shiroka also reminded Ceelyha that as a young priestess in training, one of the fundamental teachings was to be a sacred channel through which the power of the Goddess continuously flows. This energy is then to be extended, in whatever form needed, to all who have need of it, including herself.

Ceelyha had listened carefully to these words of wisdom then questioned why it seemed that she could not recall the teachings when she most needed them the most. Her mother's words of wisdom were that she was still young and inexperienced. Only time and devotion would cure that.

Ceelyha was still wounded from her reaction to the oracle. She spent the next few weeks between fasting and prayer in order to establish a closer link with the Goddess and to reflect on all the Temple teachings. She released her pain, grief and humiliation to the Goddess. When she sensed that she was once again in control of her emotions, she had immersed herself in the final teachings in preparation to become an Entu. Countless hours were spent asking questions to her superiors, studying and practicing her craft.

She stretched her arms above her head and smiled. This was the most important day of her life. Today, she would join the ranks of the other Babylonian servants of Ishtar. All of her training and experiences to date were in preparation for her to take the Sacred Vows. She felt honoured and yet at the same time humbled that that Ishtar had chosen her as an earthly vehicle to channel energy to heal the sick, to assist with childbirth, to read the omens, to translate divine symbols, to ensure the fertility of crops and to interpret dreams. The list of responsibilities was so overwhelming that it forced Ceelyha out of her comfortable, warm divan. She knelt on the cold stone floor at the foot of the statue of Her Lady positioned on a raised dais and prayed:

"Thank you, O Lady of the Moon, for keeping the nightmares of the night at bay. Guide me that I may become a worthy vehicle to carry out Your sacred work. Grant me the strength and powers I will need to fulfill Your work…" She stopped and waited, as she had been trained, for the familiar buzzing sound in her ears, the blurring of her vision and her energy field to alter with a slightly disorienting feeling. There it was! Excited, she sat up and smiled with inner knowing as the Goddess's energy descended upon her.

A compassionate yet powerful voice spoke inside her mind. *"I am pleased my child that you have chosen the way of the Goddess. I am with you at all times. Blessings be with you on this."*

"Thank you O Lady for gracing me with your presence, I shall not fail you," Ceelyha graciously replied aloud. The room suddenly felt cold and empty as the Goddess's energy retreated. Ceelyha sighed and went about her toilet and dressing. She quickly splashed water over her hands and face as the shaking of the sistrums beckoned the priestesses to the early morning tribute to Ishtar. She ran from her room along the dimly lit corridors and greeted the others with a nod as they too hurried to gather in the great hall to praise Ishtar. The priestesses, in plain white tunics, formed a line on either side of the hall to await the entrance of the High Priestess. Music from harps and sistrums announced the temple dancers. They swirled veils of deep magenta - the colour of the Goddess - clashed their brass symbols to awaken the Lady and gracefully made their way to the inner sanctum. Shiroka, the High Priestess, began her entry holding the tray of nourishment for the Goddess. Ceelyha thought her mother had never looked lovelier. Her slightly graying black hair that hung loosely down to her waist in natural waves was crowned with a golden diadem inlaid with tiny lapis lazuli stones and its protruding snake. The lapis coloured designs of snakes and moons on her tunic shimmered as they caught the light from strategically placed torches situated along the walls. Her heavily kohled eyes glowed with peace and inner wisdom as she regally made her way behind the dancers.

I hope that I can have the grace and inner beauty of my mother when I too am a high priestess in the land of the foreigners, she thought as she followed the priestesses who silently fell into line behind their Entu.

Shiroka laid her tray of cakes and cup of wine in front of the covered statue while another priestess discarded last evening's food. Then Shiroka vigilantly removed the veil that had been placed over the Goddess at the evening ritual and lit a nearby torch to awaken the Mother. Everyone fell to her knees chanting.

"Lady of the Morning, we greet You with praise and love

When sleep has ended, You are there to help us greet the day.

We sing our praises to You and bring our concerns to Your holiness.

Protect us from all that is evil;

Destroy those that are wicked;

Look with kindness upon those that serve You.

Oh, blessings to us, Lady of the Morning."

When the ritual was completed, Ceelyha walked into the outer courtyard with her mother while the others went off to have the usual morning fare of barley cakes, fish, honey and pomegranates. Both women were fasting to prepare their bodies and spirits for the evening's Divine Ceremony. Ceelyha thought Shiroka looked tired in the brightness of the morning sun, different from the time when the Goddess was upon her. She hesitantly asked, "You did not sleep well, Mother?" as she led her mother to a private bench which was shaded by an almond tree in full bloom. As they sat down, both women took a moment to inhale its sweet fragrance before Shiroka replied.

"No, I have been thinking about many things." She paused as if testing whether or not her daughter was capable of hearing what was on her mind.

"You need not hold things back from me," Ceelyha intuited. "We have not much time left as it is."

Shiroka sighed, "Tonight will be one of the most glorious affairs in your life. Since you were a small child, everything has been leading up to this moment. You have had the best teachers and have worked hard to become an Entu." She sighed and clasped her ringed hands together as if to give herself strength before she continued. "I pray that I have prepared you for what is ahead! It displeases me greatly that you will not know anyone where you are going!" Then she turned and faced her daughter as she spoke with resignation, "These people are not like us. They believe in one god,"

"Yahweh!" Ceelyha's voice broke in. Over the past few months, she had been gathering snippets of information from speaking with servants, slaves and anyone within the Temple confines that had any knowledge about the foreign land she was about to depart for.

Yahweh was the name for the Israelites one and only God. The priest caste of that land was very much against Goddess worship, but the common folk still need a Mother God.

Ceelyha was well aware that there were many names for the feminine God. In the land of her grandmother came from, She was called Isis, while the Israelis name Her

Asherah. She had learned that Asherah was not as popular as She once was and not always worshipped openly, but the ancestors' beliefs were still respected by most of the citizens of Israel.

Shiroka continued. "You will probably be called upon to aid mostly women and children. You will be asked for herbal potions to bring on menses, for assistance with birthing, and for omen reading; all that you have done here in The Land of Two Rivers. But be cautioned, there will be many who will fear and even hate you for being a foreigner and worshipping what they call a pagan god. For this open hostility, I fear I have not prepared you."

Her mother's fearful look dissolved as Ceelyha answered with resolve "I will have the protection of Ishtar, Mother."

Shiroka smiled a knowing smile as she reached out to hold her daughter. It was with a slight tremble in her voice that she replied, "Yes, Ceelyha, you will have that."

Still holding her child, Shiroka continued, "And as further assistance, I sent a message to a sister Temple in Dor. The priestess there is expecting you. She will take you into her care and protection. Not only will you learn the ways of Asherah but will teach the priestesses about ours. It will be a perfect exchange!" Shiroka released her daughter.

With a brave voice Ceelyha replied, "I will not disappoint you, the King or the Goddess," Ceelyha sounded convincing even to herself. She did not want her mother to worry unduly about her daughter. "But what can you tell me about their land?"

"I do know that they are not at peace. They have wars with the Philistines and from what I have heard, there is much infighting among the tribes." She shook her head in disdain. "They are just not as civilized as we are. I doubt they have the riches and comforts of our country." She paused then her eyes lit up with excitement, "Now, my beautiful priestess, it is time for you to begin your preparations for this evening. Away you go!"

With bittersweet feelings of sadness at leaving her mother and home combined with excitement and anticipation of the unknown, Ceelyha went back to her quarters. She was grateful that her mother was able to use her powers to delay her departure. Her magic had caused the King's assistants to be unable to immediately find a suitable caravan travelling west; enabling enough time to complete the necessary steps to allow her to become an Entu.

The halls of the Temple seemed dark and dusty after the freshness of the morning. As she entered her room, Ceelyha found Nintu kneeling among the open chests carefully wrapping stones, crystals, vials of scents, various statues of the Goddess and the medicine box in protective cloth. Folded garments lay on the bed, in preparation for packing. Nintu raised her face in greeting, her big round brown eyes filled with the glossy residue of tears.

"Oh, Lady, how will we ever get through this? I cannot believe we are departing! How can we leave all that we have ever known to travel into a land of barbarians? What will happen to us?" she wailed.

Ceelyha hugged her reassuringly. "Do not fret my friend, The Lady will guide and take care of us." She then proceeded to assist her servant.

The rest of the day flew by. After helping Nintu, two of the Temple's naditu came to take Ceelyha to the river for purification. It was required that she too be pure of body as well as spirit. Where the Temple stood, a portion of the Euripides had been channeled off to make a small pool. Over the years palm trees had grown around the area, making it a private haven, away from the curious eyes of the river vessel passengers. Several vases with long spouts stood on the steps that led down to the river some filled with water and others with oils, all of which had been blessed by the High Priestess.

The naditu helped Ceelyha remove her shift and sandals. Hyssop and other purifying herbs were tossed into the pond. As she entered the coolness of the water, she wondered what the bathing ritual would be like in Dor. From what her mother had said, she did not think that she would have a pool such as this. Then to rid herself of that distressing thought, she dived into its green depths with total surrender. When she felt that she had emptied herself of any feelings that did not serve Her, trepidation over the upcoming journey, the separation from her mother, the lack of communication with her father, sadness over leaving her beloved city, unworthiness of her talents, and the uncertainty of her future, Ceelyha returned to the steps and stood half submerged while the waiting priestesses poured water over her head from the sacred vessels. As they carried out this ritual, Ceelyha imaged hundreds of tiny ankhs, symbols of fresh life, entering her body and energy field. She chanted a prayer of thanks before exiting the water. The girls wrapped her in sheets of cotton and motioned for her to sit on the steps. They then carefully anointed her hands and feet in sweet smelling lotus oil. Her hair was braided close to her head to allow for a wig that she would wear later. Cosmetics were artfully applied to her face. Finally when Ceelyha was clothed in a clean tunic, she went to meditate in front of the Statute of Isis until it was time for the divine passage. When she was summoned, Ceelyha entered the sanctuary door with as much grace and dignity as she could conjure carrying a single lamp, a symbol of light. *My entire life has been in preparation for this!* Never, as a naditu, had she been allowed in this part of the Temple. The alabaster pillars with carved vines appeared to reach the heavens instead of supporting an arched ceiling painted with stars of the night sky. The floor tiles, inlaid with intricate designs of lapis, felt reassuringly solid beneath the bare soles of her feet. The cloying scent of frankincense and cedar, mixed with the low chant of the entus, added to the ambiance of sacredness. Ceelyha's heart fluttered when she saw all the priestesses in white flowing robes begin to assemble in a circle around the statue of the Goddess. The sacred eternal flame, that always burned in front of the womb of the Goddess, flickered vitality onto the bronze life-sized statue of Ishtar that stood out sharply in the center of the room. The Goddess held her arms out with a writhing snake in each hand. Her ample breasts, which symbolized the Mother, were bared. A golden girdle, intricately carved with Her sacred animals – goats, lambs and birds – encircled her waist. The rest of the Ishtar idol was clad in a layered metal dress etched with entwining snakes. Serpents rose up from her hips to outline the sides of her body to wrap around her neck. On her head was a gem-encrusted tiara that glowed in the lamplight.

From somewhere in the room, came the steady beat of a lone drum. The sea of white robes immediately parted as Ceelyha approached the Goddess. From the crowd, Shiroka stepped forward and prostrated before the Goddess while Ceelyha knelt behind her, placing her lamp on the floor.

It seemed that the statue spoke as one of the priestesses channeled the voice of the Goddess. "I am the Mother of All, queen of life, queen of the dead, the stars and the light of the world. We welcome you to this circle of light. How may I be of service tonight?'

Shiroka answered, "I bring one with me who has studied Your magic and seeks to become one with You."

The channeler spoke, "Of whom do you speak?"

"I speak of my own daughter, Ceelyha, who waits here behind me, seeking entry into your mysteries."

"Who has caused her to seek Me?"

"She is following her destiny as it was willed by Yourself,

O Light of the World."

"What is it she seeks?"

"She seeks to become one with You in mind, body and spirit."

"Who can vouch for her?"

"I can as her mother, teacher and guide. I have shown her Your ways and have kept her on Your path."

"Then have her come forward."

Shiroka stood, then stepped back motioning to Ceelyha to come forward.

Another priestess spoke"Welcome to your ordination. It is time to assume your official duties as High Priestess. Do you, Ceelyha, seek to devote yourself to the work of Ishtar? Do you, Ceelyha, vow to remain true to Ishtar even though you may be exposed to other deities who may try to attract you? Do you vow, even with the threat of death, that you shall not revoke your devotion to the Goddess? Do you vow that even when persons try to persuade you to renounce the Goddess that you will not abandon your resolve? Do you pledge that even when the

Goddess appears to not be present, to uphold Her beliefs and persevere in spite of adversity? Are you willing to take on all the responsibilities that being a servant of Ishtar entails?"

Ceelyha bowed before the statue of the Goddess and relayed the words that she had carefully rehearsed over the past few days.

"Lady of peace, I humbly stand before You to accept the vows of a priestess. I devote myself to You and Your work only. I shall not worship or honour any other deities but You. I shall never denounce my faith even in the face of death. I shall turn a deaf ear to those who wish to persuade me to abandon Your ways. I willingly take on all the responsibilities and demands that will be placed upon me as Your servant."

"Then it is done. Pick up your lamp and always remember you are My light on this plane of existence. Blessings are upon you."

Softly the drum beat and sistrums began to shake as the priestesses started to chant the ancient sounds of the Goddess. Ceelyha stood still as the priestess who was behind the statue, came out and placed the red girdle of Ishtar around her waist. Shiroka also stepped forward and placed her own amulet, the one with the eight-pointed star encircled by the snake, over her daughter's head while she whispered, "I want you to have this. The mystery of the snake is its extraordinary vitality and immortality through rejuvenating itself by shedding its skin. I give you now the spontaneous creative energy of the Goddess so you too may be renewed and reborn! Any time you need Her help, just touch the amulet and it shall be done."

Tears of joy poured out of Ceelyha's eyes causing rivers of black from the kohl that adorned them to run down her cheeks as she whispered, "Thank you Mother. I know how much that necklace means to you. It will give me your energy as well as the Goddess's energy. Now, a part of you will always be with me!"

Still holding her tiny light, Ceelyha turned to greet each one of the priestesses in the circle. As was the tradition, each of the ten priestesses bestowed a small gift upon their newest Entu. She was overwhelmed by the rings, bracelets, anklets and tokens that were given to her. Then the drum beat again to clear the energy as the temple dancers entered the inner sanctum. The priestesses also joined in the sacred dance to pay homage to the Goddess. The feasting went on until the small hours of the morning.

The last words that evening were the ones Shiroka imparted, "Always trust your intuition, because it is the way through which the Goddess guides. Walk tall with pride and dignity no matter in what circumstances you find yourself, because at all times you are the Goddess incarnate. Above all else, remain true to Her teachings. And lastly, You and I will stay in touch through the magic of the Goddess."

The Golden One

Chapter 4
The Journey

In the early dawn, when the Goddess brought light to Her world, Ceelyha and Nintu began to journey on horseback through the deserted streets of Babylon. They were not alone. Several palace guards flanked either side of them. It was a royal escort to the city gates. Here a caravan waited for the women and their baggage bearing mules to begin the arduous trip to the Land of the Israelis. The journey would take at least one full cycle of the moon or more. As the entourage approached the legendary Ishtar Gates, Ceelyha closed her eyes and invoked the Goddess to help her remember its beauty and awe-inspiring majestic artwork of lapis coloured dragons and bulls. She then looked up to absorb its power and symbolism. Tears of sadness flowed unabashed as she was bombarded with thoughts of how nothing in her life would ever be the same again. Never would she pass through these gates. She knew with all of her being that she would, on no account, ever again see either of her parents alive in this life. The tears continued as she passed through the thick tiled walls of the Gates. The Goddess's presence descended briefly to confirm her fears and to relay a message.

"Daughter of Light, Daughter of Mine, Weep no more for the past. The next phase of your life is just about to begin. Weep no more!"

Ceelyha gathered strength from Her message and ceased lamenting.

The fifteen men of the caravan, not use to such high profile passengers, made gestures of welcome and respect as they greeted their guests with curiosity. They were a travelling band of various merchants and hired guards who frequently crossed the desert to the Land of Judea. Their caravan consisted of pottery, spices, oils, textile, jewels, food supplies and water. Baggage was loaded onto the backs of small camels while the women were shown how to climb onto larger kneeling animals. After much adjustment to find a place of relative comfort on top of the various robes and blankets that were supposed to soften the hardness of the beast, the women accompanied by two of the palace guards, set off.

After concentrating on not falling off the beast of burden, and getting used to its wobbling motion, Ceelyha was able to relax enough to discover that the wilderness had a beauty of its own. The Goddess opened a whole new world of wonderment. The green fields of grains disappeared and palms trees; fruit trees and grasslands gave way to cactus. Rivers that were the life force of The Land of Two Rivers were a distant memory. Bright sunlight picked up the brilliance of quartz particles mixed in the sand. The busy, noisy streets, teeming with hundreds of people, were replaced with a tranquil sea of sand, a quiet, solitary world of peace. The crunch beneath the camels' hooves and the muted sound of the wind whipping over the dunes were the only sounds to be heard.

When the caravan finally stopped to make camp for the night, the women were exhausted. Even on horses, neither was use to riding for that length of time over such rough, hard terrain. After a dinner that had been provided by the Temple kitchen of dates and fresh goat's meat, Ceelyha sat apart from the men. In the deep twilight, she imagined the evening Temple prayers taking place but here, there were no statues, no shrines or inner sanctuaries, just the open sky with its bright stars. As she looked up to see the Ishtar Star and the belt of Marduk, she found comfort in the knowingness that the Gods and Goddesses were everywhere. Numb with weariness, having no strength to further delve into her emotions, she crawled into the black goatskin tent that she and Nintu shared and fell asleep immediately.

Just when it was dawn Ceelyha awoke to sobs. She pushed back her goatskin cover and crawled to where Nintu was huddled on her blanket. She whispered with concern, "Nintu, what in the name of the Goddess is wrong?"

Sobs racked through the fragile body. Her black hair that had come loose in the night made her look younger than her ten and two years. Her dark eyes appeared larger than usual and streaks of wet flowed over a brown face. Between sobs she choked, "Mistress, there are demons out there! I heard them calling all night long."

"What kind of demons?"

"The Djinns, the wrath of Marduk. I heard them scratching and clawing at our tent many times!" Her voice was full of panic.

Ceelyha responded in a soothing yet firm voice. "I heard and felt nothing. Besides, the Goddess is protecting us. She has a greater destiny in store for you and I than to die in the hands of desert demons! And that scratching and clawing could just be the wind whipping the sand around."

Relief flooded through her when Nintu ceased her wailing. She said, "Come, let us pray to the Goddess for strength and protection."

As they crept out of their tiny goatskin tent into the bone chilling night air and prostrated in the direction of what they believed was Babylon, Ceelyha had an uneasy feeling. Maybe the girl was right; maybe evil was lurking out there! She clutched her mother's sacred amulet close to her breast and tried to invoke the Goddess, but She did not come.

For the next few risings and settings of the sun, the going was fairly easy as the women became familiar with the caravan's routine. The men loaded the cargo on the beasts when the sun was just about to rise and stopped to make camp before it went down, after a check to ensure there were no scorpions or vipers close by. Ceelyha and Nintu learned to expect bone chilling nights, so cold that their breath seemed to freeze in the air, and days so hot and airless that it weakened their bodies and minds. They became accustomed to hearing the soft, padding sound of the camels' feet and the slosh of the water filled goatskin bags that hung on either side of the animals. They suffered the stink of the camels' breath, the constant cud chewing sounds and the songs of the caravan riders to urge the beasts on. They got used to the night wind as it pelted sand against the paper-thin wall of their tent followed by a dead silence when it ceased. They learned to appreciate the beauty of the bright night sky that made a surrounding protective canopy. They tolerated sand in their sandals, clothing, beds, water and food. They hungrily ate whatever fair was available: dried dates, camel's milk, meat and goat's cheese. They learned to drink their most precious commodity of water when they were not thirsty in order to ensure hydration.

One day the unbroken sand led to an oasis, which was like a succulent green island on a sea of sand. Eucalyptus and tamarisk trees spread their shade over the weary travellers. They replenished water pouches and had the luxury of washing off the sand, sweat and smell of the camels in the water pool. Although this oasis was void of human life, the men told the women that they would soon come to one with stray dogs, mud huts and women yelling at their children. Here the traders would barter wares for much needed fresh foods and goat meat after which news from various lands would be exchanged. This was a treat to which they all looked forward to in the next few days.

Ceelyha's dream recall was more pronounced away from the lower vibrations of the city. She had numerous dreams of the man speaking a foreign language, which she could now identify as Hebrew. A new stirring was beginning inside of her that she sensed had nothing to do with the Goddess's presence. It was so intense that she often woke up drenched in perspiration to find one of her hands between her legs.

Some of the men who spoke Hebrew were more than happy to teach Ceelyha words that she would need in her new home. If there were a fire at night, all the travellers would gather together to tell stories about their adventures in the distant lands which they had visited. At one of these gatherings, Ceelyha heard stories about the King of Judea and how, as a boy, he had killed a giant with one stone. As the men continued to talk of the wonderful feats of David, she began to shiver under the protection of her heavy mantle. The men's faces blurred, their words became meaningless. She closed her eyes to welcome the Goddess.

"Blessed be O Ishtar. I praise You Mother of all Light. Thank you for being with me. If it is in order for me to know, can You verify that the man in my dreams is the King they talk about? Is this the man whose destiny is intertwined with mine?" She waited for confirmation then sensed the speaking of her Lady.

"My daughter, yes, this is the man that I have been prophesying to you. All will be as it should be."

Ceelyha anxiously waited for more information, but the Goddess's energy had left. She thanked the Goddess for Her message and opened her eyes. The men were silently staring at her, completely mesmerized by what had happened. Ceelyha was uncomfortable and did not know what to do. A few awkward moments passed before one of them spoke. "Priestess, you must have been speaking to your Goddess. Your appearance totally changed as a curtain of light fell upon you. Is all well?"

Ceelyha just smiled and nodded her head. She got up and retired to the tiny tent that Nintu was now an expert at setting up. Once she was comfortably wrapped in her warm blanket, she reflected on how far she had come. *The desert finds a way to bring peace. I no longer mourn, to the degree I once did, the loss of my home or family. I am now looking forward to meeting the man in my visions!*

The calm, peacefulness of the desert was short lived. The next morning just after the travellers broke camp, the wind rose. Everyone's sun-bruised eyes were half closed as sand mercilessly whipped at them. The heat was unbearable. Progress was painfully slow, and several stops had to be made in order to huddle into a circle for a brief respite. Ceelyha reverently prayed to the Goddess for protection and cessation of the howling squall. When the storm finally ended, the night sky cleared enabling the group to glimpse rocky hills in the far distance. One of the men told the women that their journey would soon be over. They were nearing a settlement where water and rest would be found.

In the morning as the weary caravan plodded along, Ceelyha sensed that a message was about to come from the Goddess. She clutched her amulet in one hand and tried to reign in her camel with the other. But the Goddess descended in a way that was unfamiliar to Ceelyha. Instead of the usual buzz in her ears and blurred vision, she heard the thud of many feet smack on dry mud accompanied with blood curdling shrieks of terror. The sounds ceased as she saw a river of flowing blood followed by a dark nothingness as if a black curtain had fallen. Nintu, who was behind her mistress, anxiously reined in her camel.

Her voice was full of alarm. "What have you seen? What is it that has made your face drain of all its colour?"

"Oh, Nintu," Ceelyha gasped while wildly looking around at her surroundings, "The evil that you sensed so many nights ago is upon us."

"What is it? What has the Goddess warned you about? Is it us? Are we going to be attacked before ..."

Ceelyha held out her hand for Nintu to stop. "Do not ask me any more. We will just have to wait to see how it unfolds." She did not want to relate her foreboding vision and upset the entire caravan. They would all know soon enough. Word quickly passed through the men that the priestess had had a vision, and the guards were more alert.

About mid-day they sighted a grove of palm trees of the long awaited oasis settlement. The usual signs and noises of habitation were not present. Instead, an eerie silence prevailed. Guards signaled for the caravan to stop then Ceelyha immediately dismounted and ran ahead.

Nintu yelled, "Stop mistress, stop!" But Ceelyha did not heed her. There it was. What the Goddess had warned her about! A dozen or so village men hung grotesquely from spears that had been placed like beacons of warning outside the village wall. Their heads swayed back and forth in the breeze; their mouths were slack, flies droned lazily around their eyes, blackened blood caked their bodies, and buzzards circled menacingly above. The stench of rotting flesh was vile. This was the first time that she had ever seen maimed, decaying bodies. She stood trans-fixed, too shocked to even call on the Goddess for assistance. Then, to her dismay, she began to retch. She fell on the ground. When her stomach was empty, she clutched her amulet and tried to invoke the Goddess. But the Goddess was silent.

The guards and men, armed with swords, cautiously entered the village gates and began a frantic search for signs of life. Nintu caught up to Ceelyha and held onto her. The horror of the scene had taken a toll on her as well. She hid her head in the folds of her dusty mantle. A yell from one of the men snapped them both into action.

A stronger Ceelyha commanded, "Nintu, run and find my medicine box. There may be some who are still alive in need of assistance."

A breathless guard ran up to the women, he gasped, "Lady of Ishtar, come quickly. We found someone who is just barely alive."

While Ceelyha quickly followed the man into the small village, Nintu hurried to retrieve the box. In a courtyard entrance, a woman, not much older than Ceelyha, lay spread-eagle, her robe pulled up to her neck. Dried blood marred her thighs; bruises discoloured her arms and face. A contusion was evident on her forehead. Her eyes stared sightlessly. Appalled at the condition of the woman and the act that caused it, Ceelyha bent, gingerly pulled the shift to cover her modesty, then touched the woman's forehead. She murmured words of comfort as she ripped a piece of her own mantle and dipped it in a jug of water that one of the men had found. She pressed the soaked cloth against the woman's dry chapped lips.

Ceelyha ordered the man, "Help me get this woman into shelter. We must get her out of the hot sun."

Inside the crude hut, the men laid the woman on a pallet and waited for more instructions.

Nintu arrived with the medicine box and took charge.

"Open the windows! Leave the door ajar so light comes through. Fetch us fresh water and cloths; then leave us to work the Goddess's magic!"

Ceelyha knelt beside her patient and began to invoke the Goddess by fingering her amulet that lay between her breasts.

"O Lady of Wisdom. Lady of Healing, assist and guide me to make this woman whole again. Let Your hand be mine, heal through me and with me. Assist me to choose the herbs that will dull her pain and ease her soul. Blessings are upon You, O Lady of the Light."

The Goddess quickly manifested Her divine presence and took over Ceelyha's hands. Under Her guidance, Ceelyha searched frantically through the medicine box and extracted the precise healing herbs. Then, with a tone of voice that Nintu had never heard before she spoke with authority and purpose.

"Fetch the jug of water. Infuse it with natron powder. We must hurry. This woman is already more than half way to her gods. If she is to live, then Ishtar wills it. If she is to die, then we must ease the transition of the soul."

While chanting for the removal of the evil that had entered the victim's body, the women gently washed the blood away with the natron mixture. To ease the trauma, they spooned honey mixed with granules of skullcap into her mouth. Next Ceelyha placed a poultice of dried herbs on the head wound. Lastly, a small copper ankh with the serpent of Ishtar was placed over the heart to help the woman open up to the Goddess's healing.

It was dusk when Ceelyha motioned for Nintu to step outside the hut.

"We must now let the Goddess decide what the woman's fate will be. Let us get some nourishment and then I need to pray."

While the woman was being treated, the rest of the village had been searched for survivors; none remained. Anything of value had been taken, including goats and sheep. The travellers had reverently removed the murdered men from their death spears and buried them in a communal grave. Now water bags refilled, bathing and refreshing were done, dates were picked off the palm trees and a fire was started in the village courtyard to cook some vegetables that had been left behind.

Ceelyha sat in the hut with the injured woman during the night, but in spite of her administrations and prayers, she felt her slipping over to the other side. In order to assist her transition, Ceelyha invoked the power of the Goddess and projected a white light of protection around the woman's body. Just before dawn, Ceelyha felt the remains of the soul leave. She felt relief that the woman had not been left alive to remember the horrors that she had witnessed. It was truly a blessing that the Goddess released her from the shame and horror of what the rest of her life might have been. Ceelyah was lost in her own thoughts about how a woman could be so defiled, then abadonded as if she were no more important than a left over scrap of meat. There were so many things of this world that she had no understanding of.

She later woke up Nintu, who had fallen asleep in the corner of the small room, to assist her with the body. They removed the blankets that covered the woman, smoothed the tangled hair, and washed the body, allowing the rivulets of water to be absorbed by the mud floor. Together they chanted "O Ishtar, Lady of the After

World, receive this; thy daughter into Your eternal care. Give her light as she journeys into the house of shadows. Open the seven gates that she may enter and pass through. Take her into Heaven where her soul may be at rest."

While they prayed, Ceelyha fell into a trance state. She heard the voice of the woman's soul cry out for revenge, as she watched the details of the attack unfold.

A group of marauding men, with weapons of iron, had crept out of the wasteland of the desert in the dead of night and attacked. The village watch guards had blown a ram's horn as an alarm but it had been too late to arouse the sleeping villagers. The astonished villagers tried to retaliate but could not match the sophisticated weapons of the attackers and were easily overtaken. Women and children were rounded up as prisoners later to be sold in slave markets and animals and any valuables such as silver, gold and vases were stolen. The woman had tried to hide while her husband, soon to become one of the slaughtered, tried to defend the village. But she was eventually found by the attackers and was repeatedly raped; every part of her body was assaulted. Since she was then in no condition to be of any use as a possible slave, her value having gone, she was left to die. The vision ended and Ceelyha sent the woman's soul to the light of the Goddess.

After Ceelyha relayed to the rest of her group that the woman died, she asked that they remain in the village for another three days. It was during this time that she would watch over the men, ensuring that strength and support was there for these traumatized souls to journey to the underworld. Although the caravan travellers did not want to remain in the settlement, out for respect to the priestess and the dead, they obliged. There were no animals left to slaughter as a blood sacrifice, so some of the wine, which the merchants were transporting to sell, was spilled as Ceelyha and Nintu chanted for the safety of the souls.

After the third day, with heavy hearts, the caravan set out to climb the rocky hills for the last part of the journey. The travellers paused at the top. The gnarled pines and oaks were a welcome sight as the sea of sand disappeared. A new world of ox drawn plows, a shimmering river and trees with their branches laden with fruit emerged. Just before they began their descent into the cool river valley, Ceelyha touched her amulet and devoutly thanked the Goddess for Her protection over the hot sand. She was not the same person who had started out. She had witnessed the destructive side of humans and learned more about the land she was about to live in. Her childhood innocence was gone. The softness of early adolescence had been replaced by the neat, trim body of a young woman. In these past few weeks, her thoughts had matured as she came closer to Her Goddess and to her destiny.

After the Babylonians had taken their leave of the caravan in order to continue on a hard packed mud road to a small village, the two guards negotiated donkeys for the rest of the journey to Dor. Once the river was crossed, they made the balance of the journey in less than a day.

The Golden One

Chapter 5
Life In Dor

It was past midday when two very exhausted, dusty, sunburned women arrived at the village gates of Dor. The entire area looked worn out and dull. It was archaic with nothing even close to Ceelyha's beloved ostentatious Ishtar Gate. There were no golden statues or opulent villas with fragrant colourful flowers spilling over their balconies. Instead, small, mud brick buildings with tattered tents erected on flat rooftops assailed their vision. The main street, rather than the smooth stone road of the colourful Sacred Passageway, was no more than a donkey trail. A small bazaar of tradesmen – hawking wares of melons, dates, grains and spices under makeshift dilapidated awnings – did nothing to improve the newcomers' impressions. The final disgruntlement was witnessing a soldier as he vomited last night's beer in the midst of the stalls.

Trying not to let disgust register on her face, Ceelyha ordered one of her guards to inquire as to the whereabouts of the Temple of Asherah. A local man, in a robe of un-dyed wool, nodded his head in the direction outside the town's entrance. At this point, she was not overly surprised that the Temple did not even have the protection of the town. A winding path, up to the side of the hill, eventually led them to an ancient mud wall with a gate. Ceelyha hoped there was a mistake that this fallen down place could not be the home of a goddess but she motioned for her guards to knock on the gray weather beaten door. After several bangs, a shrill Hebrew voice called out, "Who is it that bangs so loudly on the door of the Goddess? State your business."

Ceelyha sighed with dismay, it was just as her mother had warned,she dismounted and went up to the rundown entrance. She noted a faded engraving of two serpents entwined around a tree, a sign of the Goddess. After yelling through a crack in the wood in her own tongue that she was the Priestess from Babylon, Ceelyha nervously waited for the gate to open. It creaked on its rotting hinges as an old woman in a faded linen shift, her gray hair falling like snakes around her shoulders, cautiously peered out. Her wizened, pale face did not portray any sign of welcome to the weary travellers. She did not speak but indicated with a crooked finger that the two women could enter. When she saw the strangely dressed male escorts, she held up a hand in a gesture that meant they were to stop where they were. Ceelyha turned to the men.

"The Goddess, Nintu and I are forever grateful for your protection. When you return to our homeland, please inform my mother, the Entu, that we have arrived safely." She proceeded to hand them a generous amount of gold coins that Nintu quickly extracted from the lining of her belt. The guards bowed, bid the women goodbye and went off to enjoy a few days of freedom before finding a caravan returning to The Land of the Two Rivers.

As Ceelyha and Nintu cautiously entered the empty courtyard, they were pleasantly surprised, as fresh air with a tang of salt and a soft breeze embedded with a hint of pine fragrance greeted them. Its coolness was such a welcome relief after weeks of dry, blowing hot sand. The courtyard's floor tiles, bleached by the sun, supported several dilapidated wooden benches that were strategically situated under the protection of sycamore trees. A large stone altar used for sacrifices, its eternal flame ablaze, dominated the center of the courtyard. To its side was the most magnificent carving of wood Ceelyha had ever seen. She recalled from previous teachings that it was an Asherah pole symbolizing fertility with two intertwining serpents that met at the up-turned crescent top. Ceelyha and Nintu bowed in respect and then bathed their hands and face in an inviting pool of spring water near a palm tree. Ceelyha silently thanked the Goddess as she absorbed the simple yet pristine atmosphere of the Temple and started to feel the layers of the taxing journey drift away. As the sacredness of the Temple filtered into her awareness, her heart opened to the new life upon which she was about to embark. It might not have the grandness of her old residence, but somewhere within the depths of her soul, a sense of coming home began to resonate.

The old woman, patiently waited, while the strangers lingered, then led them to the entrance porch beyond which Ceelyha surmised was the main room, the Holy of Holies. They entered and were ushered past a libation table surrounded by various incense bowls burning the sweet smell of cedar. Further along, there were various small figurines in bronze, silver and gold that resembled the Goddess Hathor, Isis, Osiris and other Egyptian deities. The room also had stone statues of the Canaan gods standing on various pedestals. In an alcove, with an eternal flame aglow, there was a large wooden statue of Asherah. Ceelyha thought with dismay that she did not look anything like Ishtar with her crudely carved nude torso, short-cropped hair and sagging breasts.

Nintu interrupted her reflections when she whispered, "Is this the Goddess of this land?"

Ceelyha answered back. "Yes. She aids in childbirth. She is the protector of the sea, the Lady of the Heavens, the Lion lady and…" she paused trying to recall her lessons.

An authoritative voice from outside the sanctuary added, "And the Tree of Light, the companion of El the Compassionate and Yahweh the Compassionate and Merciful."

The gatekeeper knelt and the newcomers followed her example. A priestess, long past childbearing age, wearing a single braid down her back and a midnight blue robe, entered. She bid the women rise. Ceelyha spontaneously smiled. The woman was so like her mother; tall, strong looking with dark skin and kind, knowing eyes. The priestess met Ceelyha's gaze and sent her a warm radiant beam of love and acceptance.

"I am Dinah, what you would call the head Entu in your land. Welcome to the Temple of Asherah." Her voice had a soothing quality that Ceelyha immediately liked and was visibly relieved that she spoke Akkadian. The High Priestess directed her head toward the elderly woman, " And this is Magda, the Temple's servant. As you probably guessed, she cannot speak your language. Now, You must be Ceelyha and who is this person accompanying you?" Dinah raised her voice questioningly.

"Nintu, your Holiness. Nintu is my servant and companion." Ceelyha bowed again to the Priestess.

"Of course, your mother, the Lady Shiroka made mention of her," she aimed an inviting smile at Nintu then continued, "Welcome to both of you. You must feel dirty, tired, hungry and in need of other comforts after your long trip. Magda will take care of that. We shall meet when you are rested. Go, make yourselves at home for the time being. Praise the Lady of the Stars of Heaven, Mistress of All Gods, May she grant both of you peace and happiness in your new home."

Nintu was led away by a servant to sort out their lodging while Ceelyha followed Magda to a small bathing pool beyond the main building. Magda gestured for Ceelyha to remove her dusty robes that Ceelyha gladly shed. She modestly covered her breasts in front of the stranger and gingerly stepped into water that was surprisingly warm. Magda proceeded to pour water from a narrow necked vase over Ceelyha's naked body. The liquid libation seemed to sooth away the aches and pains of the journey. So far, in her short life, it had been the hardest ordeal she had ever faced; but somehow she intuited that it was just the beginning. She now appreciated how coveted and pampered life was in Babylon where soft shifts, tasty food and a warm bed were all taken for granted. As she rose from the pool and let the elder woman rub her dry, she felt she had matured beyond her age in just three moons.

A simple draped shift was placed over her head and a pair of well-worn sandals held out by a pair of wrinkled hands, brought her back to the present surroundings. Ceelyha's hair was still wet when Magda led her around the Temple to a grouping of low buildings. She understood that this was the area where the priestesses' were housed. The elderly servant retreated and Ceelyha entered a small chamber with a tiny window, a wooden stool, a low table and a pallet where Nintu was busy unpacking their personal effects. There was barely room for the two of them in the miniscule cell let alone the belongings from Babylon. Nintu had already set a statue of Ishtar in the niche of the room and Ceelyha greeted her Lady with a quick bow.

Nintu stopped working to attend to her mistress' damp hair. As she expertly worked the wet strands into tiny braids, she asked, "Lady, will we be alright in this foreign land? I do not understand that strange language! I just assumed when a servant showed me where our trunks were located that this is your chamber and that I will be with the other servants at the back of the Temple. It is nothing like Babylon. Everything here is so primitive!"

Ceelyha gently chided, "Nintu , we will make the best of our situation. Remember, it is the Goddess who sent us here. Now, stop moaning. As soon as you have done here, go and have your bathing done then get some rest."

Ceelyha lay down on the pallet while Nintu fussed about her trying to find spots for clothing and the priestess tools. She closed her eyes wondering what the High Priestess meant by the remark of making herself at home here for the time being. *It is all too confusing*, she thought before dropping into a deep sleep.

Sounds of activity woke her. For a moment, Ceelyha did not know where she was. The room was hot and airless. She got up, opened the door and was surprised to see that the sun had already risen. *I must have slept through evening and morning prayers!* Lured by the distant sound of crashing waves, she walked up a slight incline, to a high plateau of rock that overlooked an aqua marine sea. She could not recall having ever seen such a big expanse of water! The surrounding cliffs were full of strange and wonderful trees while the air was invigorating. Raising her hands high above her head, she allowed herself to enjoy the gentle sensation of the wind as it billowed her shift. She laughed with the pure joy of the moment and chanted, "Goddess of the Sea, thank You for allowing me to be here. Today, I will begin to learn more about Your ways. I know that You and My Lady will work together with me. Praise be to Ishtar and Asherah, one and the same." Her stomach began to growl, a reminder she had not eaten since yesterday and she reluctantly retraced her steps to an anxious Nintu who waited outside the cell with a tray of food.

"Where have you been? I have been looking everywhere for you. Are you aware of the length of time that you have slept? Why are you still wearing that dowdy shift? You must be very hungry. Come and eat before you collapse."

Ceelyha laughed and playfully responded, "Stop bombarding me with questions and orders. I will eat and do exactly as you say."

Just as she finished dressing in one of the tunics and red belts from her trunk, the gatekeeper arrived. She raised her eyes at the sight of Ceelyha's outfit before motioning her to come. They walked along the stone pathway and entered the main courtyard where the head priestess sat on a bench under the shade of a tree. Dinah wore the same gown, which she had received her guests in the day before: however, her hair was tied back into plaits that were accented by a plain leather diadem. No jewels adorned her neck or hands. Ceelyha bowed in respect and waited to be asked to rise.

A gentle voice said, "Come and sit beside me, my Babylonian priestess." She patted the spot beside her and continued, " I trust that you are well rested?"

"Yes, your Greatness. I had quite a sleep. I apologize for missing the honouring of the Goddess both last night and this morning," Ceelyha sheepishly replied.

"Never mind. You have your whole life to make up for it. The Goddess is very forgiving and you needed the rest. I hope that you are comfortable in our humble Temple."

"Yes, very. But it is not humble. It may not have the opulence of my Temple but it is just as sacred, with a special beauty of its own." Ceelyha responded, eager to let the Priestess know how pleased she was.

Dinah smiled and replied, "You must have seen the sea then. The cliffs offer a spectacular view."

Ceelyha nodded in agreement then asked, "Please, my Lady, may I know more about your ways in this Temple?"

"You will do well here, Ceelyha!" Dinah seemed pleased with her new priestess. She paused then continued, "We do not wear jewels and ornaments as you do in your land. The people that come to consult us are poor. If we were adorned, they would feel that the Temple was getting rich from their meager offerings. As you can see," she dropped her eyes to her own simple attire, "we wear plain garments with only a girdle to identify us as Asherah's servants."

Ceelyha considered the logic of what Dinah had said and looked down at her garb, which was austere in Babylonian terms. She self consciously took her necklace and quickly tucked it beneath the neckline of her shift. "I am sorry, I did not know", she whispered apologetically, feeling flamboyant and disrespectful.

"Never mind," Dinah said in a soothing voice, "there is no way that you would know our ways. Do not hide the necklace; it is so beautiful. You must leave it out. Because you are a foreigner, it should have some magical appeal to the townspeople."

Ceelyha reverently pulled it out and wistfully replied, "It was a parting gift from my mother."

"I was honoured when your mother sent a message. I am pleased to take care of you until a suitable position can be found in another Temple. She said that your father's priest read the omens for you, and that is the reason you came to our land of Israel." The older woman paused then looking directly into her younger charge's eyes asked, "Do you have any idea as to the reason why you were sent here?"

Ceelyha hesitated before she answered, uncertain how much the woman actually knew.

"Just that the Goddess wishes me to do her work in this part of the world. When I was born, one of the Ishtar priestess' performed a scrying in the sacred Temple bowl. The vision was that I would be the Goddess' channel to do Her work through divining and healing."

Dinah responded, "And our work is what we are and not just what we do. We came to this earth to do Her will and to become whom She would have us be. The Goddess has given us both tremendous gifts."

She paused then asked, "Did your mother tell you what my special talent is?"

Ceelyha shook her head and replied, "No, my Lady, she did not go into detail. All I know is that she spoke very highly of you and that she knew of you through one of the other priestesses at the Ishtar Temple."

"I am known, by some, for my skills at conjuring up the spirits of the dead and foretelling events. The ancient name for what I do is called obh. Later, when you are more settled, I shall share this magic with you."

Ceelyha could hardly keep her excitement under control! To learn to communicate with the spirits was something that even her own mother could not have taught her! She cleared her throat and tried to reply with as much humbleness as she could, "Oh, Lady I would be forever grateful if you could! I am still learning my craft of interpreting the oracles and speaking on behalf of the Goddess for those that seek my help. I wish to learn as much about all the various practices of an Asherah priestess."

Dinah smiled knowingly as if she was pleased for the younger one's enthusiasm. "Well then, shall we get started?"

The High Priestess spent the rest of the morning, educating Ceelyha on the history of the Deities. Asherah or the Tree of Life, as She also referred to, was the life-giving goddess of well-being. The palm tree, particularly the female date palm, was Her living symbol. She was the living goddess of this sacred tree. Its foliage provided shelter from the sun; its leaves made thatch roofs for dwellings; its trunk was cut into pieces for building; its sap produced the sugar to be fermented into wine. The fruit of the date, both fresh and dried, was eaten and enjoyed. Her other names were Lady of the Stars of Heaven and Queen of Heaven. Her associated symbols included the solar disk and the crescent. She was often portrayed as curly haired, riding a lion with lilies and serpents held in Her upraised hands. In Egypt they worshipped Her as Hathor, regally standing on a lion, holding a lotus in each hand, and is girded with serpents. Ceelyha knew her best as Ishtar wearing the intricately knotted serpent apron and with undulating snakes wrapped around each arm.

Ceelyha learned that Asherah was the consort of El, intermediary with those who wish to petition His aid while Baal, the statue she saw yesterday, was the Storm God, source of the winter rain storms, spring mist, and summer dew, which nourish the crops.

After her short history lesson, Dinah led her student into the cool shadows of the inner sanctum. Both women took a moment to adjust their eyes to the dimness. "We call this area of the Temple, the Holy of Holies because it houses our Canaanite Gods. Here is Baal," she pointed to the God that dominated the entrance. He wore a horned helmet and carried a lightning-bolt staff. A short wrapped kilt covered his manhood.

Dinah continued her lecture, "He is also called Aleyin, meaning 'Most High'. He is the son of Dagan, a god of agriculture and storms. It was through competitions and fighting with other gods, that Baal got the status of being the one below El. He uses Asherah to communicate with El."

"Oh, your Baal is our Bel! God of the sky, clouds, and rain!" Ceelyha was excited to make the connection.

Dinah nodded and indicated two other stone statues, "And these Gods; Gapen and Ugar, are His assistants. El has dominion over all Creation, while Baal controls the fertility of the Earthly realm. Anat is both His sister and lover. Here she is as a heifer." She pointed to a cow shaped idol. "She is the Goddess of Dew. Sometimes you might see her image carrying a distaff and spindle. She can also be a warrior, armed with a spear and shield."

Ceelyha looked around the room. It was plain in comparison to the halls that housed the Gods in Marduk's temples. There was no gold, no bejeweled statues, just wooden carvings. She noticed a straw basket, then without thinking, Ceelyha went over and peered inside. There were sleeping coiled serpents! She recoiled in surprise.

Dinah's voice rang out in warning, "Let them be. They are venomous!"

Ceelyha sheepishly replied, "Lady, I must confess to you. I have no desire to touch the Goddess's snakes. I ..." her voice faltered then gained strength, "have never been able to work with serpents."

Dinah smiled a knowing smile and said, "Then you are not meant to work with them."

To move the conversation away from her, Ceelyha curiously asked, "Is your temple the greatest edifice of your land?"

"No, the one in Jerusalem is probably more familiar to what you know. It is in the city where our King David resides when he is not fighting the Philistines and other tribes of Israel."

Ceelyha felt her knees wobble and heartbeat increase just hearing his name. She haltingly asked, "Does this David ever visit Dor?"

"No, he has not of yet. Why do you ask?"

"I am just curious, that is all," Ceelyha hoped her face did not reveal her feelings. She did not want to share the Goddess's prophecy or her visions. To change the subject she said, "All the God and Goddesses are truly one, just showing themselves with different names and faces to us. I do not think I shall have a difficult time picking up your ways."

"I think you will be just fine. Now, let me introduce you to the other ten priestesses."

It did not come as a surprise to Ceelyha that the morning and evening homage to the Goddess were less formal than at the Ishtar Temple. The shaking of the sistrums called the Temple workers together in the inner room at sunrise and sunset. Although, there were no sensuous veiled dances to awaken the Goddess, she was pleased that the priestesses did form a somewhat similar line as her Temple , which Dinah slowly walked down while invoking the energy of the Goddess. Asherah's statue was not anointed and washed. Petals of flowers were offered instead of food.

It seemed that life was less formal and offered more freedom. Over the next few weeks, Ceelyha easily fell into the routine of after the evening ritual of bidding good night to the Goddess, she liked to take a small torch and climb the hill that overlooked the sea. Nintu would sometimes accompany her and the two of them would sit and watch the glowing reflection of the moon on the shimmering water. Nintu would recount the village gossip while Ceelyha listened and interjected the odd comment. Also, if there was any free time during the day, Ceelyha liked to retreat here to watch the sea crash on the rough rocks beneath the cliff and listen to the song of the wind playing through the pine trees. Sitting on a flat rock warmed by the heat of the sun, lulled by the sounds of the sea, she was at liberty to close her eyes and allow memories to emerge. It was during this quiet time that she allowed herself to fully embrace her loneliness for her mother and life in Babylon. She often chided herself, *I am too old to be homesick. I have the training to overcome and rise above these emotions.* But, sometimes the longing was so intense that she actually imagined she could hear Shiroka's gentle voice teaching the novices the sacred teachings of Ishtar. She even thought of her father and what his latest antics and conquests might be. During times like this, she would take comfort from her mother's words, "Earth is not our home, only a stopping ground, a place on the way back to the Goddess. You must connect with spirit and not the body." Ceelyha would then pray to the Goddess to remove her unhappiness.

A few moons into life in Dor, Ceelyha awoke during the middle of the night. She was restless and overheated in her airless cell so she stepped out into the warm humid air. A full luminous moon beckoned her to climb to top of the cliff. As its golden light lit the familiar path, her bare feet hardly stumbled on the stones. When she reached her favourite rock, it seemed even more sacred at this hour. As she sat down, a prayer formed in her mind as homage to Her Lady.

"I hail thee glorious Moon Goddess who blazes Her earth with light," Ceelyha lifted her hands to the heavens. "Cast Your light upon me, that I may bask in Your love." She pivoted to the east, in the direction of Babylon, where the moon disappeared behind a heavy cloud. She thought, *It would be almost time for Nisan. Has it truly been a whole twelve moons since I heard the baru pronounce my fate?* She reflected on how over the next eleven days everyone in Babylon would fully indulge in every possible sensuous pursuit to ensure that King Eulma-Shakin Shuki would once again be fertile when he had to perform on the marriage bed. *I wonder if Nanab, his last year's chosen one, will provide him with another child.* She envisioned the scents of musk that pervaded the air from all the careful oiling and perfuming that everyone indulged in. She recollected the special foods, wines and beers that were prepared for the festival. She thought about her fellow priestesses and the priests of Marduk performing the sacred duties of prayer, ceremonial dancing, fasting, and anointing the statues of the Gods.

The surrounding air grew suddenly cool. Her eyes closed as a gentle breeze billowed through her thin nightdress. Immediately, she felt her consciousness lift out of her body. She soared higher and higher above the cliff and the sea. As she floated somewhere between heaven and earth, she willed herself to travel back to the cool corridors of her mother's well-appointed chamber. There she saw the richness of the thick carpets, the soft red couches, and the flickering brazier. She deeply inhaled the cloying scent of sandalwood and felt the soft cooling breezes of the river through open balcony doors. She heard the merrymakers in the streets and felt the excitement of Nisan in the air. She drifted over to the sacred alcove where the figure of Shiroka knelt before the golden statue of Ishtar. At that moment, her mother suddenly stood and called into the night, "My daughter, I sense your energy around me! It has taken you awhile to seek me out! You must become a powerful Entu. Be patient; learn all that you can of the foreign ways. It will serve you well."

Before Ceelyha could respond, she was plummeted back into her body. Her eyes jarred open as the moon reappeared with its golden light above the treetops. *I am so happy to have actually connected once again with Shiroka. It has been a long time since I have felt this much joy!* Invigorated with hope and the sense that she truly had communicated with her mother, Ceelyha thanked the Goddess for Her gift of magic. She returned with more happiness in her heart than she could remember to the cramped crude quarters that was her home.

Ceelyha kept her own council. In all the time she had been in Dor, she still had not formed any friendships with the others. Everyone was polite but did not include her in their circle of friendship. Mealtime was especially painful as she did not fully understand the language of her sisters; she was excluded from most of the conversations. She was referred to as the 'foreigner' and knew they were in awe of her being the daughter of a King and a High Priestess. She tried not to let it bother her, as the Goddess and Nintu were all she needed, but she missed the comradeship of gathering in the hall where the older Babylonian priestesses told stories about the Creation. She longed to hear again the legends of Ishtar's descent into the underworld to find her lover Tammuz and the ancient mysteries of the land that sank beneath the seas.

To overcome her 'foreignness', loneliness and homesickness, she directed her energy into expanding and enhancing her skills by learning from and sharing with the priestesses. When the moon was full, the Temple workers gathered to ensure the fertility of the village crops. They mixed petals of flowers with honey and threw them onto the altar's burning fire while chanting to Asherah. When one of the village people was sick, Ceelyha was often summoned to the person's home. Depending on the illness, she would use her Babylonian herbs and precious stones as treatment. Often, using incantations learned from the Ishtar Temple, she removed demons, which had manifested as an illness or a series of bad luck.

Ceelyha became a student in the art of necromancy, contacting the dead for divination. Dinah told her the story of King Saul, who went to the Temple in Endor and commanded its priestess to conjure up a dead prophet. In a cloud of red mist, the spirit of Samuel rose before the King and spoke through the woman, foretelling death on the battlefield in the mountains of Gilboa. There was much talk about how such a man of Yahweh could revert to the magic of the pagans when Mosaic Law declared it to be punishable by death.

Ceelyha felt honoured that Dinah had enough faith in her abilities to learn this forbidden form of prophecy. The older woman explained that summoning spirits in this Temple had been occurring since the early Canaanites. Its location was chosen due to its proximity to water, the sea, where communication with the abodes of the dead was thought to be easier.

"To prepare for necromancy, as with any type of divination work, an obh must abstain from food for three days. Only drinking water from the sacred well is permitted. During this time, she prays to the Snake Goddess for purity of mind, body and spirit so she can be a perfect channel. She also sets up a etheric wall of protection to guard against invading and lingering spirits by making a circle." Dinah paused and asked if an Ishtar priestess was trained in this type of magic.

Ceelyha nodded, recollecting how to set the wards by using a clear quartz crystal to protect from entity invasions.

"We also use a mixture of dried frankincense mixed and sage."

Dinah nodded then continued, "When the next petitioner comes that requires this type of service, I will call upon you to observe."

"I would be so ever grateful, my Lady," Ceelyha bowed with gratitude.

A few days, before the evening meal, when the moon just began to wane, the High Priestess sent for Ceelyha to come to her chamber. As Ceelyha hurried down the ancient hallway, she pondered why she had been called. In all the time she had been here, she had never seen the High Priestess's personal living quarters. Her excitement grew when she intuited that there must have been a request to conjure a spirit! When she arrived at the room, she was not overly surprised to see it was only a fraction larger than her cell. The only sign that it belonged to a superior was a fair size window that opened in the direction of the sea. A low couch, a crude wooden stool, a small statue of Asherah and a lit brazier dominated most of the space. Ceelyha stood at the entrance, knocked timidly and bowed to her superior. Dinah was seated on a stool gazing out the window while Magda was braiding her hair.

She spoke without turning, "Rise up, my Babylonian priestess."

Magda deftly continued twisting the long graying strands while Dinah continued, "A man has requested that he contact the discarnate spirit of his missing brother. Apparently, the brother was traveling to Damascus to sell carved boxes that he and his family crafted. He left some ten moons ago and he has never been heard from since."

Shivers of dread shot through Ceelyha's body. Her ears buzzed and vision blurred as she heard the Goddess whisper, "The man was murdered!"

Dinah immediately spoke in the Canaanite tongue to Magda. The woman stopped attending her mistress's hair, bowed and left the room. The High Priestess turned to Ceelyha.

"Come closer to me!" she commanded with a look of surprise on her face. Ceelyah walked over and kneeled at the feet of Dinah.

Dinah gently put her hands on Ceelyha's face and raised it up so she could see her eyes.

"I can see you just had a message from your Goddess."

Ceelyha demurely nodded an affirmation. Dinah released her hold in order to let the girl speak.

"Yes, My Lady. The Goddess Ishtar has told me the man's brother has been murdered."

Dinah perceptively smiled and with a touch of humour in her voice replied, "Then, we will have an interesting conjuring three nights hence."

Ceelyha could barely contain her exhilaration. She was finally going to see the ancient ritual being performed!

Dinah interrupted her thoughts by telling her to begin the cleansing regiment.

Back in her small cell, Ceelyha knelt before the image of Ishtar and prayed,

"Oh, Mother Goddess, Praise be to You, the Queen of All,

Hear my prayer for doing Your work here on earth

May You cleanse my heart and mind

So that I may be a perfect instrument through which You can channel the energy of the discarnate.

I am Your servant."

When the time arrived, Ceelyha, dressed in her Babylonian necklace, her priestess belt and a dark indigo gown, went into the courtyard. Magda was already there conversing in low tones with the petitioner who had two goats with indiscernible sacks over their sides. When he saw the foreign priestess, the man bowed so low that his head touched the ground. Magda spoke to him, he rose and followed the women to the altar. The air grew tense with anticipation as Dinah stepped out of the dark shadows. Ceelyha barely recognized her clothed in a dark hooded mantle with strands of loose flowing hair escaping from the hood's sides. She greeted them with a curt nod, turned her back and set about raising her hands above the sacred flame that dimly burned on the altar. She called out "Asherah, Lady of the Serpents, Tree of Life, ignite this Your fire that represents Your womb. Give birth to this light!"

At once, sparks spewed as the fire brightened. Without facing the others, she motioned for Ceelyha to approach. "I want you to conduct the session."

Ceelyha was taken aback, her heart pounded with apprehension. Her voice betrayed her insecurity. "Me? Oh, with all due respect My Lady, I thought I would just be a witness and watch your magic!"

"I saw how the Goddess came to you. You need not watch me do it! I will be here to assist if need be and I will relay the information to the petitioner when you speak as his brother."

Ceelyha audibly gasped, then realizing her mistake of appearing powerless. *A mystic guards her thoughts, which was one of the first rules I learned as a novice*! She made a quick prayer to the Goddess for assistance. Her initial thought was that she was not mentally prepared to do this but on quick reflection, realized what a wonderful gift was being presented to her. She apologetically smiled at Dinah who returned her acknowledgement. Dinah then turned and spoke to the man in a deep booming authoritarian voice, "Who comes before the sacred altar of the Lady of Snakes?"

He meekly replied, "Kerem, Your Lady, from the family of Joshua."

"And what offering have you brought Her Holiness, Asherah?"

"I have brought two goats, three bags of barely and some wine, My Lady."

"State who is it you wish to contact and why."

His voice gathered strength as he replied it was his brother Mosheh.

"And have you fasted for a day and a night as it your soul that the spirit has a connection with and not the priestess?"

Ceelyha anxiously waited for the reply hoping the man had prepared himself since he was the beacon for the spirit while she was just the medium through which it communicated.

She released an inaudible sigh of relief when she heard him affirm that he had indeed followed through on his part.

Dinah's voice rang into the night air, "Then we shall begin. Magda, show Kerem where to stand."

As the servant backed the man away from the altar, Ceelyha took her cue and began to set the wards with the crystal that she extracted from the satchel of her belt while Dinah tossed purifying incense on the fire.

Ceelyha raised the stone high above her head towards the heavens. "I call upon the protection and power of the Great Goddess Ishtar and Her Holy sister, Asherah.

May they surround and protect me from evil and not allow the spirit to linger after it has communed with Kerem. I am Your servant."

Vaguely aware that Dinah had stepped back and was chanting, Ceelyha joined in. As the rhythm began to fill her body, she felt the presence of the Goddess. She lowered her arms and directed the point of the crystal in a clockwise direction three times around herself. She waited. When her head began to feel as if it was about to lift off her neck, the veil between her world and that of spirit dissolved. At that moment, a misty grey smoke and a putrid odour began to swarm around her. Her skin crawled as if an army of worms was attacking it. Her blood ran cold. A sharp pain as if a knife was being plunged into her chest, caused her to clutch her heart and she involuntarily sank to her knees. She was so involved in the agony that she hardly heard Dinah shouting, "Stand up, stand up. I am relieving the pain. He was killed with a sword!"

Ceelyha felt relief and stood up. She coughed as if she was being strangled and then the energy leveled so she was able to speak. But the voice was not her own; it was deep and raspy.

"Kerem, my brother! I have so much to tell you. I was murdered on the road back from Damascus by marauders. They stole all the gold coins that I had for the family. I am so sorry…"

The entity began to sob, "I had no way to tell you. They took the money and it is hidden in a cave of the hills in Gilead. The cave is near a grove of date trees beside a pool of water. You must travel there and retrieve what is ours…!"

Everything went out of focus for Ceelyah. She collapsed to the ground. The next thing she remembered was Dinah gently calling her name as she tried to coax some wine down her throat. Ceelyha sat up and sipped the warm libation then in a shaky voice asked, "Did I do a good job?" She looked around and saw that she was alone with the High Priestess, the man and Magda were nowhere in sight.

Dinah helped her up to her feet and answered with pride, "You did a great job. Kerem was happy to discover what had happened to his brother and is probably preparing to travel to the area where the money is hidden. I dispersed the spirit and sent him to the light so that he would no longer wander the earth."

"I guess I lost consciousness before I was able to do that…" Ceelyha said with shame.

"Here, here, my child. It was your first time and with experience, you will be able to hold and channel the energies much better."

Ceelyha glowed with self-satisfaction and thanked Dinah for her assistance before she was sent off to her cell where Nintu waited with some nourishment. She had done her first of many contacts with the dead!

Ceelyha learned that most of the women in the village and surrounding areas possessed small statues of Asherah to which they prayed to for help with childbirth and fertility. These same women also sought help at the Temple, feeling they were cursed if they could not conceive. Amulets and charms were made to assist with conception. Ceelyha was often present with Dinah and the other priestesses at birthings. The pregnant woman would be placed on birthing stones, her back supported by a priestess who would chant to the Goddess for a safe delivery while soothing herbs were lovingly rubbed onto a swollen belly. Ceelyha showed the priestess how to use the healing power of stones in her medicine box – onyx to prevent the draining of energy, hematite to stop hemorrhaging, a ruby to bring on the birth and a bright green stone carved with the serpents of the Goddess to dull labour pains. A prayer would be made to the Lady of the Seas to help the waters flow from the womb.

Ceelyha participated in the annual Harvest Festival, which marked the end of the crop harvesting. The entire town and area farmers gathered in the fields under a full moon. Huge bonfires were lit and maidens asked men to dance with them. Everyone ate, drank and celebrated. The priestesses performed the sacred ceremony of holding cut branches of palm and olive trees high above their heads and under the iridescent light of the moon, they danced around the fields, thanking Asherah for Her bounty. At dawn, the exhausted but jubilant priestesses returned to the Temple where they enjoyed their own feast of special foods and wine donated by the townspeople. It did not compare to anything in the Sacred Marriage Ceremony but Ceelyha was moved by how much the people took pleasure in their unpretentious celebration. As Ceelyha became more known, some of the village women would seek her out.

One such person was Miriam, a young beautiful girl with raven black hair, about the same age as herself. One day, after Miriam had left some grain as an offering to the Goddess, she approached Ceelyha, who had just sat down to rest in the outer courtyard after mixing an elixir for a colicky baby. They exchanged pleasantries. Ceelyha sensed an instant connection with Miriam and a quick friendship grew between them, one that filled some of her loneliness.

After being friends for several months, Miriam asked Ceelyha to interpret a dream that was filled with erotic details about a young man in the village. Ceelyha did not bother to invoke the Goddess's help. "Miriam, if you are dreaming so much of lying with this man, then ask your father to arrange a marriage for you as soon as possible. It sounds like you are ready to fully embrace your womanhood."

A surprised Marian nodded her head in agreement. "Yes, you are right. I am ready to love a man and start a family." A dreamy look clouded her black eyes as she added, "Every time I see him, and I feel weak in the knees and tingly all over." Then she begged Ceelyha to make her a love potion.

Ceelyha asked her to wait in the courtyard and to sacrifice some seeds of grain on the altar while she prepared the ingredients. In a small room off the inner sanctum, she mixed aromatic dried cedar and pine with feverfew, valerian and motherwort. She placed the herbs in a small goatskin pouch along with a cinnabar stone then summoned the Goddess to invoke the magic of love into the mixture. When she returned to Miriam, she placed the bag in her hands and said, "Go and put this under your pillow until the next full moon. Before you sleep each night, ask Asherah to join the two of you in love and marriage."

Miriam had tears of gratitude in her eyes, "Oh thank you my friend, the priestess. You are surely most skilled in your craft." Then she added, her voice full of curiosity,

"Will you marry and have children?"

Ceelyha, taken aback, having never considered this way of life, hesitated before she answered. "No, as an Ishtar priestess it is forbidden for me to take a husband."

"Then all your life you will be alone? Surely the Goddess will look down from above and will choose a handsome man to share your bed!"

"I am never alone, I have the Goddess and I can take lovers if it is one of our festival times, I suppose," she speculated uncertain of what the Goddess had in mind for her. "I am not a qadishtu, a priestess that you would call a holy harlot, who lays with men. I am an Entu, a priestess that heals and reads oracles."

"Then you are missing out on a whole part of life. Surely you must have desires too!" replied a surprised Miriam.

I do have desires, she thought. *So many times since coming to this Temple, I have dreamt of the one they call the King of Israel. In my sleep, he sets all my senses on fire, fills me with ecstasy and leaves me begging for more. I must be betraying the Goddess with these wanton thoughts!*

Later that same day, Ceelyha sought the wisdom of Dinah. "Oh, Lady, I had a question for which my mother did not prepare me." Her unease was evident by the reddening of her cheeks.

With a surprised look on her face, the older woman waited for the question.

"Are the priestesses of Asherah allowed to marry or have children?"

Dinah wavered, as if searching for the right words. "Long ago, prior to marriage, young people were given to the priests and priestesses so they might lose their virginity in a holy ceremony. But when Yahweh became more popular, this practice was stopped. Now, the priestesses of the various temples do not marry. They may lay with the opposite sex and even have children without being bound with any man to become his chattel!"

Ceelyha summons her courage and asked, "Have you lain with someone? Did you ever fall in love?"

Dinah shook her head and said with what Ceelyha sensed was regret, "No, that was not in the Goddess' plans for me. Because I had a calling to become a servant of Asherah, I came to the Temple when I was nine years old from a place that was south of here called Beer-Sheba. Since then, I have only known the Goddess' divine love."

"So, it is not forbidden to have love for a man?"

"As long as you always put the Goddess first, then it is acceptable. But if your love for man is stronger and more powerful than that for the Goddess, your will negate your reason for incarnating! Your soul will be in anguish. Just remember the sacred vows that you took when you were ordained as an Entu. Devote yourself to the Goddess and only the Goddess."

"Then a great love for a man would be a curse, not a gift," Ceelyha replied introspectively.

Dinah questioned her with concern in her voice, "Do you love to such a degree?"

Ceelyha lowered her eyes in shame and then told the Priestess about her dreams.

When she was finished, Dinah walked over to the altar, used the divine flame to light some incense in an alabaster bowl before disappearing into the inner sanctum. Before Ceelyha could follow, she returned with the snake basket. Skillfully she picked the two of them out of their nest, raised them to the heavens and chanted softly to herself to induce a trance like state. "Oh, Lady of the Serpents, Lady of the Tree of Light, Grant me the insight to read the dreams of your servant, Ceelyha."

Ceelyha watched the snakes with a mixture of horror and fascination as they coiled around Dinah's outstretched arms. She had seen the high priestess perform this type of divining before but never had it been for her. A rush of heat enveloped Ceelyha as she was overcome with currents of energy that jolted every part of her body. As the Goddess came upon Dinah, the High Priestess's voice sounded as if it were coming from some place deep within the bowels of the earth. Her face shone with light and her dark eyes widened glowing like shiny pools of black water.

"Oh Child of Light, Child of the Moon, Child of the Earth. You have a heavy load ahead of you. One that is called David, King of Israel, waits for you in his city. Just as he is a great leader of his brothers, you shall be a leader of your sisters. But, be warned and listen well! He will cause you as much happiness as he does pain!"

The heat and vibrations stopped. Dinah returned to her natural state and cautiously put the Goddess' instruments back safely in their basket while Ceelyha stood with her mouth open in shock. *What did she mean by as much happiness as pain? Why is my karma so heavy?* Ceelyha needed time to absorb and deal with what had just been declared!

Dinah spoke first. "You can not change what the Gods have decreed. Go to meet your destiny with joy and a pure heart. You have no choice. I will make arrangements for you in the Temple at Jerusalem."

She embraced Ceelyha with the love of a mother. As they clung to each other, Ceelyha breathed in the calm soothing energy that Dinah radiated. She could not undo what the Goddess had decreed. She gathered strength as she recalled her earlier distress with the baru's divination. All she could do was to let events unfold as they should. She needed to trust.

Chapter 6
Jerusalem

Within two full moons, Nintu was again packing her mistress's belongings, but this time it was a much easier chore. All of the beautiful robes, shifts and jewelry, not suited to life in Dor, had been left in trunks. Ceelyha would miss her friend, Miriam, who was very busy with preparations for her marriage to the young man for whom she had secured the love potion. The entire Temple staff assembled to say their goodbyes to the two women. Even Magda hugged Ceelyha. Dinah had tears in her eyes as she gave the Goddess's blessing.

"You have taught us much at the Temple of Asherah. I hope that you will take away some of our customs and incorporate them with yours. You have evolved into a powerful healer and reader of dreams. I speak for all of us, as I wish you success in the King's City. Remember, if you ever need my help, you need only send a message. It is but a few days travel away!"

"Great Lady, I can not thank you enough for all that you have taught me! Words alone are powerless to express my gratitude. I shall be your humble servant forever. I came here as a foreigner and leave with your language, your skills and so much knowledge. I shall call upon you if I am in need of your help."

With great emotion Dinah replied, "We may have finished sharing in this life. If we do not do it in person, then it will be done in spirit!"

With a heavy heart, Ceelyha, her faithful servant and an escort from the village, began their trip by donkey and oxcart to Jerusalem. It was the first time that Ceelyha had traveled outside the Temple's area. As she took one last look at the expanse of blue sea and inhaled its freshness, she hoped that she would see it again. It had been such a source of comfort. She gave a short prayer of protection for their trip as the energy of the Goddess descended upon her to confirm her thoughts.

By late afternoon, they had made their way down to the coast through the oak forests of the Plain of Sharon to the fields of barley and wheat near Joppa, where they would spend the night in a small inn. A friendly innkeeper and his wife welcomed the travelers. The women were given a small curtained sleeping space with a straw pallet and their guide was asked to sleep in the main room with other male travelers. For dinner, they all sat around a table eating goat's meat and honey cakes followed by succulent fruits from the inland orchards. The meal was washed down with a barley beer that had been chilling in the coolness of the inn's deep well. Ceelyha found herself relaxing and enjoying listening to her hosts telling about previous guests who had stayed at the inn. When she learned that David had spent time here as well, she tensed and was full of questions that she was not able to ask in Dor. She had not wanted to raise any suspicion as to why a priestess of Babylon would be interested in the love and political life of an Israeli King for fear of being accused of spying. Miriam had once described him as a 'great tall man with seductive eyes, sensuous lips, a black curly beard and shiny hair that women longed to touch', but she had never seen him in person. Ceelyha had been shocked when Miriam had wickedly insinuated that not one woman had ever been able to satisfy his lustful desires. Dinah had told her stories about his time in the wilderness where he gathered six hundred supporters to rise against Saul; however, when the King actually slept outside the cave where David's men hid, David would not allow them to kill him. When Ceelyha had questioned why, Dinah's answer was that his God had told him not to. Ceelyha also had asked how did his God, Yahweh, chose David and her answer was that Samuel the Prophet had a vision to seek out the young shepherd boy in Bethlehem. She learned from Dinah that it was rumoured that Samuel, as he poured the oil from a ram's horn over the fourteen year old's head, spoke an incantation in a foreign tongue. When he regained control of himself he informed Jesse, the father of David, that the boy had been chosen by the Lord to be King.

So it was in this inn, where no one knew her, that Ceelyha felt comfortable asking what they knew about David's life. One of the guests told her how David was the one whom Yahweh chose to be the leader of the tribes of Israel. Another relayed that David was a kind, gentle soul who spent much of his youth alone with the sheep, while he played the harp and wrote beautiful songs and poetry. A guest also related how – when Saul was in one of his melancholy moods – David soothed his madness and chased away his demons. She heard of the fight with Goliath, a giant Philistine whom David killed without any armor, just a stone. When the innkeeper began to tell what he knew about David's love for Michal, Saul's daughter, and how he paid the bride price by killing over two hundred Philistines for their foreskins, she experienced a stabbing pain in her heart. She shook her head to rebuke such as uncalled for reaction and thought, *I cannot believe that I am experiencing jealousy over a man that I have not even met and certainly have no claim over! Why is this happening to me? Ishtar, O exalted Mother of Wisdom, please help me to stop these feelings!* She thought she heard the Goddess whisper the word 'patience' in her mind. However, when she heard about his other brides, Abigail who was more beautiful and intelligent then Michal and Ahinoam whom he saved from a lion, and the exotic Macaab, his foreign wife who resorted to sorcery in order to stay in his favor, Ceelyha felt sick to her stomach. She rose from the table and went to the curtained partition of her room. It was only after meditating for an extended period of time that these undesirable thoughts were finally dissolved by the Goddess's light. She vowed to be careful and not give her power away like that again.

When Nintu came to bed, no amount of coaxing would make her explain why she left so abruptly. That night she dreamt of David. He came to her in his purple, kingly robes. She sensed his mouth press down on hers and felt the heat from his body as it lay over her. She immediately woke up, drenched in sweat. *What is the Goddess trying to tell me? I am a priestess; I should be able to find the meaning of this.* Then it became clearer. She was destined to have a deep connection with this man in mind, body and spirit. For the rest of the night, sleep would not come.

The following day, the travellers journeyed inland through the gentle hills of olive, fig and fruit trees to their last overnight stop. The host of the inn asked them where they were travelling. When he was informed that it was Jerusalem, his face lit up. "Jerusalem! It is the most beautiful city in the world! At sunset and sunrise, the entire city glows with a radiant hue. There are many great houses, crowds of people from all over the world, music, wine, temples and of course, the great Palace of David."

Ceelyha hoped that his words were a sign from the Goddess that this city would be more sophisticated than the modest village of Dor. On the final day, as the travellers began to approach Jerusalem, they could see the distant hills of Judah with their sparse vegetation and stony outcrops. The area had a haunted, desolate look. The women learned from their guide that this was the place where David and his men had sought refuge from Saul. Ceelyha admired his determination to have survived for ten years in that wilderness.

Finally, Ceelyha and Nintu were excited to see the buildings of Jerusalem gleaming like bricks of gold in the setting sun. It was just like the stranger at the inn had described it! Ceelyha now understood why a king would want this place as a capital city. Not only was it beautiful, but also it was a natural fortress with both sides guarded by deep valleys. The slopes, surrounding the city, were rich with grape vines and olive trees.

The guide explained that the city had been seized years ago from the Jebusites. They had stood on the high protective walls of their city and taunted David's troops only to be later attacked by his ingenious soldiers who entered the city through its legendary underwater streams.

It was dusk when the travelers arrived at the partially closed, thick, unadorned narrow gate. A sentry greeted them with annoyance, gruffly stating, "The ram's horn has already been sounded to call people back into the city. What business do you have here?"

Their guide answered, "We have been traveling from Dor and are on our way to the Temple of Asherah. We cannot spend the night outside the gate! These ladies are tired and in need of food and rest!" The guard reluctantly let them pass.

At this time of day, the markets were empty, the street hawkers had gone. It was so quiet that doves could be heard cooing. As the threesome progressed along the main road, cooking smells of oil and garlic from the low, flat roofed mud houses permeated the air. Moving further into the city quarters, they encountered a section of more prominent two story whitewashed houses. Each had a walled garden with almond trees spilling their flowers onto the street. When Ceelyha asked why the doors were painted a red colour, the guide told her it was for good luck. He directed her attention to a large building that dwarfed all the others, The King's Palace.

Shivers ran up and down Ceelyha's spine as she thought, *This is where this mysterious man lives with his wives and concubines. This is the palace where the political decisions for this land are made. This is where my destiny lies.* She halted her donkey and stared. Even in the dim light, she could see that the Palace was not even half as ostentatious as her father's. The unfinished building to her left led her to believe parts of it appeared to be under reconstruction. The main entrance consisted of several wooden columns enhancing an open courtyard. The outside torches were in the process of being lit, and guards stood in breastplates holding long spears in front of a pair of large doors carved with two interlocking triangles. The letters YHWH were embossed in gold above the entrance. She turned to her guide and asked what the double triangle symbolized. His face beamed as he told her it meant the joining of man's body with God's.

"My Lady, the lower part is man, and see how he is joined at the center, his heart with the upper triangle, God? The country and Yahweh are one."

"And what about those letters, YHWH, what do they stand for?"

"That is the name of the God, Yahweh."

"Lady, come on," cried an impatient Nintu as she pulled on her mistress's donkey reigns. "It is now late and we still have not found the Temple!"

Their journey ended at the Temple of the Goddess which stood at the far end of the city, situated half way up a hill. It had large white painted columns at either side of its entrance and was much more impressive than the one in Dor. The guide left as the two women gained entrance through wooden gates adorned with the symbols of Asherah. Torches lit up an extensive courtyard where Ceelyha saw a huge stone altar loaded with the spoils of the day; grapes, pomegranates and grains. Suddenly priestesses began to flow into the courtyard from the depths of the inner sanctum. Ceelyha surmised that evening prayers had just finished. One, who was dressed in a white cotton shift, stepped forward. Ceelyha judged her to be much older than the others by the grayness of her hair and shoulders rounded from years of bending. Ceelyha immediately warmed to her soft, gentle energy. "You must be the Babylonians from Dor. Would you like to sit and rest while I fetch the High Priestess? She has just finished the ritual to Asherah. Oh, look, here she comes now!"

As the slightly stooped figure of the High Priestess approached, Ceelyha thought the woman had a live red-eyed snake twined around her head! When she got closer, Ceelyha was relieved to see that it was just a realistic copy, designed as a headdress, the red eyes being rubies that caught and reflected the light from the lamps. The High Priestess was dressed in a sleeveless robe in the same dark blue shade as the one Dinah wore but even in the muted light, Ceelyha could see not only was it a better quality, but it was decorated with designs of snakes and goats. The High Priestess had the sign of the Goddess on her necklace of intertwining serpents while

rings and bracelets decorated thin hands and arms. The thought that she could finally wear her finery and necklace here brought a sigh of relief to Ceelyha.

When the High Priestess was directly in front of them, Ceelyha and Nintu fell on
their knees in obeisance. A voice which resounded with authority rang out, "Stand
up and let me see what you look like."

They immediately did as ordered, both surprised at how old the woman was. Her
hair, bound tightly around her head, was completely white; her face, like parchment
was lined and pale, her blue eyes piercing. For a brief moment, as she stood
absolutely still, the older woman's body glowed with the light of the Goddess then
in a blink of an eye, the illusion was gone. But it was long enough for Ceelyha to
realize the power of the woman.

"You will do," she said to Ceelyha. "And who is this with you?" She raised her
eyebrows in the direction of Nintu.

Ceelyha tried not to sound intimidated and cleared her throat to allow more time
to respond before she stated, "This is my servant and companion, Nintu, My Lady."

"Ha, a servant…," the older woman scoffed, "Well, it is not often that we are
graced with such royalty at our humble abode but she will have to do as well."

Ceelyha felt it was her duty to defend Nintu and replied, "Lady, as you know I
am from a foreign land. As the daughter of King Eulma-Shakin Shuki and his consort, the High Priestess Shiroka, I am entitled to my servant, who is also my friend."
Ceelyha felt her knees knocking beneath her traveling cloak and prayed to the
Goddess that she had not offended the Entu.

But the woman simply turned and called for the Priestess who had greeted them
earlier. "Dilbaha, take these women to their quarters. Get them settled. We shall con-
verse in the morning." And with that she turned, dismissing the women.

Ceelyha blushed with humiliation. There was not even a word of greeting, nothing to welcome them. She noted that all the priestesses were staring at her. One in
particular, a woman in her maturity had fastened her steely eyes on Ceelyha. Her
long black hair was pulled back into a single braid like the others but she was clad
in a plainer, less elaborate version of the High Priestess's robe. Ceelyha guessed she
was next in line to be High Priestess. She involuntarily shuddered and tried to beam
with the Goddess's light but felt that She was not with her. She was grateful when
Dilbaha ushered them from the courtyard to a side door that led to a series of low
mud brick buildings decorated with geometric shapes and symbols of various
Canaanite deities.

"Do not be upset by our High Priestess, Bernice. She is really a kind and caring
person. She has had to be hard to survive in Jerusalem. Over the years, so many of
the Levite priests have petitioned to have our Temple taken away from us but she
convinced the King to let us keep it. And," she whispered, "of late, she has not
been well."

Ceelyha murmured a quick prayer for the health of the Priestess then inquired,

"You mentioned the King; does he ever come here?" asked a curious Ceelyha.

"Oh, yes, he is welcome here. He comes every once in awhile to have the omens read!" Dilbaha announced with pride. "Now, here are your quarters. The Temple servants will see to your baggage and other needs. Supper will be brought to you on a tray."

"Oh, Lady," said Nintu with dismay, "I thought by what we saw earlier that our quarters would at least be more luxurious than Dor! Look at this place, it is not much better or larger!"

Ceelyha had to agree with her. The tiny cell, lit by a sputtering torch, was dusty and dingy. There were two worn sleeping mats, a stool, a small dais for a statue and a weather beaten chest for clothing. She replied with more enthusiasm than she felt, "It must be what the Goddess wants for us. I have a feeling…" The skin on her arms prickled, her eyes blurred, the buzzing began in her ears. Her voice became deeper and full of authority as the Goddess spoke through, "We will not be here for long! Be patient."

Nintu was all smiles when Ceelyha released the energy. "Then, we will make the best of it. At least there is room for me to sleep with you!"

After a servant had delivered a tray of goat's cheese and fruits, both women ate and then fell into an exhausted, dreamless sleep.

The call for morning prayer was similar to the routine at Dor. Ceelyha took pleasure as she dressed in one of the shifts that she had brought from Dor. Her spirits lifted as the softness of the material floated about her body. She took a spot near the back of the line, while the sacraments were being made to Asherah who was represented as a golden statue. Ceelyha chanced to look up at the ceiling that was covered with geometric designs painted in a light sky blue. It was obvious this was not a poor, country Temple. She was surprised to see another Priestess light the altar lamp of Asherah and wondered why the High Priestess did not perform the morning ritual. When she asked one of the priestesses beside her, it was explained that the Lady rested in the mornings. After the Temple services, Ceelyha curiously wandered about the expansive courtyard. Its floor was tiled with faded mosaic patterns in greens and blues suggestive of a Phoenician influence. The courtyard also had a large cistern, the size of a small pool lined with bronze. Stone benches, under the shade of palm trees, surrounded the perimeter, while an altar, with remnants of animal bloodstains, faced the entrance. The statue that graced the courtyard was similar to the one in Dor but made of bronze. There was a hall beside the inner sanctum that she had not noticed last night. She intuited it was used for outsiders who chose to stay within the confines of the Temple for healings and omen readings. Dinah had told her that there were a series of subterranean chambers beneath the inner sanctum that had been used in initiation rites and she idly wondered if she would ever be given an opportunity to see them.

A young priestess with an olive complexion and black plaited hair approached Ceelyha. She was wearing a cotton shift trimmed with a gold fringe. Around her neck was a lapis necklace from which hung a silver ankh, the mark of Isis. Even before she spoke, Ceelyha felt as if she had known this woman since the beginning of time. The Goddess descended upon her. Her head swam and vision swirled as an image emerged of the two of them climbing the steps of a magnificent temple in a strange land. There were fountains and large rocks that shone in the sunlight surrounding the scene. Ceelyha sensed they were on their way to perform a healing.

The vision faded as the girl in a cheerful voice with a slight accent spoke, "Welcome to our Temple. I understand that you came from Babylon. I have heard of its beauty and great wealth." She smiled revealing a perfect set of white teeth. "My name is Thu and I too came from a foreign land, Egypt, many years ago. Come, I will show you the dining hall." Her kind smile put Ceelyha at ease and she sensed that she and this woman would rekindle whatever their past had been. While they broke their fast with the other thirteen priestesses, a servant came to announce that after Ceelyha had finished eating, the High Priestess, Bernice would receive Ceelyha in her private chamber. Ceelyha quickly downed the cold millet and set the crude glass of date wine on the rough table with a sigh. Her stomach was in knots just thinking about the High Priestess. She could not think why she was so openly hostile towards both Nintu and herself. Earlier that morning, she had reverently prayed to the Goddess to cast some light on the upcoming meeting. In order to find some inner peace, she listened to the chatting of the dining priestesses. They politely greeted her and asked about life in Dor. She answered in brief sentences, not wanting to appear rude but neither did she want to linger at the table. She was anxious to meet the High Priestess. As quickly as possible, she retired to her cell where Nintu was busy unpacking and rearranging the stark furniture.

Breathlessly she ordered, "Nintu, find me some clothes from home. I have an audience with the High Priestess." Ceelyha hastily dressed in a snow-white diaphanous robe, tied the red girdle around her waist and donned her amulet while Nintu routed in the trunks for a pair of gilded sandals. Just as she finished smoothing the wrinkles from her gown, a servant arrived to lead her along a winding hallway over smooth well-worn gray stone floors to the High Priestess. Ceelyha bowed and fell on her knees when she entered the well-appointed chamber. Beyond the sitting area she saw a second room with carved bed on wooden legs covered with fine red linen and a thick foot carpet at its side. The sitting area had two large windows with half closed shudders to keep out the morning sunlight. On the dresser were several pots of cosmetics, unguents, wooden combs and a large silver hand mirror. A table with a large silver bowl and incense was in the far corner. For an instance, Ceelyha was reminded of her old room in The Land of the Two Rivers until she noted a basket at the foot of a bronze image of the Goddess that was slightly moving. Without asking, she knew what it contained! The High Priestess was regally sitting on a comfortable stool. She wore a loose short-sleeved gown that fell from shoulder to ankle; a golden girdle embroidered with the Goddess snakes circled her waist.

Her unbound hair, reaching almost to her waist, was thinning. The formidable presence of last evening was gone, replaced by a fragile, aging woman. She smiled and said, "For many years, Goddess has warned me of your coming and now here you are in the flesh! Stand and come forward, my Babylonian priestess, my eyes are not what they once were.

Ceelyha was flabbergasted as she obeyed. What did the woman mean that she had been warned about her? Finally she found her voice.

"I am afraid my Lady, you have me at a disadvantage. I do not know of what you speak. Does my presence here offend you? The Lady Dinah sent me here thinking that I would be welcome and…"

Bernice held up her hand to interrupt. "I have been watching you in my scrying bowl since you were a young priestess in training." She pointed to a large bowl sitting on the table. "I knew when you came to this land that you would eventually get here. The Temple of Asherah, diviners to the Royal House, has been waiting for your skills."

"Then why was your divination warning you of me?" Ceelyha was confused. The Goddess had not given her any forewarning!

"Because, it means that my time is nearly done here. I am tired and long to move into the arms of the Goddess."

So that is why she was so unwelcoming! Now it made sense. Her showing up meant that the woman was close to dying! An overwhelming feeling of sadness came over Ceelyha.

"Oh, don't you mourn for me yet!" The woman was uncannily perceptive. "Now, go and prepare yourself for this evening. The presence of Asherah is requested at the Palace. There are foreign dignitaries that the King wishes to impress. He often calls upon the Temple to send him three or four dancers."

Ceelyha's heart began to beat furiously, her remorse was replaced with trepidation as her face flushed and her hands started to sweat. Bernice noted the change immediately. "Yes, I know about that oracle as well."

Ceelyha was amazed how easily the older woman dismissed this as she carried on, "That is why I have chosen you to go. I assume that you do know how to dance?" Without waiting for an answer, she added, "Now go and pray to your Goddess for guidance."

Ceelyha bowed in respect and thanked the Priestess for meeting with her. As she followed the servant, whom she noted had been waiting and listening outside the door, back to her tiny cell, she wondered why Bernice had more knowledge about her destiny than she did. Then an answer came. *If I knew every detail of my life before it happened, then how would that serve me? Where would my growth come from and how would I learn from my experiences? Where would the joy and wonderment be of each moment? Surely I am most blessed by The Goddess!*

She released her reflections as she entered the room. "Nintu, prepare my dancing veils, get out the fragrances. Tonight we will be at the Palace!"

"What, so soon? How can that be? We just got here."

"It seems that we have come at a time when David is entertaining. I will find out what is expected of us from Thu, a priestess I met this morning. Can you arrange for a bath while I meditate with Ishtar, then practice my Goddess dance?"

"Of course, My Lady. I shall return shortly," responded an excited Nintu.

Ceelyha bathed her hands and face with water in the earthen jar outside her room then entered and prostrated herself in front of the tiny statue of Ishtar that Nintu had unpacked and placed on a small diesis. She took several deep breaths and began to invoke the Goddess.

"Oh Lady of the Light, please call upon me, Your most humble servant.

I wait for your wisdom to guide me and grant Your blessing upon me.

Thank you for allowing me to see the workings of You more clearly.

If it is at all in divine order, I ask that I see the outcome of my meeting with David."

She stayed kneeling and tried to reflect on the interchange with Bernice but her anticipation and excitement of the evening kept interfering in her thoughts. She felt overwhelmed with all the events that were occurring in the short time she had been in Jerusalem. She needed to untangle her emotions and let her thoughts be a reflection of the higher part of her being. Through her training, she silenced her mind and in finding that doorway to the silence, her mind grew calm, as her thoughts took on clarity, separate from her emotions. She intuited that the Goddess was quickly advancing her fate but She did not appear.

Once again, I need to step back and just let things unfold as they should. I need to trust.

Nintu burst into the room with servants carrying water. It was time to concentrate on the physical world.

The Golden One

Chapter 7
Meeting With David

The tiny cell was in a state of chaos. Clothing, jewelry and cosmetics were everywhere. In a flurry of activity, Nintu bathed her mistress using a rough cloth that she dipped in the jugs of water that some of the Temple servants brought then went about applying the sacred oils of the Goddess. Star of anise, with its slight licorice scent was rubbed into the ankles and thighs of her mistress. Bergamot, with its invigorating citrus aroma, was dabbed on the priestess's wrists to give her energy while she danced. Cassia, a sweet powerful cinnamon odour, was massaged into the hands. The sweet fragrance of clove oil went under her armpits while a drop of myrrh was placed in the secret part between her legs to enhance her female muski-ness. Galbanum, with its woody, spicy bouquet, was put over her forehead to stimu-late her third eye, the window between the world of the Goddess and the earth. Finally, droplets of nard were rubbed on Ceelyha's breasts to further entice her sen-suality. Nintu then carefully applied cosmetics, combed her hair and arranged so it fell loosely down her Lady's back. She adjusted the silver filigree headpiece so it perched on the top of her forehead then added the appropriate dancer's ankle and arm bracelets.

Nintu barely had time to find the traditional costume and veils of an insharitu that had been carefully packed between layers of cloth to hold in their individual scents in the bottom of a trunk. She quickly passed the materials over the smoke of dried rose petals that she had hastily thrown over hot coals in the cell's small bra-zier. The heat released some of the preserved perfumes that Shiroka had lovingly applied to the outfit before Ceelyha departed. Next, she expertly dressed Ceelyha in scented diaphanous layers of deep cobalt blue silk, which fit tightly at the bodice and hung loose at the ankles. The red girdle of Ishtar was pulled as tightly as possi-ble to accentuate Ceelyha's tiny waist. The veils were delicately attached and the amulet of Ishtar, that looked out of place, had to be worn to show her status as a Priestess. As a final touch, Ceelyha asked Nintu to pull out her medicine box. Inside was a vial of Shiroka's special gold dust, which she sparingly sprinkled on her hair. When Nintu commented on her Lady looking like a Temple Whore, both laughed until they cried.

"Oh, if Mother could only see me now! She would think that all my extensive priestess training was for nothing! I could just have been a qadishtu." They both laughed some more. It felt good to release the tension of the day with her companion.

On a more serious tone, Ceelyha added, "She must have thought I would need this outfit and all these holy oils, or she would not have told you to pack them. Can you find a pair of my jewel encrusted sandals?" Ceelyha wondered if her mother knew that she would have to stand out to attract the attention of the King in order for her destiny to be fulfilled.

When Ceelyha was finally ready, she waited impatiently in the courtyard for a sedan which would take her to the Palace with Thu and two other priestesses. She willed herself to be peaceful and to control her excitement. She wanted to appear dignified and in control while she danced. Thu was clothed all in white to enhance her dark exotic looks, while the others were attired in a deep rose colour. While Thu greeted Ceelyha warmly, the other priestesses talked in low voices and frequently glanced in Ceelyha's direction. For a moment she lost her confidence until Nintu whispered that they were full of jealously because her Lady looked so dazzling. Ceelyha immediately sent out a beam of white light to defuse their negative thoughts. She glanced at them once more and sensed now they were confused about her.

As Thu and Ceelyha shared the same ride on the way to the Palace, the Egyptian priestess asked about the meaning behind the dance that the Ishtar priestesses performed. Ceelyha explained that even though she was not an insharitu, a sacred dancer, she had learned as all of Ishtar's daughters had – the dance of the Seven Veils.

"It is a reenactment of the Goddess's passage through seven gates to the Underworld. At each gate, a piece of clothing is taken from Ishtar until she arrives completely naked in the Underworld – a symbol of not being able to take any possessions with us when we die. The removal of the clothes is likened to a snake shedding its skin, and I use the veils to portray that phenomenon. Also, each veil has its own unique aroma which when swirled arouses the sensuous nature of the audience. When I use this veil," she referred to the one draped as a shawl around her hair, "which is scented with myrrh, it creates the illusion of femininity and mystery."

Thu interrupted, "Then you are naked by the end of the dance?"

Ceelyha laughed, "No, I am wearing my dress. That is as close to being naked that I am willing to go! Then I get redressed, so to speak, as I pass back through each of the gates. In our religion, we believe that the Gods gave Ishtar back each article of clothing as she ascended to earth, and that is the part where I put the veil back on. The dance is about creation, rebirth and fertility. I become the snake moving my hips, descending to the floor and manipulating the veil. Some dances use a live snake, but my training was not that in-depth." She added with a nervous giggle, "I do not really like snakes."

Thu nodded her head in understanding then related, "I too do the sacred dance but we do not believe that you leave this world with nothing. In the Isis religion, we believe that when we die, we take our worldly possessions with us because our soul has need of them. It is through dance that I contact and link with the divine essence of the Goddess. The swirling of my veil is like the wings of the Goddess as She gently wraps around Her worshippers. During the dance, I form a lotus bud with my hands." She showed Ceelyha by folding her hands together and joining her fingers, then placed them over her heart. "It is from my heart where I experience the exquisite ecstasy of opening up to the Goddess just as a lotus flower opens to Ra, the Sun. When I ignite my inner fire, I melt the souls of those who watch me dance. But of course, I do not need to tell you that these eternal feminine mysteries are as closely guarded by the Isis dancers like your rites."

Ceelyha responded thoughtfully, "It really is all the same. The same Goddess, similar rituals, the flexing of the muscles..." she stopped and pointed, "Look we are here!"

The doors to the Palace were wide open and the light from inside spilled into the courtyard. The Temple Priestesses and their servants were ushered by Palace guards down a hallway of shining white marble into a room with several alcoves. Ceelyha watched some servants, laden with trays of meats and delicacies, move to and fro serving men who sat on comfortable cushions around low tables while others continuously filled cups with wine or beer. Smoke from linseed lamps, the heavy scent of jasmine, and the accompanying soft seductive harp music all meshed together to create a surreal atmosphere.

Suddenly the music stopped; the royal guests ceased eating and chattering as the Priestesses made their entrance. Ceelyha noted the various ages and dress of the ten or so men. The foreign guests with short gold-bordered tunics were easy to identify. They wore golden chains around their necks, were clean-shaven and had short dark hair. The Israelis were distinguishable by their simple homespun shifts tied with bronze belts, heavy beards and shoulder length hair parted in the middle.

A man, whose face was hidden in the shadows, gracefully rose from his cushion. When he came into the light, Ceelyha could see his face. Her blood ran hot, everything inside of her tensed. He was the most beautiful man that she had ever seen! She saw the inner and outer radiance that glimmered about him. He was unusually tall, muscular and well built yet with fine, almost delicate facial features. He wore a purple cloak that was fastened over one shoulder, leaving the other bare. Thick gold armbands with flashing rubies encircled his wrists. His tightly curled beard matched the black oiled ringlets of his head that shone in the lamplight. His brilliant smile showed even white teeth as he looked across the room, his deep brown eyes seemed to lock on hers. She lowered her eyes shyly, afraid that he could see into her soul. Shivers rippled through her entire being as she heard the Goddess whisper, "Here is your destiny. I have brought you this far, the rest is up to you."

Ceelyha thought, *He has an aura of strength and vitality, which must attract both men and women alike. David is more than just a king! To be in his presence is like being with a God!*

When he raised a goblet and began to speak, Ceelyha lost her concentration. His voice was of such a strength and vibrancy that she wondered if his god was not speaking through him. "Gentlemen, let us welcome our Asherah Priestesses. They are famous for their dancing and divination." He turned in the direction of one of the hidden corners of the room and commanded, "Musicians, play for our honoured guests."

For a brief moment, Ceelyha shut her eyes to feel the room with her inner senses. The heat from the bodies and the braziers would work together to help to release the seductive scents of her veils and person as she danced. She quickly sent a message by projecting the thought of *choose me first* out her third eye to David. Then she rubbed her hands together to release the aphrodisiac powers of the cassia. An unsuspecting David looked at all four of the women and pointed directly to Ceelyha, "You must be new. I see by the necklace you are wearing that you are a foreigner. You begin."

Ceelyha bowed and made a quick prayer to the Goddess to help her remember how to dance; to not stumble or make a fool of herself. She wrapped the cobalt blue veil around her face and shoulders like a shawl and waited to feel the beat of the music in her soul. Tentatively she turned her right sandal towards the center of her body. The sweet mildly euphoric scent of anise escaped as she began to clang the tiny finger cymbals that Nintu had given to her. The soft steady drum's beat was like a quickening of a heartbeat. The rattling of the sistrums filled the air as the entire room waited with expectancy. As she suggestively shook her hair and sensuously rolled her head back, her vision blurred, her ears buzzed and the presence of the Goddess descended. She then knew without a doubt that she had the power to entice him, making the other dancers pale in her glow. Her consciousness floated away from her body. She felt as if she were looking down at herself from a distant place, then she stepped back into the dance. The soft material of her veil swooshed as her arms rippled like leaves of a tree stirring in a breeze emitting the cloying aroma of cloves. Her hips undulated. She shifted from side to side with snake like movements, as she reenacted the seven initiations that Ishtar undertook when She entered the Underworld. She created a spellbinding circle around the room as she danced with unabashed sexuality. No one spoke. All eyes were on the swirling blue veil, their senses alive with the exotic mixture of fragrances. When the dance ended, Ceelyha bowed to the King, the gold flecks of her hair sparkling in the lamplight. The nearness of him made her senses reel as she breathed in his woody spicy smell of spikenard and she took a step back, about to loose her balance, when his hand reached out and steadied her. "Careful my Golden One," he whispered with a teasing masterful tone. His hand lingered on her arm and she felt as if a God had seared her. She gazed directly into his eyes, and sensed a spark of recognition ignite from the depths of his soul. He stared at her; she met his gaze, and both acknowledged the connection. She knew with the knowingness and wisdom of her craft that between them a bond from the past had been reawakened.

The claps and cheers from the other men brought Ceelyha back to her senses. The magic of the moment passed. She took her place at the side and watched as the other priestesses performed their dances. Each dance was a special tribute to the Goddess.

Thu did indeed dance like the opening of a lotus flower. Her sinuous movements captivated the audience giving them unspoken promises of enticement. But Ceelyha had a difficult time concentrating on any of the dances. Her thoughts were elsewhere. She thanked the Goddess for giving her the strength and skills to perform as well as she did, and tried to grasp the underlying raw emotion that she had experienced while dancing for David. It was for him whom she danced – no one else.

The rest of the evening was a blur. The women were invited to sit with the men and to partake of the wine and food. David retired to his alcove with a few of the guests while Ceelyha laughed and joked with a man from Phoenicia, but her eyes were always searching for David. She was disappointed that he did not approach her but understood that he needed to be with his guests. When it was time to leave, he did not wish the women good-bye. Instead, his commander, Beniah, escorted the priestesses to the waiting sedans.

Back at the Temple, Ceelyha was able to let down her guard. Her thoughts were in turmoil; her body burned with a desire that was frightening. She was not able to silence her mind no matter how many times she tried to clear her thoughts. Instead, she relived the swirling dance, the beat of the drum and her tumultuous feelings for a man that had not even bid her goodbye. Just at the sistrums called the priestess to morning prayer, she was about to finally sleep.

The day was extremely busy. An exhausted Ceelyha was glad to immerse herself in learning the work of the Temple priestesses, as much as possible, in order to stop the thoughts about David. As the people filled the courtyard waiting with their offerings Ceelyha noted that those who came to the Temple for help had similar needs to Dor. The first person she worked with was a man who brought a goat. He asked, "Priestess, I wish to ask how I can find a husband for my daughter. Her mother is dead, so she cannot look after this business for her."

Ceelyha ordered one of the Temple servants to take the goat to the back of the Temple, then she walked over to the statue of the Goddess. She threw some hyssop on the brazier and prayed for the Goddess to use her as a channel. A moment of fear surged through her as she anxiously recalled the lack of communication when she tried to pray before meeting David. When it began to smoke, she watched for images to form. The Goddess descended and Ceelyha silently praised and thanked her, relieved that she was still in Her favour. She then consulted for the petitioner. When she was done, she walked back to the man who was sitting anxiously under a palm tree. In an authoritarian voice she said, "Go to the next village, that is to the west of here, Bethany, I believe is the name, and seek out your old friend who lives there. He has a son about the same age of your daughter and will be glad to pay a bride price."

The man was so happy that his face lit up. "Oh thank you my Lady. Please thank your Goddess for me! I am grateful for the divination!"

The next person was a farmer who had a basket of fruits as an offering. He asked, "What shall I plant in my fields this year? The rains have not been kind to us of late."

Ceelyha went back to the altar not even needing to contact the Goddess but wanted the man to feel that his request was as important as any other. When she returned she said, "Whatever you planted seven years ago, will be the crop for the fields. Do not worry, it will rain as you plant." He too was grateful and seemed appeased.

Over the next few days, she filled requests for herbs for various ailments, passed on the Goddess's wisdom to pregnant women, made predictions about the futures of many young children, and even mixed potions for a herdsman who was having trouble with his sheep. Then, one day a young woman with a few eggs as an offering sought Nintu and requested a meeting with the foreigner. She pushed her unkempt hair under a dirty shawl and appeared nervous as she peered over her shoulder to see if any of the other petitioners were watching her.

"Priestess," she whispered, "Can we talk in private?"

Ceelyha sensed that the woman was in some kind of trouble and led her over to a vacant bench where she bid her to sit down.

"This is my faithful servant Nintu. She is sworn as I, to honor the privacy of your request. Now, what can I help you with?"

The woman hesitated then said, "I do not wish to have the child that is growing inside of me."

Ceelyha tried to keep the surprise out her voice as she asked, "How long have you known that you are with child?"

"Two moons."

"Why do you not want this child? Are you not married?"

The woman held her head down in shame. "No, I am not yet. The child is my uncle's." She looked up and appealed to Ceelyha, "He took me when he was in a drunken stupor; against my will while my father was away fighting in one of the King's wars." She began to weep.

Ceelyha impulsively reached out to take the young woman's hand. She empathized with this woman's plight. It reminded her of the defiled woman in the desert, the one she could not save. She was determined to assist this one as much as possible. "Does your father know what has happened?"

The woman shook her head, her fingers tightened around the priestess's. "He died in the fighting. It is my uncle and his wife and family with whom I live. I cannot have this baby. It will disgrace not only me but my aunt as well!" Her plea became more urgent, "Please, I sought you because I heard that your ways are different than the others. Please help me get rid of it!"

Ceelyha nodded and said, "Nintu fetch my medicine box," She did not know if the herbs she needed would be available in the Temple's storerooms. "And afterward bring me the largest date from the kitchen that you can find; then meet us in the healing area." She led the distraught woman into the hall down the corridor to a small private room with a stone table large enough to lie upon. When Nintu rushed in with the box, Ceelyha told her to keep guard outside the door to ensure that they would not be interrupted. She opened the sacred box and began to mix the necessary medicines together. She ground pomegranate seeds, mugwort, shepherd's purse and hypericum into a paste then stuffed the ingredients into the large date. She gave the woman the fruit to eat and had her lie on the table. She raised her hands high above her head and invoked the Goddess. She prayed,

"O Mother of All Living Life, Mother of all the Gods, Mother of Creation, if it is in divine order, assist me to abort this child that was conceived out of sinful lust. Let the womb of the woman cry to purge its unwanted seed."

When she felt the healing power of the Goddess enter her body, Ceelyha began to move her hands in a counter clockwise direction over the woman's abdomen in order to stimulate the woman's flow of blood. Then she contacted the soul of the unborn child and mentally explained that it had not come at the right time and that this person it had chosen, as its mother vehicle, was not ready. She loving explained that the soul had to return to the Goddess to wait for another mother. Then, from her medicine box, she placed some crystals and gemstones over the area of the womb before she spoke to the woman.

In a masterful tone she ordered, "I want you to go home and lie down for the rest of the day. In a short while, you will feel some cramping as if you were about to have your courses. That will be the sign that the magic has worked. You will have your monthly flow and expel the unwanted egg. May the Goddess be with you on this."

The woman thanked her profusely and Nintu escorted her into the courtyard.

Later that day, Thu came upon an exhausted Ceelyha.

"It looks as if you need to take a break from your work. Have you seen any of the city yet?'

Ceelyha looked at her and shook her head.

"Come, we will have a tour. They can do without us here for a while. Get your cloak to cover your tunic, so we can blend in with the rest of the people!"

Just outside the Temple gates, Ceelyha was overwhelmed by the amount of activity. It was so different from the quiet sleepy town of Dor. It was like stepping into another world. Shouts from vendors, voices of women, men and children, donkeys braying, the creaking of cartwheels all blended together to make up the noise of the city. Merchants sold all kinds of wares- small Teraphim statues of Asherah, live animals, farm produce, carpets, food and drinks. A physician treated cuts that a man had received in a brawl. A scribe translated messages for a foreigner. Guards and soldiers mingled with the hordes of people as they made their way through the city. Ceelyha felt alive – her Temple work and David forgotten for the moment.

"Oh Thu, this is so amazing. It is wonderful to feel the living pulse of the city. Thank you for suggesting this venture."

"Sometimes we can get too involved in the work of the Goddess and forget what life is like in the outside world. In order to heal and divine for other people, we must first understand them." She grabbed Ceelyha's arm. "Come, let us buy a piece of sweet melon and enjoy our freedom."

The succulent juice ran down their chins and fingers. Ceelyha removed her hood and was just about to wipe the stickiness on the inside of her mantle when she became aware that earlier street noises had dimmed. She looked up and noticed everyone appeared to be looking towards a rise in the road from where the sound of horses' hooves coupled with the thunder of metal seemed to be coming.

"What is going on?" she asked.

Someone in the crowd yelled, "He's coming. The King is coming!"

A luxurious chariot, with wheels of iron and decorated with golden leaves, appeared at the top of the road.

Thu whispered, "It was a gift to David from his third wife's father. It was made in Geshur."

David stood in the chariot, driving two white horses, his breastplate jewels flashed in the sunlight. He looked like a God with sun bronzed skin, muscular arms and dark hair flowing in the breeze. He slowed down and waved to the cheering crowd. As he passed in front of the two priestesses, his eyes fixed on Ceelyha and he shouted to her, "Oh, the Golden One, The Princess of Babylon!"

Thu turned to a red faced Ceelyha. "He remembers you!"

A shot of joy and longing enveloped her and she felt herself blush.

Thu stared at her then gasped, "My God, you are smitten by him. You and a thousand other women!"

Ceelyha, realizing she would have to explain her discomfort, decided to take Thu into her confidence. When she finished sharing her feelings, the Goddess's oracle and her fear of her future with David, Thu said, "My friend, let me consult my stones for you. Come, we will find a secluded spot where we won't be interrupted."

The women moved into the shade of a sycamore tree and Thu crouched down on the ground. From a pouch that was tied around her waist, she withdrew a number of shiny stones. She cast them on the ground and observed their arrangement. She cast them two more times, gathered them up and returned them to their pouch. Then she raised her eyes and spoke.

"The Goddess Isis speaks this to you. You will become the lover and confident of the King, but you will pay a price for your relationship with him."

Ceelyha caught her breath. "What kind of price?"

Thu looked as if she wanted to say something more but just shrugged and cautiously said. "That has yet to be determined. You have been sent a warning. It is out of our hands."

Ceelyha frowned, "I wonder why our attraction is so ill fated. This is not my first warning." *I wonder why the Goddess has placed a cloud of uncertainty over this relationship.* She thought for a moment and then reconsidered, "Is there anything I can do to at least to make him come to me and start the relationship? I fear that I may wait forever for him to make the first move. Even the Goddess said the rest was up to me."

Thu seemed more comfortable with this topic and took Ceelyha's arm. "Let us enjoy the rest of our outing and when we get back to the Temple, I will conjure up some magic that will bring him running to you!" Both women laughed at the idea of the possibility of making a spell then they walked back into the street.

The Golden One

Chapter 8

The Dying Priestess

When the women returned from their adventure outside the walls of the Temple, an anxious Nintu met them at the entrance. "Where have you been, My Lady? I was worried and was about to alert the guards! Dilbaha has been looking for you!"

Ceelyha and Thu exchanged sheepish glances.

"We have been out exploring the city. Why does Dilbaha want me?" Even as she spoke, Ceelyha felt a chill through her body. Something was wrong. "Is it the High Priestess?"

Nintu nodded and both women followed her into the inner chambers of the Temple. Bernice had not been at the last few evening praises to Asherah. They had been informed that she was resting, but now it was evident that it was more than that.

Thu spoke as they hurried along, "Why has she not sent for any of us earlier? It is not as though she does not have the very best healers here among her workers!"

Dilbaha, carrying an empty tray, was just closing the door to the High Priestess's room when she saw the women.

"She is deteriorating rapidly. She says she does not wish for any of us to treat her. She just wants to go in peace. See what you two can do for her." Tears welled up in the older woman's eyes. "I am going to pray for her." She left and the women knocked on the door.

A feeble voice rang out, "Come in."

Ceelyha rushed through the reception room to the bedroom. The bed seemed to dwarf Bernice. Her white hair spread over the bedcovers that were tucked up to her neck. Her eyes had a sunken hollow look about them, and her entire person seemed to have shrunk. Without her makeup and ceremonial robes, she no longer had the look of the Goddess. The women bowed. Bernice weakly smiled while Ceelyha lifted her head off the pillow and Thu picked up a bowl of soup that Dilbaha had left on the table, and prepared to spoon-feed her High Priestess. "Here, take some nourishment. You need to keep up your strength. We are not yet ready to send you into the arms of the Goddess!"

After a few mouthfuls, the woman cried, "Enough," then motioned to be helped back onto the pillow. She seemed to have gathered some strength as she looked at Ceelyha and asked, "Was the dancing successful that night at the Palace? Was David enchanted with you?"

Thu answered, "Oh, My Lady. You should have seen the way our Babylonian danced. It put the rest of us to shame! David only had eyes for her!"

"I thought so. And has he come to call on her yet?"

An embarrassed Ceelyha answered, "No, but we saw him today in the marketplace."

Bernice's energy seemed to pick up as she insisted, "We must get him here. Thu, do you still see the Lady Maccab?"

"Yes, your Great One, I do. She often comes with questions about her son, Absalom."

"Does David ever come with her?"

Thu looked surprised. "No, my Lady, I do not think he knows of her coming here. And they, from what I gather, are not on very good terms at the moment."

"Then we must work our magic and bring him here. I will arrange for Dilbaha to ask him to call on me. I have a few words to say to him before I leave for higher places!"

The talking exhausted Bernice; she closed her eyes.

Even though they had been forbidden to, the women spent a long time channeling the Goddess's healing energy to make Bernice more comfortable. When they finally finished and had stepped outside of the room, Ceelyha speculated, "She is dying and there is nothing we can do to stop it. It is her wish and the Goddess's".

Thu nodded her head in resignation. "We must form a watch. I will inform the others and we can take shifts making her as comfortable as possible. The Palace and the citizens of Jerusalem need to be told. I will see to that as well."

Later the next day, when it was Ceelyha's turn to be with the High Priestess, she walked into the dimly lit room that already smelled of decay. She was very aware of a misty veil surrounding the elder's body – a sure sign that Death was closer. But, Bernice was awake and appeared to be alert.

"Are you comfortable? Can I bring you anything?" inquired an anxious Ceelyha as she rushed over to the bedside.

"No," answered the priestess dully, "I am dying. I have not much time left." Ceelyha saw that she was even more shrunken than yesterday; her eyes were covered with a white film.

"I need to speak to you and I want you to listen."

Ceelyha bent over the bed trying not to inhale the fetid breath. "I have been a priestess here since I was a child. My parents, ancestors of the Canaanites, had no money. They sold me into Temple service in the city of the Jebusites when I was the age of eight. I began as a servant, cleaning, cooking and catering to the Priestesses but I also had a calling to be one of them. One elderly woman, skilled in the arts of Gabbalah, took me under her wing and taught me how to divine, how to heal, how to invoke spirits and how to look after serpents." She rested for a moment and began to cough.

Ceelyha, anxious that the old woman not tire herself too much, interjected: "Dinah told me about the Gabbalah's mystical skills and that they were practitioners of divination and healing. She said Moses had declared that the work was punishable by death. But, in order to avoid that law, a branch of prophets began a sect called Gabbalah. These were the only ones who could have access to the world of spirits."

Bernice nodded in agreement. Her coughing subsided; she continued with a strength that surprised Ceelyha. "Oh those old priests, what did they know about the needs of women and the people who seek Asherah? They danced in the hills, drank their secret herbs and read oracles from a God, that only a select few would ever understand!" Her voice weakened.

Dinah had told her that these priests only dealt with political issues, which forced the common folk to seek Asherah's priestesses. Even Rachael, one of the founding mothers of their religion, kept her Teraphim idols hidden from her husband Jacob. She knew that his God, Yahweh, would not give her the strength and guidance that she needed.

Bernice found her voice again. "In this age, we have the ancient teachings of the Babylonians, Assyrians, Sumerians, Egyptians and Chaldeans blended together. We are what the people want and even the kings come for our help. Many times I have conjured up dead spirits for Saul. Many times I have helped David decipher his dreams and I have predicted the outcome of his battles." She paused and looked directly into Ceelyha's soul before saying, "Now, this task will pass onto you and others in this Temple."

Ceelyha was not quite certain how to respond to her Lady. She adjusted the bedcovers and then questioned, "High Priestess, what exactly do you want me to do?"

"I want you to ensure that you will carry on the work, teach the younger ones the ancient arts and ensure that the Temple doors will always be open to the common people."

Ceelyha barely had time to nod her endorsement as the priestess continued, "The supernatural is constantly around all of us. It touches every aspect of the human world. It is up to us to make sense out of a world that is not kind to its inhabitants. Come here, my child."

Ceelyha bent over the woman. She reached out and touched her third eye. Ceelyha's mind flooded with images of a lifetime before the land sunk beneath the sea. She had quick flashes of blue sky, lush tropical vegetation, snow capped mountains, pristine rivers, crystal clear lakes and strange animals that roamed across grassy plains. She watched in utter fascination as a mother, the present incarnate Bernice, was about to give birth. She felt with absolute certainty that she was the child in her womb! Bernice, in the last throws of labour, was immersed to her neck in a container of water located in what appeared to be a dimly lit chamber, surrounded by tropical plants. Tranquil sounds like waves softly lapping on a shore filled the room. Then the scene suddenly moved to a Temple with columns of rose quartz that seemed to reach into the clouds. The steps she climbed towards two massive doors of solid amethyst that opened by themselves were very familiar. She found herself in a healing room where she intuited she worked with her mother, Bernice, using crystals and an unidentifiable source of light. Then as quickly as the entire experience came upon her, it faded and she was thrust back into the present. Ceelyha shook her head, refocused her eyes and looked to the High Priestess to explain but Bernice had removed her hand and appeared to be dozing. Ceelyha reverently bowed to the semi-conscious woman and just as she was leaving the room, a feeble voice called out: "Return to me tomorrow."

Ceelyha silently thanked the Goddess for weaving her magic and showing her the connection with this precious woman. *My mother, she was my mother in the lost land!* But she was not given the opportunity to reflect on the miracle of discovering her past as on her way back to her cell, a vivacious Thu intercepted her. "When do you want to prepare that potion to hasten bringing you and the King together?" she asked with a twinkle in her eye.

Ceelyha's eyes widened with surprise. "Are you serious? I have made many potions for other people, but never one for a fellow priestess! I do not need a love potion. The Goddess has already put that part in motion." She hesitated than added. "Well, what harm can there be in speeding things up?"

"Come, it will give us an opportunity to work together." Thu picked up two lit torches from the hallway and led Ceelyha back past Bernice's room, into the depths of the Temple. They made their way down winding narrow stone steps into what Ceelyha guessed was the original foundation of the building.

She asked as she attempted to extract a spider's web from her hair: "Why are we down here?'

"To show you this part of the Temple in case you ever need a quiet spot to work in." Thu laughed then added in a serious tone, "You never know when you may need a clandestine place. Both of us are foreigners in this land and will always not be totally accepted because we are not true followers of the Goddess Asherah. Our ways are always suspicious." She held her torch out in front. "This is the oldest part of the Temple. The ancients built this subterranean section to be a replica of the chambers beneath the Sphinx. In those days, the priestesses who were being initiated into the order, had to undergo a series of physical and spiritual tests of strength. Just as I am sure your training taught you that one must symbolically die before she is reborn."

There was not room for the two of them to walk side by side along the narrow corridor. The smell of mold and mildew alerted Ceelyha that they were over one of the many underground waterways of the city. She recalled the words of Dinah that temples built in close proximity to water provided better portals to the spirit world. *Then this should be a great place for the art of necromancy.* The idea of doing more divination work sent a shiver of excitement done Ceelyha's spine.

She called ahead to Thu. "Our temples have stepped towers and each one represents a different ascent of the seven stages in our reaching to Heaven to connect with the totality of the God."

Thu opened a heavy wooden storeroom door and from her own flame lit a torch that was hanging on the wall. There was a table with some covered pots and what appeared to be an old battered scrying bowl. The chamber was free of cobwebs and dust as if it had been recently used.

"I discovered this room a long time ago. I asked the High Priestess's permission to use it. It was in this place that I uncovered these containers. Here!" She opened the lid from one of the jars and the room immediately filled with the cloying scent of jasmine.

"These are the sacred herbs of Isis. Some past priestess must have transported them from Egypt. There is a host of special scents and herbs like musk, sandalwood, rose petals, lotus oil, and catnip. I have added some of my own and this is where I come to prepare my medicines and spells. Now, I will make a potion from these to bring you two together." She turned, her dark eyes flashing with intensity and added, "When you are ready to be fully bound, mind, body and soul for eternity to the king, then I shall prepare that potion for you. But for now, what is important for you to keep in mind is that we already know that yours and David's destinies are intertwined, we just need to give a little push to get that happening. I believe David may be here tomorrow to see Bernice, so I will need to find a way for him to unknowingly take the potion."

Ceelyha wondered if she would meet him at the time when Bernice asked her to come to her room. She longed to be in his presence. She imaged their meeting as a bright light encompassing their two souls as one. A quick shiver of confirmation from the Goddess shot through her body. Meanwhile Thu was busy opening jars and mixing. Her words formed a chant.

"Great Isis, Isis-Asherah, Isis-Ishtar, Goddess of Romance, Hear my prayers. Bring together with great haste Ceelyha and David. Great Isis, it is not for we mortals to understand the ways and workings of the heart. Help me to bring these two together. Blessings to you Great Lady." When Thu held up her vial in both hands, Ceelyha could see the Goddess's light shining through the mixture.

"Thank you Thu. Let us see what happens."

That night, after the evening ritual, all the Temple worker priestesses had just sat down to their meal when Dilbaha entered. Her face was pale and drawn. "The time is drawing near for the High Priestess's departure from this life. I read the oracles after the service. She will not live to see another sunset."

Many began to cry and sought each other's comfort. The priestess, Adah, who had assumed the position of High Priestess, taking over the ceremonial duties for the High Priestess, offered a prayer to Asherah.

"Oh Asherah, Mother of All, with Your wings of light, accept our sister, Bernice, protect her from evil as she journeys to You. Make her transition as easy as possible. Let her go from dark to light. Let her feel Your love. We surrender our loss and pain to You. Wipe away our tears. Clear our grief so that it does not hold her spirit here. Blessed be to You, Asherah."

Later, in the crowded sleeping chamber, Nintu asked Ceelyha, "Do you think our lives will change with a new High Priestess?"

Before Ceelyha answered, she sat up on her pallet aware of the concern in her servant's voice. She carefully sought her words before she replied. "I do not know what the Goddess has in store for us. Are you unhappy here?"

"No, I like the other servants and the freedom of going out into the city. It is not as exciting as Babylon but it is much better than Dor!"

"On that, my friend, I agree. But what of the young soldier Jacob, whom I have heard you talk about?"

"Yes," she answered shyly. "He comes and asks for me from time to time when he is not fighting for the King." Then Nintu hesitated as if she was gathering the courage to speak, "Could I impose upon you to read the oracles for me? I wish to know if anything will become of us."

"Oh course I would be happy to read for you. We will try to do that in the next few days when I am not so busy with the High Priestess." Ceelyha hoped her voice did not betray the foreboding feeling she was getting. Even though Nintu was her servant, she was free to leave and marry at any time, and was not bound for life. The thought of losing her trusted childhood friend, the anticipation of perhaps seeing David tomorrow, the pending death of Bernice, and her journey into the past, kept her awake most of the night.

The morning ritual did not have the same uplifting effect as usual. With heavy hearts, everyone went through the motions of awakening the new day and praising Asherah. When the day fully dawned, it was dull and gloomy to match everyone's moods.

Breakfast, a time for much talk about the upcoming day, was subdued. Every worker went about her duties without her usual enthusiasm.

It was well past noon when a trumpet announced that the King was arriving. The priestesses and petitioners, who were in the courtyard, prostrated themselves as David entered riding gloriously on a great black horse. His hair shone like the feathers of a raven as he flicked some loose strands off his shoulders before he dismounted with agility and grace combined. When he removed his deep purple overcoat, specks of dust fell about him like flecks of light. His simple short brown tunic, accented with a gold belt, revealed strong muscular legs. To Ceelyha, he looked even more appealing than ever. She felt a burning desire in her that needed cooling, as she openly gazed at his handsome features, that were flushed with the heat of the day and the ride. As Ceelyha continued to stare, a ray of sunlight burst through the clouds and shone a beam of light around him. It was as if his God was trying to tell the pagan worshippers that He had equal or even more power! Every one of the Temple workers was in awe. There was no doubt in her mind that his divinity radiated to all.

The new High Priestess, Adah, rushed into the reception area. She humbly bowed and accepted David's offerings to the Goddess of a purse of coins. His eyes skimmed over the people kneeling and he spoke with a strong authoritarian voice, "Rise up my people. It is I who should be bowing to all of you. Now where is the Her Greatness, the Lady of the Asherah?" He turned to the priestess who led him away into the labyrinth of the Temple.

When he left, Ceelyha felt as if the light had been taken away. She played with the sound of his voice in her head; it was like the music of the Gods. She knew he had not seen her in the crowd but hoped that they would have a chance to meet later. She checked her appearance. Her shift was marked with soot from reading the oracles of the petitioners. *This will not do! David has to see me at my best!* She rushed into her cell yelling for Nintu. "Come to make me presentable. The King is here!"

Nintu came running from the garden where she had been gossiping with the other servants. "My Lady, what is it you are shouting about?"

"I need to have my hair plaited. I need my fragrances and a fresh shift."

"Do you want cosmetics?"

"As lightly as possible. I do not wish to be adorned like a whore while the High Priestess is dying. But get the gold sparkles out for my hair and my mother's oil mixture so I will be sure to attract the attention of the King. Get me the myrrh and frankincense. I need to appeal to his male senses! When we are done... no," she changed her mind and gestured for Nintu to leave, "Go now and get a message to Thu. Tell her to proceed with our plans.

"What plans are you talking about? Why are you so flustered?"

"Just hurry and do as I say. Then get back here as soon as you can."

Ceelyha immediately felt her colour heighten with excitement. Her stomach seemed as if it were full of the fluttering of tiny bird wings as she eagerly anticipated meeting David. It took several deep breaths to calm down. A while later, she emerged looking and feeling more composed as she made her way to the High Priestess's room. Adah and Dilbaha were waiting outside the closed door. Adah eyed Ceelyha with displeasure before whispering, "The King is with her now. When he is finished, we will offer him some refreshments in the receiving area. Thu is taking care of that. Now, we need to clear the Temple of petitioners and visitors."

Ceelyha nodded. "What can I do to help?"

Dilbaha replied, "Stay here while Adah and I see that things are in order in the reception area. If the King leaves Bernice's room, before we are back, then escort him to the courtyard."

A small part of Ceelyha wanted to rejoice that things were falling into place but it was overridden by the sad circumstances surrounding Bernice that was finally bringing her and David together. She heard voices in the room, and then suddenly the door swung open. The King stepped out and looked directly at Ceelyha. "My Golden One!" he exclaimed as a deep glow ignited in his dark eyes.

Ceelyha felt as if the floor beneath her feet had given way. *My name sounds magical when he says it.* She felt weak and embarrassed, not used to flirting or playing games.

"You honour me, my Lord!" and she bowed to him aware that the heat from her body would be releasing her carefully applied scents to entice him further. He reached out and touched her hand to help her up from her knees. His touch was electrifying. It shot through her veins, making her blood boil. He looked directly into her eyes, and she read in his face a raw primal need that matched her own. He moved towards her, but stopped as a weak voice called out, "Is that Ceelyha? I am so glad you came. Come in here both of you."

They entered the room, which became incredibly small as the form of David occupied a great portion of it. Ceelyha was not certain whether it was his physical size that produced that effect or the greatness of his spirit.

Bernice looked much more shriveled and helpless than yesterday. With her priestess eyes, Ceelyha noted the thickening of the grey mist. Her breathing was labored; a rattling sound emanated from her chest. Yet her rheumy eyes were surprisingly keen. Bernice did not even attempt to sit up but held out her frail emaciated hand for Ceelyha to grasp. Between coughs, she wheezed, "I wanted you two to be formally introduced. Not that you are unaware of each other. King David, this the Lady Ceelyha, Entu and Princess of Babylon."

Ceelyha dared not look into David's eyes for fear she would betray her true feelings for him.

"I have informed David that you can easily take over the reading of the omens for the Royal House of David. He has given me his word that the Temple will continue to be under his protection."

Bernice's voice faded and she slipped into a deep sleep. Both David and Ceelyha quietly left the room. Dilbaha and Adah were waiting by the door. Ceelyha said in a voice choked with emotion, "She is going quickly. I think you both should be with her. I have only known her a very short time, but she has deeply touched my heart and soul. I will take his Highness to the courtyard for refreshments." With that, she bowed and motioned for David to follow her along the corridor. Her hand accidentally brushed the side of his tunic and it was all she could do to not reach out and touch more of him. The coolness of the stone walls did not soothe the fever burning inside her. She felt tongue-tied and did not speak. He also did not say a word. They entered into the brightness of the courtyard where refreshments had been laid out in honor of the royal guest.

Thu graciously directed David to a small table, under the shade of a palm tree of food, which was displayed before them, and prepared him a plate. "Here, my Lord," and she curtsied and looked in Ceelyha's direction, "I beg you please to take a bite of this delicious date." Then she waved for Ceelyha to come closer and said, "You must have the other half," and walked away. She proceeded to divert anyone who was coming in their direction by pointing them to a larger table that was laden with sweets and drink.

David willingly took a bite then held out the rest of the date in front of Ceelyha's mouth. She saw his eyes smoldering with desire as he provocatively whispered, "Taste this, my Golden One." He popped the fruit onto her tongue, his finger lingering in her mouth.

Ceelyha felt her cheeks burn, her heart quicken at his touch as a warmth spread between her legs. The fruit had a slightly bitter taste, which she recognized as the potion. She swallowed it and waited, not sure what to do next.

David began to talk, "I knew you were special and now I understand why. You are a priestess and a princess. What a powerful combination! How long have you been here?"

Ceelyha – hoping her voice would not betray her nervousness – lowered her eyes shyly, afraid that he might be able to read her shameless thoughts. "My Lord, it is going on a year and more that I have been in your country. But I have been at this Temple, only two or three moons."

"Do you like it here?"

"Very much so, My Lord." She raised her head and directly met his sultry eyes. The Goddess descended upon her and she was able to see past his airs and kingly attire into his true self, his passion, his devotion to his people, his love of his God, his creativity, his animal instincts, his driving ambition and a disturbing darkness that she could not figure out.

"I am sorry, what were you saying, My Lord?" He had been saying something while she had been delving into the depths of his soul.

"Are you comfortable in your lodging?" he repeated.

"Ah, how do I answer that?" She hesitated wondering how much to reveal then quickly admonished her thoughts and decided to be honest. She cleared her throat and continued. "No, to be honest. It is very small especially sharing the cell with my childhood servant. It is no better than what we had at Dor." She wondered if she had overstepped her limits but he had asked.

"Then you will be moved. There must be plenty of spacious rooms in the Temple. I will make the arrangements before I leave."

"Oh that would be wonderful My Lord. I sometimes do miss the luxury of the Ishtar Temple in The Land of The Two Rivers," she wistfully added.

"I can well imagine that being such a beautiful woman, you would be used to the finer things in life." He moved his body closer to hers. "I do not mean to be disrespectful nor wish any dishonor," he whispered, his breath sending shivers of delight through her body, "But I would be your lover if you will have me."

Ceelyha pulled back, needing a moment to compose herself. Either that love potion worked too quickly or she did not understand the rules of seduction!

David sensed her discomfort. "I apologize. I should be more discreet. I mean you no harm."

This is what the Goddess has willed for me. I even had a potion made to advance his interests. Oh, this is moving beyond my control, she thought.

She cleared her throat and put on what she hoped was a sophisticated look.

"My Lord, I would be honored to be your lover. When shall we begin?"

David threw back his head as a deep throaty laugh escaped from his mouth. The tension broke between them. "Well, perhaps not right here, although it is tempting! Let me arrange the time and place and I will send for you."

At that moment Adah was approaching and Ceelyha thought it best to mingle with the others. She bowed to the King as she whispered, "I will await your call, your Highness."

Thu caught up with her. "Well, it must have worked. You look like the cat that caught the mouse!"

Ceelyha nodded and whispered her thanks. She felt as if she were floating high above the courtyard, she was so happy.

She did not see David again that day. Adah had come and informed her in a tone dripping with animosity, "The King has requested that you be moved to a new room as soon as possible." She gave Ceelyha a condescending look, "One, he said that would suit your status as a Priestess and Princess. You will move into mine when I take over the role of High Priestess in this Temple." She stared hard at Ceelyha, "Unless you wish to displace one of the other priestesses in the meantime."

Ceelyha felt a shiver of dread pass through her as she replied, "No, I wish to cause no upset to anyone. I would not like to profit by having a room at the expense of another. And I especially…" she emphasized the I, "would stay where I am if it meant that Lady Bernice would live."

With that, Adah turned abruptly and left.

Nintu was ecstatic about the new rooms. Ceelyha did not tell her what the move was going to cost both of them.

Late that afternoon just prior to sunset, Ceelyha received a message from a servant that the time was drawing near for Bernice. She hurried along the corridor and found a distressed Dilbaha in the reception room, rooting through a trunk. She looked relieved to see the younger woman. "I am glad that you are here. I need some help. Bernice has asked to be dressed in her ceremonial robes. She also wants her face painted and I am so afraid there will not be time. The evening is almost upon us..." her voice faltered.

"I would be honoured to assist," Ceelyha replied, relieved that she was not too late.

Together they assisted the old woman into the elaborate robe of dark blue, the colour of lapis with its golden designs of snakes and goats. The Goddess' necklace, with its intertwining serpents, was gently placed around her neck. Rings and bracelets decorated her emaciated hands and arms. Dilbaha carefully applied red pomegranate paste to her sunken cheeks and her dry mouth while Ceelyha painted malachite on her eyelids and then added kohl to enhance their depth. The headdress, with a flashing ruby, was finally added to her white hair, which they held up with combs. The priestess looked like a tiny dressed up doll.

In a feeble voice, she rasped, "Now, I wish to be taken out into the courtyard so I can see my last sunset and look upon the face of Asherah."

Between the two women, they lifted her light frail body and carried her to the dimming light of the courtyard. A makeshift pallet of cushions had been arranged on the ground in front of the statute of Asherah and the waiting priestesses – all dressed in white, the colour of death – helped to make her comfortable.

Adah stepped forward, puffed with her importance and asked, "Shall we perform a healing so your soul might have a smooth transition?"

Bernice managed weakly to nod in agreement and the priestesses formed a circle around her as the sun began its final descent. They held the palms of their hands down over her body and began to hum, softly and slowly, the universal healing sound of Ohm. Everyone lifted her hands up to Heaven gradually increasing the chant's momentum and volume. Every priestess could feel the healing energy that was being generated, surge through her own body. A oneness was sensed as they envisioned the soul of Bernice rise out of her earthly body and soar into the waiting arms of Asherah. Twilight moved in with a soft dark blue inkiness, and Dilbaha bent down to check to see if Bernice was still breathing. She raised a hand to let the others know that their beloved leader had made the transition. The women kept on with their chanting even as the tears, a sign of sadness and joy, poured over their faces. Another priestess had found safety in the arms of the Goddess.

Later, in the privacy of her darkened cell, Ceelyha gave herself permission to grieve. She and Bernice had not had enough time to even begin to get reacquainted in this life. After she had spent her tears, she suddenly found herself being inundated with light. A feeling of intense love flooded her being. And, in that sacred field of energy, she heard the voice of Bernice. "This is why you needed to be in Jerusalem, to ensure that the work of the Goddess will not be lost!"

The voice ceased but Ceelyha basked in the glowing warmth of reassurance for the rest of the night.

Chapter 9
Life with David

For three days – the time when the soul is susceptible to wandering evil spirits – the soul of Bernice was carefully watched over by the priestesses. Temple workers fasted, prayed, and a blood sacrifice of a lamb was made. After the conventional mourning time, the High Priestess was cremated; the fiery flames permitted her soul to escape from the world of form into the world of essence. The others formed a protective circle around the burning corpse while the Goddess spread Her wings and carried Bernice to the Heavens.

David and a few members of the Royal Court came to the Temple for the funeral rites. Dressed in his royal blue robes, he picked up a handful of ashes from the funeral pyre and rubbed them onto his face. He shouted to Heaven, "Let the Priestess find peace in Your arms." The rest of the courtiers followed his example except for a woman dressed in a yellow, filmy sheath with a veil that hid the features of her face. She carried herself with such royal assurance that Ceelyha knew it was Maccab. Her first impression of the queen was she had an aura of exotic mystery until the Goddess sent a warning shiver down her spine. Ceelyha immediately sensed Macaab had knowledge of the black arts and used them to her own advantage. While she was trying to read what the woman actually was capable of, a feeling of intense heat and excitement interrupted her. Without even needing to look, she knew David was at her side.

His warm breath was full of promise as he whispered, "Tomorrow night, my Golden One, a sedan will come for you." Then he was gone as if the interchange never happened. Ceelyha was sure that her face was beet red and was not the least bit surprised to see Macaab's back stiffen as she stared. The veil was gone, revealing painted brows that arched above eyes, which narrowed, like those of a jaguar about to leap on its prey. Ceelyha involuntarily shuttered and immediately invoked the Goddess to dissipate the woman's hatred and jealousy.

Later that day, Nintu was busy, once again unpacking her mistress's belongings.

She looked up from her work as Ceelyha entered the room. "Oh, Lady, I am so happy in these rooms. Look, we have a window that overlooks the garden! You have an actual bed and I have my own pallet. There is even a basin for bathing! Of course, it is nothing like what we had in Babylon but there is even a sitting area where you can receive guests!"

Ceelyha knew that its previous occupant did not willingly relinquish this room. Adah, having taken over the position of High Priestess had filled it with a heavy dark energy that had the potential to harm its new occupants.

"Nintu, wait. Do not unpack anymore of our things. Bring me my medicine box. Stir the coals on the brazier, and then leave the rooms. Open the window and I will call you when all is clear."

When Nintu's jaw dropped, her face full of fear, Ceelyha gently told her, "Adah is not happy with the fact that David favors me. Although she might not directly wish me any harm, she harbours a great deal of ill will towards me. There are a lot of unhealthy emotional fragments that need to be cleared before we can safely move in. We certainly do not want her negativity entering our energy fields!"

Nintu nodded with understanding, got Ceelyha what she needed and left her mistress. First Ceelyha took out some dried cedar and threw it on the burning brazier in the corner of the sitting area. As its sweet odor filled the room, Ceelyha picked up two of her crystals, one clear and the other a smoky quartz, and raised them up to the ceiling. She positioned herself in front of the statue of Ishtar that Nintu had carefully placed on a dais in the tiny alcove and began to perform her magic.

"Oh Ishtar, Goddess of Light, I ask that Your powers be invoked through these crystals to clear this area of any negative thoughts, evil spells and demons. Send Your Heavenly light through this clear white stone into every particle of wood, stone, metal and fabric of this room."

She waited, carefully watching the energy swirl and move about the room. "Now, my Goddess of Light and Love remove any debris through this black crystal and send it up into the ethers to dissolve."

She waited as the mist cleared and the energy transformed. "Thank you Goddess of Ishtar, Mother of All Gods. Blessings be upon You." Ceelyha then called for Nintu to complete the unpacking.

Thu came to visit Ceelyha in her new chambers and sat on a stool.

"This area feels so light. I am pleased that you have moved from those cramped quarters! David must have used his influence," she said partly in jest.

"I am not going to deceive you, Thu. Yes, he did ask for me to move and Adah was not too pleased about it. She seems to think that I am some sort of threat to her position here."

Thu's black eyes widened. "You do not see that you are? You, my friend, are about to launch into an affair with the King! Of course her position is threatened. She can be replaced by you in an instant if David decrees it."

Ceelyha had not thought of that. There no been no forewarning from the Goddess or anything in her dreams to indicate that situation was coming up. Then she recalled Dinah's oracle. 'One that is called David, King of Israel, waits for you in his city. Just as he is a great leader of his brothers, you shall be a leader of your sisters. But, be warned and listen well! He will cause you as much happiness as he does pain!' *At the time, I foolishly only concentrated on the part about the pain David would cause and had ignored the other part. So much has yet to happen!*

This knowledge both excited and scared her. Was she ready for such a responsibility? Did David have the power to instate her as High Priestess? Would the Goddess be pleased? Ceelyha suddenly realized Thu was waiting for a response. She touched her necklace as if to gain Shiroka's wisdom and with sincerity replied, "Oh, Thu, I did not realize that. No wonder she appears to dislike me!"

"Perhaps it is time to consult your Goddess over this. See, what is in store for you before you give Adah a false sense of security."

As an after-thought Thu added, "And Macaab as well, is not too pleased with what she sees."

"I sense a darkness about her. You are her confidant, are you not? Does she not consult you about her son?"

"She has sought my services over her son Absalom, but she is not to be trusted."

Ceelyha nodded as she spoke, "I have seen something of her dark side already. But come, I will consult the oracles. I also promised Nintu that I would look into her future as well. Would you like to be present while I do it?"

Thu threw her head back and laughed. "Try and stop me! I am very curious and you owe me this."

"Thu, can you suggest a place where we can go and not have prying eyes upon us? How about the lower part of the Temple where we were the other day? You must know of a spot."

Without hesitation Thu said, "Have you broken your fast yet?"

Ceelyha shook her head.

"Nor, have I. This is a perfect time, so get what you need and meet me at the same steps we used the other day."

Ceelyha called to Nintu to gather the necessary materials for divination. Then the two of them found Thu waiting with three lit torches by the stairs. She led them down into the bowels of the Temple beyond the room she had previously used, to an empty room with a stone altar in its center. Crude sketches of various figures were barely visible on the smoke ruined walls.

"It appears this room was used for some sort of sacrifices to the Gods. It is really difficult to tell what Gods these were," speculated Ceelyha as she strained to decipher the pictures. She suddenly stiffened and announced, "The room has a strange feeling to it."

Thu's eyes flashed with interest. "Look, at this writing! It is not my language, is it yours?"

"No, it will be from the ancient Canaanites. I have no idea what it means but I am sure that the Goddess will protect whatever work we do here."

Thu immediately raised her amulet above her head and invoked the protection of Isis in her language. Then she stated,

"This was just one of the initiation rooms that the ancients used. I am intuiting that the altar was used for the slaying of sheep or goats, and then the entrails were given to the priest for divination."

Nintu spoke for the first time, "My Lady, that's what our priests do!"

Ceelyha agreed. "It is unnecessary to kill animals to read the omens but it seems as if it was a male orientated ritual. Come, Nintu light the brazier we brought. Put the crystals and image of the Goddess on the altar and let us get started."

When Nintu used one of the flames from the torch to ignite the brazier, an eerie shape was cast on the wall. While the coals were heating, Ceelyha put herself into a trance. She began to hum, a low droning sound, then closed her eyes and held up her arms swaying her body back and forth to a rhythm that only she could hear. When she felt the presence of the Goddess, she opened her eyes, took some incense that was held by Nintu and threw it into the fire. Immediately a smoky vapour began to form. Her voice deepened; she stood up perfectly straight as the energy surged through her and she nodded to Nintu that she was ready to read the omens.

Nintu, used to her mistress's sessions asked, "Will I be with my soldier?"

"To the one that is called Nintu, the soldier that you are in love with, is true in his heart to you." She paused and looked more closely at the smoke. "I see him going away on a horse as if to battle and yes… a message comes to you that fills your heart with pain." Ceelyha doubled over as she felt the anguish and then turned to her servant. "That is all."

Nintu's face looked drained. She turned to Thu and gasped, "What do you think that means?"

Thu thought and then replied, "Only the Gods know what the future holds. All we can do is read what They are trying to relay, however we do not always interpret correctly. You have to accept that you are the one that asked for the reading and only you can determine how to use the information."

While Ceelyha was still deep within her trance, Nintu threw another lump of incense on the fire. The voice of the Goddess commanded, "To the one that is named Thu, what is your question?"

"My Lady, my question is what is the past relationship between the one through whom you are speaking, and myself?"

"Look into the mist. The two of you are dancing and laughing."

Thu tried to see what Ceelyha was reading in the vapours but only saw the smoke.

"You were together in many past lives as priestesses. Two shared incarnations were in the lands that disappeared beneath the seas. Then there were two lifetimes in the land of the Pharaohs. In one, you were Daughters of Ra. It was your jobs to keep the sacred flame burning in the temple. You were Isis priestesses together in a later time… you combined your healing powers to remove entities from troubled souls…"

The voice of the Goddess trailed off. Ceelyha appeared to lose her connection to the Goddess! Shadowy images formed in the smoke. A cold force of air rushed into the room with such fury that the flames of the lamps extinguished. A sound began, first as a droning, then increasing in volume and intensity until it resonated like the swarming of thousands of angry wasps. Then an agonizing moan seeped out of the corners of the room as if an evil force had been conjured up from the bowels of the earth. The flapping of wings thundered ricocheting off the stone walls. The two women stood in fear. Then all was silent. The energy changed, light prevailed and the room was once again calm as the channeling continued, "One of you died trying to assist the other."

Ceelyha slumped to the ground and Nintu quickly threw more incense on the fire while Thu made a silent prayer for protection. Ceelyha continued to speak though her voice was muffled, "Your souls have chosen many times to share and learn. Once, again, it is as priestesses, you have come together again in this life to work and assist one another." The voice stopped.

Thu paused as if unsure if she should press for more information. Nintu nodded for her to go ahead. "Will Ceelyha replace the current High Priestess?"

More incense was scattered. "It is her destiny to do so. However, not many will be happy about it. There is much hidden beneath the surface. It is not in divine order for you to know more than that since the one called Ceelyha does have some free will. May the Light and Peace of the Gods be with you in this."

Nintu went over to Ceelyha, gently guided her to a seating position. She rubbed her hands until Ceelyha opened her eyes. She cleared her throat and said in a cracked voice, "Did the Goddess give you both what you wanted?"

Thu and Nintu exchanged quick glances then filled her in on the details.

The next day, Ceelyha was nervous about the pending liaison with David. She went about her duties in a daze. She tried several times to invoke the Goddess but was unsuccessful. She assumed it was because at the moment, she was too mired in the physical world. Immediately after the evening ritual, she took great pains with her appearance. She had Nintu pluck away all her body hair as if she were preparing for her wedding night. Nintu poured myrrh and unguents into water that had been drawn earlier from the well in the courtyard and carried back to the room. She washed Ceelyha's hair and brushed it dry so that it fell in long curls down her back. When the infamous gold flecks were added, Ceelyha smiled as she thought of the endearing name that David called her, My Golden One. She chose a red shift embroidered with gold designs. She wore no jewelry, not even her necklace; she wanted to emanate a womanly aura of desire and sensuality rather than that of a priestess. She carefully applied droplets of nard and myrrh to augment her own nat-ural musky fragrance as a further enticement to David.

A servant knocked outside the door. "My Lady, a sedan is here from the Palace for you."

Ceelyha looked at Nintu, grateful that she had not asked any questions. Instead she had only said "You look like a princess tonight. You are glowing with beauty. Good luck My Lady."

"Tonight, I return the favour for our new quarters," replied Ceelyha with a nerv-ous laugh as Nintu helped her on with her cloak. "Do not worry about me. I will be back before the morning ritual." She turned and slipped out of the Temple hallway into the dark courtyard hoping no one was watching. The ride to the Palace seemed much slower than the last time without the company of Thu. Ceelyha kept the cur-tains closed, not wanting to draw attention to herself as the burley servants traversed the city streets. In her mind, she hoped that she was doing the right thing and tried to convince herself that this was what the Goddess wished.

When she was set down, Ceelyha was surprised that it was not at the front gates of the Palace but at a side entrance. *This is very clandestine. I wonder how many others he has secretly slipped into the palace! Perhaps he is ashamed to have others see me or maybe it is for my own protection.*

A male servant with a small-lit torch stepped out of the shadows and motioned to her to follow. As they silently climbed steep, well-worn steps, soft fluttering sounds of harp music floated through the stairwell. The music stopped as an anxious Ceelyha and her guide reached an unpretentious wooden door. The servant gently knocked, and David's deep voice called out, "Enter."

The servant discreetly ushered Ceelyha into a large chamber. She noted various animal skins and thick carpets decorated the walls and floors of the room. The ser-vant bowed and departed before Ceelyha gracefully fell on her knees with her eyes lowered and head bowed. David laughed and said, "Rise up, my Golden One. There is no need for formalities here!" and he directed his hand towards a large bed on a dais that dominated the room.

Ceelyha tried to remain calm and in control as he helped her up but his touch seemed to seer deep into her soul.

"You look like a frightened lamb," he said with tenderness and concern. Then his voice grew stronger," I want you Ceelyha. Ever since that night when you danced, the images of your movements so sleek and sensuous, are in my mind day and night. I cannot think of governing my people; Yahweh has forsaken me; my wives are repulsive. You have bewitched me with your golden magic. Please free me from your spell!" He pulled her into his arms but she stepped back.

"I did not cast a spell on you that night!" she replied indignity. *Maybe after but not before. And I do not want to hear about your wives or god.* She almost blurted out "*It is our destiny to be together. It was ordained long before we set eyes on one another.*" But thought better of it and said, "You have been in my dreams for many years, so let us stop this nonsense about spells and bewitching."

David must have sensed that she was upset by his words and pulled her close again. She felt the warmth and strength of his body, his groin stiffen beneath his light tunic. Never had she been this close to a male! She tensed, not knowing what to do next and stepped back again.

"Do you still have your maidenhood?" he asked his eyes wide open with surprise.

She nodded.

"I thought that you would have been given to one of your priests when you became of age in some sort of fertility rite!" he said with astonishment.

"My father sent me away before that could happen. His priests read the omens and sent me here to this Land."

With concern, he posed the question "If I lie with you, will it be of disservice to you? Will your Goddess forsake you?"

She answered with as much conviction as she could summons, "You called me beloved, and I am here."

He coyly looked at her then held out his hand. "Come my Golden One, to the bed. I will be gentle with you. Here," he held up a cup of wine, "drink this, it will help to relax you." He knelt in front of her and waited while she took the wine, his dark irises glowing like embers.

As the warm liquid slid down her throat, Ceelyha became aware of how wonderfully alive her body felt. She could see the lust in David's eyes and sensed that she was just as powerless to resist him, as he was powerless to resist her. She drained the entire cup while he watched. She got lost in the depths of his eyes trying to read into his soul. Then, he was beside her on the bed. He bent to kiss her on the cheek but she moved and her mouth met him full on the lips. She felt a groan escape from some hidden place deep within her as his tongue sought hers. A powerful surge of raw sexual energy bolted through her and she reached out to him with her body. All she wanted was to feel him naked, to touch and be touched. He hastily pulled off his clothes. Her jaw dropped as she looked at his magnificent body. In the dull light of the room it glowed like a golden statue; it was as if she were looking at a living God! His manhood stood erect, throbbing and she gasped with desire. He fell upon her and both of them struggled to remove her sheath. At one point she heard it rip but did not care. The sensations that were flooding her body were more important. David was finally there in the flesh! He was no longer a dream! She wanted him, had to have him.

She held out her arms, saying his name over and over, hearing him say hers; then his mouth was everywhere – her throat, her neck, her breasts, her stomach, her thighs. She exclaimed, "I give myself as the Goddess to you! We both have waited too long in this life to be joined!"

She sensed David was taken aback by her words but this was not the time to explain. The need for them to connect as man and woman made her frantically urge him between her legs. He pushed into her. She screamed – he stopped. She begged for more and he kept entering her, filling her as she melted and molded around him. She journeyed through a dark, uninhibited place; then reached up into particles of indigo blue light and finally exploded with ecstasy. A deep sense of peace and a great warmth spread over her as the tempest that had been raging in her for months subsided.

"My Golden One – that was an experience unlike any I have had before!" David said affectionately. His black eyes were soft and full of peace as he pulled away from her.

"Nor I." she said with a smile on her lips, and they both fell into the deep sleep of satiated lovers.

She woke up sometime in the middle of the night, not knowing where she was. Her insides hurt; there was stickiness between her thighs, and she was covered with a musky masculine scent. Then she saw him, stretched beside her in their huge bed, asleep like a baby. She smiled, kissed his lips, forgot about her discomfort and shyly touched him. Then she began to be bolder, exploring the hardness of his chest and stomach, the long muscles of his legs. The strangeness of his male body, glowing in the weak lamplight, excited her beyond her wildest dreams. He woke up and murmured in a drowsy voice. "My Golden One, come, let us declare our love for one another.

"David, my God, David, my God," she groaned as his groin hardened with desire.

Her thighs reached up to receive him. She met his thrust with an abandonment that momentarily frightened her. She wondered where all this passion and animalistic lust had been hiding. Then her mind freed, as they became, one flesh, one mind, and one spirit.

A knocking at the door woke them. Light from the windows poured into the room. Ceelyha sat up in shock. *I have missed the morning ritual with the Goddess! I am late for the petitioners! What will the others think, what will Nintu think?* She frantically grabbed a tangled cover and shot out of bed.

"Not so fast my love," David's voice stopped her. He yelled in the direction of the door. "What is it?"

A male voice replied "Your Highness, you are late for the Royal audience."

It was then Ceelyha noticed a large door that must have led to the rest of the Palace. The entrance she had used was hidden behind a carpet! She should have been more observant last night. *I am just one of his women* she thought, but when David began to stroke her bare breasts while he called out to the voice behind the door, she did not care. "Tell them I am indisposed. Have a servant bring me breakfast. Lots of it, enough for two." He winked at Ceelyha, "I am ravenous".

She felt herself sink one again under his spell, as he began to seduce her. In the morning light, she not only discovered him with her eyes but also with all her senses. When they were done, she was surprised to see a tray of food beside the bed and she blushed with embarrassment. "Do you mean to tell me that someone came in here while we were making love?"

David shrugged as he got out of the bed and began to inspect the food. "My servants are trained to see only what I tell them to. Do not worry, your reputation will be intact."

Ceelyha was angered. "Intact, how can you say that? I will be missed at the Temple and now everyone will know that I have become your harlot!" There, she had said that dreadful word. Tears flowed and uncontrollable sobs wracked her body.

David came over and took her gently into his arms, "Oh my Golden One do not be upset. I sent a message to the new High Priestess, when the sedan came for you last night, that you were needed in my harem to assist one of the women. See," he kissed the tears that fell, "I always think and plan very carefully."

She was so taken aback that he would just assume that she would stay the night that her crying subsided.

"You have certainly thought of everything," she replied haughtily.

"I am King," was his arrogant reply. "Now come, woman, let us enjoy what time we have left. We have much to talk about. And you are not my qadesh or harlot as you referred to it! You are my love."

A bath was ordered. *It is strange that my body feels so sore and tired; yet I feel like I am floating on a cloud,* she thought as David, himself, poured the perfumed water over her. *I wonder where the Goddess is and what she thinks of all of this. Surely I will come to my senses soon. I know that I should invoke her wisdom but I want to be just a woman for a little while longer totally enjoying the pleasures this man has to offer.* As they took turns washing each other, they talked. David wanted to know about her childhood and her parents. When she told him about seeing her father only once a year; his eyes clouded over and he stated. "I too do not see my children as much as I should." She sensed that topic made him sad and steered the conversation to his childhood.

"As you have probably heard I grew up near Bethlehem in a humble home like the ones you saw in Dor."

"You mean with the stable attached to the living quarters?" It was hard to imagine this stately King living in such a lowly abode.

"The animals' body heat kept us warm in the chill of winter. We had one room with slits for air and light, not like this." He indicated the two large windows in his chamber." We did not have any beds, just sleeping mats. The house was very crowded with eleven people. Therefore, I was very happy to escape to the hills to look after my father's flock."

She listened carefully trying to understand the man with whom she had fallen in love.

"It was in the hills, away from the noise of my family and the town that I found peace."

"Did you not miss people and the excitement of the village?"

"I went home most nights, unless I was far up on the mountain. And no, I did not miss them that much. I was the youngest. It seems like my brothers were always away fighting Saul's wars. Since I could talk to no one, I started to listen to the sounds of nature. I saw the grass growing, felt the water flowing in the streams, smelled the fragrance of the flowers; and witnessed the rise and fall of the sun. I was able to see and hear God in every one of his living creatures…" his voice trailed off as if he were speaking more to himself than to her.

"I too know that the rocks of the earth are the Goddess's bones, and that the grasses are Her flowing hair. Her faceless presence is everywhere." Her affections deepened for him with those words.

David nodded in agreement and continued, "And Yahweh's presence is everywhere too. When I look back on that time, it was my forced isolation that put me in touch with Him. I opened myself up to His glory and began to praise the beauty of nature and all living things by playing His music and singing His songs."

"Tell me about speaking to your God. It must be similar to my communication with the Goddess. Do you have any warning before he speaks?"

"So, your Goddess also speaks to you?" He seemed fascinated with the fact that the Goddess spoke to her and rose out of the bath.

As she dried him in a soft thick cloth she smiled, "Of course, how do you think I became a priestess? Ishtar chose me to represent Her on this earth, just as your Yahweh chose you to speak for Him to the people who cannot hear Him. There have been many others before us with whom the Gods have chosen to communicate, and there will be many in the future. That is what makes us different and," she hesitated unsure of how much to reveal to him, "that is probably why we are so attracted to one another. We each recognize the other's divinity. You are the closest thing to the God embodied for me and I am the closest to the Goddess incarnate for you."

David responded by taking her in his arms, "That is why we are so good together. Now let us celebrate being divine with our bodies!"

Ceelyha laughed and allowed herself to be swept away by their mutual passion.

As the sun set and she again missed out on honoring Asherah at the Temple, she turned in his arms and said, "I heard that a man called Samuel came to you and declared you would be the next king. Had your God not already told you this?"

"No, not in those words. Yahweh told me that I was the chosen one to unite and then lead the twelve tribes of Israel but I did not know how that was to be done."

"So Samuel's prophecy must have surprised you?"

"Yes, I was still very much a youngster when he came and told me the Lord had chosen me to be King."

"But how did Samuel know?"

"I never asked. He was a prophet of God; I was just a mere shepherd boy."

Ceelyha looked him directly in the eyes. "Yes, but you too were hearing the God so Samuel was no more divine than you!"

David thought over her words before he answered. "I suppose you are correct but I just assumed that he was more enlightened. We were raised to believe that the High Priests were the servants of the Lord."

Ceelyha tried to diminish her annoyance over such a preposterous statement as she looked at him firmly and spoke with her inner wisdom. "I think that he did not count on King Saul being such a good leader. He probably thought that Saul was gaining too much popularity with the people. Was it not the priests who had more power than a King? Was not Saul the first king in your land and did not the priests appoint him?"

"Samuel chose Saul because the priests could not guard Israel from her enemies. He did a good job winning a battle against the Philistines until he sacrificed beasts to the Lord without waiting for Samuel. Samuel was so angry that he cursed Saul and told him that the Lord no longer favoured him. But in Saul's mind, he had proof that the Lord was on his side because he had won the battle. He began to question whether the High Priest could really communicate directly with the Lord. Then something happened to Saul's mind; maybe he used his powers to bring on the madness. We will never know for sure. He used to cry out, see demons and hear voices in his head. And that is where I came in. I was called upon by Samuel to go to soothe the King with my songs and music."

Ceelyha interrupted him with the idea that maybe Saul was communicating with the one called Yahweh and just did not know how to channel the energy properly. Then she repeated her earlier question of how did David know when his God was speaking to him.

"Priestess, I can not answer that. That is a private matter between Yahweh and me."

Ceelyha looked at him to see if he were serious or not. His face was solemn and his jaw was stubbornly protruding outwards. She assumed he was serious.

She changed the subject by asking, "I also heard you killed a giant without a horse or armor. Is that true?"

"Yes, I did kill the Philistine, with the help of the Lord, my sling shot and my expert aim. I remember how I tried to put on a soldier's armor but was not used to it and frankly; it did not fit very well. The Lord spoke to me telling me that I had nothing to fear and I trusted His words. I instinctively aimed at the enemy's forehead because that is how I killed the lions that tried to attack my sheep. I got him on the first attempt. I do not even think that I had any fear. I just wanted to prove to my brothers and father that I was worthy of being a soldier."

David paused then almost wistfully added, "My family thought I was too young to be in the army, but I wanted to fight for my country, fight the heathens for my God."

Ceelyha immediately had a vision that she did not share with David. She intuited that each passing year, the size of the giant was exaggerated. She sensed that the man had very poor vision and with the added disadvantage of having the sunlight in his eyes, he did not see David sling the rock. These thoughts she kept to herself and instead responded, "And is that when you became a warrior?"

"Yes, no one could deny me that! Now, enough of this talk, I want you to hear something."

David picked up the harp that he had been playing before Ceelyha arrived and began to pluck its strings thoughtfully. Then he sang. "The Golden One is full of grace and beauty, she wove a spell that binds my heart to her. Ishtar is her protector and I her servant. The Golden One has granted me part of her heart."

Ceelyha's soul was touched by his words of devotion. It sounded so strange that such a gentle voice could come out of such as gigantic man! Goose bumps accompanied her though that he definitely has the voice and demeanor of a God.

It was late at night when Ceelyha left the King. She had asked about their next meeting and he had answered it would be arranged in a few days. As she rode in the sedan, she was comforted by his distinct scent that lingered provocatively on her skin. She stole like a thief back to her rooms.

Chapter 10
Temple Life

The night of her return, Ceelyha was too late for evening ritual. She was dismayed to have once again missed the opportunity to gather through ceremony with the others. Dusk and dawn were when all Goddess worshipers, whether it be for Asherah, Isis, Demeter or Ishtar came together as one consciousness. Not only was it a sacred time to show Her their love and have Her, in return, bless their minds and spirits but it was also when she felt connected to Babylon. Each time she praised Asherah, she imaged her old Temple with the veiled dancers as they swirled their magenta clothes and Shiroka in her ornate tunic with its golden designs offering nourishment to The Lady.

When Ceelyha entered her room, an eager Nintu greeted her, full of curiosity. Ceelyha, somewhat shyly but with a touch of vanity, told her that she and David had become lovers. She could hardly believe it herself. *A foreign priestess and the King of the Israelites in love with one another!* Nintu's response was that she was not surprised and she was happy for them. She then told Ceelyha how she too was now more involved with Jacob, and they had discussed the possibility of marriage. Ceelyha had a flash of regret that she, herself, would never be a wife but the feeling quickly passed as she told herself, *I am no man's chattel. And yet, I am tied to David emotionally and physically so it seems I am exactly that, waiting for him to come to me!*

She quickly veiled her thoughts and replied with as much joy as she could manage, "How happy I am for you! Nintu, come, let me hug you!"

As the women embraced, Ceelyha added with what she hoped was detachment, "You are, of course, free to do whatever you please."

"You do remember the reading that you gave me? It did seem to indicate that this was coming up for me. Do not worry, I will just let things happen as they are supposed to take place." Nintu must have sensed her mistress's dismay because she added almost apologetically, "Jacob is away most of the time, anyway."

Ceelyha smiled to relieve her friend of any feelings of guilt, "It is all as the Goddess wishes. We are merely Her instruments playing the parts She has chosen for us."

At the dawn gathering, Ceelyha could not find the usual portal to the Goddess's world.

Some part of her felt sullied, as if she was still with David and she was not worthy to partake in the sacredness of the act. *Up until my coupling with David, since I was old enough to partake in the rituals, this was when I felt most alive! Now I am not sure which one arouses the most energy in me!* Then she quickly chided herself, *how can love making and praising the Goddess even be compared?* She desperately desired the opportunity to make the recommitment of her heart to the Goddess and time to sort out her feelings.

With a heavy heart, she tried to immerse herself in the ritual but not a moment passed without thinking about David. She relived that first time of his touch and her response, over and over in her mind then was consumed by guilt to feel so wanton without him even being present! She came to the awareness she was lonely without him, as if a vital part of her life was absent, and even more worrisome, was the realization that the Goddess was presently not filling that aloneness.

Thu spoke to an exhausted Ceelyha just after the Goddess ritual. "You look as if you have had several hours of love making," she teased." You have the look of a satisfied woman."

Inspite of her feelings of despair, Ceelyha could not help but smile as she replied with a touch of immodesty, "Yes, I have, and my entire body aches. But Thu, I am worried that my feelings for him are stronger than those for the Goddess. He has consumed my thoughts, my body, my emotions and my spirit. It seems that I have betrayed Her for him."

Thu thoughtfully answered, "You are just tired. You need to concentrate on getting back into your routine here. By the way," she whispered, "Adah has not been too pleased about your absence. She asked Dilbaha to bring you to her when," she imitated in a sarcastic tone, "'it is convenient for the princess'."

Foreboding arose in Ceelyha. "What can she possibly want with me? I have done nothing wrong. A message that I would be detained at the Palace was given to her by the King's own servant."

Thu merely shrugged her shoulders and sent Ceelyha a look of sympathy. Together they made their way to breakfast. As soon as they approached the table, the others fell silent and avoided looking at her. She turned to Thu in surprise.

"What is being said about me? Do they not believe that I was helping at the Palace either?"

"Apparently not. I will get to the bottom of this later."

Ceelyha's throat felt as if it had closed during the uncomfortable meal. After, she looked for Dilbaha and told her she was ready to see the High Priestess. Dilbaha informed her that she would be received the following morning.

Between assisting a petitioner, who had a pain in his hand that prevented him from tending his vineyards, and a woman who wanted help interpreting a dream about a wolf eating a mule, thoughts of David kept intruding on the Goddess's work. Ceelyha did not sense Her presence when she mixed ash leaves with burdock or when she deduced that the wolf was the woman's husband and the woman was the mule that he was trying to control. Discouraged with her work, Ceelyha returned to the quiet of her rooms. She bowed down in front of Ishtar's statue and poured out her heart.

"Oh Lady of Love, Lady of Light, I pray that You will not forsake me in my time of need. I know that the mortal, David and I were fated by Your divine wisdom to be together as man and woman but I fear that I have offended You by giving him my heart. I ask for My Lady's divine guidance to remove the lustful thoughts I have of him by replacing them with only Holy ones of You. As Your servant, I vow to put You before all others. I fear that I am no longer filled with Your light. Assist me to release the feelings of abandonment and to move back into Your clarity of being as I no longer sense Your presence when I heal or give prophecies to others. I ask that You guide…"

A blaze of white light suddenly surrounded the golden statue. Ceelyha felt the familiar signs of the Goddess and heard an imposing voice that resonated to the corners of the room.

"Ceelyha, my priestess. Do not fear. I have not abandoned you. You and I still have much work to do. It is only your perception that I have withdrawn my divine gifts from you. This will not happen unless you break your sacred vows!"

The light dimmed and the presence of the Goddess was gone. Ceelyha sunk to the floor. Tears of gratitude poured down her cheeks and she finally slept.

In the afternoon, Nintu found her mistress crumpled at the foot of the statue and immediately concluded she was ill. She called for Thu to assist her to lift Ceelyha onto bed. Ceelyha kept insisting that she was just tired, but Thu mixed an elixir, which helped her have a dreamless night. She rose on time for morning rituals but ached all over as if she had been beaten with a stick. Thu must have sensed that Ceelyha did not feel up to the humiliation of being shunned by the others at break-fast; so she took her aside from the rest of the priestesses who were just about to break their fast and whispered, "They think that you and David are close, maybe not lovers yet, but soon will be. Remember, you were seen talking to him when Bernice was ill and then you were again seen consorting with him at the funeral. Then, your status suddenly elevated with your new rooms. When it was heard that you were at the Palace, they put two and two together. You should also know that Macaab was here yesterday afternoon asking me many questions about you." She quickly added: "I did not tell her anything that was not public knowledge. I would never betray our secrets!"

Ceelyha trusted her friend and thanked her for her loyalty. "Oh Thu, what am I to do? I seem to have upset a lot of people. I fear that things are not going favorably for me. Now not only are the priestesses jealous of me but so is his wife, and there is more than just one wife!"

"I do not know what the repercussions will be. I guess only time will tell," Thu paused to think then added, "Use your training and surround your situation in white light. And, we must consult the oracles on this. But now, you had better go to your audience with the High Priestess."

Ceelyha heeded Thu's advice and flooded herself with harmonious thoughts as she hurried to her appointment. She briefly stopped at the entrance thinking how strange it is to be in the rooms that were occupied only a few days ago by Bernice. There was little trace of her left; Adah had filled up the room with her belongings and energy. Even with the brazier on, the atmosphere was cold and dismal. Ceelyha bowed in obeisance to the new High Priestess and was left for an undue length of time on her knees before she was given permission to rise.

She was greeted her with open hostility, "I do not know what kind of upbringing you have had but I do not approve of you becoming another one of the King's harlots!"

"What are you talking about?" asked Ceelyha as calmly as possible. "Were you not informed that I was called to the harem?"

"You were not called to the harem, you were the harem!" Adah spat.

Ceelyha lower her eyes and mentally asked for the Goddess to remove her anger so that she could answer calmly and honestly. She looked at the older woman and stated flatly,

"The King requested my presence at the Palace. You are right. I was not at the harem. I was with him. But my Lady, pleased be advised that as the Goddess is my witness, I did not have anything to do with the message about being called to the harem. I did not know about it until much later."

She could see Adah was struggling to get control of her emotions. "The King obviously favors you, at this time, "with an emphasis on the word 'time', "But think about when he tires of you, and, he will tire of you as he has tired all the rest. I hear that he has already named you!"

Ceelyha was confused, "What," she faltered," Are you referring to, My Lady?"

Adah condescendingly replied, "He has followed in the Hebrew's tradition of his Adam naming Eve. He is asserting his authority over you by naming you the Golden One, I believe it is."

How does she know that already? I cannot believe how news travels so quickly! I will not bother to correct her!

Adah did not even wait for a response. She continued on, "As High Priestess, I forbid you to see or consort with him anymore and if you disobey me, then I shall seek another post for you. Perhaps it is time for you to return to Dor!"

Now Ceelyha understood the depth of Adah's jealousy and fear for her position. Ceelyha opened her heart and silently prayed while sending a beam of healing light to alleviate the older woman's fear *"May Your light shine in me that I may extend it to this troubled soul."* The Goddess came upon her with more force than late. Her ears buzzed, eyes closed and she clutched her necklace in her left hand. She heard Ishtar's words in her head.

"Do not back down or fear this one that wishes to disregard your divinity. She is not as connected to the Goddess as she would like to be. Stand up to her. That is the only way to gain her respect."

Ceelyha opened her eyes and was aware that the High Priestess witnessed the Goddess's energy by her ashen face.

Ceelyha spoke in a calm authoritarian voice. "High Priestess, I mean no disrespect to you or the Temple of Asherah. But, if the King asks for my services whether it be to warm his bed or to read omens for him, I will oblige. The Goddess Ishtar has arranged for us to be together, and you, of all people as the High Priestess of Asherah, must understand that to disobey one's calling is to break one's sacred vows."

Adah backed away, narrowed her eyes and sternly replied, "I have nothing more to say. Return to your duties." She turned her back on Ceelyha so abruptly that her lapis robe rustled. Ceelyha was shaken by what had occurred and wished that she could speak to David. Did Adah have the authority to send her back to Dor? Would David allow that? Would the Goddess permit that? She was so deep in thought as she walked back to her rooms that she almost ran into Dilbaha.

"Ah Priestess. Here you are. Did the time go well for you at the Palace?"

Ceelyha did not know how much Dilbaha knew. She dared not to speak and just nodded.

"Good, then I need to remind you of the promise that you made to Bernice."

Ceelyha confused, looked at her. What was she talking about? Then she remembered and blurted out "To teach the dancing? To teach the younger priestesses the dance of Ishtar!"

Dilbaha smiled and replied, " I have some new recruits that would be honored if you would teach them."

"Of course, I would be more than happy to instruct them." Suddenly she was happy, grateful to be given a chance to do the Goddess's work, grateful to forget her problems for a while.

Under the shade of the courtyard's palm trees, Ceelyha addressed four young women. "The technique of the dance is the secret of inner muscle control which is basic to the sinuous movements that glorify the Goddess." She flexed her arms, then thighs to demonstrate and clanged her finger cymbals.

"But first you put yourself into a trance – like the state where you implore the energy of the Goddess. You become her instrument. How each of you achieves that condition is personal, between you and Her. Once you have the mystical connection then you must become the serpent and move like a serpent with each part of your body."

"When I dance, I express the serpent wisdom by undulating, circular flowing movements like this;" She swayed her pelvis. "This is the center of life, where creativity begins, where control over emotion begins, where the feminine manifests." She kept undulating and then used her arms to show the flow. "From here the energy rises like the snake ready to strike with grace and fluidity, ever so slowly, in calculated and timed movements."

She turned her back to the students saying, "Visualize my energy as it rises up my spine, as it coils up to my chest and shoulders, and moves through my arms," She raised her hands in a graceful fluid movement, "up towards the house of the Goddess." She stopped and instructed her students to try to follow what she was doing.

As she demonstrated how to use a veil like a shimmering cloud of light, to tie the dance together, she thought, *this is so enlightening to be teaching and concentrating on bringing my knowledge to others that perhaps it is time for me to teach the initiates other things I have learned.* But she remembered the words of Adah that she could be sent back to Dor.

Several days passed with no word from the Palace. Although Ceelyha was content to do the Goddess's work, it was as if some vital part of her was missing. It was time to consult the Goddess. She fasted for three days then called upon Nintu and Thu and the three of them descended into the bowels of the Temple.

In that same room where Ceelyha had done her last divination, with the brazier lit and with the necessary preparations, she began to connect to the Goddess. She closed her eyes, stretched her hands up to the ceiling searching for a humming vibration that would elevate her spirit. Finally she swayed her body back and forth as Nintu threw incense onto burning coals. When the Goddess was upon her, Ceelyha opened her eyes. A smoky vapour began to form off the coals. Her voice deepened as she tuned into the images.

Nintu called out, "Oh Goddess, what can you tell us about your servant Ceelyha and King David?"

"I see the one called David. He is a strange mixture. I see him as a loving, kind man, connected to his God … yet I also see him as cold and calculating. Ceelyha believes that she has lost her heart to him … in doing so, thinks she has forsaken her sacred vows. I see her floundering... not knowing which way to go. I see her following this man even though it is against her vows. He needs her Goddess connections and will use her as he has used the others … his is a greater destiny than hers… her contract in this life is to help him, as he has helped her in past lives. In this life, for a short period of time, they will fulfill their destinies together. Then, her use will wane... it is My greatest desire that she will heed her lessons…"

Ceelyha stopped speaking and Nintu quickly threw more incense on the coals but the connection was gone. Ceelyha slumped to the floor and was assisted back up by Nintu who slowly rubbed her hands to bring her back to full consciousness.

When Ceelyha opened her eyes she looked intensely at her partners to see what emotion they were experiencing. Detecting sadness she said, "I was fairly deep but I was aware of some of the message from my beloved Ishtar. But I do not see it as being depressing! What did I miss?"

Thu gently answered, "I think you missed that you and David have a contract together. When you both have fulfilled that commitment, you will no longer be of use to him." She turned to Nintu. "Is that what you perceived as well?"

Nintu responded nervously, "Oh, it is not my job to question what the Goddess predicts. I am just here to look after Her channel, my mistress."

Thu's eyes narrowed and she had a far away look as she spoke to Ceelyha. "Look, I am not sure what your past was with David but I am going to find out for all our sakes. I will read the Goddess's cards that were handed down from my mother. They will tell us what we need to know. Meet in my room after the morning ritual."

That same evening while honouring the Goddess, Ceelyha did not feel well. She alternated from a sweaty hot to a frigid cold. Her head ached and it felt as if tiny needles were being stuck into her body. Just as the food was about to be offered to Asherah's statue, she felt faint and rushed out into the courtyard, not caring about the questioning eyes of the other priestesses. She took several deep breaths and tried to get in touch with her body while vaguely aware of Thu's hurrying footsteps behind her. She felt herself slide to the ground as her consciousness completely severed from her sick body. She was aware of all that was happening around her, yet was not part of it. She hovered over her body while Thu frantically screamed for help, then watched as Thu, Dilbaha and some of the other priestesses lifted her up, carried to her room and put her in bed. She saw Nintu bring a cup of wine and pour a tiny amount down her throat. The heat from the harsh liquid briefly brought her back into her body, but the aching, chills and fever drove her quickly out again. She hovered over the scene while Thu ordered Nintu to get her medicine box and Dilbaha applied compresses to her brow. Ceelyha waited as Thu examined her body to discover it covered with tiny red dots. When Thu cried out that it was like a thousand needles stuck in her body, she floated away. She traveled through the darkened evening streets to the Palace and into David's chamber. She viewed him on the huge bed, where they had made love only a short time ago, with a woman in his arms. It was Macaab with a satisfied look on her face! *My God*, Ceelyha thought, *she has somehow invaded my body with her black arts! I thought from what Thu had said that she and David were at odds. In the name of the Goddess, she has used her magic to seduce him once again. She knows that I have been with him!* Shock abruptly pulled Ceelyha back into her body. She felt cold and weak as if her life force was being drained. Thu was administering poultices and laying crystals around her body, which was wrapped in cloths soaked in strong medicines. Ceelyha tried to sit up to tell Thu what the Goddess had shown her but she did not have the strength.

As she spooned a hot sour tasting tincture into Ceelyha's mouth, Thu must have sensed Ceelyha's return because she whispered, "Hush, quiet, it is alright, you just need to rest now. I have taken care of it. You will return to good health in a few days."

Over the next two days, Ceelyha wandered in and out of consciousness. Snippets of the priestess's conversations 'curse from the Queen,' 'almost dead', 'the King's lover' floated into her awareness as they administered to her needs. She thought she had heard David's voice in her room but was not certain whether or not it was a hallucination. In fact, she was not certain she could tell reality from fantasy as she felt suspended in an altered reality; neither dead or alive. She thought that she had visited her mother in Babylon and sensed her worry about her daughter. She thought she heard her say, "Never look to another human to complete you. Only the Goddess can do that!"

When she thought she saw her father, riddled with gout, planning his next conquest, sadness for the fact that he never made the effort to get to know her flooded her soul. She thought she saw Dinah frantically praying for her to get well and wondered how she knew that she was ill. She thought when she saw Macaab screaming with anger as she threw a doll, stuck with needles, into the fire, Ceelyha sent her the Goddess's white light and the message that she forgave her but it got lost in the ethers. She thought she saw Adah begging the Goddess to forgive her thoughts of jealously. She thought she saw Nintu telling her soldier that she could not come to him now. She thought she saw Thu divining with her Egyptian magic cards.

She woke just before sunrise feeling weak but knew with certainty that she was going to be well again. She was not quite sure what had exactly happened to her until she looked at fading red spots on her arms. *Macaab; Macaab used her black magic to try to kill me!* Nintu got up from her sleeping mat and smiled. "My Lady, you gave us all quite a scare. Shall I fetch you some food?"

Ceelyha answered feebly, "Please tell me what happened. I dreamed many strange things and am no longer sure what is real and what is not."

"You have been very ill for the past ten days with a high fever and a rash all over your body. At first we did not know if it were contagious, something you had caught from one of the petitioners but Thu intuited that it was a curse by the Queen. All of the priestesses have taken turns watching over you, healing and administering Thu's herbs to exorcise the evil out of your body."

Ceelyha spoke with resignation, "Then I was not dreaming. Tell me, was David here?"

"Yes, my Lady, He came as soon as he heard you were ill. He was very concerned for your well being."

So, everything she had experienced was real. She felt not only depleted physically but also spiritually as well. Whatever the Goddess was trying to teach her through this experience, she hoped the lesson had been learned! She sighed and said, "Bring me some soup and a little bit of goat's cheese. I have to get my strength back as soon as possible."

Nintu bowed with a smile of delight, "Welcome back, My Lady. I have missed you!"

As soon as she heard of Ceelyha's recovery, Thu ran to her chambers. She hugged her patient and started to feed her some of the warm soup while she filled Ceelyha in on everything she had missed.

"David came and I practically had to remove him physically from your chamber, so I could strip the sheets and perform a healing on you. He was beside himself with worry. Adah has often visited you and seemed genuinely concerned. I think she thought that she a hand in causing your illness, until I told her that it was a dark, evil magic from one of David's wives. She seemed relieved about that. Personally, I do not think that Adah has enough power to do that sort of thing, nor the knowledge."

Between spoonfuls, Ceelyha asked her friend why she had been so open to picking up the negativity that Macaab had projected on her. Thu answered, "We do not know from whom or where this woman learned her black arts. She is a priestess of Anubis, the God of the Underworld and just as powerful as you or me. She wanted you removed from David's life and probably would have succeeded if I had intuited what was happening. Did you not guess it was her?'

"Yes, I saw her first in bed with David mocking me. Then I saw an image of me in a crude doll with needles stuck in it. What was she trying to do?"

"She put poison on the tips of the needles and using a magic spell, pricked the doll as if it were your skin. But she did not deceive me that day when she asked about you. I knew she would attempt something but I just did not know what. It was the rash that gave it away. It showed up in perfectly arranged lines. It was not sporadic like a disease would be. That was my clue."

"Oh Thu, I can not thank you enough for saving my life! I could have died!"

"No, the Goddess arranged for me to help you. You must know this!"

"But Thu, as a priestess of Ishtar, an Entu, Her light in me should have repelled the evil."

"I think you left your energy field wide open when you had sex with David. It is not that you forsook the Goddess; it is that you let your guard down. You opened to him in mind, body and spirit and were vulnerable. Macaab would have waited until you were at your weakest point, then pounced. Also you were tired when you returned and that too lowered your resistance to the dark forces. But never mind, you are going to be well and will fight off anything anyone throws your way. I have strengthened your energy field so it is like a metal shield!"

"So that is my lesson, to protect myself from outside forces!" Ceelyha was so grateful for her friend and the Goddess. She laughed, her face full of relief as she added, "So I can repel even your magic?"

Chapter 11
David's Gift

"My Lady, my Lady, the King is here. The King is here!" Nintu ran into the chamber, her face aglow with excitement. "Hurry, get up and I will put some paint on your face and some flecks in your hair. He is in the courtyard, waiting to see you!"

Ceelyha impatiently allowed her servant to comb her hair, put kohl around her eyes and scent her body. She was feeling much stronger, but still had not been out of bed for several days. Her heart was racing; she was beside herself with happiness that her beloved had come to her but some of the joy dimmed when she remembered that he had not contacted her for days after their lovemaking and even worse, he had slept with Maccab. Immediately she caught herself. She flooded her unsavory thoughts with the white light of the Goddess. *Of course he is free to sleep with whomever he chooses! He is both a man and a king.*

David entered the room with a worried expression, rushed to the bed and gathered Ceelyha into his strong arms. He huskily whispered, "My poor Golden One, this is all my fault! I had no idea that Macaab would be so vindictive. I see now that she is a jealous, evil woman. I have banished her from the harem. No woman has the right to interfere with my affairs whether it be personal or political!"

While he was hugging her, Ceelyha felt protected and loved. Desire swept over her as his body ignited her longing for him. *Even though I am weak, I still crave his lovemaking!* she thought with surprise. David must have felt her stirring because he released her and tenderly said, "Not now, My Golden One. Later, when you are recovered enough to match my passion!"

Ceelyha blushed a deep red and nervously straightened the bedcover. She cautioned herself not to convey hurt and disappointment as she asked, "Why did you not send for me sooner? I remember your parting words to me that you would arrange for us to meet in a few days."

She could see that he was annoyed with the question and was also trying to compose himself before he answered! *If only I knew how to play the game of the coquette!* She berated herself.

"You just came into my life. I was not expecting this to happen. It takes time for me to clear myself of duties. I cannot come and go as I please. Surely you, of all people being the daughter of a King, should understand that my life is not mine alone."

Immediately the vision of him with Macaab arose. *Yes, and you do need to satisfy all your wives and concubines!* she thought. But instead of saying what was on her mind, she was learning, the hard way, how to massage his ego and for the second time within a few minutes, called upon the cleansing white light.

"Yes, of course, you must forgive me. I too have duties to attend to and understand how one's life is not their own." Then she thought it best to change the subject and began to tell him about the attitude of the High Priestess and the others towards her since she started to see him and Adah's threat to send her back to Dor.

He was enraged. "This cannot go on. I will not have these women seeing you as my harlot. You will not be treated in this manner. The High Priestess can easily be replaced and she should know this. I will speak to her at once. She will be the one who will be sent to Dor!"

"No, David, I implore you, do not do that. It will only make matters worse. I will attend to the situation by asking the Goddess for help!" she pleaded. To have him intervene on her behalf would not only be humiliating, but also the repercussions would be too great. None of the priestesses would respect her. Then she began to cry. He held her again and promised he would not interfere yet.

With her fears alleviated, he said, "Since we were last together, I have been thinking that it is not safe for us to meet at the Palace anymore."

Ceelyha's heart skipped a beat and a sense of foreboding washed over her.

He looked straight into her eyes and said in a matter of fact tone, "I have taken the liberty of securing a small house in town. The servants there are very discreet."

He was not ending their relationship! A wave of relief swept through her.

"I had hoped that we could meet there tonight, but I see that you are not strong enough so I shall try to meet you within two days time."

"What do you mean by a house? Do you want me to live there?" asked a confused and flustered Ceelyha. "I cannot leave my work here at the Temple."

"I am not asking you to forsake your work or your Goddess. It would be safer there for you, away from prying eyes and death threats. You could be my private advisor and still do the Goddess's work." His eyes gleamed with hidden meaning. Ceelyha immediately tensed. *He seems to have it all worked out, assuming I would naturally want to leave the Temple to be his mistress.* Just as no woman could interfere with his affairs, no mortal would with hers!

He must have seen or read the hostility in her expression because his parting words were: "Think about it then. I had hoped you would be happy to be with me. Will you at least come to see the house?" he added with almost a plea and then gave her a beauteous smile that melted her heart.

"Of course, my beloved. I will be there in two days. Send a sedan. Nintu will accompany me, so there will be no gossip." She reached up and pulled him down onto her body to kiss him full on the lips. She felt his groin harden and teasingly replied, "There will be more of that soon!"

Thu came to Ceelyha shortly after David left. Her eyes were full of mischief as she teased, "Well, what did the King want with such a weak maiden? Did he sweep you into his arms and declare he was your champion?"

Ceelyha laughed and replied, "As a matter of fact, he did just that. He has located a house for me in the city, which I will go to see it in a couple of days. So there, he is my champion!"

Thu's joking was replaced with surprise. "A house? He wants you to live there? What about the Temple?"

"He seemed to assume that I would just move in and forget who I really am, to be there at his beck and call. I told him that I would think about it but I cannot see how that would work. I can never renounce the Goddess and the vow I made to do Her work."

Thu cried out, "But he will not have it both ways. With him, it is either all or nothing. You will surely lose him if you do not comply with his wishes."

"Then what shall I do? I serve the Goddess first! He has to understand that!" she cried. "Thu did you ever make that spell that will bind him to me in this lifetime?"

The other priestess pursed her lips. She hesitated before answering. "Yes, but it might go against what has already been destined for you."

Ceelyha had been pondering this fact ever since Thu had made her last potion. Did that magic really work when the Goddess had already set out her fate with David? Did Thu's last potion really bring she and David together faster than if they had just allowed events to unfold? A shudder of cold passed through her but it was difficult to discern if that was from her illness or a warning.

Thu carried on as if oblivious to Ceelyha's reflections. "But this should please you, I consulted the Isis oracle symbols about your history together. Would you like to hear about that?"

"Oh Thu, that would be wonderful." Ceelyha sat up in bed full of curiosity.

"Well from what I could intuit, you and he have had a few past lives together, the most recent being in Egypt." The Goddess sent a confirmation through Ceelyha.

"It appears that you were an Isis priestess in the Luxor Temple and that he was a scribe. The two of you had a forbidden love affair; you broke your sacred vows as a priestess to be with him. Interesting that the same situation has presented itself in this life! It seems that you made a final choice to stay with the Goddess and let him go even though it broke your heart."

"Oh, I feel by the shivers in my body that what you say is truth. And here I am again, being given the chance to be with him, yet having to choose my spirituality over my emotions." She thought over the situation and asked, "Was there anything else in the reading?"

"Yes," answered Thu with reluctance. "There was a previous life. It was during the cataclysmic upheaval when the great floods occurred. You were a priestess and he a priest, but in that life, you were able to publicly be with one another. The earth upheavals separated the two of you. I am not sure which one of you died trying to rescue the other."

Ceelyha responded with an uneasy laugh, "So, at least we were happy for awhile. Oh Thu, what am I to do?"

"I guess you will consult the Goddess, go to the house and see how things present themselves. You have to learn to trust your instincts more. Perhaps that is the lesson for you in all of this," she added kindly.

"But I do not know anymore what my instincts are! When I am with him, they are pure lust, when I am away they are of reason!" she cried out.

"That is what love does!" answered Thu wisely.

Early the next day, Adah dressed in a traveling robe came to visit a surprised Ceelyha. "I wanted to see how you were feeling and to let you know that I am going to make a visit to the Temples in Dor and Acco. It seems that my assistance is requested. Dilbaha will take over my duties until I return." She said formally.

Ceelyha replied anxiously, "Is Dinah not well? Is that why you are going?"

Adah hesitated then answered, "As far as I know she is well. The King has requested that I, as High Priestess of Asherah, Royal Diviners to the House of David, extend my expertise to the other Temples of Israel. That is my first destination." She puffed up with importance. "Also the King has requested that you be released from Temple duties for the next little while, until you are feeling better."

"Thank you for coming to tell me. I hope to be recovered and back at my duties long before you return. Could you please take a message to Dinah for me?"

Adah nodded and waited. "Tell her about my narrow escape from death. Tell her I know she was aware of the situation and thank her for her prayers. Give her my love."

Adah's expression was one of surprise. "Oh, she knew about your illness?" Then she composed herself and replied, "Yes, of course I shall relay your message. Now I will take my leave. Goodbye Ceelyha." With a swoosh of her mantle, she abruptly left the room.

David has really thought of everything. He has given me a reprieve from my duties to lessen my guilt over being his lover and he has temporarily removed both of my adversaries. Once he sets his mind on a course of action, nothing stands in his way. I will take this as a warning. I, too, am now caught in his web. Do I want to risk losing him again as I have lost his love in our previous lives? I want the best of worlds, David and my work. But can I have both?

Then she remembered how the shock of seeing him in bed with Macaab and the stab of envy that immediately manifested. She would always have to share him with his various wives and concubines. *How did other women deal with this emotion? How did my mother feel when she was in love with the King and he took other women? Does one turn a blind eye and accept that is how things are? My own Goddess lay with many men but only fell in love with Tammuz. Look at how She followed him into the Underworld and sacrificed for him. Did She feel the human emotion of envy? Look at all the qadishtu ceremonies where the priestesses take lovers. Did the men feel jealous when new lovers were taken?* There was so much of this world that Ceelyha did not have knowledge or understanding of. Pushing back the tears of longing to speak to Shiroka that welled up in her eyes, Ceelyha made a decision. She would have David on her terms and not his. Now it was time to accept Thu's offer of a love potion that would bind their two spirits together.

She called Nintu to fetch Thu. When the priestess arrived with her medicine box, Ceelyha was fully dressed in her tunic wearing her necklace and red belt.

"You look much better. I see how just one visit from David revived you!" she teased then spoke in earnest. "I have the potion. It has taken me a full two weeks to prepare. Are you sure that this is what you really want? Taking it will mean that you are bound to him for eternity. *"*

"And he to me?"

"If he is a mortal then yes, but if he is a god, then no!" Thu smiled at her own humour. Then with questioning eyes asked, "You obviously already have him; why do you need this?"

"I want the potion so I can have him and can continue to do the Goddess's work. I am hoping to have the best of both worlds. I am also afraid of his other women from the past and perhaps even the future." As she finished verbalizing her fears, she felt the Goddess's energy descend. Her ears buzzed with the familiar sound of Ishtar's wings and she closed her eyes, anxious to hear the Goddess. *"There will be more women in his life than you. That is not something that you have any control over. You will own his heart but not his affections."* Then the Goddess released the energy.

Thu anxiously waited for her friend to tell what had happened. When Ceelyha did not speak, she asked "What warning did the Goddess give you?"

Ceelyha paused then quietly answered, "She says I will never completely have David to myself." She became introspective, and not quite certain of what to think about this message. She knew the potion was not the solution but Thu had gone to a great deal of trouble to concoct it. In order not to hurt her friend's feeling, Ceelyha summons enthusiasm as she brightly said, "Let us go ahead with your magic brew but first will you share how it was made?"

Thu looked sympathetic. "But before I do that, do you know the Hebrew position on the status of women?"

Ceelyha responded dully, "I suppose a man can marry and keep numerous concubines and then dismiss them when they are no longer needed."

Thu nodded "In the tradition of this land, the man literally becomes the master of the woman with marriage. Some of their forefathers took more than one wife. Esau took three, Jacob took two wives and of course David has many.

Did you know that Sarah gave permission to her spouse, Abraham, to engage in sexual intercourse with her maid in order to give him children? Concubines are just sexual partners of even lower standing than a wife."

"Women do seem to have a very low status. They are the property of the man." Ceelyha was reminded of the woman who died from multiple rapes and her recent petitioner who was assaulted by her uncle. With determination and a distress for the plight of women, she added, "In my country, a woman can hold property and is not at the mercy of her husband. As Entus, we hold the same status as a male priest and if one is a qadishtu, then you too are independent from the ruling of any man.

I shall never become the property of a man. So Thu, please tell me about your magical potion." At the moment, the idea of a potion seemed even more attractive.

"The process is rather complicated. I first gather rose petals in the fullness of bloom during the full moon between dusk and dawn. Then I added clear-flowing spring water. While the moon was shining I mixed the petals and water with salt from the sea. Afterwards, the elixir was strained through fine Egyptian cotton and placed in this small vial." Thu picked out a tiny bottle from her medicine chest." I asked Isis to bless it. You must keep this vial under your pillow until the next full moon, then put it in David's drink and he will be yours for eternity."

"You know Thu, at a deep level of my being, I feel he is already mine. It seems that we have certainly shared some past lives together and no doubt, if it is the will of the Goddess, we will share this one and perhaps many more. But, being only human and, "she felt herself blush, " I am a woman in love and in this particular moment of time, I want to make certain of our bond. Besides, what harm could there be to try your potion?"

"I cannot answer that for you. Do any of us truly understand the ways of the Gods? Do we dare to go against Their wishes? We are told that every aspect of our lives is predetermined by these omnipotent beings. So, do we really have any choices, and are those choices really choices or just what They wanted us to do anyway? All we really have is the faith that a more evolved being is guiding our lives. Ceelyha my friend, if I had all the answers, then I too would be a Goddess."

"Then we just have to trust our instincts, play out Their script and pray for the best outcome."

That night, as Ceelyha finished her nightly prayers, she was once again thinking of her mother. She climbed into her bed but lay awake, her eyes moist with tears. She must have fallen into a light sleep for suddenly she awoke. The soles of her feet tingled and then a push came as she felt her spirit forced out of her body. Immediately, she called upon the light of the Goddess as protection as she began to float through the roof into the star lit night. When she sensed Her wings of protection, Ceelyha instinctively knew to concentrate on the Temple in Babylon. Her vision expanded and she sensed she was once again in Shiroka's quarters. She deeply inhaled the rich scent of sandalwood, relishing its heady effects. She found her mother once again kneeling before the golden statue of Ishtar. As she brushed against Shiroka's thin sleeping robe, her mother looked up and spoke into the night air, "My daughter, I am pleased you have once again found your way to me. I too sense your plight with the one called David. Just remember, you are not in his life to serve him, or to have a marriage of convenience or bare him children. Instead, it is a pure and simple love affair that you are having, a meeting and joining of two souls. And when that time of sharing is done, you both will move on. You see, how simple it all is. There is no need to become his chattel, no need for jealousy or envy of his other women. Those are not emotions for you to be involved in. Rise above your earthly wants and needs and reflect on the higher light of the Goddess."

With those words, the images faded and Ceelyha sensed she was back in her bed where sleep quickly enveloped her.

The next day, true to his word, David sent a sedan for Nintu and Ceelyha. Nintu had arisen early to bath and paint her mistress. Ceelyha had asked her to pack a few of their belongings: her mother's necklace, medicine box, holy oils, a dancing costume, some clothes and sandals. The night before, the temple workers had been told that Ceelyha would be recovering at the house of a friend. Ceelyha had told Thu that she would send word as soon as she knew where they were going to be staying and that she would see her friend when David was out of the house. As they hugged each other, Thu reminded Ceelyha to put the love potion under her pillow.

After a short ride through the city, with the curtains of the sedan drawn so no one could see its riders, the women found themselves in front of a house in the fashionable section of the city, through which they had travelled on their first night in Jerusalem. A thick mud brick wall that surrounded the property ensured its privacy. The cooing of doves greeted them as they entered a courtyard inlaid with mosaics of black, white and red clay. Flowering bushes and a shady eucalyptus tree filled the air with a fragrant mixture of sweetness. The sound of running water gushing from a fountain gave the yard an aura of peace. Both women were delighted with a stone covered well that provided easy access to water. The entire setting reminded Ceelyha of a luscious oasis, a tranquil retreat after her bout with illness. A silent servant bowed to the women as he held open the red painted door of the sprawling house. They entered a large reception area, which had divans, low tables, stools, carved wooden chairs, gold vases, and silver ornaments tastefully arranged.

"Oh Lady, it is quite beautiful," sighed Nintu. "Look at the rich carpets, I can sink my feet into them.'

Ceelyha laughed at Nintu's child-like behavior. The servant led them up the stairs to the sleeping areas. The first chamber had a small divan. The thick goat's hair carpets on the walls gave it a cozy effect. The next room had a low table and a cot where Nintu would sleep. The final room, the master chamber, was dominated by a large stately wooden bed carved with floral designs, plenty of thick cushions and a deep blue cover trimmed with gold moons and stars. There was a cedar chest for clothes, plenty of carpets and a divan. A large mirrored dressing table was neatly arranged with silver combs. A separate dressing room with a generous sized brass basin and several alabaster jars for fetching water added a touch of luxury to a room fit for royalty. A window near the center of the room led to a small balcony, which overlooked the gurgling fountain of the courtyard. Ceelyha imaged that the soft sounds of falling water could be heard all night from the bedroom. A harp stood in the corner, as if waiting to be played by David's talented fingers. On the left side of the room was a narrow set of stairs that beckoned the women to climb to a roof, which provided a view of the city and its surrounding hills.

Ceelyha exclaimed her delight and stretched out her arms to the sky. "Oh Lady of the Sun, Lady of the Moon, Lady of all that is, grant Your blessing on this house. Thank you for allowing me to recover here in this little piece of paradise. May peace and love flow through its walls." She felt the Goddess descend as a warm breeze around her and knew that she had Her blessing. This was where she was supposed to be for the time being.

In the reception room, servants had placed trays of fruits and sweet cakes on one of the low tables. Silver goblets filled with wine were passed to the women. Incense had been lit. Nintu asked her mistress to lie on one of the couches and proceeded to cover her with a fur skin. Then she quickly devoured some of the sweets before begging Ceelyha to let her go exploring. She wanted to see the kitchens, the servant quarters and inspect the food. She wished to unpack some of their belonging before David arrived and set up the small room upstairs as a working area for Ceelyha to consult the Goddess. She also needed to let her young man know where she would be staying.

Ceelyha was content to be alone. She needed to think about what being in this house meant in terms of her relationship with David and the Goddess. So far, the Goddess seemed to approve, but at what price? David was surely the kindest of men to prepare this house for her but she still did not completely understand him. *I hope to know more about him during our time together; I have many questions.* But how much time would they spend in this house? How long could she stay before people would talk? How long would the Goddess allow her to have this reprieve? How long before David would tire of her and return to his wives and concubines? Before she could ponder any more, there was a commotion at the door. She pushed her cover aside and was getting up to see what was happening when David burst into the room. Her knees weakened, her previous worries forgotten. She had the same rush of excitement as when she saw him the first time. A spasm of desire and longing overtook her. She practically threw herself into his arms. He picked her up and swung her around saying "You look much better. Are you feeling up to seeing me?"

Before she could answer he continued, "Do you like it, Golden One? Do you like our little love nest?"

"Put me down you brute," she laughed trying to tame her unbound hair. "I absolutely adore it. It is beyond my expectations. And yes I am feeling up to it." To prove it, she kissed his soft lips while he carried her upstairs. She admired the perfect muscles of his arms as he laid her on the bed. He removed his cloak before putting a small soft satchel in her hands.

"What's this?" she asked with surprise.

"Open it and see," he said with a twinkle in his eyes. "It is just something small for you to remember me by."

"I need no gifts to remember you by, My Lord!" But she opened it anyway. Inside was an amber necklace with delicate gold strands linking the beads. Each stone seemed to sparkle with its own life-giving force.

"It is delightful, I love it!" Ceelyha kissed him on the cheek.

"I bought it to match your eyes and the gold flecks that you always have in your hair. I hope that you will wear it in good health and as a reminder of my love." His eyes momentarily misted over and Ceelyha was not sure what she read in them. She held the stones to her neck and turned for him to lift her hair and close the clasp. But David got side tracked by seeing her delicate bare neck and began to cover it with tiny soft kisses- the necklace forgotten. After a few moments of experiencing this new sensation, David removed her gown, exposing smooth white shoulders, full breasts, and a flat stomach. She shivered more with than anticipation than cold as she watched him undress. She caught her breath, as his tunic fell in a heap to the floor, becoming more and more aroused at the sight of the perfect muscles in his regal body. His shoulders were so broad, his legs long and muscular. She breathed in his familiar scent. She felt his heart pounding against her chest as she melted into his arms, murmuring his name. They reached for one another. A slow heat moved like the Goddess's serpent as she felt him enter her. Every part of her was alive, on fire, aware of his mouth, hands and thrusting.

When they were both satiated, Ceelyha braced herself on one arm and looked into his eyes. His guard was down and she was able to see his love for her in the depths of his soul. She sighed with relief and touched his forehead, brushing away the black hairs. "I wish it could always be like this, the two of us in our own world."

"That is why I have the house," he said drowsily, "So that we can be like this forever."

At least we have a short while to be together, she thought but did not want to ruin the mood; so said nothing.

For the rest of the day, they dozed on and off waking only to make love. At sunset, a servant brought a meal of cheeses, grapes, rice and goat meat that they both ate with relish.

"What would you like to do this evening, my darling? I do not want to tire you out. Are you feeling well enough?" He asked with concern.

Touched by his caring, Ceelyha announced that she was just fine and why did they not go up to the roof to enjoy the evening? As they quickly dressed in matching white sleeping robes from the dressing room, Ceelyha wondered who had picked them out but thought it was better not to ask. She also wondered whose house this used to be and who had decorated it. *So many questions*, she chided herself, *and none of them important. The important thing is that he loves me and we are together.*

From the housetop, the lights of the city twinkled like fallen stars. The narrow streets were lit here and there from orange lights, which emanated from clusters of houses. The wind was calm; the night air warm. A mixture of flower blossoms and heady eucalyptus balm filled the air. The sky was a deep cobalt blue hosted shining stars while the yellow waxing moon hid behind a puffy cloud. The only sound to be heard was the distant splashing of a waterfall. Ceelyha silently thanked the Goddess for making the evening perfect. She was more content and happy being here with every minute.

"Do you see that distant hill over there?" David pointed to the east. "That is Mount Moriah. That is where Abraham, one of the fathers of the Jews, went to offer his son Isaac as a sacrifice to the Lord."

Ceelyha was surprised. Her religion had no human sacrifices. She asked "And did he?"

"No, the Lord came to tell him it was only a test of his faith. That hill is also where Jacob dreamt of a ladder going up to Heaven. He believed that this spot connected Heaven to earth. And that is why I have chosen this city to be the center for my kingdom. Moriah is where God's presence can be felt more than any other place."

Ceelyha thought that it was unfortunate that God had to be experienced in a place while her Goddess was the faceless presence in every day life; She was everywhere, the channel that linked the temporal with the divine. David left her side to move some pillows away from the wall, which he then arranged like a bed on the mosaic-tiled floor. He motioned for her to come into his arms. For a long time neither spoke, just enjoying the peace of the night and each other's company. Then David said "This reminds me of my childhood, sleeping under the stars among the flocks of sheep."

"Were you happier then as a simple shepherd boy without the responsibilities of a King?"

"No," he cuddled her closer, "because I did not have you!"

Ceelyha laughed then solemnly asked "But you have had many others before me. What about your first wife? Were you not happy with her?"

"Michal? I was so young and inexperienced in the ways of love and war when I met her. I thought I loved her more than life itself, but she did not return my affection. When I fled to the wilderness to escape Saul, she did not follow me. If it were real love that she had for me, then she would have gone anywhere I went, to the end of the earth if need be."

"You must have been terribly crushed. So why did you take her back after you were made King?" Ceelyha turned her face away from his to hide her resentment. Her pulse quickened, anxious to hear his response. Her mother's words repeated in her head to stifle any potential jealously that might come up.

"Without her by my side, the northern tribes would never have accepted me as king. By calling her back, I united the tribes of Israel and secured my kingship."

"So, you didn't love her anymore?" Ceelyha tried to calm the erratic fluttering of her heart while she waited for his answer.

"Saul married her to another man before our bed was cold. By that time I had taken others, some as my wives and others as my concubines. I was no longer the love stricken boy that once adored the earth she walked on. I lost my passion for her."

"Then you will also lose your passion for me!" mumbled Ceelyha. *How can I ever understand this man, who professed his undying love, then changed his mind and find fulfillment with another?*

"Men by their very nature are not loyal to their mates. As King, I may take as many wives and concubines as I wish. But dear Golden One, know that you are the first woman to please me both physically and spiritually. I am getting on in my years and have no need to rut like a bull anymore. You are all I need now and will ever want." His voice sounded so full of conviction that Ceelyha was certain he truly believed it. But, her woman's intuition gave her a premonition that there would be more after her!

He turned and stared into the night sky. "I will tell you something, that I have never told another soul. I am a lonely man. My only true friend was Jonathon," his voice quivered, "It even hurts to say his name! He was killed at the battle of Mount Gilboa. All the rest of my so-called friends see me first as King, then as a man. Each one of them wants something from me." Even in the darkness of the rooftop, Ceelyha could see the tears in his eyes. She held him closely against her breast while willing the Goddess's loving energy to flow into him. It surprised her that this great man still mourned for the one called Jonathon. There was so much that she had yet to discover about him.

"Tell me about your friend,' she begged when he had his emotions under control and lay back down to look at the stars. "Would I have liked him?"

"Everyone loved him, it was impossible not too. He was a strong, capable man but gentle at the same time. Together we would have mock battles with our swords. We would ride our horses until they were soaked with sweat. We would swim like fishes in the cool waters of the river. I could tell him anything and he never judged me. When I would play my harp with him, songs just seem to flow from my lips. He loved and trusted me so much that he gave me his girdle and sword. He was everything I could ask for...." He hesitated then added, "in a friend. He so often professed his love for me. And the best part was I was not a King then, just a poor soldier in his father's army. He was the Prince, the next in line for the throne and he thought of me as a brother."

It would be hard for any woman to compete with that type of love she thought. No wonder he has had a difficult time finding his true match in a female. Then she remember Thu's love potion and hoped that she would be able to slip it under the pillow tonight. *With the blessing of the Goddess, I am going to make certain that I am all that he desires,* she thought without any shame.

Finally, after several moments of silence while they each had their private thoughts, Ceelyha said, "David, I am your friend. I see you first as a man, then a King. I want nothing from you but to share my heart. I cannot be your wife or concubine, as my vows are to the Goddess. I do not want your wealth. My own father is a richer King than you. As for power, I have my own source of the Goddess for that. Therefore, my beloved, I make the perfect friend!" She was proud of how she presented that to him. Surely he could see that she was after nothing from him.

"Then let us seal our friendship with this," and he proceeded to make love to her under the light and blessing of the almost full moon that had made its way from behind the clouds. Just after Ceelyha reached her climax, she silently prayed to the Goddess:

"Oh Lady of the Night, Goddess of the Moon, Bless this union with Your magic. May I love this man for eternity and may he return his love to me. Lady of the Night. Goddess of the Moon."

Later when they finally went to bed, Ceelyha had found the vial in her medicine box and placed it under her pillow. Just before she fell asleep she thought that perhaps David only thought he was in love with Michal because she was Jonathon's sister and therefore the closest way to be near to him. Perhaps he killed the giant and slaughtered the Philistines and brought back their foreskins because of his need to impress Jonathon more than the King. The Goddess sent her a shiver of confirmation. Ceelyha smiled as she fell into an exhausted sleep with the knowledge that David had never really been truly in love with a woman – yet.

Chapter 12
The House

Together, David and Ceelyha spent three glorious days and nights. They were never apart; eating, bathing, sleeping, making love, playing music and talking together. During that time, Ceelyha was able to find out more about the life of the man with whom she was in love. He had rescued a young woman, Ahinoam, from a lion, while he was hiding from Saul in the wilderness. She had followed him into the mountains and they became lovers. Ceelyha learned the circumstances surrounding Abigail, who had defied her husband's orders by taking cartloads of food to David's six hundred men and how her husband, Nabal, became suspiciously ill and died. David married the rich and powerful widow, an act which helped to further his cause to later become God's chosen King of Israel. Ceelyha, did not sense that either of these women was a threat to her relationship and was certain he did not visit their beds anymore. It summoned a great deal of courage to ask about Macaab. David told her that he had been intrigued with Macaab's exotic dark looks while visiting her father, King Geshur, and how she had been given in marriage to the Hebrew, to secure peace between their people. Ceelyha suspected that Macaab continuously used her wiles and magic on David and that until recently, she had been his favourite. According to David, his other women were in fear of Maacab and had as little interaction with her as possible. She bore him two children, a daughter named Tamar and a son, Absalom whom Thu said she wanted to secure the throne for when David died. Ceelyha felt a shiver of warning as the Goddess's wings surrounded her about his children but could not ascertain exactly what the Goddess was trying to convey. *If I were in the same position, with my knowledge of magic, I too might resort to trickery to keep him,* she thought with compassion. Then it dawned on her! *Essentially, I am no better than Macaab! I am basically doing the same thing with Thu's love potion!* She made herself a promise to get rid of it at the first opportunity.

As they talked at length about David's time in the wilderness, Ceelyha admired the six hundred men who had risked everything, family, homes and lives to support this man who had a mission to unite the twelve tribes of his country against its enemies. She had difficulty understanding why David did not kill Saul when the opportunity presented itself.

David explained, "He was sleeping right at the entrance of our cave! I could not believe that he did not sense our presence. My men, of course, wanted to kill him and could not understand my reluctance. But the Lord had told me that my time would soon come and I should not cause any more unnecessary dissension among my tribesmen by killing the King; all I needed to do was wait."

"But surely you must have known that Saul needed to die! Surely, your God must have forewarned you that there was no other way for you to get the throne except through his death!" exclaimed Ceelyha.

David was thoughtful, "I guess I never questioned it. Do you question what your Ishtar tells you? Do you ask for details and reasons why?"

Ceelyha shook her head no.

"Well, it was the same with me. I devoutly follow what Yahweh tells me. What He did not tell me was that not only would I lose my king but also my best friend in that same fatal battle at Mount Gilboa! I had no idea Jonathan would die!" His voice drifted off then came back in full force, alerting Ceelyha to the underlying hurt and anger that was festering in his soul. "And do you know something? I was angry with Him for not forewarning me!"

She felt his anguish. *I am so connected to this man, more than I have ever been to anyone on this earth!* It was a strange feeling for her, one that she had no control over. Her heart went out to him as she replied, "But David, even if you knew, you could not have prevented it. I believe that your god just did not want you to be tormented about something that was about to happen. He actually did you a favour. Think of how upset you would have been if you had known in advance!

You are just feeling separation from your god. That is what is really causing you pain. He did not forsake you!"

"Oh, that is why you are my Golden One! The God and Goddess shine Their wisdom on you. How did I ever live without you for this long?"

She admired David's loyalty when she learned how rigorously he continued to be in his determination not kill to Saul. She sensed that he would have that same fierce protectiveness for any one who was in his life that did not wish him harm. Her thoughts were further confirmed by the fact that while he lived among his foreign enemies the Philistines, and joined forces to attack the Amalekites; when Achish, the King of the Philistines, asked David to join his army and fight Saul, he refused. David returned to Israel having gained the skills to make sturdy armor out of iron instead of flimsy copper, along with the ability to plan strategic attacks. In David's own words, he emerged, a stronger, one knowledgeable commander to lead his people.

David asked Ceelyha if she had heard the story about the priestess whom Saul had consulted with to conjure the spirit of Samuel. She replied that yes, she had heard of that particular incident. As she was in the process of informing David that she had learned that particular technique of necromancy from Dinah at the Temple of Dor, her skin became clammy. She abruptly stopped talking as a foreign energy invaded her body.

David exclaimed, "You are not ill again, are you?"

Ceelyha managed to shake her head and hold up a hand to silence him. She needed to follow through on what was happening. *It must be a spirit trying to enter my being!* She took a deep breath to center herself and silently reached out to the entity.

To invoke the Goddess's protection she spoke aloud,

"Oh Lady of Light, Lady of Love, assist me now and let my consciousness know what is invading my body. Praise be to You, oh Lady of the Light."

Suddenly she intuited that it was the spirit of Saul trying to send a message through her to David. But the timing was not right; she was not properly prepared to be a clear and accurate channel. She called out, "In the name of the Goddess, I demand you to cease. I am not prepared to be your host! Be gone, spirit!

Then she mentally thanked the Goddess and requested Her to delay the contact until a more suitable time.

As quickly as the energy had descended, it left. Relieved that she was now void of any connection with the vibration, she turned her attention back to David. He was visibly shaken; sweat had broken out on his forehead. His face was white and his hands gripped the edge of the table where they had been sitting while having a meal. Ceelyha reassured him that she was well and that a message was trying to come through from a discarnate spirit but she was not able to channel it properly.

"What are you talking about?" he cried.

"I need to use incense, be pure of body, wear my protective amulet and invoke the Goddess, if I do not wish to be harmed by the energy of the dead person. That is all." And she smiled as an attempt to alleviate his fears.

"Who or what was trying to come through? Your face was distorted and twisted! A mist; no, it was more like a gray film forming around your body! Then you spoke to your deity!" he exclaimed.

Ceelyha, shocked that he was so upset over what she considered to be a natural occurrence, replied, "I have no control over it. Until meeting you, I have never been with a person who has not expected it of me. I am surprised that She has not come through in your presence before. I am not just a woman but also a priestess so you now have a better idea of what I do. I hope it will not frighten you if it happens again. Did you not have Bernice perform such divination for you?"

"No, she used always used her scrying bowl. I always assumed it was the Goddess that descended upon her and not some other spirit." David's voice betrayed his indignation. Then he added more gently, "But that was different because I was expecting it. Just now," he paused and looked at Ceelyha with such love and concern that her heart skipped a beat, "I was not thinking of you as a priestess but as my lover and was naturally worried for you."

Ceelyha sensed that she had somehow hurt his feelings and tried to make light to the situation by kissing him. "See, I am still your lover!"

David returned her affections by gathering her in his arms. Then very much in control of himself he asked, "What was the message?"

"I believe it was Saul who wanted to use me as a channel to communicate with you."

"Saul? But why?" David asked in a perplexed tone.

"David, is it up to us, mere mortals, to question the higher realms? Maybe he wants to advise you on some war strategy. Whatever it is, I need to fast and prepare myself in order to channel the energies of a dead person. Let us forget it for now and enjoy the rest of our afternoon," she said in a matter of fact tone.

David replied, "I am needed at court. I have been away too long. Matters of state need my attention so I shall leave shortly. But you, my Golden One, will stay in our house and I shall return as soon as possible, probably by tomorrow evening." As if to make her comply, he gave her a long, promising kiss, which temporarily appeased her disappointment.

"I shall be here, my Lord, waiting for your return," she replied breathlessly as she reached up and wrapped her arms around him, missing him already. He carried her to the divan and together they reassured one another of their love.

While David was there, Ceelyha had no time to speak privately to Nintu. She called for a servant to heat some water for a bath and asked Nintu attend to her. As the faithful servant poured water over her shoulders, Ceelyha asked," What have you been doing my friend?"

"Do you mean, am I as in love as you, My Lady?" Nintu threw back her head and laughed. "I have seen Jacob a few times while you have been occupied with the King." She beamed with happiness. "It is now certain, we are to be wed!"

Ceelyha was overjoyed. "When?"

"We have not set a date; Jacob is waiting for his next orders from the King's commander, Beniah. Do you remember him? He was the one who escorted us out of the Palace on the night you danced for David."

"I think David is meeting Beniah tonight. Maybe Jacob will have his answer and we shall have a wedding sooner than you hoped. This is all very exciting. Do you know where the two of you will live?"

"If it is alright with you, I will stay with him in his mother's house when he is in Jerusalem; then return to you while he is away fighting. My first allegiance is to you, My Lady."

"Of course, you may do that. I am so happy that you have found love. When will I meet your young man?"

116

"If you do not need me further after your bath, I would take your permission to meet him later this evening. I will bring him here to receive your blessing." Nintu bowed her head in obeisance.

"I would indeed be honored. Hurry and finish my washing. Then go and make yourself ready. Oh, I also need you to send a message to Thu. I want her to come here tomorrow if she can. Then bring me my medicine box, honey and some boiled water in a goblet."

"Yes, My Lady. I will take care of everything before I leave," Nintu replied.

After Nintu brought a tray with the items, which Ceelyha had requested, she left to meet her soldier. Then Ceelyha carefully went through the contents of her medicine box. *I should have not left this for so long,* she thought remorsefully. *With all the lovemaking we have been doing, especially before the full moon, I should have been more careful. I do not want to be with child.*

She ground some acacia spikes into a fine powder then put the leaves of a silphion plant in the hot water and waited for it to brew before adding the powder and honey. She took the infusion to the rooftop and held it up to the waxing moon.

"Oh Mother Goddess, Goddess of Fertility, Goddess of Mystery, Bless this brew and allow my monthly courses to flow. Praise be to Ishtar, Mother of all Goddesses. Praise be to Asherah, Lady of the Serpent. Weave Your magic to make me barren."

She drank the brew as she looked out to distant hills that stood like sentinels watching over the city wondering if David's God watched over him as much as the Goddess watched over Her worshippers.

Ceelyha reflected that even though she enjoyed being with David, she needed some time alone. Reminding herself that she was not fully recovered from Macaab's attack and needed rest, she lay down on the pillows. As she stared up at the stars, she recalled listening to David bare his soul. Although she felt that she knew him somewhat better than before, there were many layers she still had yet to uncover. She did not fully understand why he did not have more trust in his connection with his God. Why did he need the priest, Achitophel, to tell him whether or not the people were in favor of him? Why did he not just ask Yahweh directly? And Nathan, the prophet, who seems to have taken over for Samuel, why did he listen to him instead of his God? Did he fear the priests could take his kingship away if he did not heed their wishes? In her mind, David was every bit a priest. She would have to speak to him about his doubts.

There were so many deaths around him. Did he have a part in killing Abner, Saul's general? Did he have a hand in Saul falling on his sword after that fateful battle with the Philistines? Did he have Saul's successor, Ishbosheth, killed? He had told her how he kept going out to search the night sky for his God to give him a sign as to what to do about Ishbosheth being crowned the new King. He prayed and prayed for guidance, night after night but instead his God speaking to him, two of his men brought the head of Ishbosheth to his feet. She thought that he should have been grateful that his problem was solved but instead he was furious, ordering the two men killed and dismembered. Their body parts were hung in Hebron as a sign to everyone that he would not tolerate the destruction of the House of Saul. When she asked if he was furious that his god had not directly communicated with him, he was quick to anger and indignantly replied, "He will speak to me when I am worthy to receive his words."

Ceelyha was certain that her clever lover realized that if his hands were clean of murder, then his people could not fault him. Circumstances arranged their deaths, he had said. But she truly wondered if he was as innocent as he let on. Her thoughts and solitude were suddenly broken by the excited voice of Nintu calling,

"My Lady, my Lady. Where are you? I have Jacob here to meet you."

Ceelyha called that she would be come down immediately. She pulled a shawl over her night robe and hurried down to the reception room. The happy couple was standing together, very much smitten with each other. Jacob was at least a full head taller than Nintu and Ceelyha guessed his age to be near ten and ten. His hair was jet black and it lay in curly locks around his head while his skin looked blackened from over exposure to the sun. Nintu's large brown eyes looked adoring up to him, her hand possessively touching the shoulder of his simple knee length woven tunic.

Ceelyha's heart quickened as she wondered how she had never noticed how beautiful her servant was! *That is what love must do*, she thought. Nintu's dark skin glowed like polished mahogany in the dim candlelight. Her hair was pulled tightly against her head to accent her delicate features. Her ears were adorned with a pair of ornate gold earrings that hung down almost to her shoulders. As if the girl could read Ceelyha's mind, she said, "The earrings, look, aren't they beautiful? They are a gift from my betrothed! My Lady, this is Jacob and Jacob this is the Priestess and Princess Ceelyha of Babylon."

The soldier bowed respectfully. "I hope that you do not mind that I have asked Nintu to become my wife. I do not know the protocol for marriage in your country but I will love and cherish her. I do not expect a dowry. I just want your blessing." He straightened and smiled at Ceelyha who immediately told him of course she and the Goddess would bless the marriage.

"Lady," said a hesitant Nintu, "We do not have much time before Jacob receives his next orders. If you have no need of me, would it be all right if we went out? This may be our last night together for a while."

"Of course you must go. I am off to bed for an early night."

As the couple bowed then took their leave, Ceelyha felt the wings of the Goddess surround her. A premonition of dread surged through her body and she prayed that Nintu would survive whatever the Goddess had in store for her.

Ceelyha woke in the middle of the night with sharp pains in the area of her abdomen as her courses came. Normally, this was the time when a priestess had a more powerful connection for divination and manifesting work but the herbs she had taken earlier dulled these abilities. As another cramp sliced through her, she cried out for Nintu only to remember that she was with her fiancé. The rest of the night was a blur as she fell in and out of awareness. She desperately wanted David's comfort and reached to embrace him, only to grasp thin air. Suddenly, she heard the words of Dinah's prophecy, "But be warned and listen well! He will cause you as much unhappiness as he does pain!" Then she dreamt of coldness – a bitter chill unlike any she had ever experienced – followed by a foul odour, like the stench of rotting flesh. Shadowy forms danced on the walls before a hollow voice spoke, "David will shed more blood. See all that he has done! See what he has yet to do!"

Ceelyha cried out, "Saul, is that you?" and woke up. Despite an unnatural cold in the room, she crawled out of bed to the idol of Ishtar with the intent to pray for the Goddess's protection for David and herself.

In the morning, Ceelyha awoke, surprised to be back in her bed with Nintu asleep on a pallet. "What are you doing here? I thought you would be with your handsome soldier."

Nintu rubbed the sleep out of her eyes and replied, "He is off to battle again. When he returns, we shall immediately marry. I met with his family last night and all the arrangements were made. But you," she looked at her mistress with surprise, "were on the floor in front of Our Lady and had a fever again. Are you ill?"

"No," Ceelyha emphatically shook her head. "I took a herbal remedy to bring on my monthly courses. The cramping was uncomfortable. That is what made my night so restless, but I am in perfect health now." She smiled to convince Nintu while pondering what messages the Goddess and Saul were trying to convey to her last night. Again, she chided herself for taking the herbs! *If only I had trusted that I was not with child then I would have been able to decipher my dream.* She involuntarily shivered recalling the frigid temperature mixed with the putrefying smell when Saul began to manifest.

Nintu did not seem to notice her mistress's reaction as she stood up and began to fold the sleeping mat. In a reproachful voice she said, "My Lady, you have given me too many scares in this last couple of moons. Now stay put while I arrange for breakfast and then help you dress before Thu comes to visit."

Thu, who arrived later in the afternoon, rushed into the reception room and carelessly discarded her mantle while she exclaimed, "This house is beautiful. It suits you perfectly!"

Ceelyha was pleased to see her friend. She missed her fresh perspective on life and her uncanny wisdom. They embraced then stood back to face one another. "You have grown stronger since I last saw you. It must be all that good love making!" Thu teased.

"And the good food. David eats like a horse and insists that I keep up my strength and I need to, to match him!" Ceelyha laughed. "You look every bit the priestess with your Isis amulet and sheath. Tell me, what have I missed at the Temple. Are they still gossiping about me?"

Thu reclined on a stool and told Ceelyha that Dilbaha was doing very well filling in for the High Priestess. The talk had quieted down about Ceelyha and David especially after the incidence with Macaab. No one had seen her at the Temple since David had banished her from the harem. Then, Thu informed Ceelyha that the priestesses were getting ready for the New Year's Festival of Asherah. "I hope that you will be back for that. We probably have a more elaborate ceremony than you were exposed to in Dor. When are you coming back?"

Ceelyha told her about the dream of Saul and how his spirit had tried to come upon her. "So," she finished, "I need to be in the Temple in order to find out what his message is. I'll spend one more night with David and then return."

Thu commented on the brilliance of the necklace on Ceelyha's neck and asked, "Have you replaced your mother's for his?"

Ceelyha hastily responded with annoyance, "Of course not! I am not doing the Goddess's work here and feel that I do not need Her power. When I wish to invoke Her energy, I will put it back on." She fingered the necklace self-consciously, then added, not certain if it was for Thu's benefit or her own, "I will not allow my spirituality to diminish by being here with David. The time spent with him will only increase it. This is what the Goddess wants me to do."

When the priestesses had finished catching up on one another's lives, Ceelyha showed Thu the rest of the house. They spent the remainder of the afternoon in the courtyard enjoying the fountain and the gardens. Thu had a light meal of cheese and fruit before she needed to depart for the evening ritual. She noted Ceelyha only drank water and asked her why she was fasting. Ceelyha told her about the herbs and how she was still cleansing them from her system.

After Thu had gone, Ceelyha felt restless and for the first time in her life, experienced a sense of emptiness as if her life had little purpose.

Here I am playing housemaid to David. I sit and wait for him to return to make my life meaningful. This will not do! I am a priestess not a harlot! She sent for a servant to see if there had been any word from the King. There had been no message so she spent another restless night alone in her bed.

On the fifth day of having no communication from David, Ceelyha, in a rage, called for Nintu to pack their things. They were returning to the Temple. *How dare he treat me like this; at least he could have sent a message.* Her anger was fueled further by feeling as if she had been discarded like an unwanted concubine. They had almost finished packing when David burst into the house, ran up the stairs to the bedroom, flustered and out of breath.

"Ceelyha," he got down on his knees, "please forgive me!" He sounded so sincere that she was afraid to look at him for fear he would see her smoldering anger. Instead, she formally said with lowered eyes, "I rejoice to see you again my Lord. I trust that you are well." Then she turned to her servant and said: "Nintu, please continue with our arrangements to depart. I will speak to his Highness in the reception area." She abruptly left the chamber, started downstairs, never once speaking or looking at David. He came lumbering down the steps and roughly grabbed her arm.

"What do you think you are doing? Are you angry with me? Are you leaving?" His tone of voice was flat.

"Yes, I am returning to the Temple. The New Year festival is almost upon us and my services will be needed. You are obviously much too busy to have time for me." She met his black eyes expecting to see the same hostility that she felt. But instead, she could not read what his emotions were. She faltered, annoyed at being locked out.

"I apologize for not getting back to you. I had urgent matters to attend to."

"There is no need to say that to me. Let us just forget this matter." She nervously stepped away from him but he pulled her roughly into his arms. He invaded her mouth with his tongue. Her anger and body softened at the same time as she met his passion. When they finally pulled apart, Ceelyha led him over to the couch and motioned for him to sit. "What has happened David? Why did you not come sooner?"

"My troops were needed to fight the Philistines near Gath. The villains are trying to overtake us again. I had to lead my men part of the way as a show of my support and improve their morale. I told you my life is not my own!" He voice expressed his exhaustion.

"I know David, I should be more understanding but why did you not send a message to me?" Ceelyha was ashamed of her lack of trust in him.

"There was no time and I thought I would be back. I promise to be more thoughtful next time…"

A noise behind them made them turn to look at Nintu who was trying not to interrupt. "My Lady, shall I unpack or are we leaving? The sedan is waiting in the courtyard."

Ceelyha looked at David and he replied, "The Lady will stay another night."

Nintu looked at her mistress for confirmation and then bowed when she saw her nod. "Yes My Lord." Then she left them alone.

"Ceelyha I must speak to you about a dream I had last night when I was sleeping with my men. It is troubling me. I need you to interpret it for me."

Ceelyha now understood the distress that she had picked up earlier. She was relieved that it had not been caused by her childish behavior. "Come, we will go to consult the Goddess." She was thankful that Nintu had left her priestess tools still set up the spare room. As they climbed the steps Ceelyha said, "Have you found Asherah's wisdom helpful before?"

David responded that he did and she replied, "In that case, are you amenable to anything that may come about?" He nodded and they went into the room. She positioned David on the small divan while she closed the door and the window shutters. She took a light from a torch that had already been lit by a servant in anticipation of the coming darkness, and ignited the brazier. She said, "I will be back in a few minutes. I need to get my amulet."

Nintu was waiting in the dressing room. She helped Ceelyha put on her red girdle and unclasped David's necklace. With the priestess amulet once again around her neck, Ceelyha was surprised to feel how heavy it was compared to the amber stones. She lovingly fingered each of the eight points of the star to get in touch with her mother's energies. Sadness flooded over her, she missed her home and her mother's guidance. Shiroka would certainly know how to handle David! Ceelyha pushed her personal feelings aside and told Nintu to place the serpent bracelet around her upper arm. Something told her, she would need lots of power to decipher the meaning of David's dream.

When the women went into the room, David was lying on the divan with a far away look in his eyes. The coals were red, so Nintu took a handful of hyssop that lay beside a small statue of Ishtar, and threw the cleansing herb on the fire. She stood aside and waited.

"King David, My Lord David." Nintu gently called his name.

"Yes?" he quickly sat up.

"My Lady needs to know what your dream was. Tell her the details."

"Of course." He cleared his throat and spoke in whispers. "I heard the powerful, all knowing voice of God telling me to advance on a tabernacle. I could not understand why, as I have no quarrel with the Levites. But my army advanced and captured a golden calf that lay upon the altar. We began to march the idol back to the city of Jerusalem. Half way along the road, Yahweh sent a terrible storm over the land. A bolt of lightening struck the idol, and the soldiers, who were supporting the calf on their shoulders, caught on fire. They were unable to let go, as if their very flesh were attached to the statue. I could smell their burning flesh! I pleaded and begged God to release them from this terrible torture. Then I woke up in a sweat. I prayed to God for an interpretation but got no answers. So..." he turned to Ceelyha with pleading eyes, "please help me. Was the dream just a whim or was there a divine message in it for me?"

Ceelyha stirred the herbs on the brazier, stood in front of the smoke and closed her eyes to invoke the Goddess.

"Oh Lady of Dreams, Lady of Light, Ishtar Great Goddess. Answer me with truth about which I am to inquire. Bestow your wisdom upon me so that I might read the true meaning of what, the King of Israel, one of Your divine children, has seen in his dream." She began first to chant in low tones and then raised her voice higher and higher as the energy of the Goddess came upon her. When she had completely raised her vibrations to Ishtar's level, Ceelyha gazed into the smoke.

In a deep powerful voice she divined, "The Temple of Shiloh, in your land of Judea, is the place where the mysteries of your people reside. The time is right for the people to take possession of this gift from your god. It is not a golden calf but some sort of memorial. The fire that you saw is a warning that only the pure of heart must carry it. It is not a soldier's job. It must be transported only by Holy Ones." She motioned for Nintu to put more incense on the coals. "Someone will die in connection with it. It is an ordinary man, not a priest. It appears that many have lost their lives already over this artifact. That is all. Blessings be with you on this, David."

Ceelyha released the Goddess's energy; Nintu discreetly left the room. David was excited, his earlier reflective disposition gone. "My Golden One, "he grabbed her hands and had her sit down.

"My dream was about the Ark of the Covenant! I am to bring it here to Jerusalem to be with my people! It has been with the Levites in Shiloh for too long. Of course, God would want it closer to His energy at Mount Moriah!" His eyes narrowed. "Who is to die? Your goddess said many have already died over it. But who will die because of this?"

Ceelyha shook her head. "David, I do not think that the death will be someone who is close to you. It will serve a purpose to make the crowds fearful and in awe of whatever it is you are transporting." She paused and then in a perplexed tone asked, "What is this Ark?"

"The Ark, "he said lovingly, "was brought by Joshua, another father of Israel, to Shiloh and placed in a temporary structure. Shiloh is to the north of here and was where the Twelve Tribes use to gather for prayer. It is said that Yahweh rested in Shiloh after creating the Universe. The Ark is an acacia wooden chest that houses the stone tablets of Moses' Ten Commandments, the history of my people. Many have died protecting it. At one time, the Philistines captured the Ark and put it inside one of their pagan temples. We finally got it back, but at the cost of many lives."

"Good, I am glad that you are pleased with the outcome of the dream. Now, can we continue with what we started?"

David scooped the priestess into his arms and carried her into their bedchamber. Ceelyha's arms encircled his neck as their tongues slid over one another. He gently placed her on the bed and Ceelyha arched back as his kisses followed his hands and when he pushed aside her tunic, she gasped with pleasure as the cool air of the room made her nipples hard. Glorious sensations cascaded down her body as he entered her.

"My Golden One," he murmured in a guttural moan as he eased himself deeper within her.

After a slow, sensuous pairing of their two bodies and just before sleep enveloped them, David said, "You are my other half. You are the outer manifestation of my wishes."

Ceelyha, deeply moved and overcome with the joy that he too had felt the same as she did, told him that he too was the missing half of her soul. Then she asked. "When will we meet again?"

David mumbled in her ear something about as soon as possible, and then fell asleep. Ceelyha lay quietly beside him reflecting on how close she felt to him. He had openly shared his hopes, his dreams and his insecurities with her. The resonance of his husky voice, the scar on his upper arm, the hardness of his muscles, every soft hair on his head and the feel of him inside her, were all embossed in her memory. His love was seared into her heart.

"I love you, my beloved David, I love you," she whispered into the night air. "There is no way that anything or body will threaten our love. The Fates must not have been right..." she murmured as she fell into a deep sleep.

Just before the light of dawn filtered through the windows, Ceelyha was jarred awake by a crushing sensation on her chest. She sat up, pushed the energy away and called on the Goddess to remove the unwanted energy. Fearful of whom the spirit was and what it was trying to relay, she reached for David. To her dismay he was gone. It was at that moment she recalled Thu's potion and yanked it from under her pillow.

She yelled, "Nintu, Nintu!"

The girl came running into the room, wiping the sleep from her eyes.

"Nintu, finish packing. And here," Ceelyha trust the vial at Nintu, "Get rid of this!"

Later that morning, as the servants gathered to bid them farewell, Ceelyha sensed a segment of her life was closing. Her heart filled with grief as she intuited that she would never share the same intimacy with David again. It was time to return to the Goddess.

Chapter 13

Back At the Temple

On the return journey to the Temple, Ceelyha and Nintu's sedan blended into the early crowds of religious pilgrims and families travelling with their provisions, veiled women walking to the market place, children playing, donkeys braying, stray dogs barking, the loaded carts clinking and soldiers staggering home after a night of drinking.

What a cloistered life I have been living, thought Ceelyha with excitement. *My world before David consisted only of the Temple and now it includes so much more. This is where real life is, in the streets, the pulse of the land. It makes me feel so alive!* As they came closer to the Temple, Ceelyha was surprised to see so many people lined up outside Asherah's gates. The servants carrying the sedan had to yell, "Make way, make way," before a path cleared for them to enter.

Once inside, Ceelyha dipped her hands into the sacred well, scooped water over her hands and face and then prostrated before the statue of Asherah while Nintu waited.

"Oh Lady of the Snakes, Lady of Light, Accept my return to Your sacred Temple and allow me to fully serve You and Your people. Bless me with Your light and wisdom. Praise be to Asherah and Ishtar."

The two women then went to their chambers where Ceelyha quickly changed into a plain tunic, tied the Goddess's girdle about her waist then put on her amulet. She instructed Nintu to place David's gift carefully away then replace any herbs that she used from her medicine box before proceeding to the courtyard. She greeted various petitioners waiting for assistance with their dreams, aches and pains, agriculture and relationships. It was not until mid afternoon that Ceelyha had a moment to seek out Thu, who was busy along with Nintu in the medicine room.

"There you are my friend, I thought you too had found a lover and had left for a clandestine meeting!" Ceelyha teased as she stood in the doorway watching Thu mix herbs on a stone table.

"I should be so lucky. No, I have to prepare a poultice for a woman who has sores on her eyes." Thu stopped and turned to look at her friend.

"You are fully recovered?" she asked with concern.

"Yes, and already at work! I am going to need your help to conjure up a spirit. I thought we could do that two nights from now. I need to give David time to arrange to be here."

"Of course, I would be happy to aid you. By the way, did you keep the love potion under your pillow?"

"I did and it definitely worked because I am in love!" Ceelyha laughed at her own joke. She did not wish to hurt Thu's feelings by telling her that it was destroyed. She quickly glanced in Nintu's direction as a warning to not tell Thu but the servant was busy refilling Ceelyha's depleted jars.

"But is David in love?" asked a serious Thu.

"As far as I know. Am I finished with needing to sleep with it under my pillow?"

Thu nodded. "Now the vial can be worn close to your body in a belt, or it can be hung around your neck."

"Since I have many things to put around my neck, I will sew it into my girdle. Thank you for doing that for me!" Ceelyha walked across the room and hugged her friend. She felt guilty about not revealing her thoughts and was just about to, when a spark of divine energy flowed between them. She was glad she did not. Thu gently removed herself from the embrace saying she had to give the medicine to the woman and reminded Ceelyha that the Festival of the New Year was tomorrow.

"Ah, that explains the extraordinary number of travellers in the streets, "reflected Ceelyha. She felt a stab of homesickness. Was it just two years ago that she had heard Marduk's priest prophesize that she was go to the Land of Judea? Has it been that long since she left her homeland?

Thu asked, "What is wrong? Your face has gone pale. Are you getting ill again?"

Ceelyha forced herself to respond with a smile. "I was just thinking about the time when I was told that I was coming here. Look how much has happened since then."

"I too get homesick. I have been here since I was nine years old, over five and one years ago now. But it is what the Goddess wished and we know that a greater hand than ours directs our lives. Now, I really must go. That poor woman has been waiting for this remedy too long!" And she rushed into the hall with a quick wave to Ceelyha and Nintu.

The next day was the new moon festival of the New Year. Instead of the shaking of the sistrums, the sounds of bells ringing and the blowing of a ram's horn awoke the priestesses at dawn. They gathered in the courtyard to bathe in the sacred water of the pool. After cleansing, they tossed petals from various flowers into the water as a token of thanks to Asherah for Her cosmic waters of creation. After, the women dressed in their traditional tunics. Servants deftly wound ropes of flowers into their loose flowing hair. Masks were handed out – serpents, scorpions, lions, fish and goats. Everyone laughingly exchanged jokes about the symbols they were representing. Ceelyha was relieved that no one seemed to hold any grudge toward her. When Dilbaha, in her lion mask, held up the Asherah pole, silence prevailed. Led by the High Priestess, they left the protection of the Temple and walked into the city streets, chanting praises to Asherah for creating the world. In the market place, Ceelyha recognized a familiar face amongst the crowd of well-wishers. She broke away from her place in the procession long enough to run up and cry, "Miriam, whatever are you doing here?"

When Ceelyha dropped her serpent mask, Miriam smiled affectionately and exclaimed, "O Lady, I am here with my husband. I had hoped to see you!" It was then Ceelyha noticed the woman's enlarged abdomen. The priestesses were getting ahead of her so she hurried to rejoin them shouting, "Come to the Temple and ask for me. I need to stay with my group."

When they reached the city gates, Asherah's daughters removed their sandals then filed out one by one. Thu whispered to Ceelyha that no one must step on the earth, the Mother's body, with footwear for this ceremony. Dilbaha, dressed in the blood red robes of the High Priestess, raised her pole, a signal for everyone to fall on their knees. The crowd and priestesses invoked the Goddess, "Hail Asherah, the Holy One, Oh Asherah, Lady of All Fertility, bring Your rains so that we may enjoy the fruits and crops of this Your sacred land. Hail Asherah, the Holy One."

When thunder rolled in the distance, everyone cheered, danced and sang to the beat of drums and the clang of tambourines. Wine flowed and good wishes were exchanged. Everyone was in a festive mood.

On their way back to the Temple, devotees handed the priestesses small cakes that were specially made for the Festival of Asherah. At the Holy Gates, a feast of special breads, apples, fresh figs, dates and carobs were set out by grateful petitioners.

After the evening ritual of praising the Goddess, Ceelyha heard a knock at her door. A servant announced there was a woman in a delicate state who wanted to see her and claimed she was expected. "Miriam, I had forgotten about her! Yes, I will see her in the courtyard immediately."

She hurried out to the torch lit reception area. "How are you? It is so good to see you again." Ceelyha affectionately embraced her old acquaintance.

"I am in very good form, Your Lady," she giggled and pointed to her belly, "and so is this little one."

Ceelyha led her young friend to a bench and signaled for her to sit down. Her awkwardness and the way she held herself alerted Ceelyha that Miriam's time was very near. Ceelyha graciously said, "Congratulations. You must be very happy. Did the priestesses at Dor predict whether the baby would be a boy or a girl?"

"The barley grew before the wheat, so it will be a girl!"

"That is wonderful!" Ceelyha responded and then asked, "How is Dinah, do you ever hear of her?"

"I went to the Temple for a potion to help me conceive. She was there and doing well. Everything is much the same as when you left."

"And what of married life? Is it everything you had hoped it to be?"

Miriam hesitated before she responded, "I do not think that anything quite prepares you for it. I am in love with my husband. I enjoy the status of being a married woman and talking to the other wives each day at the well. But, you were right. I wait on his wishes. It is 'Miriam, fetch me some food, fetch me my cloak, prepare the lanterns, slaughter the lamb, weed the garden.' It is no different than being in my father's home! I just exchanged one man for another!" But" she lovingly patted her swollen tummy, "a child will make a difference." Then she looked at Ceelyha.

"You look radiant. There is definitely something different about you and it is not just that you have aged since we last met."

Ceelyha only smiled and Miriam knew immediately. "Of course, there is a man! You are in love! You, who said that you would never be bound to a man! Now look at you! He must be very special for you to have chosen him."

Ceelyha could feel herself blushing. "He is very special, and yes, I am in love but I cannot be his wife. I am married to the Goddess."

"Then how often do you meet? Who is this man?"

"We meet when we can but I cannot tell you who he is. Just know that he is powerful and is already married."

Miriam looked disappointed so Ceelyha changed the subject and asked when her baby was due and how much longer she and her husband would be staying in Jerusalem. She explained they would be staying with her husband's uncle until some family business was cleared up.

"Then you will be here for the birth of the baby! You must call on me when the time is upon you."

Miriam's face lit up and she reached over to hug Ceelyha. "I was so hoping that you would say that! I begged for my husband to let me come with him so you could help me give birth!"

The two women spoke for a while longer, exchanging news about people whom Ceelyha had healed in Dor. When they parted, Ceelyha told Miriam they would be seeing one another before the next half moon.

The next day, after the New Year's festival, Temple life went back to normal as everyone went about her regular duties. Ceelyha sent a message to the Palace asking for David to come to the Temple just before midnight.

Late in the evening, when the moon rose high above the Temple, Thu came to Ceelyha's chamber.

"Are you ready for this?" she asked.

Ceelyha nodded. "I have been fasting, have had my cleansing bath and have just sent Nintu to find some goat's milk."

Thu had a puzzled look on her face so Ceelyha explained that Dinah had told her that it assisted with purification before divination. She wished to be a perfect channel for David. *I do want this to go well. It is important to me that he thinks of me as more than just a mistress. I desire him to see me as an Entu, one who can summon the dead, interpret dreams and heal the sick.* She had been struggling with how David might react to tonight's session. A part of her feared that he would have the same conviction as his forefather Moses, who decreed death to all those who divined. All day she had been sending white to light to David, along with prayers to Ishtar, that all would go in her favour. When David was relaying the story of how the priestess used the art of necromancy to predict the death of Saul, Ceelyha had meant to ask if he would have condemned her to death if he were Saul. *Perhaps I really did not want to know what his answer might have been,* she wondered. With these thoughts weighing heavily upon her, she asked Thu about David's previous interactions at the Temple.

"I know he came to ask Bernice about the outcome of some battles that he was worried about, but of course, she never shared his confidences. Why do you ask?"

Ceelyha replied with concern in her voice. "I hope to be in trance before David arrives. I do not want to be aware of him as a man, my lover; I need him to be like a regular petitioner. But I want you to get his assurance that I am under his protection while I do the conjuring. Promise me that Thu."

"Of course. However, I do think that you are being overly cautious. Was he not the one who wanted this done? Surely he is used to divination through Bernice."

Ceelyha explained, "Unexpectedly, a spirit came upon me while we were discussing Saul and Samuel. I sent it away because my energy field was not protected. I did not want to be possessed by a ghost even for David! David wanted to know what was going on so I said that I needed to be back at the Temple in order to communicate with the spirit. I wanted you, the Goddess and Her wisdom breathing through the wall of the Temple before I would allow this spirit through. When I asked him what type of work Bernice did with him, he stated it was by scrying. I do not think she ever used necromancy directly in front of him."

Nintu returned with the goat's milk drink and the conversation ceased. She assisted Ceelyha into royal purple robes and fastened the red girdle around her waist. Ceelyha indicated that she wished to wear the golden headdress from Babylon, the one with the large black sapphire so Nintu secured it on her mistress's loose flowing hair. Shiroka's necklace went around her neck.

"Oh," exclaimed Thu. "You look every inch the High Priestess tonight. I am sure that even David will be awed by your presence and power!"

Ceelyha nervously answered, "Let us hope so." Then she turned to Nintu and said, "Pick up my bag of tools and let us proceed to same the room where I did my previous divining. That way we will not be disturbed. When I am ready, you can bring the King to me. I will instruct Thu how to assist me, rather than you, Nintu, so the King will not think there are too many of us privy to his secrets. You must wait outside the door until I am finished."

As the women made their way down the ancient stone steps into the bowels of the Temple, Thu said, "In my country, the dead are not summoned for prophecy since it is believed that they have no knowledge of the living."

Ceelyha replied, "In Babylon and other parts of Mesopotamia, it is quite customary to retrieve information from the dead for those who are still living. Powerful people, who have died, such as the Prophets and Kings, would have the same powers in death that they had in life. I cannot guarantee what will happen tonight but I believe it is King Saul who wishes to communicate a message to David, which means Saul still has an attachment to this plane of existence."

Thu clutched her chest with her hand that was not holding a torch. "How did this man die? By the pain in my chest, I sense it was by sword."

Ceelyha's voice had made a hollow sound as it rang out from behind, "I do not know but there may have been many forces involved." Secretly, she wondered if David had a hand in it but did not voice her thoughts.

The rest of the trip along the dark, dank, dusty corridors to the room where the necromancy would be performed was made in silence. Nintu used her torch to light the brazier and the wall lamp. She deftly unpacked the contents of her mistress's bag and arranged the three statues of all the Goddesses, Ishtar, Isis and Asherah in the center of the altar then placed two tall candles on either side. A smoky quartz crystal was placed it in front of the statues and the clear quartz was handed to Ceelyha. Sandalwood and lavender incense to be later thrown into the fire were passed to Thu.

When Nintu made certain that Ceelyha had everything, she hurried back to the main part of the Temple to wait for the King while Ceelyha gave some last minute instructions to Thu. "You must ensure your safety and that of David's by not allowing him to step inside the magical circle of protection that I will make with my crystal. I can not be responsible for anyone's safety if that line is broken."

When everything was in order, Ceelyha stood in front of the altar. Above her head, she raised the crystal, with its point directed up to the Heavens. After a few minutes, she began to sway back and forth to an inner rhythm that coursed through her body. Then she prayed, "I call upon the protection and the love of Asherah, Ishtar and Isis, the Goddesses of Light, to surround me. I ask Your lights to protect me. Oh, Goddesses, hear me now, I pray, protect from evil those that will be in this room. Oh Goddesses, do not allow the spirit of the deceased to linger after it has said its piece. I am forever, Your servant."

She began to hum, first softly and then with more volume as she connected with the Goddesses. She sensed the presence of David as Thu threw some incense on the brazier's burning coals. A chant raised her vibrations higher and higher, and with her crystal she cast a circle in the air three times in a clockwise direction. She silently prayed for the protection of the Goddesses as she allowed the borders between her world and that of the spirit to dissolve. She knew that she had broken the barrier when a foul odour permeated the tiny room and a wind manifested out of nowhere. The lamp and fire flickered and Ceelyha allowed herself to be taken over by a foreign energy. In a voice that sounded as if it were coming from outside her being, she was aware of saying, "I am protected by the power of the mightiest Goddesses on earth. I bid the spirit to reveal its presence to us."

She opened and widened her eyes as her body felt as if it were shriveling, getting more stooped and smaller. She took a deep breath and expelled a gust of air from her lungs. She took three steps backwards from the altar and turned to face an anxious Thu and David. Then a voice, deep and gruff, spewed from her throat. "David, David, my son!"

At some level of her mind, Ceelyha was aware of Thu nervously leaning toward the circle of protection and calling out, "Who are you?"

"I am Saul, King of the Israelites," Ceelyha answered in a hollow voice that sounded as if it were coming from the depths of a deep well. "I have a message for the one called David."

David attempted to step forward until Thu reached out to stop him.

"Take heed my son. There are many more challenges ahead of you. Watch your back for sons that are already born and those yet to be born. Just as there was rivalry for my throne, there will be many who will contest yours. Beware of your second born and watch your daughter. Your hands, already smeared with blood, will shed more."

Thu tossed more incense into the fire before she asked if there was a further message. Ceelyha again spoke in the strange voice as the spirit pressed upon her. "Put your kingdom before your personal life, for the Lord will sorely test you in this. Take care, my son."

The room went out of focus, the energy released itself and floor rose up as Ceelyha slumped to the ground. When she was revived, three anxious faces greeted her. Nintu was rubbing her hands, David's cloak was around her, Thu was calling her name and David looked gravely shaken. When he saw that she was fully back in the land of the living, he hugged her and when he began to murmur endearments into her ears, the other two women discreetly left the room.

"My Golden One, you were magnificent. You never need to worry that I would not support the work that you do! Do not ever let that concern you!" He held her and kissed her face and hands. They talked about what Saul had tried to convey to David and then he escorted her back to her rooms. He left just before the sun rose and promised to meet Ceelyha at the house after he got back from supervising his men who were still closely watching the Philistines at Adullam.

A week later, while Ceelyha was overseeing the preparation of herbs for a sick man, the Gatekeeper interrupted her healing. "I am sorry Lady but an urgent message has come from one called Miriam. Apparently her time has come."

Ceelyha called for Nintu, "Get another priestess to administer to this man. Call Thu and anyone else who is not occupied and tell them our services are needed at a birthing. Get a set of birthing bricks from the hall. Fetch my medicine box and hurry!"

The uncle of Miriam's husband had a cart waiting at the gate. Thu, Nintu, Ceelyha and two novice priestesses climbed in. They quickly wound their way through the crowded streets while the driver yelled, "Make way for the Women of Asherah! Make way!"

The women found an anxious Miriam lying on a pallet, at the house of her husband's uncle. Tears flowed down her pale face. The aunt exclaimed, "We thought you were not coming!"

As a pain surged through the expecting mother's body, Thu placed a scarab amulet around Miriam's neck to ward off evil. She then ordered the young priestess, who had accompanied them, to arrange the birthing bricks painted with scenes of a mother holding her new born and decorated with colourful symbols of Asherah. The women helped Miriam onto the bricks. Ceelyha gently rubbed arnica over the distended belly while they waited for water to boil in order to make a blackberry infusion that would help relieve some of the labor pains.

The priestesses began to chant the traditional birthing songs to soothe the mother and to beckon the soul of the unborn child into its waiting body. The day wore on. Several times the Goddess was called upon to release the child into the world. Thu took out her birth charms that would be secured in the cloth wrapped around the newborn's body while Ceelyha prepared an herb to induce the birth and placed a bright green stone of the Goddess on the top of Miriam's stomach. Finally, just as the sun was about to set, Miriam gave a final push and a baby girl slid into Ceelyha's waiting hands. The women immediately broke into a celebratory chant of welcome. While Miriam's aunt helped her back onto the pallet, the baby was quickly examined; then bathed in clear, fresh water that had been drawn from a nearby well. The tiny body was anointed with oils and swaddled along with the birthing charms. The exhausted mother beamed with happiness as the newborn was placed in her arms.

"My daughter is so beautiful. She is perfect!" Miriam smiled blissfully. "Thank you, all of you. Would one of you priestesses please read the omens for her!"

Thu looked at the cracks in the birthing bricks and consulted her Goddess Isis.

When she was finished, she announced the child would become a priestess.

Everyone exalted in the future of the child. Miriam, the most jubilant of all, looked at Ceelyha and said, "I suppose that is why our destinies are intertwined.

You will be the caretaker of my daughter when she is of age to come to the Temple! In your honour, you must name her."

"I could not do that. That is for you and your husband to do!" replied a flattered Ceelyha.

"No, it is you that brought me together with my husband, you who aided at the birth and you shall name her," Miriam was insistent and held up her child to Ceelyha.

Ceelyha tenderly held the tiny bundle in her arms. Her heart melted; the child was so innocent, so dependent and so precious. She touched the pink fingers and smoothed the black fuzz on her head. She knew she would never have a child of her own but if she did, she would want a daughter just like this one. And now the Goddess was giving her to the Temple! Just as she was making a silent pledge to care for the child and teach her all she could, a cold chill shot up her spine. In that instant, she knew that she would not see the child grow up.

"Ceelyha, what is wrong!" cried an anxious Miriam struggling to sit up. "Have you seen some evil omen for my daughter?"

"Oh no," Ceelyha responded quickly "She will grow to be a fine priestess. I see no evil for her." Then a name came to her. "In the name of the Goddess Asherah, I name this child Bernice."

She gently gave Bernice back to her mother wondering why she would not see the child become a priestess. What did the Goddess have in store now for her?

Chapter 14
The Making of a High Priestess and A Wedding

Jacob returned from the battlefield to marry Nintu. The bride, not being of the same religion and culture as the groom, arranged for her bridal preparations to take place at the pool of Asherah, instead of at the mikvah. On the day of the wedding, just shortly after dawn, Jacob's closest women family members arrived to assist the bride.

Servants had swept the bathing area, by the bronze pool, clean of any debris and meticulously scrubbed the faded mosaic tiles. A striped awning and comfortable cushions in celebratory colors added to the ambiance of festivity. Trays of fresh fruits and spiced wine were brought to the guests and priestesses.

Everyone dressed in her best clothes. For the occasion, Ceelyha had chosen her royal blue sheath, accented by the necklace that David had given her. Since Nintu was too busy to attend to her, she wore her hair long, accented with the golden sparkles that David admired. She applied her own cosmetics. As she placed the gold diadem on her head, she speculated for the hundredth time when she and David would be alone again. It seemed like ages since they were last at the house.

When she was dressed, Ceelyha hurried to find Nintu who was in the servants' quarters with her friends. Many Temple workers, both priestesses and servants alike, and Nintu's soon to be female in-laws waited under the awning as Ceelyha led a glowing Nintu, dressed only in a unflattering robe, over to the bathing area. Amid much clapping and cheering the bride's robe was removed. Nintu stood naked on the tiles, trying modestly to cover her breasts, while heated water mixed with sweet smelling herbs was poured over her from ornamental alabaster jugs. The bride was then led to the pool where she submerged three times, once for her body, once for her mind and lastly for her spirit so she would be entirely cleansed for her husband. A thick white cloth was used to rub her dry while the women made jokes and suggestions about how a woman should please a man. Her skin was oiled, her hair braided into plaits then interwoven with the petals of roses that Jacob's mother had brought. Her hands were painted with intricate designs of flowers and fertility symbols. A clove was stuck into the bride's mouth to freshen her breath as more comments and jeers were made about lovemaking. Finally, Nintu was dressed in a long diaphanous sea green robe, one of Ceelyha's from Babylon, its rich colour setting off the luster of her mahogany coloured skin. Ceelyha noted how the thick gold bracelet from Thu and long lapis earrings which she herself had given Nintu, transformed her old friend into a woman of beauty and means. *I wish her all the happiness in the world,* she thought and silently prayed for the Goddess to grant her a good life. Nintu had been her servant and confident as far back as either could remember. She had been left at the Temple when she was just a baby, her origins unknown, to be raised by the Ishtar priestesses. Since they were close to the same age, Nintu had become a companion and later a servant to Ceelyha. Tears of happiness streamed down Ceelyha's face as she thought about her friend becoming a wife and possibly a mother. Then the tears changed to fear as a foreboding thought clouded Ceelyha's happiness. The wings of the Goddess surrounded her as the message came, "Her happiness will turn to sorrow. The one she loves is not long for this world."

At that same moment, Nintu happened to look over at her mistress and saw the familiar signs of the Goddess. She removed herself from the women who were busy applying her cosmetics, walked over to Ceelyha and nervously inquired, "Oh Lady, what is it that you just received? By the expression on your face, it is not good news. It is about my wedding isn't it! What will happen?"

Ceelyha paused and tried to put a bright smile on her face. Nintu looked so worried, on the verge of tears. In order to gain time to recover her composure, Ceelyha reached out to massage a bit of pomegranate juice that had not been fully rubbed into Nintu's cheek and explained, "It was not about you, my beautiful bride. I just felt a shadow fall over my life." She directed Nintu back to the women who were waiting to finish her makeup. "Go! This is your day to be pampered, not mine. Enjoy."

A none too satisfied Nintu rejoined the giggling women to have the finishing touches applied – a circlet of gold on her forehead followed by draping a gossamer veil over her face. When Thu held up a mirror, Nintu gasped with pleasure. "I can not believe that I am actually getting married! Who would have thought that a poor orphan from The Land of Two Rivers would ever marry a handsome Israeli soldier?"

Thu replied, "It is the Goddess's wish that you do so or you never would have traveled so far to meet your beloved!" Then she turned to the guests, "It is time for the bride to be taken to the groom."

Dilbaha gathered the women who were part of the wedding party, and they surrounded Nintu. The lyres and drums started to play as the Temple dancers began to swirl and move about the circled group. Everyone's voices soared in the bridal song as the gates to the Temple opened and the women spilled out onto the street. The crowds parted to let the party through while singing their well wishes. As they proceeded towards the groom's home, Nintu managed to catch up to Ceelyha and grasp her hand. "You once prophesized that I would fall in love with Jacob, but you never told me my future. Can you tell me if we will be happy together and live a long life with plenty of sons and daughters?"

Ceelyha turned to her friend and gently replied. "For the time that you will be together, you will both be very happy. That is all the Goddess has given me. I wish you a long prosperous life with Jacob and many children to bounce on your knee!"

I hate to not tell her what I have seen, but I have not told an untruth. They will be happy while they are together. We cannot undo what the Fates have cast for us.

Nintu's face was full of gratitude. "I thank you my Lady." Then she added anxiously, "I have arranged for another serving girl, Sarah, to attend you while I am gone. But as soon as Jacob is called back to the army, I will return to you."

Ceelyha, recognizing that the girl wanted to please her, replied, "I am fine and can even do my own hair and bath. Now go. This is your day!" and then she added with a naughty smile, "And night!"

The bridal procession congregated before they reached the home of the groom's father. The dancers stepped forward, followed by the rest of the women and lastly, the bride. The door to the courtyard of the humble house swung open to reveal a group of men, dressed in their finery of cloth shifts in various stripes and colors, impatiently waiting. The invited soldiers were in full uniform, proudly wearing metal breastplates and tunics. Ceelyha's heart quickened when she saw David standing among his men. He wore a simple tunic with a heavier breastplate than the rest of the soldiers. Since he appeared as if he were trying to be just part of the crowd and not the King, no one else in the women's party seemed to notice him. But, his eyes sought hers and his mouth parted in a smile of pleasure. A current of energy passed between them. Ceelyha had not known that he was back from commanding his army in the south. *Why did he not send word to her?*

While the ceremony was taking place, Ceelyha's awareness of his nearness almost superseded the vows that the couple were taking until Jacob held out his large hand, adoration radiating from his face, to receive Nintu's small brown one. That simple gesture of the acceptance of their love overwhelmed her. She sighed and wiped tears away as she looked in David's direction. She wondered if he too wished that they could be joined in marriage. But his face was impassive; she could not read what was in his heart. There were shouts of joy from the guests as the groom lifted his bride's veil and the couple shared a cup of wine as a symbol of their union. Then the dancing, feasting and celebrating began. Ceelyha congratulated the bride and groom before moving towards David. She bowed in respect and when he reached out to take her hand, tiny jolts of electricity shot through her. She inhaled his fresh fragrance that reminded her of the outdoors and willed herself to stop the desire that spread throughout her body. He too, must have felt the yearning in her for he whispered,

"My Golden One, sneak away to the house as soon as possible. This is a far too public place for such wicked thoughts," he teased in a low sensuous tone of voice.

She murmured a yes as he left her side to congratulate the couple. She told Thu where she was going and not to expect her at the evening ritual. As soon as possible, she snuck away from the merriment and walked out of the courtyard. David must have arranged transport since a servant signaled her to enter a waiting royal sedan.

David was already waiting in the reception room of the house. She ran into his arms and they embraced. She felt his passion ignite hers as his strong hard body pressed against hers. Without either uttering a word, their lips met and his tongue searched for hers. After a long passionate kiss, he picked her up and carried her to their bedchamber. Kissing all the while, they urgently fumbled to remove one another's clothing. Ceelyha felt as if she was unable to let go of him. She needed his body to mold and fit into hers in order to feel whole again. All her teachings and promises to the Goddess, slipped away as he entered her. The cry that escaped from her lips as she reached her climax was more like that of an animal rather than a priestess.

When they both were satisfied and had lain contentedly in each other's arms for a long period of time, David suddenly rose up on his elbows and looked at Ceelyha. He tenderly ran his finger over the delicate features of her face, and she got lost in the depth of his eyes that at that moment emanated love. Then he broke the magic of the moment when he spoke in an authoritarian voice, "I have some news for you. Your high priestess, Adah, will remain at the Asherah Temple of Jezreel."

Ceelyha sat up. "Why?"

"I think it is better suited to her skills. I have already sent the order." His voice softened as he gathered her into his arms. "Now, that means that you, my Golden One, will be the High Priestess of the Jerusalem Temple." He appeared quite pleased with himself as he relayed the news.

"What?" Ceelyha cried. "I am not ready to have such a high position."

Then she thought better of her response remembering a mystic guards her emotions. *How could I have blurted that out! What must he think of me!* she reproached herself. *Will I ever learn?* As she reigned in her surprise, she added, "I am so very flattered but is not the priestess, Dilbaha, a better choice?"

Immediately she sensed David's annoyance. He released his hold on her and got out of bed to search for his tunic. "I thought you would be pleased. What higher honor could a woman in your position have than to be High Priestess? I have given you a gift that only a King could give. Are you throwing it back in my face?" His voice was terse, his face red with anger.

Ceelyha silently prayed for guidance. *What am I to do? Am I ready for such a big responsibility? Is this what the Goddess has in store for me? The prophecy is coming true, too quickly! If I become the High Priestess then David will cause me pain! I know I will lose him! Can I postpone the inevitable? If I refuse, I will lose him and if I accept, I will lose him. Please Lady of Light and all knowledge guide me in this time of need!* She momentarily waited but did not sense an immediate response from the Goddess. She knew David was waiting. She bit her lip and spoke with more assurance than she felt.

"My Lord, do not be angry with me. You have taken me by complete surprise and I am honored that you would wish me to hold such an esteemed position." She looked to see if his anger was abated before continuing, "If you believe that I am worthy of such a gift then I gratefully accept your generous offer." She took a deep breath wanting more time to think about the sudden change in her life. *What about Dilbaha who was been acting as the High Priestess? How is she going to react to this? What about the others in the Temple who do not hold me in very high regard because of my liaison with David? And now, what will they think if he makes me their High Priestess?*

He stopped searching for his discarded clothes, once again took her in his arms and spoke. "You are my choice for the position and so it is decreed. The Golden One from the Land of the Two Rivers is the new High Priestess. That way, I shall have easy access to you and there will be no more gossiping behind your back. You may come and go as you please from the Temple and this house. What could be simpler? You will read the oracles for me whenever I wish."

A chill of foreboding crept up her spine as she felt the Goddess's wings surround her but Ceelyha pushed the premonition aside by kissing David to show him her gratitude in the best way she knew how.

It was later in the evening, after another session of lovemaking, and a simple meal, that David picked up his harp from the corner of the dressing room and began to play. Even in the dim light of the wall torch, Ceelyha sensed an aura of light and peace surround him as she listened in earnest as he praised his God with a song.

O Lord, our Lord.
How glorious is Your name
over all the earth.
When I behold Your heavens,
the work of Your fingers,
the moon and stars which You set in place –
What is man that You should be mindful of him,
or the son of man that You should care for him?

You have made him little less than the angels,
and crowned him with glory and honour.

"You sing like a god, David! You have such an astonishing way of combining harmonious music with such inspirational prose. You provide a journey into the Light and awaken the soul to its natural state of harmony. Sometimes it is difficult to connect the hard, ruthless King with the sensitive artist."

David sighed, the surreal glow still around him as he laid his harp aside. Ceelyha still in awe continued, "Before hearing that song, I had the impression that your God only appeared to His people with smoke, fire, thunder and lightning. To me, He is a force to be feared and yet you have portrayed him as gentle and as loving as My Goddess."

"I have seen all sides of Yahweh. He is all the Gods of all pagans compiled into one."

As David began to explain some of the history of his people, he continued to be bathed in a radiance that Ceelyha could only conclude meant that spirit was with him. It was difficult to concentrate on his words, she was so fascinated by his God like presence. *Surely he is as connected to his God as I am the Goddess.* She wanted to point this out but was reluctant to interrupt in case the link severed. So she forced herself to attend.

Like her early people, his forefathers, the Canaanites' worship was tied to the land. If a man prayed hard enough to the God Baal or to the Goddess Asherah, rain would fall and there would be a bountiful harvest. But if he was not devoted, then his crops would fail. The Gods had to be constantly appeased and made happy. If They were angry, the belief was that They would destroy human life and the world. So, if sacrifices were not made at the right time, crops would not grow, the world would be chaos.

When David drew a similarity to her ritual of honouring the Goddess each dawn and dusk, Ceelyha forgot the unnatural light as she felt her jaw drop. David turned and looked at her, obviously picking up her dismay and added, "I am not belittling what you do but do you actually think that if the Goddess was not praised that the sun would not shine or the rains would not come?"

Ceelyha quickly composed herself, noting the glow had indeed gone and thoughtfully answered, "But because we do that, we will never know. Perhaps it is we, the pagans, as you refer to my beliefs, who keep the world running for the rest of you! If we did stop our rituals then who would heal the sick? Assist with childbirth? Ease heartache? Foretell the future? Celebrate the harvest?"

"That is why we allow you to co-exist along with us." David went on thinking more out loud than conversing with Ceelyha. "My people understand that sacrifices do not make rain and growing crops. We have no need to make the Gods happy. God simply wants a relationship with each of us, a personal relationship."

"Here," he picked up the harp and began to sing,

I have set the LORD always before me: because he is at my right hand, I shall not be moved. Therefore my heart is glad, and my glory rejoiceth: my flesh also shall rest in hope.Thou wilt shew me the path of life: in thy presence is fulness of joy; at thy right hand there are pleasures for evermore.

Ceelyha listened carefully to his song, noting the presence once again around him, then responded. "So you do not believe in sacrifices to your God but your ancestors believed in them. Did not your God ask one of your forefathers to kill his son as a sacrifice?"

"Yahweh does not need placating through sacrifices of humans, animals or even flowers that you put on your altars. These offerings are meaningless. To Him, it is the faith of humankind that is all-important. And, you do not have the full story about the time when He asked Abraham to sacrifice his son Isaac." David was getting more and more excited with the conversation. "He told Abraham to place his son on the altar as a test of faith. It was proof of Abraham's commitment to a God who has supreme domination over man and earth. After that incident, Abraham believed that we were His people, His chosen ones. God gave us laws to live by and we must abide by them or suffer the consequences."

"And do you think that you have ever broken one of the rules of your God?"

When David answered that he was not aware of any, Ceelyha sensed the earlier radiance beginning to dim.

"But have you not killed another man, in fact many other men? How do you justify that?"

"The prophets have told us that we must fight for our land. I have not knowingly killed another of my own people. It is the foreigners, the pagans we are removing. Remember, we Israelis are His chosen ones. You must hear the song I wrote about that very issue."

In the LORD put I my trust: how say ye to my soul, Flee as a bird to your mountain?

For, lo, the wicked bend their bow, they make ready their arrow upon the string, that they may privily shoot at the upright in heart.

If the foundations be destroyed, what can the righteous do?

The LORD is in his holy temple, the LORD'S throne is in heaven: his eyes behold, his eyelids try, the children of men.

The LORD trieth the righteous: but the wicked and him that loveth violence his soul hateth.

Upon the wicked he shall rain snares, fire and brimstone, and a horrible tempest: this shall be the portion of their cup.

For the righteous LORD loveth righteousness; his countenance doth behold the upright.

As he sang, the light once again strengthened. He put the harp down and thoughtfully added, "You see, I have prayed to God to help me with this. I know that He will help my people to destroy thine enemies."

"Then perhaps I am your enemy? I, according to Him, worship the wrong God." Ceelyha had a tremor of fear in her voice. *Surely this could not be happening? I have never doubted my faith in the Goddess. Am I about to allow this man to alter my entire belief system in order not to lose him?*

"No my love. It is not my duty to convert you. I honour your beliefs and would never ask you to change them for me. I am just so happy that we can have conversations like this. None of my wives has ever understood me the way you do.

I have no fear that I would ever stray from my God, as you have no fear of leaving your Goddess. Let us just celebrate our differences. There are no children from our union, no ties of marriage to cause either one of us sacrifice for the other. Just mutual friendship and love."

Ceelyha breathed a sigh of relief. "You are correct, David. I accept you as you are and am grateful that you support my work." She was glad to rid herself of the need to choose because of course, there was no choice. She had simply let her emotions overrule her heart.

Later, after more food and wine, they continued their discussion about their different religions. Ceelyha was pleased to explain how to her people, all the Gods are related to the elements of nature. People worship the sun because of its light; the moon because of its mystery, the water God because of its life giving force and each facet of nature for its divine purpose. She told him how each country or group of people has its own Gods. Her Babylonian Gods are different from the ones in Egypt just as the Canaanite Gods are different, one and the same.

Then she asked, "So your God is all the Gods tied into one?"

David nodded. "Yahweh is all the Canaanite Gods in one. There are no separate Gods in my religion and no image of God."

"But your ancestors worshipped many Gods. How do you justify that? Even your Rachel, the Mother of your people, worshipped idols."

"Idols are man made. They have eyes that do not see and mouths that do not speak."

"Why are your people so opposed to the ancient ways of learning? The teachings of Asherah could be classified as witchcraft since we do not worship your God. Do you not think it is of utmost importance for the people to have choices? Your priests only cater to the political climate of the country. They do not address the needs of the poor farmer, or the woman who wants to be with child, or the man who has hurt his foot. They really do not have any idea about the common day to day issues of the people."

She continued on, "Don't you agree that the people just want to have food on their table and will honor whatever god provides that for them, like Baal?"

Ceelyha recalled Dinah teaching her how the people mourned and mourned when they thought Baal, the God of rain and thunder, had died and gone to Heaven; forsaking them when their land became barren. They believed that their tears brought him back to life because He returned the following season with the rains. It was only natural that He was their most important God at that time.

David thoughtfully rolled his eyes as if trying to recall the history of the Canaanites. "Not so with Yahweh. He never leaves his people."

"But is not the name Yahweh the same as El?"

"Yes, the name is the same. But, Yahweh, the chief god, replaced the need for all the pagan Gods and Goddesses."

"But here in your land, some still worship Asherah. Is Asherah not Yahweh's feminine counterpart?"

"She was El's consort. Some of my people still believe that she is the mother of the Gods and shares in El's work. My God, Yahweh, has no mate. But when my people came from Egypt to Israel, they intermarried and integrated with the Canaanites so it was only natural that they incorporated Canaanite gods and beliefs with those of their own. Abraham was told by Yahweh to not worship these other Gods, and that the arts of divination, the making of potions, healing remedies and the worshipping of idols were punishable. The Leviticus Priesthood was the only group that was allowed to perform any type of mystical arts. The priests of this order claimed that they were the only ones who could receive messages from the spirit world.

Until the time of Saul, our people were free to seek help at Asherah's temples for healing and divination. But Saul, under the direction of Samuel, tried to discourage consulting the Asherah priestesses."

"And what of your prophets? Do they not believe that they have contact with your God just as the priestesses of Asherah do with their Goddess?"

David answered. "Yes, that is correct."

"And how do these prophets of yours receive the word of Yahweh?"

"I suppose it is through visions and dreams."

"Then some of their dreams would require a symbolic interpretation and others would be taken quite literally, use smoke from a brazier as a divination tool to interpret what the Goddess is trying to convey. However, when I am in trance, I am the channel through which Her divine words flow. And you, yourself, once said that God spoke to you in words." When she looked at him, she sensed his distress over their conversation and was aware that the iridescence had vapourized.

David wavered before he answered. "He has not spoken to me for a long time. That is why I have to rely on priestesses such as you and have to listen to Nathan." He sounded angry and his voice rose in agitation. "God has not communicated with me since I took over Jerusalem. Do you know how frustrating and alone that makes me feel?"

Ceelyha pitied him, recalling the times she had felt deserted by the Goddess. "But David, you are His chosen one. You are His living representative here on earth. You are so connected to Him that His words are yours."

"What do you mean by that?"

Ceelyha cleared her throat before she replied. "I mean that your God uses you as His channel. When information needs to be relayed, then God speaks to you and you in turn speak His words for the betterment of humanity! As you spoke, you positively radiated His presence. Just look at how beautiful your poems and songs are. Were they not inspired by a higher source than you?"

David reached out and took her lovingly into his arms. "That is why I have you in my life, to remind me of who I really am. You see why, my Golden One, that you are the new High Priestess?"

It was at that moment that Ceelyha remembered Dinah's prophecy. "Just as he will be a leader of his brothers, you too will be a leader of your sisters." That is what was meant. She would be in charge of the priestesses! It suddenly made sense and the Goddess descended upon her with the message, "Here lies the rest of your destiny. You have not deserted me. Take the gift that is being offered and soar with it."

Ceelyha disengaged herself from David's arms and looked into his eyes. She searched the depths of his soul and found many layers that even she could not uncover. Finally she said, "My Lord, I accept your offer of the position of High Priestess. I shall not fail you, the Goddess Asherah or my priestesses."

His face beamed, his eyes lit up. He raised his hands to the ceiling and said, "It is the least I can for my Golden One. Did you know that Bernice requested that you take over for her as soon as things settled after her passing?"

Ceelyha was shocked. "I had no idea that is what Bernice wanted. Why did you not tell me before? Why did you make Adah the High Priestess? Is that why you sent her away?" The thought of his deception fueled her anger.

He laughed. "Did you know that those fascinating gold flecks in your sea green eyes become a deep amber colour when you are upset? You have never looked more beautiful than right this minute." And he proceeded to cup her breasts in his hands.

"Stop that," she pushed him aside. "You are not taking me seriously. How dare you treat me like one of your concubines!"

Now it was his turn to anger. "I am the King and whatever I decide is the way things are." He turned away from her.

Realizing yet another time how quick he was to anger, she sent a beam of white loving light to him. In a moment he turned back to her.

"I never endorsed Adah as High Priestess. Her talents could never hold a candle to yours. If you must know, I needed to test you first. I needed to know if you were as connected to your Goddess as Bernice was to hers. You have proven yourself and now it is time to assume the role to which you were born." He placed his hands back onto her soft breasts and both of them tuned the world out as they lost themselves in one another.

It was almost midnight when they left the house. Ceelyha insisted that David personally speak to Dilbaha about his decision. They rode in a chariot that was waiting outside – in silence – each lost in thought. A sleepy gatekeeper who opened the

Temple door, was surprised to see the King and one of the priestesses. He bowed and kept watch over the horse and chariot as its occupants entered the darkened court-yard. Not wishing to wake a servant to light the torches, they made their way more by sense than sight to the rooms of Dilbaha. Ceelyha gently knocked on her door.

"Priestess, I apologize for the late hour but the King is here and wishes to have a word with you.

They heard Dilbaha quickly get out of bed and open the door to her chamber. She nervously clutched a small-lit torch.

She was just about to go down on her knees when David ordered her to stop. She looked in confusion from David to Ceelyha as she waited for the King to speak.

In his commanding voice he announced, "I am now proceeding with the dying wishes of your late High Priestess, Bernice. She had decreed that the priestess from Babylon take over her position as head of this Temple. Let it be known that Adah will be staying in the north to reside over a sister Temple and that the Priestess Ceelyha will be in charge beginning now."

Dilbaha went down on her knees and bowed before an embarrassed Ceelyha. "Please Dilbaha, it is I who should bow before you for the remarkable work you have done since Adah left. I want you to continue as my assistant to help me to run the Temple. Would you do that with me? And would you be the guardian of the snakes as well?"

As Ceelyha helped the older woman up, she was relieved to see acceptance and not hostility in her eyes.

"I would be honored My Lady," she replied. "I will make your new rooms ready as soon as it is light. Will you be doing the morning ritual?"

Ceelyha had never performed the morning or evening ritual at any Temple. A feeling of insecurity and incompetence rushed over her until she looked into David's eyes.

He was waiting for her to take a stance, to be in charge and seize what was rightfully hers.

"Yes, that is a good idea. Will you honour me by taking it with me?"

The older priestess nodded.

"Then I will see you at the ritual," she replied with more confidence than she felt. "Now, please return to your bed." She turned to David as the other priestess had closed her door. To convey to Dilbaha that there was nothing but business between David and herself, Ceelyha formally announced, "My Lord, I will escort you back to the gate."

"Before you do that, High Priestess, I have need of your services."

Ceelyha though he meant making love to her again so she held up her hand in mock protest. In a teasing voice she whispered, "Here, in the Temple?"

David's reply was stern. "No, I mean your other services!" with an emphasis on 'other'.

Ceelyha was grateful that the hall was too dark for him to see her blush with humiliation. In a muted voice she answered, "Of course, what is it?"

As they walked to the altar of Asherah with its eternal flame, David explained that his troops were scouting the enemy south of Jerusalem near Abdullah. He needed to know if the time was appropriate to advance. Ceelyha's response was that she had not been fasting and had lain with him without washing and therefore would be unable to go into a deep trance. David did not seem to mind that her powers might be diminished so she positioned herself directly in front of the flame, took several deep breaths and raised her hands to the Heavens. She chanted for the Goddess to assist with the reading. When the Goddess came upon her and vapours began to take shape, she began to divine. "I see chariots rushing forward and many cloaks full of blood and toppled helmets with plumes. And I think that …yes, a victory banner. Does this help you?"

David grabbed her, swung her around and around all the while laughing. "That is why you are the High Priestess. Even in your so called contaminated state, you are the Goddess's channel!" He lowered her to the ground and steadied her on her feet before strolling away into the darkness.

Chapter 15
The New High Priestess

Ceelyha knew there was no sense trying to sleep; she was too anxious about her new position as the High Priestess and the conversations with David. She felt as if she was now much closer to the man whom she was in love with and had a better understanding of the person under the crown. His relationship with his God was just as deeply ingrained as hers with Ishtar. She felt that with her new status as head Entu, the Goddess would be pleased that She was first rather than David. But, Ceelyha wondered how she and David could possibly have more time together if she ran the Temple and he made arrangements to bring the Ark to Jerusalem. Everything seemed out of her control.

A few hours before dawn, Ceelyha slipped out of bed and prostrated before the Lady.

"Oh Ishtar and Asherah, one and the same,

Brilliant Mother of All Gods,

Bringer of the Dawn,

Be with me now as my ever-guiding light.

To You I pray that I may be Your faithful servant here on earth

And take charge of this Your Temple.

Guide me to make the highest and best decisions for all those that seek our assistance.

Be with me when I praise You at the morning and evening rituals.

Be with me to guide my sisters in their healing and divination.

Blessed be, My Lady."

At the end of the meditation, Ceelyha felt stronger, more connected, at one with Her source. It was as if the Goddess were blessing her with an extra amount of light. It poured through her removing any insecurity about her new role. She knew what had to be done and how to do it. She picked up a torch and made her way to the servants' quarters in search of Nintu's replacement. Sarah was just rising when Ceelyha approached. When Ceelyha saw that the slight girl was several years her junior, she realized with a shock that she was aging and right now, was in the prime of her life! *I am at the age of my mother when she had me! I am certainly old enough and experienced in both the ways of Asherah and Ishtar to reside over this Temple. I just need to assert my power and authority to make this work.*

"Sarah," she startled the girl. "Come immediately. I am in need of your assistance. I am to perform the morning ritual and I need a bath!"

Sarah self-consciously bowed, then straightened the night wrinkles from her tunic before she rushed to do her mistress's bidding.

Just before the sistrums called the priestesses to the morning ritual, Ceelyha was ready, garbed in an ornate Babylonian robe that her mother had packed in one of the trunks. Ceelyha recalled Shiroka having said that one could not count on the barbarians having the materials and colours that would properly glorify her daughter if she ever became head priestess. Thoughts of her mother threatened to bring tears to her eyes; there had been no news from her in such a long time and she had been too busy with David to try and make a connection through the Goddess. She mentally sent Shiroka a white, healing light and a quick prayer for her well-being.

When all the other priestesses had gathered in the outer courtyard to usher in the dawn with their chants of praise, Ceelyha made her entrance. She was aware of the statement she was about to make with her flamboyant robes and sparkling jewels. She would stand out like an exotic flower especially beside the plainer tunic of Dilbaha. When the dancers clanged their symbols to awaken the sleeping Goddess, she was taken back to the ceremonies in Babylon. Shiroka's eyes always radiated peace and inner wisdom as she regally made her way towards the Goddess. Dilbaha's nudge to begin the procession, brought Ceelyha quickly back to the present. With her head held high, she proceeded to walk beside the elder priestess. She saw the shocked faces and hesitated as she heard snippets of "A foreigner... what is she doing beside Dilbaha...a foreigner is now the High Priestess...what about Adah... just because she is consorting with the King!" But when her eyes met Thu, whose face was glowing with support and approval, she held herself up straight and followed the dancers into the inner sanctum. At the statue of the Goddess, Dilbaha handed Ceelyha the tray of flowers while she removed last night's offerings. As Ceelyha bowed to present the gifts, she heard the others fall to their knees and take up the chant with her.

"Lady of the Morning, Praise be to You.

Accept our thanks for this new day.

Help us to be a reflection of Your radiance here on earth.

Give us Your powers to heal and nourish those in need.

Accept our humble gift of refreshment that You might be satisfied in Your heavenly abode

And grant us Your blessings.

Praise be to Asherah, Mother Goddess of All."

After performing her administrations, she accompanied the priestesses into the courtyard where she announced that she would speak to all of them at breakfast.

The whispering and speculations stopped when Ceelyha stood at the head of the table. She cleared her throat while fingering her mother's necklace for support.

"As all of you are probably aware, I have the honor of being the Head Priestess at this Temple of Asherah, Royal Diviners to the House of David. The King announced his decision to Dilbaha, whom as you know, has been doing an exemplary job of fulfilling the duties of Adah."

She paused, taking the time to make sure that she made eye contact with each of the twelve priestesses; she needed to establish her power. *I am the daughter of a King!* she reminded herself and tried to copy his intimidating stare. *Now, I have a better understanding of his ruthless attitude towards his subjects. I must never let them see my weaknesses or they will never acquiesce to my authority!* She sensed a few of the women flinch while the others carefully disguised their feelings. *Do I want to rule like he does by fear or by mutual respect?* She quickly prayed to the Goddess to guide her as she continued, "Adah has been given the post of High Priestess at Jezreel, and if any of you wish to join her, arrangements will be made for your passage." She stopped and intuited that some of the women would indeed, out of principle, ask to leave. Then Ceelyha soften her approach and added, "Dilbaha has graciously agreed to assist me with the day to day running of this establishment. I will not change any of the Temple rituals. I promise to uphold the tradition of Asherah and incorporate my teachings from the Ishtar School of Mysteries. And," she looked over at Thu, "my dear friend, Thu, is willing to share her knowledge of Isis. I think we all need to understand that even though some of us come from different cultures and teachings, we are all united as one under the Goddess. It does not matter if her name is Asherah, Isis, Aphrodite, or Ishtar.

Over the next few days, I would be honoured to meet with each and every one of you to discuss any issues you might have, whether it is about me or how to improve this Temple. But, I will not have any gossiping about the King or me. I hope that is understood." At that point in her speech, Ceelyha felt the Goddess descend upon her. Her ears buzzed, her vision blurred and she incorporated Her energy. She was aware that her entire body was bathed in glowing light as the Goddess spoke through her. "I invite all of you to welcome my daughter, Ceelyha, as the new Entu. Blessings be upon all of you."

The Goddess departed and even though her knees shook and heart raced, Ceelyha turned her back on the group and attempted to walk proudly back to her chambers. She silently gave thanks to Ishtar. *Thank you O Lady for manifesting Your energy through me. Those women needed some assurance, and I as well, that I am the right person to lead them.*

Her thoughts were interrupted as Thu called "Ceelyha; rather, Your Greatness, please wait!"

Ceelyha faced her friend and waited for her to catch her breath. She was definitely not use to being called by that title. It thrilled and surprised her at the same time.

"You were magnificent. You were every bit the Lady of Asherah. There was not a person at that table that did not respect you, especially when your Goddess came upon you!" She grabbed Ceelyha and held her tightly. "I knew this was coming. You are the best candidate for the position. I hope you will be happy and successful!"

Ceelyha disengaged herself from her friend's hug. "How did you know I was going to be given this position?" she asked with surprise.

Thu threw back her head and laughed, "It was already written!"

Later that day, Ceelyha moved into the quarters where Adah had resided for a short period of time. The only reminder of Bernice was the large scrying bowl, which Ceelyha ordered Sarah to remove and give to Thu. *If any priestess will be able to use this form of divination, it will be Thu,* Ceelyha thought. *And, it is a momentum of Bernice to be treasured.* She breathed a huge sigh of relief that the snake basket had already gone to Dilbaha. There was no sign of Adah ever having lived in the rooms. *She must have taken all her belongings with her when she left. She knew she was not coming back! That meant David has been testing me all this time to see if I was worthy of this position! How dare he!* Her anger flared. It took several deep breaths before she was calm and once more in control of her emotions. *I never tested him! I just trusted! I must love him more than he does me,* she thought. This truth did not bring her any comfort.

A few nights later, when the air was cool with the bite of winter and the night sky blazed with stars, it was the first night of equinox, the night when the veils lifted between the worlds of the earth and heavens. The priestesses gathered in their ceremonial robes to welcome their new High Priestess. The tinkling of bracelets and anklets were the only sounds heard. Just as the heavens grew luminous with the rising of the moon, they formed a circle around Ceelyha, who stood in front of the eternal flame of the altar. There was no need to cast a circle of protection, the place was already sacred. Ceelyha was dressed in a royal blue tunic that bared her breasts to symbolize the Mother of All Life. The red girdle of the Goddess encircled her waist. Her cloak was decorated with silver snakes that appeared to slither as they glowed in the torchlight. Her head, covered with a black plaited wig, was enhanced with a golden circlet that had been her mother's and around her neck hung the silver amulet of Ishtar. She was glad of her heavy cloak, it hid the shaking of her knees. She knew not if the reaction was from the cold, or her excitement. Tonight, she was the Goddess Asherah incarnate. She gazed into the flame on the altar to gather courage, made a silent prayer for assistance to her mother and all the priestesses in her family before her, then turned to face the east. She raised her hands high above her head in shape of a V. She felt ribbons of light flowing out from her. In a voice she willed to be steady, she sang:

"We hail thee, Lady of the Snakes. We salute You as the Goddess of the Moon, Goddess of the Stars. We honour those who have gone before us. May they watch over us tonight. Come out and greet us, Lady of the Moon!"

They all turned their faces upwards to watch the stars fade in the glow of the moon. Sistrums rattled and the beat of a drum filled the air with anticipation. It was important, tonight of all nights with her ceremonial initiation as High Priestess, that she command the moon in order to gain the respect of her priestesses. A lone thick cloud threatened to cover the moon and Ceelyha silently prayed to the Goddess to remove its presence. The cloud moved closer and she concentrated, gathering all of her energy into one forceful act of will power and called upon the energy of her ancestors to have it dissipate. She sensed Thu and the others working with her as its mighty vapours separated. Relief shot through her as Ceelyha thanked the higher powers.

All at once the Lady of the Night shone down, her sides tinged with gold. In unison, the priestesses lifted their hands in adulation. Dilbaha's voice rang out:

"Our Lady of the Moon has risen!"

"Lady of Light," the others chorused in return.

"Fair Light, be upon us to welcome this our new High Priestess!"

"Welcome our High Priestess," they chorused.

The energy of the circle was rising. The priestesses began to sway to the rhythm of their song.

"Lady of Light, cast Your light on our Temple!"

As the ancient homage continued, Ceelyha found herself growing warmer and cast off her cloak. It fell to the ground with a dull thud and a hiss as if the snakes were angry at being cast aside. She swayed and moved as the Goddess descended. Her voice sang the praises with the others, the harmony of the notes resounding through her being. She felt her consciousness begin to rise out of her body. She saw the city of Jerusalem nestled among the purple hills of Judea. Her vision expanded until it compassed the entirety of the Land of Israel. To the east, the sea, with its silver water sparkled in the moonlight. The dark hills of the coastline jutted out like sentinels protecting the Land of Asherah. To the west, the flat plains of the Jordan Valley were parallel to the desert sands stirring in the night wind. This was Her land and she, Ceelyha was in charge of protecting it with Her magic. She was the living Goddess!

"Fair be...," she was aware of opening her arms in blessing as her awareness returned to the circle. The circle had opened and the priestesses were gathering around the sacred pool. Ceelyah joined their ranks. Their chanting had become a low hum as they joined hands. Ceelyha raised hers up and the rest followed suite. She sang out to the Goddess, "Lady of the Moon, bless us with Your divine presence in this Your cosmic water of creation!"

The rest chanted, "Lady, come down to us, Lady show us Your presence." They repeated the chorus three times and then waited. Silence prevailed. Everyone focused on the pool. A shaft of light from the moon shone on the still water. Suddenly a light manifested so brilliantly that it blinded the group. Ceelyha first thought the moon had fallen into the pool but that was impossible. A murmur of wonder passed through the circle. As the women adjusted to its brilliance, or it dulled – Ceelyha was not sure which – out of nowhere a breeze arose and the water rippled. Two snakes formed, splashing and undulating furiously beneath its surface. Then a face, not from this world, of such beauty and radiance, formed between the serpents and gazed back at the priestesses.

"Lady…" Ceelyha gasped in spite of herself. Never had she seen the face of the Goddess! The others were shocked and cried out their thanks. Then as quickly as the apparition came, it vanished.

Whatever Ceelyha had conjured that night was beyond everyone's expectations. Not even Bernice had ever been able to manifest the Goddess! The priestesses welcomed their powerful High Priestess by bowing before her. Ceelyha was thrilled and touched by their devotion as she thanked the Goddess for making Her presence known.

Thu later asked how Ceelyha had managed to conjure the face in the pool. Even Ceelyha had no answer. She simply trusted that the Goddess would somehow make Her presence know to secure Ceelyha's position as the High Priestess.

That night, Ceelyha had difficulty falling asleep. She kept visualizing the snakes cavorting in the water. She willed her mind to be still but was inundated with images of what she assumed must be a past life. At one point she felt herself being pushed into a dark pit as evil laughter and the taunting of several spectators, in an unfamiliar language, echoed in her ears. Horrifying fear accompanied her fall as hissing noises drowned out all other sounds. She landed head first on a soft pile of something moving. Then serpents, hundreds of them, slithered and slid over her as they broke her fall. She could feel their scales as they intertwined around her limbs. They were in her hair, her face, her eyes, everywhere injecting her with poison. She tried to fight them off but it was futile. She was powerless. The vision ended. She sat up now knowing that she had died a slow torturous death through being paralyzed by the venom of hooded snakes.

Although Sarah did her best to fill in as her servant, Ceelyha missed having Nintu to organize the move and share her news. When she was settled in her new quarters, all of the priestesses requested an audience to declare their loyalty and support. Dilbaha came with the accounts and explained how much they depended on the petitioners to run the Temple. It was through their donations of grains, meat and wine that they survived. Very few coins ever came except when a plea was made to the King. When Ceelyha asked if something could be done to improve the living quarters of the priestesses, Dilbaha shook her head.

"Lady, there are no extra coins for that."

Ceelyha thought that David could surely help. "Then get a message to the King that I need to speak with him about the condition of the Temple. I am sure he will assist."

Dilbaha nodded and sent the request. The next day a bag of gold coins came with a message that it was on behalf of the King; however, there was no personal communication for Ceelyha.

Over the next two moons, Ceelyha made some aesthetic changes at the Temple. Along with remodeling the priestess's living quarters, she had directed Thu to move from her cramped cell into Ceelyha's vacated rooms. She thought it was important to keep Thu's friendship and loyalty. Thu thanked her profusely, and then with her uncanny sense of intuition added, "I told you before that we are connected from the past. You do not ever need to doubt my affections for you. You never need to secure my loyalty with these rooms."

Ceelyha responded with embarrassment, "I think I knew that but I have so few friends here." She had trouble meeting Thu's questioning eyes as she added, "And I wanted to show my appreciation in the only way that I could. This is my gift to you."

The two women arranged gatherings where they taught the other priestesses about herbs from their respective countries. Ceelyha continued to teach dance classes to the newest priestesses and Thu demonstrated the reading of omens using Egyptian methods. Ceelyha was pleased to see how the Temple workers functioned together; only two of the priestesses had requested to join Adah.

Three moons after her wedding, a tearful Nintu appeared in the courtyard. She ran to find her mistress; surprised that her status at the Temple had changed.

"My Lady, is it true? Are you now head of this Temple?" Nintu fell on her knees in front of Ceelyha who at the time was supervising some workmen rebuilding the cells.

Ceelyha laughed and pulled Nintu to her feet. "Yes, I am. Apparently Bernice had requested that I succeed her. It just took David a long time to tell me!" She tried to withhold the bitterness she still felt over his keeping the promotion a secret for such a long time. "Now, why are you here? Was the honeymoon not a success?"

Then she realized why her faithful servant was back and she cried, "Oh Nintu, I am so sorry! I did hear the ram's horn this morning but did not connect it with the army. This means Jacob has rejoined the troops, but I thought the law was that a newly married man had leave to be with his bride for a longer time than this!"

"I thought so too, but the King summoned all of his men, no matter what their personal commitments were! They are advancing on the Philistines to the south of here." Nintu hesitated, "No one knew until dawn today."

David must have acted on my divination. To change the subject Ceelyha enthusiastically said, "But look at you, a married woman. You have certainly filled out since you last were here! Too many sweets or not enough exercise?"

Ceelyha sensed the Goddess descend on her and prayed that Nintu would not notice.

153

Nintu hugged her mistress and whispered, "I am so in love. And let us hope that it is more than too many sweets that has made me plumper."

Ceelyha stepped back to try to compose herself by shaking off the message of dread she had just received. "Are you trying to tell me something?"

Nintu lowered her eyes and said, "Maybe, I can not tell. I have been so caught up in the wedding and as you may have guessed, the honeymoon was not the first time that we shared a bed. I want you and Thu to tell me if I am with child. But first, I will inspect our new quarters and send Sarah back to hers." She hesitated and searched Ceelyha's face, "That is, My Lady, if you still want me!"

"Of course, how could I not want you back even if it is for a short time!" Ceelyha responded with enthusiasm.

It was later in the day before Nintu had a chance to consult with Ceelyha. Thu having just finished teaching a priestess about combining various remedies to smooth rashes joined them in the private consultation room. While Ceelyha searched for her divination rods in the medicine box, Thu ran to her chamber and returned with a small pouch. She jokingly stated that they no longer needed to resort to the subterranean rooms for any type of work. Everything could be done openly.

Ceelyha answered, "I rather enjoyed that area of the Temple. Maybe we need to resurrect it and put it to use. I think that will be our next project as soon as the cells are remodeled. Thu, what do you think?"

"It's a wonderful idea! Each room could have a separate purpose or just be available if anybody wants to work in private. But let us see about the possibility of a child for our dear friend Nintu."

They helped her to lie down on the stone table that dominated the room. Ceelyha raised her hands up to the heavens to invoke the Goddess.

"Oh Ishtar, Lady of All Things Growing

Grant me the wisdom that I might tell whether or not a seed of life is growing inside the one who lies before You."

Ceelyha felt like a fool for going through the motions of holding dowsing rods over the belly of Nintu. *Of course she is pregnant; but would the child ever be born, was the question,* she thought with dread. Thu sensed that Ceelyha was having difficulty with the divination and spoke, "Yes, Nintu it appears that you are with child. But I want to place some stones on your abdomen to ensure that your unborn child is protected."

She took a lapis stone from her pouch and gently placed it on Nintu's stomach before she raised her hands to invoke Isis. She channeled Her energy around the body of Nintu as she chanted in her native tongue. When the ritual was finished, Thu smiled and announced, "This protective stone should be worn close to your body. It will purify your blood and cause the unborn child to fasten to the womb."

Nintu sat up full of joy. Her face beamed and she reached out to hug the priestesses. "Now I will be never be alone. When Jacob is away, I will always have a part of him with me! Thank you both. I have to tell the others!" She hurried off the table and went into the Temple halls to spread her good news.

Thu turned with concern to Ceelyha. "What did you intuit?"

Ceelyha replied with trepidation, "The baby will not live. There is something not right in the womb. Did you feel it?"

Thu nodded, "She will not carry to full term. But I will do as much as I can to ensure that will not happen, even though the decision appears to have been made already."

Ceelyha answered, "Even we cannot undo what the Goddess has already decided. I need to think about whether or not to inform Nintu. She is so excited right now and to give her the news that the baby will not live would be terribly cruel. I will pray for guidance."

Just as Thu was about to respond, a servant came to the door of the healing room. She bowed in respect and said, "Lady, there are a couple of men at the gates who speak a foreign language. The keeper thinks that they are asking for you."

A chill ran up Ceelyha's spine and for the second time that day, the Goddess descended upon her. She felt her body drain of energy as she followed the girl to the gate. There, standing at the entrance, were the two Babylonian soldiers who had accompanied her and Nintu to the Land of Judea. They looked out of place with their shiny brass breastplates and conical hats. As she approached, they knelt.

Ceelyha bid them rise and called for a nearby servant to prepare food and drink for the visitors. She led them to a secluded area of the courtyard and after exchanging polite conversation for a few minutes; she waited for them to relay their message. The larger of the two soldiers cleared his throat and spoke,

"My Lady, Princess Ceelyha, it is my unfortunate duty to inform you that your father, King Eulma-Shakin Shuki is dead."

Ceelyha felt her hands and feet grow cold as a sharp pain stabbed her chest. She quickly sent the pain away, knowing that her father had died of a heart attack.

"How long ago did this happen?" she asked in a raspy voice. Her throat felt dry and tears threatened to pour from her eyes. *I was not close to him but still he was my father.*

"Your mother, the Lady Shiroka, sent us as soon as she heard. It was about two months ago. It has taken us this long to find you. We first went to Dor and then we were told you were here in Jerusalem. We have a trunk that the Lady sent to you. We left it with your gatekeeper."

Ceelyha answered, "I thought the message that I had moved would have been sent to her by now! But thank you both for taking the time to find me and for bringing the trunk. How is my mother, the Entu?"

The soldiers replied that she was in good health and seemed relieved when the servant approached with their refreshments. Ceelyha told them to eat and rest in the courtyard. She needed some time to be alone.

Now that my father is dead, I am free to return to The Land of Two Rivers. These circumstances would mean leaving David. I am definitely not willing to do that! Also, I cannot leave my responsibilities here or Thu or Nintu, so I am not really a free woman. My life is here so this must be where the Goddess wants me to be.

She knelt in front the statue of Ishtar and prayed for the soul of her father and for guidance with what to do about Nintu but the Goddess had no words of comfort. She did not speak.

Ceelyha sent Nintu with some coins to give to the soldiers, ordered them to wait and asked for the trunk to be brought to her chambers. There she wept quietly as she unpacked fine linen sheaths, rare herbs and a precious bottle of lotus oil that her mother had so thoughtfully sent. When she felt more composed, she called for a scribe and dictated a message to her mother for the soldiers to take back to Babylon. She told Shiroka all about her time in Jerusalem, her feelings for David and how she was suffering because of loving too deeply. She made mention to meeting her mother several times through the magic of the Goddess and about her new position as Head Priestess. She closed by saying that she would stay in Jerusalem to fulfill her destiny. After pouring out her heart, Ceelyha felt better but still asked Dilbaha to take the evening ritual and retired to her rooms. That night, she had terrible dreams. She dreamt that her father, who had become grotesquely fat with enlarged feet and hands, was begging her forgiveness for banishing her to the Land of Judea. She sensed his regret in not taking the time to get to know his daughter better. Then, his piercing green eyes seemed to scorn her decision to stay when she was now free to return to her homeland. The vision of him faded as she heard her mother screaming with agony and knew her anguish was not over the death of the King. She watched in horror as Shiroka rent her gown and tore out chunks of hair. When Ceelyha heard her cry, "My child, my child! You have taken my child before me!"

The nightmare ended and she opened her eyes. It took a few moments to figure out where she was. When she was about to climb out of bed to pray in front of the statue of Ishtar for guidance to interpret the dream, she thought she saw something out the corner of her eye move. The one small torch that was always kept lit suddenly sputtered and flickered. Ceelyha blinked to make sure she was not seeing things, but there in front of her, were the silhouettes of two people entangled in an erotic position. They appeared to be rubbing against each other in sexual frenzy. When the coupling was over, the figures drew apart. From the shadow's muscular form and the scent of the outdoors that permeated the air, she intuited that it was David. She could not discern who the woman was but was certain that it was not she. The vision evaporated and Ceelyha let out a scream.

Nintu, her hair loose and sleeping robe disarrayed, rushed into the chamber. She found her mistress sobbing. "What is it? What is wrong?" she cried.

Ceelyha could not answer. All she did was hold onto her servant as grief for her father, pining for her mother, frustration over David, worry about Nintu, and now fear of the future, poured out of her. They stayed that way until it was time to prepare for the morning ritual.

Three days after David had left to join his men, the gatekeeper came to inform the priestesses that the King and his army had just entered the city. Nintu begged to be excused from her duties and ran into the throngs of the gathering crowds to welcome the return of their soldiers. Ceelyha and Thu, along with several others, went to the roof of the Temple to catch a glimpse of the victors. The distant shouts and cheers alerted the women that the army had been triumphant. For a brief moment, before the crowds swallowed him up, Ceelyha saw David driving his chariot. She silently thanked the Goddess for bringing him safely home. Later she heard how David had driven the Philistines back, proclaiming that Yahweh had promised victory to His people. There was of course, no mention of the Goddess or Ceelyha's role in the conquest.

On the same day a message for the High Priestess arrived from the Palace. The King's request that some of the Temple's dancers be sent to perform the next evening at the celebratory feast sent Ceelyha into a quandary. There was no personal note. *Is this a cryptic message? Is David asking me to dance or does he truly want just some dancers to entertain his commanders? It has been so long since we have been together that I cannot believe he is not sending for me.* She tried to invoke the Goddess for assistance but when no response came she decided to consult Thu.

Thu answered, "I have never known the Head of the Temple to ever dance. Bernice always sent others, but then she was very old. I do not know how to advise you."

Unfortunately, it was Nintu who solved the problem for Ceelyha. A servant from the house of Jacob's parents arrived and requested an audience with the High Priestess. As Ceelyha rushed into the courtyard, she knew with all of her being that Jacob had been killed in battle. The tearful servant confirmed her fears. Ceelyha briskly told the gatekeeper to let Thu and Dilbaha know that she had to leave on an urgent matter and to ask them take care of the King's request for dancers. She ordered a cart with a donkey, and then set off with the servant.

The colourful awning of the wedding and the festivities in the courtyard of the modest mud brick house were long gone. Instead, the haunting sounds of the weeping and wailing of mourning women greeted Ceelyha. Their dresses were torn; their hair hung in unkempt strands about their grief stricken faces. Their mournful howls caused shivers to rush through her body as she searched for her friend. When the servant finally directed her to a slumped figure in the corner of the courtyard,

Ceelyha ran over and threw her arms around Nintu. To try to lessen her sorrow, Ceelyha invoked the Goddess's white light into her friend's energy field. Ceelyha noted Nintu's ripped dress and the scratches on her face and arms. She took off her own cloak and wrapped it around the shocked woman. She then bowed and prayed for the soul of Jacob.

One of the women watching her screamed, "Get these barbarians out of here! It is because of her," and she pointed to a distraught Nintu "that Jacob is dead! Yahweh does not want us mixing with pagans. Get her out of here!"

Ceelyha surprised at the outrage of the woman, quickly pulled Nintu onto her feet. She stood erect and with her priestess voice called out, "This is not the fault of my countrywoman. It was ordained long ago by your God" – she put a special emphasis on the word 'your' – "that Jacob has died. I am sure that it is just your grief that is making you blame my friend. Believe me, she is innocent."

She then maneuvered Nintu out of the courtyard and into the waiting cart.

On the trip home, Nintu did not speak. Instead, she continuously whimpered holding her hands over her abdomen. As soon as they entered the gates of the Temple, Ceelyha called for assistance. Nintu was carried and placed on Ceelyha's own bed.

Thu quickly came with some arnica to ease the shock and worried about the unborn child. "We have to ensure that she does not lose this baby. She is in so much distress that I fear that the child is already beginning to dislodge from the womb."

Ceelyha told her about the accusation from one of Jacob's relatives and both agreed that they had to do as much as possible to stop the unborn child from aborting. Together they mixed herbs, placed rubies and red jasper stones on Nintu's belly to prevent premature birth and prayed to their respective Goddesses.

They kept watch over Nintu into the late hours of the night. Just before dawn, the cramping became worse, the bleeding came and she lost the baby. Both Priestesses sat on either side of the bed and tried to instill as much healing energy as possible into the poor woman that had lost a husband and child within hours of each other. They administered a dose of a natural narcotic and Nintu finally slept.

In the morning, a message came from the King. This time it was more personal. The scroll read,

"My dear High Priestess, please pass my condolences to your faithful servant, Nintu. I just heard about Jacob's death. In respect to my fallen men and their families, I have cancelled the celebration. I request a meeting with you in your chambers this evening."

Ceelyha could not ascertain if the King wanted to meet with her for political or for personal reasons and showed the note to Thu who sat beside a sleeping Nintu.

"What do you think of this?" she asked with a worried tone. "Is he coming to see me to make love or to have another reading?"

Thu shook her head and then her eyes opened with excitement. "Let us find out! We have the power to read what he wants in the smoke." She called for Sarah to watch over Nintu and told Ceelyha to prepare whatever she needed to take with them to the lower room in the Temple. "We do not want any of the others to know what we are doing!" she winked. "You have not eaten since yesterday because of Nintu so your body is somewhat prepared for omen reading."

Ceelyha obediently followed her friend into the cells beneath the main floor of the Temple. It seemed as if they were always going to need the services of this subterranean area. When they reached the room, Thu lit the brazier from her torch and waited for Ceelyha to set up her statue and stones on the altar. But Ceelyha did not make a move to unpack her divination tools. Instead with concern in her voice she said, "Thu, I am not so certain that I want to do this. I am not sure if I want to know what David really wants. Maybe I should just wait to see how things turn out." Then she proceeded to tell Thu about the strange vision she had about David and another woman.

Thu responded, "All the more reason to be prepared for what lies ahead."

Ceelyha meekly nodded, prepared her tools and then went into a trance by invoking the Goddess. When the coals were hot enough, Thu threw on hyssop. When the only sound in the room was the hissing of the incense, Ceelyha stepped back from the brazier and waited. Just when she was about to give up, thinking that her talent could not be used for her own personal purpose, a shape took place in the vapor. She cried out, "I see a woman. It is the one who was in his arms in my vision. What Oh Lady Ishtar does this have to do with me?"

Thu prompted her. "What is the woman doing?"

"She is heavy with child."

"What does it have to do with you and David's visit tonight?"

"Wait. Now I see his shape forming. It is full of love and concern. He is stoking the belly of the woman! It is his baby!"

Thu interjected, "What does it have to do with you?"

But Ceelyha lost the connection as she felt the emotion of betrayal come over her.

She screamed out to an absent David, "How could you do this to me? How could you proclaim undying love to me and have love for another?" Then she fell to the floor crying with the pain of having lost his love, the death of her father and Nintu's losses. Thu ran over and just held her.

David came as promised to the Temple that night. Ceelyha met him in one of the healing rooms since Nintu was still recovering in her chambers. He was regally attired in purple robes. When Ceelyha bowed in greeting, he gently ordered her to stand and took her hand in his and kissed it. She, in state of confusion, did not know what his intentions were and formally greeted him even though her senses reeled at his closeness.

"My Lord, what brings you to this humble Temple?"

As he pulled her to him, she reminded herself not to let her passion and emotions rule over her head. Her resolve weakened when he whispered, "I just heard about your father's passing, My Golden One. You have been through so much these past days. I am so sorry."

Ceelyha broke down in his strong supportive arms and cried. He held her, mindless of the tears staining his robe, and tenderly rubbed her back. When her grief was spent, she withdrew from him and apologetically said, "I am sorry for this. I thought I was handling everything until you came."

"Come with me." His voice was soft yet firm as he led her out of the building to the courtyard. He called to the gatekeeper to tell the others that the High Priestess was called away on official business with the King. He then seated her in an elaborate partially enclosed carriage that waited by the door. Ceelyha saw him give a command to the driver before he settled beside her. She had never seen a chariot in like this before. David, reading her thoughts, said it had been a gift from Egypt but he hardly ever used it. "I was on my way to pick up a foreign dignitary who is visiting here in Jerusalem but I needed to see you. As of this moment, I am canceling the meeting. You are more important than anyone else."

Ceelyha could not imagine that she was hearing those words. *How could I have doubted his love for me? It seems that when I am parted from him, I lose faith in him. I must have misinterpreted the visions.* She sighed and laid her head against his shoulder. She closed her eyes delighted that she felt so safe and secure. It was difficult to detach herself momentarily from his side when they arrived at the house.

Once inside, David led her to their bedchamber and begged her to dance for him.

"Dance?" Ceelyha was confused. "Why my Lord, do you wish that?"

"Because you have more beauty and grace than any woman I have ever laid eyes on. I want to see your flat belly and soft breasts move in that sensuous way that you have perfected. And," his eyes flashed with mirth, "I, as your King, command it!"

She expelled a sigh of relief. *There was no possibility of him having forsaken me for another. My vision must have been symbolic; I just did not interpret the message correctly.* She lowered her eyes in playful submission and ran into the dressing area where she quickly rummaged through the trunk that held her clothes. Finally she found her costume at the bottom of the pile. She lovingly extracted its layers of cobalt silk, remembering how she had enticed David. When she shook out the material, the scent of rose petals filled the air. She had no other oils to enhance her own scent but she quickly reasoned that she had already seduced him so they were not needed. When she stepped back into the bedchamber, David was lounging on the huge bed with his arms folded behind his head. Since there was no drum, Ceelyha clanged her finger symbols and made eye contact with him. She batted her lashes in a slow sultry manner as she stepped into her dance. He immediately sat up, his face full of pleasure and began to clap in time to her undulating movements. When she began to unwrap the first layer of her veil, he got off the bed and fell on his knees. As she provocatively swayed her hips and shook her breasts, he could not stand it any longer. He reached up and grabbed hold of her and began to run his hands over her body.

"I so wanted to do this when I first saw you bewitch me and now," his eyes were full of lust, "I can!"

Ceelyha laughingly fell into his arms, the idea of finishing the dance completely forgotten. Her need to feel his naked skin against her was so great that she could hardly wait to get the rest of her costume off. He cupped her breasts and she moaned as his thumbs rubbed her nipples. He pushed her legs apart and began kissing and stroking her until she could no longer contain her lust. She arched towards him further ignited by his fire and opened herself to feel relief as he entered her. She strained against him as if she could reach something beyond her own mortal body. When they had finished their lovemaking, the closeness returned as if they had never been apart. After a light meal they wrapped themselves in robes and climbed to the roof. Everything looked magical. For a brief moment, it appeared to Ceelyha as if she and David were the only two people in the world and that the Goddess had arranged the canopy of brilliant flashing stars just for them.

She contently sighed and said, "I am so grateful that you took the time to be with me. By the way, what was it you wanted to see me about?"

David cleared his throat and answered. "I am going to pursue bringing the Ark to my people in Jerusalem. I wanted to know if you had intuited anything more on it."

Ceelyha responded, her voice full of interest, "You mean the dream about the golden calf?"

He nodded.

"Well yes, you have already mentioned what you would like to do. And no, I have not had any more information from the Goddess. So," she pondered, "I guess it is the right time for you to proceed with it. When will you leave?'

"In the morning. I have already arranged to have it brought to Jerusalem in a white cart drawn by two white oxen." He turned and spoke, "You might not be aware of this, but when the Philistines captured it, the people of Israel felt that God had forsaken them. When the enemy housed the Ark in a pagan temple beside their god, Dagon, the idol fell over and broke into pieces. Desolation followed with a devastating plague that came upon the infidels and they decided to return the Ark to us."

"Tell me more about this Ark. What does it look like?" asked Ceelyha as she snuggled up against David.

"It is much bigger than the trunks in our dressing area. As I explained to you before, it is made of acacia, overlaid in pure gold within and without. On top of the chest, facing one another, are two winged figures. I have heard that it is also trimmed with a rim of gold. The Ark is transported by two wooden poles which pass through four golden rings."

"But what you are describing to me is but a golden idol, the calf of your dream."

"No!" David was adamant and she felt his body tense. "It is not an idol. It contains the laws of our people. It is a sign of His presence."

Ceelyha knew better than to pursue her argument but wondered why such a God who was invisible to all of his people had told their prophet Moses that if anyone looked upon His face, he would not live. Did not the people need to have an object as proof of the deity's existence? She also sensed that the box held more mysteries than just the laws of the Israelites.

But instead of revealing her thoughts, proud that she was learning to hold her tongue, she asked, "Where will you house this Ark? Will you build a temple for it?"

David had an odd look in his eyes. "Strange that you should ask that. I recently had a visit from Nathan. Remember I spoke about him before."

"The prophet?"

"Yes that is he. He travelled to meet me, when I was with my troops, to say that he had a message from God."

Ceelyha interrupted, "Then your God did not speak directly to you?"

David slightly annoyed answered, "No, He has forsaken me of late. But He spoke through Nathan that I was not to build a Temple for the Ark. I had already begun to make plans to build a cedar house; however, Nathan advised against that idea. He said that one of my sons would do that, long after I am gone. The Temple needs to be built by one who does not have blood on his hands."

David held up his hands and examined them as if they were covered with blood. Ceelyha sensed his dismay and gently placed her hands on his. *Yes, he has much blood on his hands and will have more!* She involuntarily shuddered as the Goddess wrapped Her wings as a warning around her.

David must have felt her twinge for he looked directly at her and asked, "Are you confirming that Nathan's words are true?"

Ceelyha did not know what to say. The message she had just received was for her, not for David. She paused to gather her wits before replying. "Yes, my Lord, the message seems to ring true. It shall be another who builds the Temple."

David smiled, then stood and pulled Ceelyha up with him. "Come, you must return to the Temple, and I, to the Palace. Watch for me before the next full moon, when I arrive with the Ark. Everyone will be in the streets to celebrate!"

Ceelyha quietly followed him down the stairs to return to the Temple. The earlier joy and playfulness they had shared was already gone. She sensed their time as lovers had run out.

Chapter 16
The Ark Returns – Bathsheba Appears

Over the next few days, Nintu was not well enough to get out of bed. Thu had done her best to heal the girl's tortured soul with crystals and herbs while Ceelyha had spoken to her at length to try to alleviate some of her grief. Then both priestesses decided it was best for Nintu just to mourn for the loss of her husband and unborn child in her own way. Ceelyha's last words on the subject were she would be there for her when Nintu was ready to rejoin life.

When Thu had questioned Ceelyha about her time with David, she was told that nothing was amiss; they were still intimate and that, whatever the message was from the Goddess about their relationship, it did not seem applicable at this time. What Ceelyha did not share with Thu was a sinking feeling that whatever had been prophesized had not yet manifested.

Ceelyha heard that David had left to make his trip to collect the Ark. He had taken a handful of Levite priests to load the chest onto a white cart decorated with flowers and tree boughs. He had donned the ephod, usually only worn by priests, under his Kingly robes as a message to his people that he represented the link between religion and politics. A chorus of youths had been selected to sing and clang brass cymbals as the procession made its way along the bumpy journey to Jerusalem.

Thu, who had been perfecting her divination skills with Bernice's ancient scrying bowl, invited Ceelyha to her chamber, to see if they could 'follow' the procession.

The big bronze bowl, filled with water from the sacred well that sat on a small altar, was covered with a black cloth. Thu closed the window shutter, lit a small torch and placed it beside the bowl. Next she stirred the brazier and threw on some myrrh. She motioned for Ceelyha to move closer and said a prayer of invocation to Isis:

"Oh Isis, Lady of divine wisdom and light

Daughter of Nut, Beloved of Osiris,

Clear my sight and assist me to see through Your all-seeing eyes

The one called David

As he makes his way with his sacred box.

Praise be to You, Isis, Lady of Light."

When fully connected to the Goddess's energy, Thu removed the black cloth and both women took several deep breaths, in and out, inhaling the magic of the burning incense and looked at the water's surface. Through half closed eyes, they willed their vision to expand. Thu had earlier told Ceelyha that she must think of the water as a mirror that reflects the future. After what seemed like ages to Ceelyha, the smooth surface of the water began to cloud. A white mist arose. Ripples formed. It was the most amazing form of divination that Ceelyha had ever seen! There, in the water, through using an unfocused gaze, images began to form. She knew that Thu was seeing the same festive cart drawn by two white oxen! It was like being right there! When Thu motioned for her to be less emotional in case the connection was lost, Ceelyha willed her thoughts to be still. The image blurred for a few moments then the priestesses watched as it cleared to reveal a man whom they surmised was not one of the priests because of his rough tunic. As one of the cartwheels hit a rut in the mud track, his arms reached out to prevent the ark from slipping off. The procession stopped. The priestesses looked in astonishment as the man clutched his heart then fell to the ground.

"I predicted that would happen when I interpreted David's dream!" cried Ceelyha. "The man is definitely dead. I could not tell if it would be from natural causes or due to the energy in the Ark." The image blurred and the water returned to its normal flat smooth state. "Oh my!" Ceelyha exclaimed as she covered her eyes with her hands in dismay.

Thu turned to her and said in a matter of fact tone, "There was nothing you could have done to prevent it! It was already written by the Gods that the man would die at this particular time."

"I know," replied a shaken Ceelyha, "but that will cause David's people to mistrust his judgment. He is trying to bring this sacred item back to his city and it has destroyed the life of yet another. I wonder how David will manage this."

Thu had no answer for her. The connection with the scrying bowl had dissipated with Ceelyha's outburst.

It was several days later, when an excited gatekeeper came to Ceelyha to announce that the procession of the King had been sighted just outside the city gates. Ceelyha rushed to climb the Temple roof to see what was happening. There was a parade of people coming towards the city! The excitement of seeing David, rushed over her like a flash of heat. As she strained to have a better look, she decided that the priestesses should join in welcoming of the King and his Ark. When she later reflected on this decision, she did not know if it was because she wished to observe David or if the Goddess had a hand in it. She quickly descended the rough stone steps and asked one of the servants to tell the priestesses to cover themselves with a hooded mantle if they wished to go into the streets. Sarah brought her a cloak and Ceelyha joined the jubilant crowds.

The ram's horn sounded to announce the procession was at the city gates. As the people streamed out of the city to welcome their heroes, Ceelyha was surprised to see a totally uninhibited David, dancing with the priests and maidens that flocked around him.

There is no indication of a death having occurred! Had the priests concealed the tragedy or was the divination wrong? she wondered as she watched David, full of vitality and enthusiasm, prancing about wearing only the apron of the priests. Ceelyha caught snippets of his song of praise through the cheers of the people.

Lift up your heads, O ye gates:

And be ye lifted up, ye everlasting doors;

And the King of glory shall come in...

When Ceelyha heard one of the women beside her yell, "There are some of the King's wives!" she felt as if someone had punched her in the stomach; she actually felt physically ill. *These women have been intimate with David! They have born his children, shared his love and secrets. Does he love any of them the way he loves me? Will I always have to share him, or will he grow tired of me too?* Her emotions were in turmoil. It irked her that she would react in such a manner. *I am not of this world;* she repeated to herself, *I need not be involved in such lower emotions.*

Whenever thoughts like this occurred, she knew she had separated from the Goddess. But when she called upon Her energy to transform her pain into light, nothing happened.

This was the first time that she had ever seen his women with the exception of Macaab. Protected by the Palace guards, they walked as a group to meet David's procession. Ceelyha surmised from previous descriptions, that the older stooped woman dressed in a dark blue mantle was Haggith, and beside her must be Abigail who was dressed in a pale blue loose gown. Ceelyha knew that David had not been intimate with either of them for many years. A younger, plain, stocky woman in a simple gown of a nondescript colour held her head demurely, as she passed near where Ceelyha was standing. *She must be Ahinoam, the one he saved from the lion.*

Next, as Ceelyha anxiously looked to see if Macaab was present, her attention was diverted to a woman who was distinctly walking apart from the others. *That must be Michal,* she thought with an appreciative eye. Michal wore the royal purple colour of the House of David in a gossamer sheath that was dramatically attached at one shoulder with a gold clasped pin encased with rubies that flashed and sparkled in the mid-afternoon sun. Her cloak was a deep violet with golden embroidery. Rings, anklets and gold bracelets adorned the exposed parts of her body and a gold headband encircled her forehead. A thin, almost transparent, veil adorned the black plaited wig she wore. Ceelyha noted Michal's face looked drawn and pinched as she watched the antics of her husband. Before she could ponder on why the queen was disturbed, Ceelyha's attention was diverted to a young woman with exquisite loose, flowing auburn hair wearing a gown of white linen, who was stepping into path of the King. David was just turning his head away from the laughing maidens, when the young woman caught his full attention. His entire face lit up with a slow easy smile and the woman returned his greeting with a glowing seductive expression. During that brief exchange, it was very obvious to Ceelyha that something magical had passed between the two of them. And knowing David, it would not stop at a look! Then a realization struck Ceelyha. *This is the woman I saw in my vision! She was the one coupling with David!* Her heartbeat quickened, her body temperature dropped as the wings of the Goddess confirmed her suspicion. Immediately her knees weakened. She tripped over the hem of her cloak and began to fall. Horrified, she helplessly watched her girdle, the Goddess's red sash, loosen and drop to the street. When she reached out to retrieve it, an unaware passerby stepped on it. The sound of pottery breaking and crunching resounded deep within her soul as a dark stain seeped through the red girdle. "The love potion!" she screamed aloud. *Nintu must have sewn it into my belt! Whatever would possess her to do such a thing!* A thoughtful person reached down, grabbed her elbow and pulled her up, then handed her the soiled belt. Ceelyha mumbled a thank you through tears that streamed from her eyes. Then she hastily tried to move herself away from the elated citizens, not wanting David or anyone else to recognize her.

Somehow, Ceelyha navigated through the teaming merrymakers back to the Temple where she fled to her chambers. With the stained sash clutched in one hand, she shook off her mantle then prostrated in front of the statue of Ishtar. She fervently prayed to keep David. Then she waited and waited on the cold stone floor for some type of message from her Goddess. Finally she sensed Her presence as she slipped from the world of form into the world of essence. A blaze of brilliant white light filled the small room as the familiar deep voice of the Goddess resonated throughout the chamber.

"Ceelyha, my daughter of Light, You have tried so hard to give yourself to me and this does not go unrewarded but you are too involved with the mortal, David. You seem to have forgotten that you are first a priestess, then second, woman. You are allowing lower emotions of jealously, lust, judgment and selfishness to overcome the unconditional love that I have taught you. You have not chosen wisely. You did not heed your lessons."

The room became dark and cold as Ceelyha sensed the Goddess leave. Sobs racked her body as she lay on the cold stone floor. She had no one to turn to, not even the Goddess. More torrents of self-pity overwhelmed her as she realized she was truly alone. She did not have the powers to help anyone, let alone herself!

"Now, now," Nintu soothed, drawing a blanket over Ceelyha. "Don't cry." She removed the stained girdle from Ceelyha's hands.

Ceelyha wondered from where her servant had come and how Nintu was able to console anyone after what she had just been through. Through sobs, Ceelyha inquired why the potion was in her belt. A fearful Nintu explained that she had not wanted to throw it away in case it brought bad luck to her mistress and had forgotten all about it until she heard that David was in the city. Ceelyha learned that the day that she had been in the medicine room with Thu, restocking the medicine box, Nintu had asked the other priestess what to do with a love potion. An unsuspecting

Thu had advised her that it was usually sewn into a belt and she did just that. She cried, "I always wanted you to be happy with David! I never meant any harm! See, it brought him home today," she exclaimed with hope in her eyes.

"That it did but after I saw him, the potion was destroyed," answered an emotionally drained Ceelyha. *Is it not significant that on the very day that I see David engage with another woman and the Goddess forsakes me that the potion breaks? Damn that potion and all the trouble it has caused! The only benefit of this is that Nintu seems to be more herself.* She could not reprimand her for fear she would slip back into her earlier darkness. Instead, Ceelyha mutely allowed Nintu to hold and comfort her until it was time to prepare for the evening ritual.

It was during the ritual that Ceelyha knew for certain that the Goddess had deserted her. She did not have a sense of the glow or warmth of Her presence as she lay the flowers before Her likeness. In confusion and with dismay, she went through the motions, not knowing what to expect. *Should I be performing this sacred duty of leading the daughters? What if the others should discover that I have lost my powers? How can I lead and counsel them?* With these concerns, she entered the courtyard. A priestess, who was animatedly talking, temporarily distracted her. She,having attended the entire celebration of the Ark was telling how David had made a speech about light coming to the Land of Israel because God had not turned his back on his people. He spoke of the long, ongoing battles with the Philistines and how with the Ark now in David's city, the Israelites would be united and win all future wars. The priestess was very excited when she added, "He arranged for a public feast and we were all given wine and bread. He smiled at each and everyone, making us feel so special!" Ceelyha thought with dismay, *he certainly does have the gift of making each person feel that way, especially beautiful women!*

As she lay in bed that same night, Ceelyha tried to imagine the Goddess's light surrounding her. Instead, she experienced an emptiness that seeped into her soul. She reprimanded herself to not allow darkness to reign over her. Nintu's display of caring had taught her that even if one is hurting, there will always be others who are in just as much pain or even more pain. Nintu had set her grief aside to help her mistress, so now it was her turn to set her feelings for David aside and to concentrate on her work. It was her destiny as a priestess, to heal and to aid those who were in need of the Goddess's help. She would prove to the Goddess that she was worthy of reclaiming Her precious gifts. *I cannot go back to fearful thinking. I must recall my vows.* She then repeated the sacred pledges, concentrating on 'that even when the Goddess appears to not be present, she would uphold Her beliefs and persevere in spite of adversity.'

Although, she did not have a real sense of inner peace, in the morning, Ceelyha again performed the ritual without divine assistance. The gossip at breakfast was that David had left the Ark in a makeshift tent outside the city gates and had spent the night with the relic in meditation and prayer. She tried to disassociate herself from feeling anything about David and concentrated on the day-to-day running of the Temple. She dared not let herself slip back into the feelings which had overpowered her yesterday.

As if the Goddess was testing her loyalty, a message came from the Palace that David requested an audience with the High Priestess after the evening ritual. A part of Ceelyha was excited at seeing him; another dreaded her reaction to him. *Will I be overcome by my attraction to him and fall into his arms or will I be strong in my resolve and tell him what I suspect already might be, or is about to happen, between him and the woman?*

Ceelyha had Nintu prepare a bath, apply cosmetics, anoint her skin with fragrances, loosen the braids of her hair and add the golden sparkles. She chose to wear a simple white tunic and the Goddess's necklace. She had decided that since she had no inkling as to why he was coming to visit, it was better to present herself as both a priestess and as a mistress.

She greeted him in the quiet, darkened courtyard with a lit torch. In the dull light, she noted that he wore just a plain tunic under a dusty mantle with no jewelry or overt signs of his royal position. His face looked haggard, having none of the joy that she had witnessed yesterday as he danced and sang with the crowds. His obvious desolation tugged at her heart as she began to bow before him.

"No need for formalities, my Priestess. There is no one here but us," he said in a weary voice.

Ceelyha nodded and stood up with her heart pounding and said with as little emotion as possible, "Where would My Lord like to go? My chambers or perhaps you want to sit here?"

David motioned toward a bench, which the two of them walked towards without touching. Ceelyha was very aware of the distance between them. When they were seated, David placed his head in his hands as he spoke.

"I have spent many hours trying to contact the Lord. He appears to have forsaken me."

Ceelyha waited for him to go on.

"I had a terrible row with Michal yesterday."

Ceelyha recalled the woman's face as she watched her husband in the streets and was not surprised but innocently asked, "What happened David?"

"When I danced with the priests and the common people, it was with total abandonment. I felt such joy and elation here," he pounded his heart, "I was truly one with my people. You know that feeling of oneness, when we are joined in the act of love." He looked at her with tenderness for the first time. "But even more so when I am joined with God or you with your Goddess…that sensation of surrender and bliss."

Ceelyha nodded with understanding and took his hand in hers. The warmth from that touch spread like fire through her body. *How can I give him up?* she cried to herself. *I am not alone when I am with him. Why can I not have both him and the Goddess?*

David resumed talking and she pushed her turmoil aside.

"I went to the Palace to change my clothes and bathe off the sweat of dancing, or rather, add to my clothes, for I had cast away the heavy garments of a King somewhere along the road. Michal unexpectedly barged into my chambers. She was more than her usual bitter self, she was angry beyond words. She mocked me for my behaviour saying that I truly lived up to being a poor shepherd boy by a display of commonness in the streets. She told me how humiliated she was to see me dance half naked and to shout and carry on as if I were drunk. She would not listen to how I danced and sang for the Lord. In fact," he paused and looked at Ceelyha beseechingly with tears in his eyes, "she misinterpreted all that I had done."

Ceelyha forgot her resolve not to become emotionally involved and reached out to hold David. He wept in her arms as she tried to comfort him. She had never seen him lower his guard to this degree. *Does he have such a deep love for Michal and is hurt that she has let him down by not sharing his triumph with his people? Or, is he just tired? Or, is there more that he is not telling me?* But with the Goddess gone, she was blocked from seeing into his soul.

When he has more in control, he withdrew from her arms.

"I cursed her, sent her to the harem, and vowed never to share her bed again."

Ceelyha, shocked that David still shared her bed, flinched.

He continued, not cognizant of her reaction. "I left her and went to be with the Lord. I prayed all night and into the morning at the foot of the Ark. He did not speak to me. I wanted to know where to build a temple to house the Ark but could not connect with Him. It is horrible to experience nothingness."

Ceelyha had no trouble identifying with those feelings since the Goddess had left her. Empathy for his plight washed over her.

Suddenly David reached over and tilted her face towards the light of a wall torch and begged, "My darling Ceelyha, I need your strength to carry on. Come away with me to our house and let us pick up where we left off."

With his plea, Ceelyha surmised he had not followed up on his feelings for the woman in the crowd. *Perhaps I misread the entire exchange and that he was just caught up in the excitement of the celebration.* Her heart soared with joy as she quickly left him to make arrangements for Dilbaha to take the morning ritual. David needed her and that was all that mattered. Since the Goddess had forsaken her, this must be her only option; to be a woman, not a priestess.

Later at the house, their lovemaking took on a different dimension. David penetrated her with a tenderness that astounded Ceelyha. He led, she followed. Her urge to possess him totally rose until it exploded in a climax. All thoughts, emotions, time and space blanked out. Then his needs brought her back as he sent wave after wave of delight throughout her body. She cried out his name as he slowly shuddered, sweetly releasing his life force into her. She clung to him as tears poured down her cheeks, trying to imprint his essence into her memory, as if this was the last time they would ever be together.

As they lay contented in each other's arms, David asked Ceelyha about an upcoming battle he was planning. She did not have the courage to tell him that the gift of prophecy had been taken away from her. Instead, she led him believe that he would be victorious.

Ceelyha asked about the man she saw touch the Ark. David's body tensed and he halting asked, "What do you know about that?"

Ceelyha told him, half in jest, that she had her ways of knowing everything about him. *Especially the woman in the street,* she thought miserably as the closeness of lovemaking dissipated. After an awkward period of silence, he explained that he and the Levite priests had done their best to soothe the distraught crowd that had witnessed the man's tragic death. "The man was not a priest and he should not have tried to touch the relic. Remember, you had warned me that no one but the Holy Ones should handle it." David had wanted nothing to impede his promise to bring the Ark to Jerusalem and had insisted that the journey continue. The man's body had quietly been sent to his family with a purse of coins.

David seemed so disheartened and upset that Ceelyha responded,

"It is not our place to question what the Gods willed for that man."

David's only reaction was to hold her tighter.

That night she dreamt of a past life. Just as Thu had divined, David appeared as a priest. Although his features were altered, she instantly knew it was him by the depth of her feelings and the familiar essence of his soul. She was a priestess in the same foreign land that Bernice had given her access to. She saw a Temple, larger and more opulent than the one in Babylon, with columns of rose quartz that seemed to reach into the clouds. But she was not able to focus on it. Her vision was drawn to a sea of red-hot lava that illuminated a nearby mountaintop. Before she could question what was happening, she found herself clutching a heavy cloak to protect herself from torrents of rain that pelted down on a steep cliff overlooking a turbulent sea. Suddenly the ground beneath began to shake with violent spasms followed by water from tempestuous waves surging up. Without warning, she found herself being dragged into its murky depths. She screamed. She frantically tried to fight her way back to the surface, coughing and sputtering only to succumb to another surge of current. She willed her spirit to rise above the watery grave and sped on a gust of wind to her lover. The moment she found him, the familiar longing scorched her body as she looked into his dazzling blue eyes. "Aileomna, my priestess" he cried out as he reached to embrace her but the waves reached up and claimed her once more. The intensity of her own screams woke her up. The vision ended.

The first light of dawn was just beaming through the drapes of the window, when a heavy knocking at the door of their chamber, jarred both of them awake.

David, in a sleep filled voice called, "Who disturbs me at this time!"

An apologetic servant answered, "Sire, I apologize for interrupting your rest but an urgent message has come from the Palace."

Ceelyha wondered who at the Palace would know where David was but did not ask. David began to pull on his clothes as he murmured, "Promise me that you will wait for me here. I will return as soon as possible."

Ceelyha agreed even though it was against her better judgment, she needed to get back to the Temple. She was hoping to tell him about her dream. Although it was not up to her to remind him of the link between them since he would have to come to that realization on his own, she had hoped to trigger some of those forgotten images within him. She wondered if she loved him more, less or the same. But, now the moment had passed and he was gone.

Ceelyha was still worried about Nintu's frame of mind and she had not spoken with Thu for several days. She closed her eyes and just before she fell into a light, restless sleep, her thoughts were overwhelmed by her inability to predict the outcome of David's battles. She knew this was her punishment for being too mired in the physical but wondered if the Goddess would return Her gift if she was not with David. When she awoke, dark images clouded her consciousness – she was filled with dread. To try to alleviate this overbearing feeling of trepidation, she called one of the servants to prepare a bath and searched through a trunk for some fresh clothing. After bathing and dressing, she sent the servant away, wanting to do her own hair. She sat down at the bureau, picked up a silver brush and was about to use it when she spotted some long reddish brown hairs. She immediately called for the servant who had attended her bath.

"What is this hair doing in my brush? To whom does it belong?" The girl stood silently and shrugged her shoulders. "Answer me at once!" Ceelyha demanded.

"Oh, Lady," she cried, "I do not have any idea whose it is!" The girl began to shake she was so filled with fear.

Ceelyha briskly replied, "Run and question the rest of the staff!" Then the realization hit as if a dagger had pierced her heart.

The deep voice of David booming from behind startled the women. "That will not be necessary. Kassra, return to your duties while I talk to the Lady."

His voice was icy, "How dare you complain to a servant about this! The servants at this house are trained to be discrete and even if they know whose hair it is, they would not answer to you. They are my servants."

Ceelyha could not control her emotions. "And whose house is this? Did you not get it for US? Is this not Our secret place where only the Two of us come? It is quite obvious that you have brought another here, or," her lips curled up in disgust, "do you share the sacredness of our bed with several?"

"Do you not understand the rules of this relationship? Do you think you are the only one who shares my bed?" His face was red with anger. By the look on her face he got his answer.

"Then my Golden One, you are a fool. I am the King! I gave you my heart and still you want more?"

"Yes David," she answered, the fight gone out of her. "If I have lost your love then tell me. I will not stand before you begging for the crumbs of your affection." To her horror, her eyes stung with tears and she began to weep.

"Why do you weep? Are you trying to make me feel guilty for something that cannot be undone? Are you trying to make me exclusively yours?" David waited but she could not respond.

"I weep because it seems I love you more than I love the Goddess!" There; she had voiced what was deep inside of her.

She saw the anger drain away from him as he replied, "My love will always be yours."

"I wanted you the way I gave myself to you, exclusively. I abandoned the Goddess and she gave up on me because of the depths of my love for you. I saw the woman whom the hair belongs. I have known about her for some time but was in denial that you would do this to me." She stood up to leave the dressing room then sorrowfully added, "You are right, I do not understand your rules of love."

David crossed the room to try to embrace her. More tears ran down her cheeks as she stepped back from him. "No, David. You will only hurt me more by doing that. Do not contact me again to be your lover. From now on, I am only available to you as the High Priestess."

Ceelyha fled from the house into the street. Never again would she share her body with David. She had now lost the two loves of her life, David and the Goddess.

Chapter 17
The Goddess Returns

As an oppressive summer heat replaced the cool days of spring, Israel suffered. The land was parched; the people were fearful of the future. David sent troops and hired Syrian mercenaries to fight the Ammonite army in Rabboth Ammon,

Ceelyha tried to resume her role as Head Priestess without the Goddess's powers. She preferred that no one knew about the humiliation of losing the divine gifts bestowed upon her by Ishtar, and of David's betrayal. She asked Dilbaha to perform the sacred duties to Asherah for the morning and evening rituals. All healing and omen reading were delegated to her priestesses. The only task she felt capable of doing well was supervising the workmen's painting and refurbishing of the Temple cells. She was able to arrange for new sleeping pallets and to commission the building of larger storage trunks. She spent the rest of her time hoping to reclaim her life's purpose though meditation and prayer. On that day when she had left David and wandered about the streets like a lost soul, she had vowed that she would never have intimate relations with him again. As a priestess, she was supposed to have the training to control her heart and will but it appeared she had failed to do either. She had a double lesson – not only had she lost David, but also the Goddess.

Ceelyha noted that Nintu was beginning to make more of an attempt to pick up the pieces of her life. When she waited on her mistress, she now spoke of trivialities and gossiped about the other Temple workers but refused to discuss her feelings. Neither Thu nor Ceelyha was able to break through the barriers that Nintu had erected.

One particularly hot night, Ceelyha lay awake, bothered by the heat and unruly thoughts. For the thousandth time, she reminisced about her relationship with David, wondering how she could have handled things differently. It was difficult to accept that he had not tried to contact her. *Surely by now, he must miss me and has tired of the other woman.*

Not wanting to dwell on her sorrows, Ceelyha got up, tiptoed past the sleeping Nintu and went into the courtyard. The palm trees that swayed in the night breeze brought some relief from the heat. She listened to the songs of the nightingales and drank in the peace of the night. As she was about to sit on one of the stone benches, she changed her mind and went over to the statue of Asherah that glowed luminously in the light of the full moon. She bowed before Her and prayed.

"Oh Asherah, Isis, Ishtar, Goddess of many names,

Please heed my prayer. Forgive me for putting my needs ahead of Yours.

Forgive me for not devoting myself wholly toYour work.

I see the error of my ways and do respectfully beseech You to forgive me.

I humbly kneel before You this evening to re-establish my vows as a Priestess.

173

I devote myself toYou and our work only.

I shall not worship or honour any other deities but You.

I shall never denounce my faith even in the face of death.

I shall turn a deaf ear to those that wish to persuade me to abandon Your ways.

I willingly take on all the responsibilities and demands that will be placed upon me as Your servant."

With the appeal completed, Ceelyha felt some of the darkness lift from her soul. She made a decision. As soon as the pink light of dawn rose in the east, she woke Nintu. Ceelyha informed her that under no circumstances was she to be disturbed for at least the next four days. She did not want any food, just water from the sacred well.

A sleepy, confused Nintu nodded her understanding and Ceelyha closed the door of her bedchamber. She used all of discipline and training to maintain a constant state of meditation.

It was not until the morning of the second day that she received any inner guidance. She had to separate from David since she had already separated from the Goddess. In truth, she had walked away from both David's and Goddess's love. Initially, in her highly charged emotional state of anger and jealousy, she believed David had pulled his love away and given it to the new woman in his life but now she saw that his love had never been withdrawn. It was only her perception that it had because love to her meant total devotion. That is how a priestess was raised, to totally devote oneself to the Goddess and she transferred that fanatical devotion onto him. Then when he became involved with the new woman, she chose to see this as a severing of his love. The same truth applied to her choice to feel unworthy to receive the Goddess's presence in her life because she believed that loving David too much would anger the Goddess. She had already set in her mind that David would leave her and that clouded her relationship not only with him, but with the Goddess as well. Somehow she had intertwined David with the Goddess. Her burden lessened.

On the morning of her third day of reflection, it occurred to her that Ishtar had mourned and mourned for Her beloved Tammuz when he was held prisoner in the Underworld. She cried out, "You, who have had many lovers and each one of them met with ill fate! And I but one! Am I not following in Your divine footsteps? Just as you followed Your beloved into the Land of No Return, am I not the same? I would have followed David into the depths of darkness to rescue him as well! Does this not truly make me Your daughter? Have pity on I beg You, My Lady! Give me back Your light so that I may make this world a me, better place!"

A further truth surfaced on the night of the third day. It was she who had shut herself off from the Goddess, not the other way around. As a daughter of Ishtar, no matter what she did, she was still a part of Her. *When I am disheartened, I as Your living incarnate no longer emanate the light that You gave me. My world is dim and lustreless since I have shut You out. And I, in turn transmit that darkness to those who come in contact with the entire world and me.* Momentarily, her heart filled with tranquility as this ancient truth arose in her awareness. If she could forgive herself for putting David first, forgive him for not loving her in the manner with which she expected, then she would be able to allow the Goddess back into her life.

She appealed once more to the Goddess. "Oh Mother God, help me forgive myself for my transgressions. Free me from my pain and allow me to love myself once more so that I in turn can fully love and devote the rest of my life to You. Allow me to forgive David in order to return to inner peace. Help me not to judge him."

She rose from her kneeling position and walked over to the open window. After taking several deeps breaths, she exclaimed with relief into the night, "I feel lighter, spiritually I feel lighter!" Immediately, some of the pent up tension in her limbs released and she celebrated by dancing a few movements of a sacred dance. As she twirled and raised her arms to the heavens, a slight buzzing sound resounded in her ears and her vision began to blur. She stopped her dance and waited, hoping beyond expectation that it was the Goddess. Even when no more overt signs manifested, she was not entirely disappointed, having felt that at least some small reconciliation had transpired.

Her energy was spent but she was at peace. Then another profound thought surfaced. At some level, David feared totally devoting his heart and soul to her as it meant he would lose his place with God. If his God deserted him, then he would lose his kingdom. It was the same situation as she had encountered with the Goddess! Then, by having several relationships with other women, he would never forfeit his devotion to his God. With this new revelation, she threw open the door to find an anxious Nintu and asked for a meal of fruit to break her fast. She was resuming her life as High Priestess.

That morning, as she resided over the opening ritual for the Temple, she sensed a slight presence of the Goddess as she laid flowers before Her. When the ceremony finished, Thu approached, her dark eyes flashing with excitement. "Welcome back High Priestess! Welcome back!"

Ceelyha looked in astonishment at her loyal friend. "Thu, you don't understand. I am not sure that I am back. It just seemed the right time to resume some of the duties that the rest of you have been doing for me."

"For a brief moment, as you led the prayers, I saw a glow about your face. I have not seen any signs of divinity around you for awhile."

Ceelyha pointed to an empty bench for them to sit on. Ceelyha took a deep breath and noted her throat was blocked. "I…I…" she rasped.

Thu held a healing hand over the base of Ceelyha's throat. In a few moments, Ceelyha was aware of an intense heat being channelled into that part of her body, then her throat opened and she was able to express herself. "Thank you. I was so blocked that I could not even speak my thoughts aloud. You are such a wonderful healer." Ceelyha smiled with relief.

"I am just so pleased that you are finally allowing me to help! You have no idea how difficult it has been for me not to approach you and offer my assistance! Nintu as well has been uneasy about you. Now, tell me what has been happening to you. Why have you shut me out?"

Ceelyha lowered her eyes in embarrassment. "I have been so humiliated. I lost David and my divine gifts! Thu, I lost my ability to heal and prophesise because I was too caught up on the lower vibrations of jealously, conceit, greed, judgement and all the other unwanted feelings that you could name!"

Thu clutched Ceelyha's hands and waited while Ceelyha poured out her heart. She listened carefully as she explained the vision of David and a woman being intimate, what had happened when she saw the royal wives greet the Ark, the auburn hairs in her brush, and the argument with David.

"And the love potion that you so carefully made for me is gone! When I saw that woman on the day David brought the Ark to the city, I realised that I had lost the ability to hold him. I tripped and as I fell my sash loosened and came off. Someone stepped on it and broke the vial!"

Thu hugged her friend." I am so sorry, so sorry," she cried. "I should not have made you that potion! Look what it has done to you!"

Ceelyha gently removed the priestess's arms and looked into the depths of her soul and quietly stated, "Thu, he was making love to that woman before it broke!"

Thu lowered her eyes, turning away her face. Ceelyha wondered what she was trying to hide and forcefully said, "Thu, what do you know?"

Her voice was apologetic. "Macaab came to see me awhile ago. I think she came to gloat because David had left you for a younger, according to her, more attractive mistress. Can you image the audacity of that woman?"

"How long has his affair been going on?" Ceelyha asked, keeping her emotions carefully under control, recalling her earlier resolve to forgive David.

"From what I could gather from Macaab, and it is difficult to believe anything that woman says, at least two moons ago." Thu cringed while she waited for Ceelyha's reaction.

"How did they meet?"

"Do you recall that David was adding onto his Palace?"

Ceelyha merely nodded.

Thu continued while nervously fingering her Isis amulet. "Well, he built a pavilion on the roof. He apparently liked to go there at night to think and watch the stars."

Ceelyha was very aware of how much the night sky reminded David of his child-hood days as a shepherd and how he felt closer to God when he was under the stars.

"According to Macaab, this woman Bathsheba, who is married to one of David's commanders, carefully calculated when David would be pacing on his terrace. She ordered a bath on her roof, which his balcony conveniently overlooked. So, there was she night after night, brazenly displaying herself, in hopes of attracting his interest. Bathsheba had heard that no woman could please David and she was determined to end rumours!"

"Did you say that she was married?"

"Yes."

"But could she not be stoned to death for lying with a man other than her husband? Does her husband know about this?"

"Ceelyha, David is the King, above reproach. I guess the laws that govern the commoners do not apply to him. Your father was also a King. I am sure he broke many laws."

"I suppose he did." *David does remind me of my father. If he wants something, no obstacle or person will stop him from obtaining it.* Ceelyha kept these thoughts to herself and continued, "But is that not dangerous for both of them? David must be very infatuated by her or he would not risk the shame. Or, perhaps she and the entire situation are a challenge for him. He does like to have challenges."

Ceelyha could see how he would be smitten by Bathsheba's beauty. "Do you know how hard it is for me, Thu, to understand how he could declare undying love for me and yet turn around and fall into the arms of another?"

"Neither one of us has experience with men. I have no guidance for you except that whenever I saw him look at you, his face glowed with genuine love.

Maybe as women, we can never understand the inner emotions and workings of a male's mind. Who knows, he may be the type of person who thrives on stimulation and excitement."

"You would think his battles with the enemy would be enough!" replied an indignant Ceelyha.

"Or, it may be that having all these women in his life, gives him an excuse not to have time to search within and really examine his deepest thoughts."

"You know Thu, you may be onto to something there. I sense he harbours a great deal of guilt over the many people who have died because of their connection with him. Whether he had a direct hand in their deaths or not, knowing David, he feels responsible. Maybe he thinks a new woman will help him forget his past and that she will play the role of some type of saviour."

Thu nodded and said, "Or, maybe, just maybe, you and David have worked out whatever the Goddess needed you to, and now you can get on with the rest of your life's journey. But," she added with a grin, "I am glad that I have my High Priestess back. We still have to make plans for the lower part of the Temple."

"Yes, but will we have the means to do it now that I am no longer the mistress of the King?" Ceelyha joked for the first time in weeks, feeling much more like her old self.

It was as if the Goddess was testing her once again when a message came from the Palace that the King would be arriving the next day to discuss some outstanding business. Ceelyha fasted and spent much of the day in meditation and prayer asking for strength not to fall off her path again. She wanted to resist David with every particle of her being. The only preparation she made for his arrival was to have Nintu sparingly apply some cosmetics, but, no gold dust was sprinkled on her hair. She suddenly recalled Adah's words about naming. *Perhaps he has taken his pet name, The Golden One away from me- a sure sign of his disassociation and lack of need for authority over me!* she thought as she donned deep blue robes and her mother's necklace and waited for him in her chambers. She asked Nintu to bring some wine and a tray of fruits.

She sensed his fresh outdoor scent even before he arrived at her chamber. She willed herself to remain calm, in control and detached from any romantic feelings she might have. David entered the room, filling it with his presence. He was dressed in a purple tunic with a light mantle attached at the shoulders. His beard was carefully oiled and curled, his hair in place. Ceelyha obediently rose from her stool, lowered her eyes, bowed and knelt with grace. As always, his hand, which reached to help her up, sent shock waves through her system, transforming every particle of her flesh. Against her resolve, she looked at this face. She noted his skin darkened from the sun, the wrinkles in the corners of his eyes, his full sensuous mouth and eyes that looked lovingly upon her. For a split second, the Goddess gave her access to his thoughts. *He thinks that we can pick up where we left off! This man has no concept or idea of how hurt I am!* To cover the awkwardness of the moment, Ceelyha said in an even voice, "Welcome My Lord. What is it that has brought you to the Temple of Asherah?'

David's face portrayed surprise; he was taken aback. It was obvious to Ceelyha that he expected her to melt into his arms. He cleared his throat and spoke, "I came to see how you are." His voice portrayed dismay.

In an icy tone she responded, "As you can see, I am fine. And you?"

His eyes clouded over, shutting her out. "I am well. Have you come to your senses yet?"

She coyly answered, "About what, Your Highness?"

"Damn it woman! You know quite well the matter of which I speak!"

She sighed, "That is finished, My Lord. I told you that it was over at our last meeting. Now, would you like to sit and take some refreshment so we can discuss the 'outstanding business' that was in your message?"

His facial expression betrayed his anger as he sat on a nearby stool. He took a large gulp from the wine goblet as if to fortify himself. Ceelyha, overly aware of him both sexually and spiritually, took a moment to pray silently for the strength to not weaken her resolve.

Finally David broke the silence by speaking in a voice that betrayed his emotions, "My Golden One, please forgive me for my indiscretion. It is you that I love; you of all people know that. This other woman means very little to me. You are the one who makes me feel complete. Can you not understand that?" he pleaded.

At least he did not remove my name. "David," replied Ceelyha with an exhausted tone, "You will always require someone new and exciting to share your bed. If it is not Bathsheba, then it will be another one."

He appeared to be shocked at the mention of Bathsheba. "How do you know of her?" His voice rose in alarm.

"I am a priestess. These walls have eyes and the court talks," she replied arrogantly.

He stood up and began to pace back and forth in the small room. His voice hardened as if to elevate himself above human emotion. "So be it. Enough of this talk! I need you to prophecise for me."

Ceelyha's anger mounted. *So that was his business! He wasn't even going to try to convince me that he could be faithful. Well, I too can play that game.*

She crisply said, "As you wish, My Lord. But," she paused for effect, "We are in need of more funds to restore the Temple. Do you recall…."?

"Fine, fine. Let us get on with this." He dismissed her request with a shake of his head.

"I will call Nintu to assist. Is this a request for divination?" she asked in a businesslike manner.

He curtly responded, "Yes."

Ceelyha was glad to escape from his close proximity; her heart was wildly beating and hands sweating. *I can do this! The Goddess has not forsaken me. I am almost certain that I have my gifts back and now is the time to prove it.* She straightened out her robe and willed herself to stand tall. She found Nintu waiting in the corridor, her eyes wide with curiosity.

Ceelyha, grateful that she had been fasting, marveled how the Goddess had intricately arranged circumstances to test her again! *So it is not just a coincidence that I have not consumed any meat for the past few days. Here I thought I was purifying myself for the Goddess, when in reality it was to divine for David. There really is very little free will!* Smiling at the synchronicity of her life and the lack of free will one has when devoted to the Goddess, she entered the small sanctuary. She had insisted this room be set up for divination work when she became the High Priestess removing the inconvenience of having to trudge into the dungeon to set up the brazier. It was lit, ready to be used all the time. She prostrated herself before the golden likeness of Ishtar and raised her arms in invocation. A small sigh of delight escaped from her lips when she felt Her energy descend.

Nintu brought the King into the room and threw some incense on the brazier then timidly asked, "What is your request, My Lord?"

He answered in almost a whisper, "I wish to know if my troops will triumph over the Ammonite army."

Ceelyha, aware of David's presence and the question, sent out his request to the Goddess. The brazier sizzled and crackled with the mixture of cedar and sage. When the fire began to smoke, Ceelyha spoke in the deep voice of the Goddess.

"There are chariots... horses... men shouting in tongues that are foreign to this land you call Israel...rivers of blood flow over dried mud."

Nintu put more dried cedar on the coals and waited until Ceelyha was ready to speak again.

"David, you are in your ... short tunic and breastplate of bronze... riding into battle. You are holding a sword up high ...and yes; there is a divine light that glows around your entire person... Your God will be with you in this."

David sighed with relief and bowed his head in thanks. Nintu asked him if he wished more information. He nodded and she put more incense on the brazier.

Once more the powerful speech of the Goddess rang out through Ceelyha's voice. "To the one called David... you will be victorious in your battles... but not in your family or love life... Be warned... there is much ahead for which you will be held accountable... The enemy is in your own bloodline... The eyes of a dead man will haunt you... a babe will die... and a woman's grief will destroy part of your soul ... pestilence... famine and drought...the wrath of the Gods is coming your way!"

David was stricken. He held his arm over his face as if to defend himself from what was being prophesized. Nintu took his arm and directed him out of the pungent smoke filled room before running back to assist her mistress. She quickly rubbed Ceelyha's hands and picked her up from the floor where she had slid. When Nintu was certain her mistress was fully back in her body, she said with concern, "I think David needs you. Go to him."

Without a second thought, Ceelyha rushed into the hallway. David was on his haunches, slumped with his back against the wall, his face in his hands. He appeared to be totally unaware of Ceelyha's presence. She looked around to make sure no one else was in the vicinity to witness his vulnerability. She gently called his name, and then touched his arm as a signal for him to stand up. She held his hand and led him, like a child, to her chambers. Once inside, she indicated he was to sit down and then gave him some of the left over wine on the table. After drinking a mouthful, he seemed more himself; the colour had returned to his face. Ceelyha gently asked if she could get him anything else but he just shook his head. He picked up the jug and poured the rest of the wine into a goblet. When he drained the vessel, in a weakened voice he announced, "It appears that my future is not too promising. It seems that stormy times are ahead."

"David," Ceelyha had been thinking, "Why don't you ask your own God what lies before you? You need not trust what my Goddess has foretold. I may have seen things wrongly."

"You have never before," he said in a flat tone of voice.

Ceelyha came over and knelt in front of his chair. She took his powerful hands in hers, marveling how small and fragile hers seemed next to his. She laid her head down in his lap and he stroked her hair. She felt his caressing touch through to her very core and willed herself to control her response. But as she reveled in the closeness to him, tears of sadness welled up behind her eyelids. She prayed to the Goddess not to lose her resolve and spoke in a shaky voice, while he continued to stroke her hair. "David, my beloved. I need to tell you why the reading may not have been true. The Goddess removed Her divine gifts when I became too mired in your life. I lost my spirituality and place in the universe when I became jealous over your desire for other women. I put myself first, instead of Her. The Goddess gave me warnings but when I am with you," she looked into his big brown eyes, "I lose who I really am. I become a woman rather than a servant of the Goddess. Do you know how hard it is to sit here like this with you and not have your kisses over all of my heated body? Do you know how much I want you to enter me and give me pleasure? Do you know how much I yearn to pleasure you?"

David tried to stoop down to kiss her and she put up her hand to stop. "See, that is what I mean. I can no longer be that woman for you. It would kill me to do so. I would just be another conquest for you, to be cast aside when your loins stirred for another. You yourself have said as much."

He shook his head and said, "My Golden One, you are my only love."

She reached up, touched his beard and sighed. "Oh David, our souls are eternal and you and I shall be together again. Let us hope that sometime in the future we will be able to love with total abandonment, with no social status or religion to come between us. I have worked out what the Goddess deemed I needed with you, as David." She paused and waited to see if he understood what she had said.

"I think I understand. You are saying that we are finished being lovers, that we have shared and loved but if you stayed with me, it would destroy you in the end. You are first a priestess then a woman and I fell in love with both the woman and priestess."

With a catch in his throat he added, "I am a lucky man to have had both parts of you. I would give up everything for my God if He asked me to. So, I shall respect your wishes and the Goddess's. I will take my leave and come to you in the future as only your King and friend. Is that alright, my Priestess?"

Uncontrollable sobs erupted from the very depths of Ceelyha's soul. Her tears stained his tunic as they streamed out. He picked her up off the floor and carried her into the other room and set her on the bed. He lay beside her and they hugged, relishing their closeness for one last time, until the sistrums called the priestesses to awaken Asherah.

Chapter 18
Life Without David

Ceelyha was more content than she had been for months. *It is so strange not to look forward to seeing David anymore. I miss him yet feel such a wonderful freedom at the same time, as I am no longer riddled with guilt or resentment. I feel that I have matured way beyond my years.* She was once again fully in touch with the energy of the Goddess happily residing over rituals, teaching dancing, guiding other priestesses to learn her unique method of divination and with Dilbaha's help, attending to the running of the Temple.

Together, Ceelyha, Nintu and Thu supervised the cleaning and restoration of the Temple's lower level. They took great delight discovering old jars filled with dried herbs, unguents and oils, most of which Thu surmised, were from the land of Egypt. A variety of primitive small clay statues of various goddesses, some holding babies and others with swollen bellies were uncovered. Each statue was carefully cleaned and taken up to the sanctuary for the other priestesses to use. In a dusty, rat infested corner of a tiny cell, a scroll was found stuffed in one of the jars. It was written in a text that no one in the Temple could decipher. When Ceelyha invoked the Goddess to inquire as to its meaning, she was told that it was scribed by the ancients in order to record Asherah sending a great flood to Earth. The scroll told how, during the cataclysm, some of Her people had been spared in order to start new civilizations and that some of those same people would come back to earth again and again to help humanity. From its message, Ceelyha and Thu were able to intuit that the two of them had incarnated many times, always in service to a higher deity, for the purpose of assisting others less spiritual than themselves. The unearthing of this scroll gave Ceelyha further validation that she had made the right choice by ceasing to be David's lover, in order to serve others as a high priestess. It inspired her to begin to scribe her own times with David, because just as the information from the ancients was important to her generation, she sensed her recording would serve a higher purpose sometime in the future.

One sunny afternoon, Nintu burst into the herb room where Ceelyha and Thu were preparing ointments.

"My Lady, you will never guess what I have just heard!"

Both women stopped their work and waited while an excited Nintu told them that Bathsheba's servant had told a Palace attendant that her mistress was pregnant and it was not possible it was her husband's Uriah's since he is away fighting. The Goddess instantaneously manifested as energy around Ceelyha. "Oh, no," she cried to Thu, "This gossip is truth! The woman is with child but some shadow is falling over her!"

"Well, she will now be branded an adulterous, whether or not the King commanded that she lay with him. Even David can not control what people think and see!"

Suddenly the vision of Macaab with her skills in the black arts entered Ceelyha's
thoughts. She asked Thu, "Do you think Macaab is that evil shadow? Would she
dare attempt to destroy Bathsheba or her unborn child?"

"I would not put it past her. She may be trying to destroy this woman just as she
tried to kill you. The only recent joy she has, is knowing that David and you are no
longer a couple."

"Should we warn David or Bathsheba?"

"Then it might appear as if you were the jealous one, starting a rumour that you
could not prove. I think it is best to just let things unfold as they are supposed to."

As it turned out, a message came from David that he needed to see Ceelyha on
urgent business. Since she knew he was not coming to rekindle their love affair, she
sensed it had to do with Bathsheba.

Ceelyha tried to hide her surprise at the way David looked when he arrived at
her chambers. It seemed as if he had aged over night! His once beautiful jet-
black glossy hair was streaked with grey, his broad shoulders were slightly
stooped and he had lost a great deal of weight. *This was not the same David!*
she thought with dismay. *Where is that beautiful strong warrior whom I fell in
love with? The affair with Bathsheba must be tormenting him at a deep soul
level.*

His manner and voice did not betray his inner thoughts as he greeted Ceelyha
with warmth and affection. "My Golden One, how wonderful you look!" She had
dressed with care in a long flowing diaphanous pale blue gown with the red girdle
of Ishtar encircling her slender waist and the Goddess's necklace around her neck as
she wanted to appear to him as a priestess, not a woman.

She prostrated before him and he knelt down to pick her up. "Come, let us
embrace as friends. We have no need for formalities."

As they reached out to hold one another, Ceelyha was aware that she no longer
felt that lustful burning that she used to experience when their bodies touched. He,
as well, did not display the usual stirring in his loins. Instead, they shared an intimacy that went far beyond their physical needs. David was the first one to break away
from the embrace and she saw that his face was flushed. Ceelyha did not know if it
was from the embrace or what he wanted to talk about. He cleared his throat as he
removed his royal purple mantle and sat on a stool near the brazier. "We are having
a cold spring this year. Are you comfortable enough?"

"Yes, I am, My Lord," she replied and waited.

He seemed reluctant to begin, as if he were searching for the correct words. His
eyes were wide and unfocused. To make it easier for him, Ceelyha gently said,

"David, whatever it is, you can share it with me. There is almost nothing that I do not know about you."

He nodded, and with some apparent relief, launched into his story. He spoke about Bathsheba and how he first encountered her one moonlit night while she was on her rooftop. He had been pacing back and forth on his balcony trying to work out the logistics of bringing of the Ark to Jerusalem, when he saw a vision of loveliness across the wall of his terrace.

For a brief moment, Ceelyha had a window opened for her to choose. She could revert back to envy that would coil like a snake up her spine or embrace forgiveness and be set free. While trying to focus on listening, she silently prayed to the Goddess to block the latter.

"I was so intrigued to see this beautiful young woman who disrobed, bearing her ripeness in the moonlight, while her maid poured water over her pale skin that seemed almost luminescent in the light of the moon. Her waist was tiny, just like yours. Her breasts were full and her hips were as slender as a boy's." He stopped and looked over at Ceelyha. "She reminded me so much of you! I could see the Goddess in her!"

With that comment, Ceelyha was not able to hide her shock. "Me? Goddess?" *Surely this woman did not worship the Goddess! He must have seen the light of her soul. That can only mean that they are meant to be as one.* She quickly regained her composure. "Then, why did you not come to me that night?"

"I must have gotten totally carried away with the moment." He had the graciousness to at least lower his eyes in shame. In what Ceelyha believed was an apology he continued with a pleading look in his eyes, "I had no control over my lust. I ordered one of my servants to fetch her to my room and I bedded her." He paused to stroke his beard, the previous humility gone and then added with what Ceelyha detected was a tone of Bravo!, "She was a most willing lover."

"Of course! You are the King! Why would she not be?" Ceelyha tried to be as civil as possible. *This is not an easy conversation for either of us. It is hard to hear him talk about the new love in his life and remain detached.* As Ceelyha recalled the sultry exchange between the two of them on the street she knew Bathsheba was in love with the King.

David did not pick up her tone of voice and continued, "She shared my bed many times, always in secret, because of her marital status. Then one day she came to me in utter devastation to inform me she was with child." He appeared to be upset and Ceelyha felt a rush of sympathy for him. She immediately sent him the white healing light of the Goddess then nodded for him to continue.

"It is mine. Uriah, her husband has been at Ammon for the last three months." David accepted the goblet of wine that Ceelyha quickly offered. When he had drunk his fill he went on to explain that Bathsheba had told him that her husband, a wealthy Hittite, never had any affections for her. The marriage was an arrangement to elevate his social and political status.

With a voice full of sympathy David added, "Bathsheba is in a loveless marriage living with a vindictive mother-in-law who continuously enforces her strange customs and pagan beliefs on the household. She was not allowed to bring a servant with her when she married so even the servants of the household are against her!"

David then informed Ceelyha that Bathsheba's life would be ruined if the general population found out that she was with child. She would be stoned as an adulteress. When he was done, he looked at Ceelyha with beseeching eyes and pleaded. "Can you help us?"

A perplexed Ceelyha responded, "Help you how?"

David answered in almost a whisper, "To think of some way around this?"

Ceelyha was astounded. *How could he even think that I would abort this child? Does he not realize that he must see this through just as much as I need to! The Goddess would never allow that! She certainly is testing my devotion!* She hesitated to give herself time to control her thoughts before she responded, "David, it is no secret that your mistress is with child. We have known about it here at the Temple for days. She is too far along to miscarry from the Goddess's methods." She paused before adding with a hint of hope in her voice, "Why does she not pass the child off as her husband's?"

"I had already thought of that. So a few days ago I ordered his return from the fighting in Ammon on the pretext of discussing battle strategies. When he met with me, I suggested that he return to his home and visit his wife, but he did not. I wanted to dispel the rumours and keep her from being branded as an adulteress but he spent last night sleeping in the palace with the rest of the soldiers."

Ceelyha replied, forcing herself to say David's new beloved's name with as much detachment as she could master, "He must have been forewarned that Bathsheba was already with child."

David answered "Perhaps, but if that were the case why would he choose to disgrace his wife by not sleeping with her and not letting on the child was his? Why would he wish to humiliate all three of us? I heard him, just this morning, say to some of the men that he would not go and lie with his wife in the warmth and comfort of their bed while his comrades were forced to sleep out in the cold with war raging about them. Is the man that much of an outstanding citizen that he would have his wife stoned?"

"What message did you receive from your God when you prayed to him about this?"

David's face reddened and he looked uncomfortable again. "I did not want to burden My Lord with such matters. I could not ask the priests for help either so that is why I am here."

Ceelyha sighed and prayed to the Goddess for advice. Her vision blurred and ears buzzed as a message came through. "David," Ceelyha said when the Goddess had left, "It was Uriah's mother who told him about your affair with his wife. This news angered him because he had yet to produce an heir and now the two of you have. He was hoping that the Israel people would take care of his wife by stoning her for being an adulteress. I believe that one of the commandments from your God that is housed in the Ark is thou shalt not covet thy neighbour's wife?"

David nodded.

"So she will be killed, leaving Uriah free to marry another who might produce his heir. It is obvious that he does not love his wife and you have given him the solution to getting rid of her!"

David stood up, paced back and forth then in a rage said, "You know, I now know can absolve myself of any guilt as to what happens to that man! He is a barbarian to start with, a pagan, and now he has gone too far. How dare he use me to do away with his wife!"

His voice softened as he went over to where Ceelyha sat and kissed her on the cheek. "You have helped me immensely, My Golden One. You are the only one whom I can bear my soul to. Only you would never judge me."

David gazed into her eyes with all the tenderness and love of their earlier meetings and she felt her heart melt, her knees weaken as the old yearning for him returned in full force. It took all of her resolve to not lean in and kiss him on the lips when he stated in a matter of fact voice, "I must leave you now but will be in touch soon."

A surprised Ceelyha did not even have time to bid him goodbye. She wondered how she had helped to solve the problem and what the possible repercussions might be. Then Goddess's energy descended as a warning.

Many days later, the gatekeeper rushed into the courtyard to find the High Priestess. He said breathlessly, his eyes wide with astonishment, "High Priestess, there is a holy man at the gates. He asks to see you. My Lady, I have never seen the likes of him before at the Temple of Asherah."

Ceelyha requested another priestess to help with the petitioner with whom she had been working. She took a deep breath, wondering what this could be about as she made her way over to the gate.

He stood outside, wrapped in a dusty black cloak made of goat's hair that had seen better days. His small beady eyes were as black as obsidian. He was slight of body and one wiry hand held onto a wooden staff as if it were his protection against her. His long unkempt hair was in need of washing. His entire demeanor reminded her of a mountain cat ready to pounce at any moment. She spoke with trepidation. "Yes, how may I be of assistance to you?"

His voice, although of a higher pitch than most males, was extremely powerful. "I am Nathan. I wish to speak with you." His beady eyes darted back and forth between the gatekeeper and some of the petitioners who looked on with curiosity before he added, "Alone."

"Yes, of course. Would it be too much of a sacrilege for you to enter the sacred Temple of Asherah?" She fully expected him to refuse to set foot on Her hallowed grounds thinking that to him, it would be committing some sort of sin, but he did. As she escorted him to one of the empty healing rooms, curious eyes followed them.

She signalled for Nintu, who had followed them, to bring some refreshment. Nathan took his time calculating the contents of the small room. He took in the altar, the small bronze statue of Asherah and the stone slab where healings were done. Although he did not speak, Ceelyha felt his revulsion at being in such a pagan room. To ease his discomfort, she asked him to sit on the only stool in the room while she stood. He refused and went to the other side of the slab. He stood across from her, his eyes cold and calculating. They were both about the same height, so it made for easy eye contact. *What a repulsive man* she thought. *He looks at me as if I were some freak of nature. He is so filled with his own godliness that he thinks I should fall down on my knees in front of him!*

"Priestess, I am here because of our mutual interest in the affairs of the King," he paused as if mocking her. But Ceelyha just waited, her face expressionless, her posture straight and regal.

His face coloured, with what she assumed was embarrassment for not getting the reaction he wanted from her. "I know that you and David were intimate and that the woman Bathsheba has taken your place in his affections." He watched again as if to see if she would cringe, but her body language did not betray her thoughts, so he continued.

"Well it seems that David sent orders to have her husband put at the front of the battle lines and that he has been killed."

Ceelyha's surprise registered on her face in spite of her resolve not to show any emotion in front of this man,

Nathan quickly singled this out. "So, you did not know," he said thoughtfully.

At that moment, Nintu entered with a tray of fresh figs and wine. She poured a goblet for each of them and waited for further instructions. Ceelyha nodded to her to leave, and the two of them were alone again.

The silence was uncomfortable, as Nathan drank his wine and greedily ate most of the fruit. When he had had his fill, he spoke. "You and I need not be enemies. We both have the King's best interests at heart." He looked coyly at her, "Besides, I have wanted to meet the woman who stole his heart and advised him on so many issues."

Ceelyha found her voice. "I advised him only when he asked. I never went to him with unsolicited messages from the Goddess. I never proclaimed that I spoke for his God."

"You are a clever one, aren't you? It is too bad that your charms were not stronger than Bathsheba's or he would not be in this situation. The wedding arrangements are already in progress with Uriah hardly cold in his grave. My God will punish David for his sins! He has sullied the Laws of Moses!"

In a loud resonating voice he held up his staff in front of his face and rolled his eyes upwards," God will deny the Land of Israel rain. He will send famine so all shall know the sins of His Chosen One and that is only the beginning of his wrath. Just you wait and see!"

Ceelyha was not about to ask for details from this strange man but his words brought to mind the last divination she had done for David. *The Goddess really must have channelled through me on that night. It was something about his real enemy being his family and the eyes of a dead man who will haunt him and a child who is dead! My heavens, that was about David killing Uriah and Bathsheba's child dying! And now, there is a curse on the House of David from his own God!*

Nathan watched her with his razor-sharp eyes while she processed what he said. "So, you have seen it too. God is not pleased with our David."

"What is it you would have me do?"

Nathan, with more sincerity than she anticipated, shook his head in despair. "I know not. I guess we both need to pray for the salvation of his soul."

Ceelyha hotly responded, "You pray for his soul. I, on the other hand will send him the Goddess's healing white light to ease his pain and be at his side if he has need of my services. We can not undo what the Gods have decreed!"

Nathan appeared taken back as he softened his voice and replied, "Priestess, you are a good woman. Now, let us part in friendship. We are united in our resolve to help David. I have already told him that the people are saying that he is no longer a true King; he is negligent in his duties. They are looking at Absalom to replace him."

Ceelyha's immediate response was that Macaab was working her black magic to put her son in the throne but dared not voice these thoughts. Nathan made a slight bow with his head to indicate the meeting was over and she did the same. He could not leave the Temple fast enough.

Sometime later Ceelyha heard that the wedding had taken place. She wondered if David had only married the woman to save her from being stoned or if he truly loved Bathsheba. Whatever his reason, Ceelyha speculated what cost it would be to himself, his family and his kingdom.

One afternoon, as the late spring sun warmed the ceramic tiles of the courtyard, Ceelyha was working with a woman who had hurt her ankle when Nintu came rushing up to her. "My Lady, a messenger has come from the Palace. You are to go immediately to attend the new queen."

Perplexed, Ceelyha excused herself from the woman and led Nintu to a private spot where she demanded, "What are you talking about?"

Nintu, in an exasperated tone responded, "Bathsheba. She must be in labour."

Ceelyha's tone of voice relayed her surprise. "She can not be. It is too soon.

Nevertheless tell Thu to get ready."

"No, My Lady. The message was specific; you, and only you are to come. Transportation is waiting outside the gate."

Ceelyha, not knowing what to make of the request, asked for Nintu's help to change her clothing and apply some cosmetics. *Was she to appear as a healer or a guest?* When she was satisfied that she was presentable for either circumstance, Ceelyha carried her medicine box to the gate and stepped into the sedan. Two Palace servants skilfully navigated the chair through busy streets. When Ceelyha arrived at the Palace gates, a female servant escorted her through the main building into a courtyard. Gurgling fountains, shady palm and sycamore trees and the scent of exotic blooming bushes impressed her. Since leaving Babylon, it was the most beautiful place that she had ever seen. But as she walked further along, a powerful energy overwhelmed her. A force of darkness and ill will negated the sense of peace and tranquillity. It was so overpowering that the skin on Ceelyha's arms prickled. She immediately mentally called for the Goddess's protection and heard Her voice. *There is evil lurking here and it is of the human kind.* Then it struck Ceelyha that this was the harem, where David's wives, concubines and children lived! Where Macaab had dwelled! Ceelyha was picking up feelings of jealously, hatred and envy that the women held for one another as they waited day after day, night after night to be called for service to the King. She breathed a sigh of relief that her destiny did not involve being part of harem life and that she had hopefully moved beyond those sentiments!

Ceelyha felt eyes watching her as she dutifully followed the servant to a large porch. Paper-thin drapes parted and Ceelyha was ushered into a small reception room. She noted various coloured cushions, silver artefacts and a low brass topped table with its tray of fresh fruits and gold goblets. Ankle bands and bracelets announced the sureness of her movement as a woman appeared from the back room. Ceelyha knew it was Bathsheba. She was every inch a queen with her flaming auburn hair elaborately dressed in cascading curls. Ceelyha could see why David would be attracted to this woman with her ivory coloured skin, her fine delicate features and full red lips. She certainly did not see why David said that there was a resemblance between her and Bathsheba! Ceelyha, with her trained eye, noted the queen's belly beneath the layers of the soft white linen sheath. She estimated her to be well into the seventh month. For a moment, both women looked at each other, until Ceelyha remembered her position and slightly bowed.

Bathsheba raised her hand with its heavy glittering rings and in a forced sweet voice said, "Welcome, High Priestess. I have been expecting you."

Ceelyha frowned and waited; she did not want to be near this woman or want to find anything to like about her. It was difficult enough imaging the possible pleasures she was sharing with David without having to be in her presence.

Bathsheba gestured to a pillow and said, "Please sit and take some refreshment."

Ceelyha, not wanting to sit or take any food, had no choice. It would appear rude not to partake in the offering. In retrospect she thought, *I should have asked David how much this woman knows about us so at least I could have been prepared.* She quickly found her answer, when for one brief moment Bathsheba let her guise of welcome down, as Ceelyha was just starting to sit. Like a waterfall, jealously and envy poured out of her. Then as quickly as it had manifested, the Goddess closed the veil, and the woman flashed Ceelyha a bright smile.

A servant appeared and passed a tray to Ceelyha.

Ceelyha took an apricot and said, "Your Majesty is very gracious."

"You are welcome," she replied. Then she cleared her throat as if to announce that formalities were over. "David has told me that you are an excellent healer and that he places a great deal of faith in your abilities."

Ceelyha had the courtesy to blush as she replied, "The King is most generous in his praise."

"We would like you to preside over the birth of our child."

Ceelyha almost choked on her fruit. She gasped, "But surely there are trained harem midwives who are experienced enough to be by your side!"

Bathsheba looked at her then turned away as if to hide her emotions. "No, it is you that we have chosen. You are the Head Priestess and the most skilled. " In almost a whisper she added, "I do not trust anyone associated with the harem. This request for your assistance comes directly from the King."

Now, Ceelyha understood. The others did not welcome David's newest wife. They would be all too happy to see some ill fortune fall on her or the unborn child. She considered David's request and like the food, had no choice but to accept. If she did not, David could withdraw his support from the Temple.

Swallowing her unease, Ceelyha replied, "Then I shall be honored."

After Ceelyha asked how Bathsheba's pregnancy was progressing. Upon hearing that everything was fine, Ceelyha sensed a shadow around the unborn child. From her position on the cushion, she mentally tried to clear it with white light while not alerting Bathsheba.

It wasn't until Ceelyha was back in the sedan that she had time to gather her thoughts. She never realized how entangled her life with David had become. She knew that the child was fated not to survive and that somehow she, as a foreigner, a pagan priestess and ex mistress of the King, would be blamed. The wings of the Goddess descended to confirm her worse fears.

Chapter 19
The Birthing

David was far from being successful in squelching the malicious rumours that Bathsheba carried his child and that he had Uriah murdered. As spring changed into summer, Yahweh vented His wrath on Israel. Never had the land been so dry or the crops so poor. Without rainfall, olives and fruits withered on their branches, wheat stalks stiffened and yellowed. It appeared that both Nathan's and the Goddess's prophesy were coming true.

Ceelyha and Thu consulted with their respective deities about the upcoming birth. Both knew that if the child was not born alive and healthy, not only would David be in trouble with his people, but also Ceelyha's personal safety would be threatened. If the High Priestess of a pagan temple was accused of wrongdoing, then the zealous Levite priests would finally have the ammunition to eradicate the entire cult of Asherah. If the goddess sect were lost, then women would become totally subjugated to male oppression in all aspects of their social, physical and spiritual lives. At least, with David as King, there were still some choices of worship. And she recalled Bernice's dying request to carry on the work, teach the younger ones the ancient arts and ensure that the Temple doors will always be open. It seemed to Ceelyha there were a great number of issues at stake.

The two priestesses carefully examined the various statues they had recently uncovered from the bowels of the Temple. They wanted to find a perfect image of a goddess giving birth and project that magic into Bathsheba's birthing room. The one that they finally chose was a bronze replica of the Goddess Asherah, standing on a lion holding a suckling child at Her breast. It seemed to symbolize the strength and determination that the queen would need to ensure an effortless birth, especially since the Gods had already spoken against the child surviving. Both Ceelyha and Thu hoped that if the child lived beyond birth, then Ceelyha might not be held accountable for its future well-being.

They questioned Dilbaha and the other priestesses about alternative methods of assisting with childbirth, so when the time came, Ceelyha would be prepared. She knew that she would be on her own as Bathsheba had made it very clear that no one but Ceelyha and her servant were to attend.

On the next full moon, Thu and Ceelyha combined their magic to consult the scrying bowl. After the purification ritual, they were able to divine that the child, a male, would be born without mishap but they were blocked from seeing his future. Thu could only visualise ripples in the bowl while Ceelyha saw an ominous murky dark shadow forming in its depths.

In preparation for the event, Ceelyha had ordered a new set of birthing bricks to be made, with no symbols or signs of the Goddess. She had made sure that all of her birthing stones and crystals were clear of any previous energy and that they had been blessed by the Goddess. She thought she was prepared until the message came from the Palace one late autumn afternoon. She nervously said her goodbyes to Thu as she and Nintu, who carried the medicine box, rushed to the waiting sedan. Thu promised to channel energies through the birthing statue at all times.

Bathsheba's piercing screams resounded throughout the courtyard. The women of David openly watched as Ceelyha and Nintu were quickly escorted through the harem. *They are also afraid. They too sense that their futures lie in the outcome of this birthing,* Ceelyha intuited. Snippets of their conversations drifted past her as the frantic servant led the way to Bathsheba's chambers. "Look, it is David's old mistress…who is that other woman with the pagan… How much longer do you think the harlot will be in labour? Premature birth; not likely… She is nine months for certain. Do you think David is with her? Did he attend your child's …?"

Just ahead on the porch of Bathsheba's rooms, Ceelyha saw a frenzied David pacing back and forth, his hair uncombed and his tunic wrinkled. He had the appearance of a man who had not slept for several days. When he saw Ceelyha, relief spread over his worried face.

"Here you are, My Golden One. Now I know everything will be well!" He held out his hand in a gesture to prevent her from bowing before him and ushered her into the bedchamber of Bathsheba. Her servant, for no other midwives or relatives were in the room, clutched a cloth over Bathsheba's mouth to try to stifle her cries. David rushed over to his wife who lay on a divan, and picked up her pale, listless hand. "The Priestess is here, my Beautiful One," he cooed, "you are safe now."

Ceelyha tried to ignore the endearing way he spoke to Bathsheba but was not successful. To hide her dismay, she firmly told David to leave the chambers then barked out orders to Nintu and the other girl, whose name she learned was Jessica. While they were preparing the bricks, water and herbs, Ceelyha spoke softly to the distraught mother to be. "Bathsheba, my queen, I want you to know that you are not alone. You and I will face the pain together and you will be successful in giving birth to a healthy baby boy. We will show the harem that you are truly blessed with... " Her encouraging words were interrupted as the queen groaned with the onset of another stabbing pain.

From questioning Jessica, Ceelyha found out the contractions had started shortly before the mid day sun. After a thorough examination of Bathsheba, she knew they were in for a long wait. She set about rubbing the unguent of ground poppy seeds and lotus oil that had been carefully prepared by Thu, on the queen's distended abdomen. As a further aid to ease the pains, she had Jessica give her mistress strong blackberry tea. Ceelyha did not put a charm around Bathsheba's neck in case it offended the woman's religious beliefs but openly asked for Ishtar's protection as she had Nintu throw some cedar incense on a nearby brazier. Next, she took out the statue of the Mother and Child and placed it on a make shift altar beside the brazier before silently praying to connect with Thu. Bathsheba appeared to be too wrapped up in another bout of labour pains to take much notice of what Ceelyha did. During one of the contractions, she screamed, "I do not want this child of sin! Take it from me Yahweh, before it kills me!"

Upon hearing the delusional cries, Ceelyha hushed the hysterical woman with soothing words, "My Lady, most mothers feel the same way. You did not conceive in sin but in love. Now, the pain is passing…" She quickly took six clear quartz crystals from her medicine box and arranged them around Bathsheba's bed in a triangular formation to assist with the physical and spiritual release of the child. Knowing that the pregnancy was not a happy time for the mother with her feelings of guilt, ridicule from others, the murder of her husband and the idea that she broke the Laws of Moses all combined to take away the natural joy, Ceelyha tried her best to ensure a pure bond of love and acceptance between the mother and child. She prayed:

"Oh Great Mother, Lady of all Goddesses together,

Protect the soul of this unborn child.

Protect the mother and guide me to assist in helping this woman

To joyously give birth.

Watch over the mother as she gives entrance to the child

Watch over the child as he pushes his way into our world."

It was nearly midnight when the Goddess alerted Ceelyha that it was time for the child to make his appearance into the world. Ceelyha had the other two attendants help put Bathsheba, who was weakened by the length of the labour, on the birthing bricks. She then told Jessica to ask a nervous David, who had been hovering outside on the porch, to leave for the last part of the birthing. Ceelyha did not want to feel the added pressure of his presence at this time. She instructed Jessica to support the queen's back while Nintu held her arms. She mentally connected with Thu and together they linked with the child's soul to tell him that he was accepted and loved. Then she knelt in front of Bathsheba to coach her breathing. She softly said, "It is time to allow the birth. All you need to do is to bear down and push." As one last intense pain ripped through the queen's womb, she shrieked, past caring if the entire harem could hear her, as the child made his way into the world.

When Ceelyha held up a wriggling, crying baby boy to a relieved Bathsheba, tears of joy poured down her face. The afterbirth was quickly expelled. Jessica hugged her mistress and helped her back into bed. She and Nintu packed the queen with cloths to stop the bleeding, while Ceelyha washed and swaddled the newborn. Someone had already notified David, who had been frantically praying in his chambers to his God for the life of the mother and child. He immediately rushed to Bathsheba's side. When she held out the tiny bundle wrapped in the royal purple robe of the House of David, he took his son and raised him up to the heavens crying openly with joy and pride, "Thanks be to Yahweh, thanks be to Yahweh!" When he finally handed the child to Ceelyha, he said from the depths of his soul," Thank you, my Golden One, for bringing me the greatest joy possible. I will never forget this." He turned, kissed her cheeks then bent to his weary wife and proclaimed,

"God has forgiven us, my Beautiful One. Everything is fine now. Rest. I will be back." He smiled with such deep admiration and affection at his wife, that Ceelyha felt a tinge of regret that she had not been the one to provide David with another heir. She quickly dismissed this unworthy thought as she watched David depart to inform the entire kingdom of his new son.

After the queen suckled her child, Ceelyha had Nintu administer herbs to help her rest. Ceelyha then examined the birthing bricks. She looked carefully for crack lines to help her determine the future of the child. She was astonished that there were no faults! The only marks were the imprints of the soles of the mother's feet. Ceelyha felt a shadow pass over her and knew she was not alone. She jerked her head around. Out of the corners of her eyes, a shadowy vision manifested of a cloaked woman, reached out to grab the babe. The name 'Macaab' came to mind. She was quickly followed by a dark image of a man wearing the skins of a black goat who was zealously waving his hands above his head. Ceelyha immediately called in the protective wings of Ishtar and chanted, "Oh Ishtar, banish evil from this room! Send it to the light to be cleansed and purified!"

The images faded. It was then Ceelyha noticed Jessica watching her with curiosity. *I hope she does not ask about the bricks. I will not reveal anything to these people!* Instead, Ceelyha willed her voice to be calm as she asked, "Shall I remove these bricks or do you think your Lady would like to use them for her next birth?"

Jessica haughtily replied, "Leave them for now. I will ask my mistress when she is feeling better. I will take over. You and your attendant are free to go."

Ceelyha, furious at being dismissed like a servant from a servant, wisely said nothing. Nintu gathered their belongings and the two women were escorted through the dimly lit courtyard. Ceelyha was too exhausted to even care what the harem women said as she walked through the walled garden to a waiting sedan that would take them back to the sanctity of the Temple.

Chapter 20
The Curse

The Goddess was about to bring Her light to the Land of Israel as the Asherah priestesses assembled to pay homage to their Lady. As the women spilled into the courtyard, Ceelyha and Nintu entered the Temple gates. Thu rushed over to her exhausted friend and gave her a powerful hug filled with the potent healing energy of the Goddess. Ceelyha sighed as she accepted the surge of vibrations into her depleted body, mind and spirit then walked with Thu, while Nintu ran ahead to make sure the chamber was ready to receive the High Priestess. Ceelyha told Thu the child was born alive and from what she could tell, healthy. Thu indicated that she knew that much and waited while Ceelyha explained the condition of the bricks.

She looked horrified. "That is very bad news. The babe will surely die."

Ceelyha sadly nodded in agreement then began to recount her vision of Macaab, without revealing anything about the man in the goatskin who she assumed was Nathan. In a troubled voice she asked, "Do you think that Macaab will use her black arts to bring harm to the child?"

"I do not think we can put anything past her. Did you protect the new-born with any stones or an amulet?"

Ceelyha shook her head. "That would not have been acceptable since the mother does not believe in the power of the Goddess. All I could do was to surround the child in white light."

"What about the other women in the harem? Were any of them present at the birthing?"

"Although none was there in body, I sensed their unease, not only for themselves but also for their sons. Bathsheba is envied and even hated by most of them. The only one that helped was her servant, Jessica."

"And I suppose she carefully watched all that you did just in case you wished to injure the mother or child?"

Ceelyha hesitantly answered, "I guess so. What are you thinking Thu?"

"I just want you to make sure that what you did for the queen was impossible to fault. If it ever came back that you performed some pagan magic to harm the child, it would not go well for any of us."

Ceelyha thought about the implications of how she could easily be the scapegoat. "I shall pray to the Goddess for the child to live, and if he does not, I shall pray that the fault will not fall on me."

With a heart full of foreboding, Ceelyha had a restless sleep accompanied by terrifying dreams. In one, David's women, their faces masked as ghoulish creatures, stood over the child's bed. In another, she assisted Bathsheba to give birth to a dead rat. The final dream was of Macaab menacingly standing over Ceelyha, while directing David's sword towards her throat as she chanted in a foreign tongue. Ceelyha woke up, her body shaking with fear. Too exhausted to rise and properly pray to Ishtar for guidance, she lay in bed and requested divine assistance to interpret her nightmares. The Goddess's only response was to wrap softly Her wings around Ceelyha.

That same evening, Dilbaha took Ceelyha's place in honouring the Goddess while Ceelyha and Nintu continued to rest. Later they were eating a late supper when Thu came to check on them.

"You both look more refreshed," Thu said with relief. "I have just heard that David is preparing a feast. It will take place two days from now to celebrate the naming of the child. And apparently, he has ordered special foods for his honoured guests and cakes to be given to everyone in the city."

"I wonder if that will stop the speculation about the child being born early and who the father really is," reflected Ceelyha.

"May his God be with him on that!" was Thu's response.

Just after midday, on the fourth day of the child's life, Ceelyha received a message from the Palace that Bathsheba urgently required her assistance. A foreboding feeling accompanied the priestess as she gathered her tools and said goodbye to Thu and Nintu.

Once again Ceelyha rode through the winding streets to the Palace. A teary Jessica waited at the Palace gates. She spoke in a choked voice. "The baby is not well. He will not suckle and is feverish. The King acquired the services of a wet nurse from one of his concubines who recently gave birth, but still the child will not feed. He is getting weaker and weaker."

Ceelyha tried to suppress the news about David's fathering another child with one of his concubines while he was still her lover, but a pang of sorrow flowed through her. *He had such a secret life while we were together! I wonder about the other women with whom he had relationships. Obviously, I was not enough for him!* As she followed Jessica to the queen, she forced her mind to move away from him and to focus instead, on what she could do to help his son.

The courtyard was full of activity with women sitting outside their rooms, laughing, gossiping and enjoying the warm spring day. Eyebrows rose at the sight of the High Priestess again with a medicine box, and Ceelyha could just imagine their tongues wagging. When Jessica and Ceelyha got to the chamber, a very pale, tense Bathsheba, listlessly lay on the cushions of her reception area, holding a tiny bundle. Ceelyha was surprised at how dishevelled the queen appeared with unwashed hair pulled back into two braids which lifelessly fell against an ashen face. Her usual vibrant green eyes were dull; her cheeks shallow and her lips drawn. Ceelyha bowed and then reached for the child. She quickly noted that his healthy glow was gone. He had lost weight and his breathing was laboured.

"My Lady, your servant has told me the current condition of your son. Yet when I left, he was healthy and content at your breast."

In a feeble voice, Bathsheba replied, "At first he took my milk, but then it was as if something disagreed with him and he stopped feeding. The wet nurse got no further, so I have to assume that my milk was not the problem. There is something wrong with my son!" In between sobs she pleaded, "Please make him well. Perform whatever magic you need to. Call up your pagan Goddesses! I will not object!"

Ceelyha willed herself to remain calm as she asked, "My Lady, what does the King make of all of this?"

"Since the day before yesterday, he has been fasting and praying in front of the Ark to Yahweh. He has left strict orders that no one is to disturb him unless it is about his son."

Ceelyha thought, *David must blame himself for the child's condition. He will see this as his God's revenge for the adultery and murder of Uriah.*

Ceelyha nodded her head as if she agreed with David's decision to go into seclusion then asked, "My Lady, has the child ever been out of your sight or that of your maid's?"

"Not that I am aware of… unless Jessica left him alone with the wet nurse while I was sleeping. What do you mean? In the name of Yahweh, do you think he has been poisoned?" Bathsheba rose on her elbows from her reclining position, her expression fearful.

Ceelyha quickly answered, "I do not know. I just want to eliminate the possibility of any treachery."

Bathsheba's face clouded with alarm.

Ceelyha hastily responded, "You said yourself that you did not trust David's other wives and therefore would not have them at the birthing. Let me examine the infant for any signs of foul play."

The first thing Ceelyha did was to smell the child's breathe for traces of poison. There was nothing. She opened the tiny mouth and peered inside to see if there were any sores or cankers. Nothing was amiss. When the wrapping was removed around his emaciated hot little body, there were no visible bruises or marks. *Was this truly the act of a vengeful God or did Macaab have something to do with the sickness?* She opened her medicine box, took out some ground fenugreek seeds, mixed them with oil then gently massaged the medicine on the baby's stomach. She had Jessica fetch some hot water and honey to make a tea out of the seeds and while it steeped, she also made an infusion of peppermint leaves, which Jessica would drip from her finger into the child's mouth.

"Here," Ceelyha said to Bathsheba when the tea was ready, "drink this and then rest. In a few hours I want you to try nursing again. Jessica should continue to administer the drops to reduce your son's fever for the next hour or so. If you need me, I will come back."

Bathsheba shook her head and firmly stated, "No, Priestess. You will stay with my son and me. I want you close by until he is better."

Ceelyha did not have a choice. She had a palace servant send a message back to the Temple that she would be detained and for Dilbaha to take over for her again. As she settled back in the reception room to wait, she noted the baby never cried or fussed. Later, the mother tried nursing. The milk flowed but the child was so dehydrated that he did not seem to have the energy to suckle. They tried feeding him droplets of milk from Bathsheba's fingertip but to no avail. At one point, Ceelyha set up her small statue of the Goddess, bowed in front of it and prayed out loud in her own language with the two Hebrew women in the room.

"Oh Mother of all life

Give this child back to his mother.

Do not send him to the gates of Heaven.

Do not let his God punish him for his parents' sins.

Oh Mother, hear this plea for salvation."

Neither Bathsheba nor Jessica commented. As night fell and the mother slipped into an uneasy sleep, Ceelyha took the baby from her arms. She unwrapped the blankets and noted that there were no signs of the child having urinated. She was on the verge of invoking the Goddess's help with a healing, when a powerful message came from Ishtar. The voice resounded deeply inside her head.

"The child that is born to the one called David will not live beyond another night. The soul volunteered to come into the body of the babe to teach its parents a lesson. The body of the child was never meant to live past a few earth days. Even the evil sent by human forces to shorten the child's life span cannot alter what has been preordained."

When Ceelyha inquired as to what the lesson was for those involved in the child's life, she received the message that, if one believed he had sinned in the eyes of God and feels he must be punished, then suffering was certain to come. After Ceelyha thanked the Goddess for the information, she thought how over the years David had lessened his spiritual connection with God as he became caught up in worldly pursuits. She had done the same with her choice to become involved at an emotional level with David rather than doing her spiritual work. But at least she did not have any blood on her hands! By his son dying, Ceelyha knew that David would believe that God had forgiven him for his sin of breaking the Commandments. Then she thought, *look at me now! Here I am helping his wife with their baby because I am still not able to disconnect from him. I am truly like Ishtar trying to rescue my beloved and also I am like the people of his kingdom, unable to resist him, willing to risk everything for him.*

Just after midnight, Ceelyha sensed David's approach, before he physically arrived in the queen's chambers. He burst into the reception room startling Bathsheba out of a light sleep. Even in the dim torchlight, Ceelyha noted his wrinkled clothes, bloodshot eyes and unruly hair. He seemed to take no notice of Ceelyha as his voice boomed out, "Where is my son? Give him to me!"

Ceelyha took the child out his cot and handed him to David. Tears flowed unabashed as he rocked the tiny limp body back and forth. He spoke to no one in particular in a voice that betrayed his fear, "Nathan barged into the tabernacle and cursed me and my family! The child is as sure as dead, even as I speak."

Bathsheba sat up, her arms held out to take her son as she tearfully shrieked, "What in the name of God are you talking about? My son will live!"

With pity, David looked at his wife. "No, Bathsheba. Yahweh is punishing us for our sins against Him. He will take our firstborn, then even more punishment will fall upon my family. I begged the Lord to take my life instead of our son's but Nathan proclaimed I was to live and suffer His wrath. God sees into my soul and it," his voice weakened, "is not without darkness. I shall be at least partially redeemed in His eyes with the death of my son."

He reluctantly gave the child to Bathsheba, his face registering surprise as he finally noticed Ceelyha. Without a word, he stormed out of the chambers. Ceelyha experienced a surge of hurt that he had not spoken or acknowledged her presence then quickly reproached herself for such selfish thoughts. *I am nothing to him right now*, nor *will I be in the future. I am just someone he once loved, like all those other women in the harem, and like Bathsheba will be one day too.*

Ceelyha kept watch over the sleeping mother and child until nearly dawn. When Bathsheba woke, Ceelyha ordered Jessica to bring a meal, one that would sustain them for whatever lay ahead. When roasted lamb on a bed of millet, cheeses and grapes arrived from the palace kitchens, Ceelyha pressed Bathsheba to take nourishment for the sake of the child. While the women ate, Bathsheba questioned the priestess about her relationship with David.

With reluctance, Ceelyha answered, "What is it you wish to know?"

"I can see by your expression that you still love him. Am I right?" Bathsheba's tone of voice betrayed her jealousy.

Ceelyha saw no need for deception and answered, "Yes."

When Bathsheba sighed, Ceelyha could not tell if it was with resolve or dismay.

"You know, he talks about you a lot. He has told me how you read the oracles for him, how he made you the High Priestess and how you contacted the deceased King Saul." Her voice took on a harder almost boastful quality as she stared directly into

Ceelyha's eyes. "And did you know," her voice rose with her emotion, "that he took me to the house that the two of you shared while he thought about a solution to our predicament?"

Ceelyha felt her throat close as if to prevent her from lashing out in anger.

The Hebrew continued, "He told me how you knew that I was in his life even before it was out in the open, and how he informed you about my pregnancy and the situation with Uriah, and how you helped him solve that problem. There is nothing about our lives that you do not know!"

Ceelyha's eyes widened with surprise and her voice was somewhat shaky as she responded, "I had no idea that he had told you all those things." *What does she want from me? How am I supposed to respond to her? Is she blaming me for Uriah's death? Please Ishtar guide me to reply in the safest way possible!*

Bathsheba continued. "It was you he wanted to have with me when I was ready to give birth. He said that you were the only person that he could trust to take care of me." Her eyes narrowed to tiny slits betraying her envy, "Now, do you not think it strange that he would ask for his ex mistress to assist with his new wife's birthing?"

Ceelyha lowered her eyes to ward off the attack and prayed to the Goddess for protection before she replied, "Lady, I am the High Priestess. I am the one skilled in arts of the Goddess. He could have asked for any of his wives and concubines to assist, as I believe is the custom. But I understood from you, when you first sent for me, that they were not your choice. I did not wish to attend you for obvious personal reasons. Do you think this has been easy for me? To be here with his new wife? To see him so distraught over the child? To have the burden of his child's future lie in my hands?" She could feel her voice divulging her tension and calmed it by taking a deep breath. "But, David knows my abilities. So to answer your question, I do not think it is strange. I am in his service and must do as he commands."

"And you think that this…" Bathsheba's anger fully surfaced as her face flushed and she gestured to her room and baby, "is what I expected? I had no thoughts other than admiration for David. It was he who commanded me to come to the Palace to be with him. So, I too did just as my King told me."

That is not the full truth! You're a seductress, a woman who stops at nothing, even going to the extreme of risking death by stoning until you get what you want, thought Ceelyha. Then it struck her, the similarities between the two of them. She intentionally seduced David with her tantalizing dance then resorted to magical spells to bind him to her. In the name of the Goddess, she was no different! And she thought, *like Bathsheba, I gave up what was important in my life for David. What an extraordinary man he is to have all these people willing to risk everything for him!*

With this thought in mind, Ceelyha gently whispered, "I guess that we are very fortunate women to love and be loved by this incredible man. What you may not know is that the Goddess decreed that it was my destiny to be with David. And for a short time he was my entire world. Then you came along, and all of that changed. I hold no malice towards you as it is also your destiny to be with him."

It was now Bathsheba's turn to register surprise. "You hold no malice? In all honesty, I am envious of the times that you two spend together and how he still holds you in such high esteem."

Ceelyha sighed and spoke as if she were talking to a young child. "But, My Lady, you have him now. I do not."

"At the moment, I have nothing, only sorrow and remorse."

"I can tell you that all will change. One day, you will be exceptionally powerful and have the son you dreamed of. There is much in the future for you to look forward to."

Bathsheba sat more upright, her curiosity and vanity tweaked. "Priestess, you see this for me in your omens?'

Ceelyha nodded and carefully replied, "I believe it will happen as I said."

Bathsheba appeared to be pleased with this prediction and called for Jessica to remove the rest of the food. She no longer seemed to notice that Ceelyha was in the room and closed her eyes.

Ceelyha kept watch over the mother and child until just after dusk. On the seventh day of his short life, the baby passed away. Bathsheba, with no more tears left to shed, involuntarily handed the tiny bundle to Jessica to prepare for burial. Word was sent to the King, who did not even make an appearance to comfort his wife. Ceelyha worked to release the child's soul from its tiny body, then she quietly slipped out of Bathsheba's rooms and made her way out of the Palace with a heavy heart.

At the Temple, the priestesses had gathered in the courtyard and were just about to begin to awaken Asherah, when Ceelyha wearily passed through the Temple gates. Her downcast face portrayed the fate of the child. Thu rushed forward and hugged her friend as she guided her back to her rooms. "You look as if you have not slept since you left here. Are you alright?"

Ceelyha nodded, too numb to speak, and allowed Thu and Nintu to remove her soiled tunic and tuck her into bed. Thu administered a sleeping drought and Ceelyha fell into a dreamless sleep. She slept straight through to the next sunrise and woke with a start.

Her room was filled with the priestesses from the Temple! Led by Thu, they placed their hands just above Ceelyha's body and began to give her a healing.

Their soft high voices blended harmoniously as they chanted the ancient sounds of the Goddess and channeled Her healing energy into their High Priestess. Ceelyha felt as if she were floating on air as the aches and pains, emotional and mental stress of the past few days flowed like rivulets of water out of her body and mind. She smiled and allowed herself to drift with the celestial sounds and harmonizing energy. Layer by layer she released her pains, pleasures, tragedies and joys of the world.

Chapter 21
The Aftermath

Over the next month, the Temple buzzed with the news of David. The rumours were that while his son lived, David fasted in hopes that Yahweh would be merciful but when the baby died, David refused to observe the sacred rites of mourning. He disregarded his forefather's traditions. He did not fast for seven days, did not roll in ashes, did not shave his beard, or have professional mourners at the burial site. Instead, David returned to his politics and wars telling everyone that no matter what he did now, it would not bring the child back to life.

After the babe's burial, Michal, David's first wife, publicly announced that David was finished as King since his sins far exceeded any that her father, Saul might have had. She sided with the Benjamin tribe who demanded Bathsheba be stoned. The general population, influenced by Michal's lust for revenge, blamed their King for the poor harvest. The grain stores were empty. Many of these people, too overcome by the drought and pestilence to do no more than try and survive, turned to the Goddess's daughters to rid the land of the transgressions of their king.

The priestesses fervently prayed to Asherah to stop the dust storms, to kill the insects and to bring rain to the parched physical and spiritual Land of Israel.

For many months, the Jerusalem Temple could not keep up with the number of people lined up each morning outside the Temple Gates. Ceelyha instructed the gatekeeper to let only a few at a time into the courtyard. It was as if in times of trouble, the people turned away from David and his God, to return to the ways of their ancestors. The priestesses made poultices for sickly cows and sheep and amulets for farmers to wear. They passed blessings on all personal statues of Asherah and made remedies to prevent pregnancies, since there was not enough food to feed more children. They said prayers to end the plight of the drought, gave encouragement, healed and listened to the woes of both women and men.

One morning, Nathan, along with some petitioners appeared outside the gate, and blatantly demanded to see the head priestess. Ceelyha, who was at that time working with a man to heal an ulcerated leg, told the gatekeeper that Nathan could wait either in the courtyard or outside at the entrance. She thought that she was allowing him a concession, as he abhorred being inside the Temple grounds. When she had finished wrapping the leg with an herb soaked cloth, she went to the entrance to find him pacing back and forth. He had attracted such a large audience from both inside and outside the Temple, that the gatekeeper was having difficulty keeping order. Ceelyha noted Nathan appeared to be quite agitated. When he saw her, he stomped his staff and yelled for all to hear, "Who are you, the daughter of a pagan god, to make me wait in this heat?"

Ceelyha, cognizant of the gathering crowd curiously listening to the interchange, made a quick prayer to the Goddess for help and replied in a composed manner, "I am the High Priestess, that is who! I was administering to one of the people of your land, as is my job here at the Temple. That is why you had to wait. You could have come inside."

His beady eyes were black with rage; his nostrils contracted with disgust. In a voice that portrayed venom, he hissed, "Be warned, this is the last time that I will ever wait to be let into this pagan house of sin. Now, Priestess come out here!"

As Ceelyha, having no idea why the Levite was upset, stepped beyond the Temple into the street, she recalled her dream of the man in the goatskin gibbering in a strange language. As she came closer, she was shocked at the alteration of his appearance. His cheeks appeared more hollow, his skin more leathered and his eyes burned with an unnatural brightness. She could not tell if he was in touch with his god or if fanatical thoughts just made him look so fervent. She nodded her head as a sign of respect but refused to bow before him. He ignored her salutation, motioned for her to come closer and grabbed her arm. He roughly led her away from prying eyes and listening ears to stand under the partial shade of a palm tree. Ceelyha felt fear creeping slowly up her spine as she waited for him to speak.

"David has disgraced the nation and the entire House of David. Someone must pay for this! In their confusion, the people are turning to the old ways, the ways of evil!" he ranted.

Ceelyha sensed the wings of Ishtar surround her. This was a dangerous man; she needed to keep her wits about her.

In an even tone she replied, "How would you have me help the situation, Nathan?"

"Close your gates before I do!" he retorted ramming his staff on the ground as if to make his point more relevant.

Ceelyha's pulse raced. How could he tell her to do this? The Temple was not under his jurisdiction; it fell under the authority of the King. She carefully chose her words before speaking. "Nathan, under whose authority do you request this? The King has not ordered me to close the Temple."

" David no longer has any authority!" He spat out each word to emphasize its importance. "The Lord has spoken. Now, send these people home to pray to Yahweh for help. Do it, Priestess, or suffer the consequences!"

Before Ceelyha could respond, he stalked angrily into the crowd with his staff held high above his head yelling, "In the name of the Lord, throw away your idola-trous worship before Yahweh sends more disasters upon you! The King's son, Absalom, is already gathering his troops to take over the City of David."

Some of the crowd dispersed while a few people stood nervously outside the entrance. Ceelyha was in a quandary. *If I close the Temple, I concede to the Levites. Surely Absalom cannot take over the city and even if he did, he might not harm us since his mother, Macaab, relies on our magic to help him! Until David brings the people back to his side, and I know with his charismatic powers that he will, Asherah is needed. Unless I receive direct orders from David to shut the Temple, I will carry on as usual.*

Fortified by the logic behind these thoughts, Ceelyha slowly entered through the gate then turned to face the loyal petitioners. In a loud voice so all could hear, she announced, "If any of you are in desperate need of assistance today, then you will be seen. If your questions or issues are not pressing, then please return tomorrow. We will only see those that are the neediest today." She motioned for the gatekeeper to let any of the few remaining people into the courtyard.

Just after evening rituals, Ceelyha called all the temple dwellers – the cooks, servants, priestesses and gatekeepers – to relay what had happened. She warned that the status of the Temple might change if David did not take back control soon. She advised that their personal safety was in jeopardy and that caution, needed to be exercised around petitioners' requests. She counseled the priestesses to administer only to people whom they had previously treated. If any type of remedies or potions were requested, anything other than healing, they were to notify her immediately. Then she added, "These are trying times. We may be blamed for using black arts or for causing a religious and political upheaval. We shall go about doing the Goddess's work as best we can but restrict the use of magic. No divination for the time being."

Ceelyha sensed the temple dwellers needed time to talk freely, without her presence, so she left for her chambers. Even after that miraculous healing that the priestesses had so generously given her on the day when she returned from the Palace, she felt the pressures from the outside world cloaked about her. She desperately needed time alone to release her fears to the Goddess. The responsibility of Asherah's followers and Her daughters, lay in her hands. She was very aware that her emotions had become entangled with her thoughts. She prayed,

"Please, Lady of the Snakes, Lady of the Moon, Mother of all that is,

Project Your light on this situation. Guide me in the highest and best way to protect all Your Children.

Let Your strength take the place of my weakness. Take away my fear.

I chose not to be victim of the enemies of the House of David.

Grant us a miracle. I will be Your light."

Nintu later found her mistress meditating in front of the Ishtar statue. Ceelyha looked up and managed a weak smile. "Nintu, you and I took on a heavy burden when we came to this land. We could be back in The Land of Two Rivers enjoying a pampered life, but, instead, we are here among barbarians whose priests do not believe in the light of the Goddess. I am afraid for all of us. Nathan will act without David's approval or knowledge. I must get a message to David."

For months Nintu had been a ghost of her former self. Now she suddenly appeared to be more talkative and animated as she responded with, "My Lady, if we had not come here, we both would have missed the biggest loves of our lives. I, for one, would not have traded that even if it is the death of me."

With a sigh, Ceelyha agreed. "My life would not have been as blessed without David. You, my friend, are wiser than I…"

She was interrupted by a hysterical Dilbaha, who appeared at the door of Ceelyha's chamber screaming, "The snakes, the snakes are gone! The basket is empty! It is a sign from the Goddess! Asherah has deserted us!"

Ceelyha tried to calm the older woman by asking what had happened. Between sobs she learned that the snakes had been in their basket in the morning but when Dilbaha went to feed them just after dark, they were gone, even though the lid still was secured. Dilbaha had already searched her rooms and the corridors so Ceelyha asked Nintu to alert the others to fully search the entire Temple.

When Thu heard the news, she rushed to Ceelyha's room. "I think we had better find those missing snakes or there will be bedlam! The rumours are already spreading among the priestesses that Asherah is not pleased with us. They are saying that if we do not do the Goddess's work, we will all suffer Her wrath."

"Have the serpents ever escaped before?"

"Not in the time that I have been here. And it is too dark now to do a full scale search."

Ceelyha thought for a moment and then said, "Fine, we shall use the scrying bowl in your room to see if the Goddess will allow us to track them. I shall fetch Dilbaha and bring her."

She ordered Nintu to assist Thu with the brazier.

In the dim light of the courtyard, Ceelyha found a frantic Dilbaha searching under benches and trees. Ceelyha gently touched her arm to send healing energy to the distressed older woman, and then asked whether anyone had access to her rooms during the day. As the two priestesses hurried to Thu's room, Dilbaha replied that it could be anyone who worked in the Temple.

The sweet scent of myrrh smoked on the brazier. Thu motioned for the women to move closer to the scrying bowl and said a prayer of invocation to Isis.

"Oh Isis, Lady of divine wisdom and light,

Daughter of Nut, Beloved of Osiris,

Clear my sight and assist me to see through your all-seeing eyes

The serpents of the Goddess are missing,

Please allow us to see where they have gone.

Praise be to You, Isis, Lady of Light."

Thu nodded to indicate that she was connected to Isis; her eyes sparkled and were almost luminescent as she removed the black cloth that protected the scrying bowl. Ceelyha and Dilbaha each said short prayers to link into their respective Goddesses' energy and willed their minds to become empty vessels-open channels through which divination could flow. The combined powers of the women soon had the smooth surface of the water rippling. A white mist began to form. After the vapour cleared and the water settled, they peered into the bowl to read the fate of the snakes. From the depths of the water, two swirling shadows formed. The women gasped as the serpents, held by two large hairy hands, frantically darted their fangs in and out. Then the divination changed to display a sackcloth bag, before ripples began to spread across the smooth surface of the water. No one dared to speak for several minutes in case the Goddesses wished to reveal more information. Finally Ceelyha broke the silence by whispering, "By the appearance of those hands, it was definitely a male who took the snakes!" She turned to Dilbaha and thoughtfully said, "I believe the only male that has access to the Temple is our gatekeeper, and he is not allowed beyond the courtyard."

Dilbaha shook her head and replied, "No, it is not Kassja, I have known him since he was a young boy. He would never betray us!"

Thu, still connected to the energy of Isis, said in a loud powerful voice, "He was sent by the one who wishes to harm you. Take heed my daughters and be careful." The voice stopped as Thu released Her energy.

The women looked in astonishment at one another. Thu, the first to speak said, "It seems that Nathan staged quite a distraction when he came to visit. I think that while everyone was watching his antics, someone portraying himself as a petitioner must have slipped in and taken the snakes."

Ceelyha responded with "But how did he know it was Dilbaha who kept the snakes and not me? That really is my job."

Thu asked, "Who else knew about your aversion to snakes?"

"David, of course, but no one else." Then it hit her. "In the name of the Goddess, he must have told Bathsheba! She said he talked about me all the time and maybe that was revealed!" She sat down on a nearby stool, overcome with the realisation her Temple was in grave danger.

Thu answered, "It could be any of his wives and not just Bathsheba. Do not forget your incident with Maacab."

More to herself than out loud, Ceelyha muttered, " Oh my! Why would anyone want to cause trouble for us?"

"Because you know too much and are too connected to David, " Thu replied then she paused as if searching for the rest of her thoughts, "That must mean that Nathan has become quite close to one of David's wives. It could be Michal,

Bathsheba, Macaab…any of them. Whomever it is, the two of them must be plotting against you!"

"What shall we do?" The severity of the situation was increasing.

Dilbaha said, "First, I will end the search, then tell the others what we suspect has happened. That will at least bring a semblance of calm among our priestesses."

Ceelyha nodded in agreement. Then she recalled her earlier need to send a message to David. "Nintu, see that David receives the message that I must speak with him." She turned to Thu. "I want to consult the Goddess as to what our next step should be. In the meantime, tell the others that we will carry on seeing petitioners." Her voice faltered, " I do not know what else to do until I hear from David."

Thu agreed, and as Ceelyha went back to her chambers to meditate and pray, she recalled the restless sleep images that had come to her after the death of David's child. Not only had the Goddess shown her Macaab but also the goatskin man who she now recognised as Nathan. *In the name of the Goddess, she did try to warn me but I did not see the signals!* Later that night, she had a dream similar to the one she had before but instead of Macaab holding the sword, it was Nathan with Bathsheba at his side. She woke up, got out of bed to prostrate before the Goddess.

"Oh Great Ishtar, Lady of the Night,

Blessed are those whom You watch over.

Please assist me to see the message in this dream.

Give me Your divine guidance.

Protect me from evil.

Great power of Ishtar, be with me now."

Ceelyha waited. When Ishtar's divine presence flowed throughout her body, Ceelyha was able to sense Her golden light of love. Her ears buzzed and vision blurred as she expanded upward and outward. She heard Her voice clearly from somewhere deep inside the recesses of her mind.

"Daughter of Light, Daughter of Love, your time here is almost spent. You have fulfilled your destiny. You will soon be coming home, my Priestess."

The warmth and light ceased leaving Ceelyha shaking and bewildered. *My time is up? Does that mean here in Israel, or will I be going to home to Babylon or to the world of spirit?*

There was no way that sleep would come, so Ceelyha got up, quietly dressed so as not to disturb Nintu and went into the empty courtyard. A chill in the air caused her to clutch her mantle close as she gazed up at the brightly twinkling stars in the direction of Babylon. *I wonder if my mother is staring at these same stars*, she pondered. She had not thought about Shiroka for some time. *Does she know that my time is near to either come home or to leave this plane of existence? Mother had said we would not meet again in this life, but I cannot be certain of that. Either way, I shall look forward to seeing her shortly. Whatever the Goddess has in store for me, I will face it with the grace and dignity of an Entu.* Try as she might, Ceelyha could not rise out of her body to travel to Shiroka. Somewhat distressed, she went back to her chamber to prepare for the approaching day.

Two days later, and still no word from David, Ceelyha began to wonder if he had ever received the message, of if he was too involved with his own issues to care one way or another what happened to the Temple. *I find it hard to understand how he could not be concerned about the Asherah priestesses. We have never done anything that would have jeopardized him.* When news finally arrived that his tribesmen in the south had declared Absalom as the new King, she understood that David had long since fled Jerusalem and now the chances of his ever getting her request were very slim. It seemed that Macaab's magic had finally paid off.

In the days following the threat from Nathan, the priestesses were very cautious and particular about whom they treated. The number of petitioners had definitely diminished; it appeared the people were listening more to their prophet than to their Goddess. When a woman inquired as to what herbs would abort a pregnancy, Ceelyha was alerted. She approached the woman who immediately changed her story to wanting to be with child and not aborting a pregnancy. Ceelyha had her escorted from the Temple as quickly as possible. Another man demanded that he see the High Priestess because he wanted the omens read by the person in command. Ceelyha listened carefully to his request to try and ascertain if it were a ploy on Nathan's behalf. The man wanted to know if his wife was possessed by demonic influences. According to him, she would rant and rave while talking to unseen beings. Ceelyha purposely gave him no advice but instead asked that the wife be brought to the Temple for treatment. The man promised that he would bring her the next day, but he never returned. It seemed that Nathan was testing them.

A few days later, a group of Levite priests arrived in the early morning and blocked a few brave petitioners from entering the Temple. They lectured to any listening ears that it was against the Laws of Moses to worship or come before idols. Any who disobeyed would be punished by Yahweh. Ceelyha heard and watched all that went on. She ordered the priestesses not to leave the confines of the Temple and to pray to Asherah for guidance.

Since the workers were still upset about the stolen snakes, Ceelyha decided to accept the High Priestess Dinah's generous proposal of help that she had offered, so many years ago, when Ceelyha left Dor. She sent a priestess and a guide to the Temple of Dor for the purpose of bringing back a pair of snakes to increase the dwindling morale of her priestesses.

At last, Ceelyha received a verbal message from her gatekeeper that someone from the Palace had replied to her request. David, who was not able to come himself, wanted the Temple to remain open. The message also said that Nathan and the priests would not interfere with the priestesses' work. Initially Ceelyha was apprehensive about the validity of the message thinking it odd that David did not write the message or have the messenger tell her personally, but then reasoned that since things had changed so much between them, anything was possible. She ordered the gates open but only a handful of people sought help; the rest were too intimidated by the words of the Levite priests to openly seek the Goddess.

The priestesses, under a heavy cloud of despair, went about their duties as best they could. They wished that their sister would soon return with a new pair of snakes, so the Goddess would be appeased. Ceelyha knew that serpents would not resolve the situation as the entire country was in a political upheaval. When Thu finally suggested that Ceelyha consult the oracles to find out the fate of their Temple, everyone was in agreement. There would be a full moon shortly, so Ceelyha asked Nintu to make the arrangements. She then fasted to ensure that she was pure enough to read the oracles accurately. On the night she was to divine, Dilbaha took over the evening ritual to allow Ceelyha time to have a ceremonial bath and to meditate. Even though she felt she already knew the outcome, it was important to clear her mind and be a clear and perfect channel. As she stilled her mind, she was swept away by a maelstrom of energy that she could not control. Her spirit soared upward through the dull gray walls of the Temple, higher and higher into the realms of magic. She willed herself to find Shiroka and once again found herself within the confines of her mother's chambers. This time Shiroka was not at prayer but was being attended to by a young serving girl who was busy braiding her mistress's hair. Heartache descended on Ceelyha's chest when she saw how much her mother had aged. Gone was the lustrous black hair, replaced with dulling strands of gray. No longer did she sit tall and erect, her shoulders now rounded as if she carried a heavy burden. Her face sported several wrinkles and her eyes lacked their usual brightness. Not wishing to dwell on things that were out of her control, Ceelyha glanced around her surroundings. The chamber was in disarray with open cosmetic pots and robes of various colours and styles slung carelessly over stools and tables. *She must be preparing for a festival of some sort.* Then it struck her, this was the end of the period of mourning for Tammuz! Ishtar annually mourned the loss of Her beloved and tonight would be the reenactment of the Goddess finding Tammuz in the Land of No Return. The head Entu, her mother would be leading the lamenting then the celebratory resurrection. Shiroka must have become aware of her daughter as she hastily dismissed her servant who was not nearly done her task. She went over to the replica of Ishtar in the niche of her chamber and knelt down in front of the Lady. Ceelyha sensed she was praying to get a stronger link to enable communication. She was not sure if her mother spoke aloud or if it was through the magic of thought but she heard, "Welcome my daughter. I have been expecting you."

Ceelyha telepathically willed her thought; *I have tried before Mother but have been blocked from connecting with you.*

"Perhaps you were to figure things out on your own and that is why you were blocked."

I need your strength Mother and the combined energy of the entire priesthood to save my sisters and the Goddess's Holy House. Can you please all pray for us?

"Ask and it is done. Are you all right? Is there anything else I can do for you…"

The conversation ceased as Ceelyha was thrust back into the world of time and space. But she was not displeased because she knew she could count on her Babylonian sisters to send energy and healing light to the Temple of Asherah's inhabitants. This knowledge relieved some of her burden. She profusely thanked the Goddess for allowing the contact with Shiroka then tried to silence her thoughts.

Later that night when the moon was full, the three women gathered in the small cell with the lit brazier. Ceelyha discussed what information they wished to find out before she began her invocation. Her chants reverberated off the stonewalls as she went deeper and deeper into the depths of trance. The brazier sizzled and crackled with the holy herbs that Nintu sprinkled. After the fire began to smoke, misty forms and shapes leapt up to the ceiling. Ceelyha felt the doorway open between her two worlds, and in a deep voice began to speak.

"There is trouble brewing. A thin man in an animal skin is frantically dancing around a fire in the dead of night. He is working himself into a frenzy, trying to contact a higher power."

Ceelyha stopped and Nintu quickly threw more hyssop onto the coals. It hissed and crackled as another image formed. " He is consorting with a woman. It is a woman who…her face is covered by a thick veil…a black cloak hides a multitude of sins… They have been collaborating and have made a bargain."

Nintu again repeated her administrations.

"When the son of David takes the throne, The Temple of Asherah will crumble! The entire building is about to be destroyed… Wait… the Temple dwellers are fleeing! There is fear and sorrow in their faces."

Nintu did not know if she should continue feeding the fire but Thu nodded and she went ahead.

When the next image formed, Ceelyha wrapped her hands around her own throat then screamed with pain. The walls in the tiny room seemed to breathe with fear. Thu started to come to her rescue until Nintu gestured for her to stop. Then as suddenly as the screams began, they ceased. A calm, composed voice spoke. "The child of Ishtar will take the sword to free the House of David and the Temple of Asherah." The brazier extinguished itself in a large puff of smoke and Ceelyha slumped listlessly on the stone floor. Nintu rushed over to her mistress and began to stroke her hands to enable a full release of the Goddess's energy. When Ceelyha opened her eyes and noticed droplets of smeared blood on the palms of her hands she cried, "What is this? Did I hurt myself?" She looked at her two friends whose faces registered fear and dread. She immediately sat up and demanded to know what had happened.

Nintu, reluctant to speak, looked to Thu to explain. In an unstable voice full of emotion, Thu related what had taken place. When she finished, Thu said, "So, it seems that Nathan and a woman who might be Bathsheba or any of David's women are in this together. They both want you and the Temple destroyed. But, it seems the Temple will remain until the future son of David has it demolished. The blood is a definite sign from the Goddess that harm will come to you!"

In a shaky voice with more courage than she felt, Ceelyha responded, "It seems that I am to be the scapegoat. I have known about this for quite a while. Did either of you think that the Goddess would not have forewarned me? But I am still not any clearer on the outcome of the Temple." Ceelyha hugged her two devoted friends and expressed her gratitude for their loyalty and companionship. "Without the two of you, none of this would be bearable. But, I am confident that when the time is right, all will be as it should be."

The three women continued to hold each other.

Chapter 22

Destiny

Nathan met Ceelyha at the Temple entrance with a cruel sneer and announced in a powerful booming voice for all to hear, "Against my orders, you have opened your Temple of sin! By Israeli law, I declare you a witch! You came here from a foreign Godless country to wile your evil ways. You have used pagan magic to abort children and prevent natural conception in our women! You heal the sick with herbs and stones. You consort with the devil to cast omens and you bring back the dead to speak as if they were the living. You use your evil spells to bind a man and woman together with potions. You even killed the child of Bathsheba by casting an evil spell upon it. You were heard to pray in a foreign tongue to your pagan God! You destroyed an innocent woman, the Queen Macaab, with your accusations of treachery and witchcraft! You put David under your enchantment and made him write the orders to have Uriah killed! You are a seductress and fortune hunter who deliberately cast a spell on the King to make him fall under your powers. Because he consorted with a pagan priestess, David has brought pestilence, famine and war to the Land of Israel! Lady, there is nothing in your life that the Lord and I do not know about! And all those that dwell within these walls shall perish along with you. Gone are the pagan ways! The only God is Yahweh! You and your witches will be stoned!"

Ceelyha's mouth went dry, her throat was blocked and her bowels loosened. So this was the Goddess's message! Her time was done on earth; she would not be returning to Babylon! By sentencing her to death, Nathan would entirely wipe out the worship of Asherah in this city. And, since this was the heart of Israel, the other Temples would soon meet a similar fate. *But sentencing all the priestesses to death because of the jealousy of Bathsheba and Nathan's need to have a scapegoat for David's sins, that is going too far! My religious sect is being blamed for all the woes of the House of David and the current state of the land of Israel! With my death and the destruction of the Temple, David will be back in favour because I will take the blame for his sins. My life will be sacrificed in order to free him. There is no way the Goddess can undo this but it is not fair that my sisters should suffer because of my so-called sins.* She recalled her mother's advice to never become powerless in times of adversity. She had too much pride to allow one such as Nathan to intimidate the daughter of an Entu and King! This last thought gave her strength. Her throat opened and her voice rang out with authority, "You may accuse me of whatever you wish. But I know the truth as does David, the Goddess and your God as well. As The Temple of Asherah's appointed High Priestess, I will strike a bargain with you. I will confess to your outrageous accusations of witchcraft if you allow my Temple workers to live. They were not David's lovers, I was. They did not attend the birthing and death of Bathsheba's son, I did. They did not make the potions for love nor the remedies to abort unwanted babies. They are not to blame.

Take my life instead of theirs, otherwise I will make public to your queen Michal, to the court and the general population, every minute detail that David has revealed to me about his relationship with God, his wives, his political views, his ambitions and how you Nathan have consorted against him."

It was obvious to Ceelyha that Nathan had not anticipated her response as his face registered surprise. He dramatically rolled his eyes upwards as if to show Ceelyha that he was consulting his God but she could see right through him. He wanted to take her place in advising David. As long as she was still around, Nathan and the priesthood would never have enough power over the King and the people.

After a few minutes of silence, Nathan ruthlessly glared at her. "Yes, I will consider this deal of which you speak – your life for the crimes of witchcraft. I will also allow the others to disperse to their respective homelands or villages."

Ceelyha looked into his beady eyes and proclaimed, "As an assurance that you will keep your word, be advised that I have been scribing all the events of the past few years – all the intimate details of my times with David. And," she paused for affect. "I know all his secrets. So, if one single priestess is harmed, it shall be released."

Nathan took his time as if he needed to create more drama for the watching crowd. He raised his staff above and his head as he agreed. "You have until the first quarter moon to get your affairs in order and to send your priestesses away from this den of iniquity. The public stoning will take place after that."

Ceelyha bowed in mock courtesy and watched as the little man turned and marched victoriously into the crowded street. She tried to walk back into the court-yard with as much grace and dignity as possible, weakly smiling at the gatekeeper and those who had gathered at the beginning of the commotion. She could tell by the shock and dread that registered on their faces that not only had they heard the fate of herself, but the entire Temple. Someone must have alerted Thu and Nintu since they rushed to meet her. She clung to their arms and let them lead her back to her chamber. They listened with grief and horror as she relayed all that Nathan had said. Nintu began to cry. Thu was stoically silent until Ceelyha asked her to take Nintu under her protection and asked that she keep in touch with Miriam concerning her daughter Bernice – Ceelyha needed to honour Miriam's request to have her daughter trained as a priestess – then, Thu burst into tears. She could hardly answer Ceelyha when asked if she would go back to Egypt.

It took several moments for the priestess to collect her emotions and then she answered with sadness, "Yes, I suppose I could return to my country but I would rather not. This is really the only home that I have known. I will need to think on this." She fell into silence and then declared, "It is of utmost importance and urgency that we get a message to David immediately. I, myself shall go to the Palace to try to find out where he is."

Ceelyha shook her head. "Thu, you witnessed the divination, David cannot stop what is about to happen." Then she felt lighter as she said, "But he may be able to save the Temple! I did not think of that. Yes, hurry and get the message to him!"

Later that day, a tearful Dilbaha came to Ceelyha. In an apologetic voice she haltingly spoke. "High Priestess, the others are fearful. Some of them want to take up swords and fight Nathan and Absolum's soldiers. Others want to flee. You must tell them what to do!"

"Tell them?" Ceelyha was upset. "Do you think my magic is so powerful that all I have to do is invoke the Goddess to save us all?"

"You are the Head Priestess. You are our leader, chosen by the King himself. Now is your chance to prove it! The rest of us may not have the same training or background as you but we do know that fear and hopelessness is ruling over our spirits!

Of course these women would not have the same faith in the working of the Goddess that I have. I had forgotten that. They do not know how I am praying for their safety and trying to figure out how to assure this. She weakly smiled at the older priestess and replied, "Of course, I was intending to speak with them at the evening meal but gather everyone together now, including all the workers."

Dilbaha quickly gathered the Temple dwellers together in the courtyard. The priestesses cried and pleaded with Ceelyha not to sacrifice her life for theirs. Dilbaha spoke for all of them when she said, "If anyone is to die, let it be the entire Temple population rather than one person. You will not die alone to save us. We are in this together." Then she added as if to make a final plea, "Many of us have no other place to go."

Ceelyha had anticipated this response and answered, "The Goddess has decreed that only I shall die, as is my destiny, while the rest of you shall carry on with Her work. Dispatches have already been sent to Dinah in Dor and Adah in Jezreel. Room will be made at these temples for any who wish to go. The servants will also find employment in these locations as well. But I urge any of you who wish to, return to your homes. Times are changing, and I fear for the future of all priestesses of Asherah in this land." Ceelyha mournfully hung her head and walked away from the assembled group. There was nothing more she could say or do. She could not tell them what the future would hold, but from her divination, it would not go well for the followers of the Goddess.

Thu was able to find out that David was at Gilead. Since there was no one in the city that she could trust she dispatched Kassja, the Gatekeeper to deliver the plea from Ceelyha. She returned with the latest news that Absalom's troops would soon have the city surrounded and those within the walls would be unable to leave. It gave little time for some of the serving girls to return to their family homes, the younger priestesses to go back to their villages and some of the others to travel to the temples at Dor and Jezreel where they could continue bringing the Goddess's healing light and energy to those who sought Her wisdom. Just five priestesses chose to wait with Ceelyha to see if the Temple would remain open, Dilbaha included. They were hopeful that the King would receive Ceelyha's message and save the Temple. They also secretly prayed that David would return and save their High Priestess from the sentence of death before the next phase of the moon.

It was decided that in the intern, Ceelyha would move into the house that she and David had shared. Thu would go with her. Nintu went ahead to see if they would be welcomed there. She returned with the message that there were only a couple of staff left but they had received long standing orders from David that the house still belonged to the Priestess and she would be welcomed there anytime. Dilbaha and the remaining priestesses would stay at the Temple and let Ceelyha know if anything changed. Ceelyha made the remaining priestesses promise to take immediate refuge at the house if there was any trouble.

The house was the welcoming oasis that Ceelyha remembered. In the courtyard, almond trees were in full bloom, their scent blending with the heady aroma of eucalyptus balm. The fountain still sprayed its cooling waters on the mosaic tiles. It seemed like ages rather than two years since she had last been there. So much of her life and David's had changed but the house remained as it was. The reception room still had the golden goblets resting on a silver tray. The divans and cushions were in their usual place. The brazier was lit. Upstairs the sight of the large bed on the dais brought tears to Ceelyha's eyes, as overwhelming memories of all the passionate times she and David had shared flooded her thoughts. She lay down on the richness of the deep blue cover and absentmindedly fingered her mother's necklace. *I could take this apart, or even better, the amber jewels that David gave me, sell them and escape to Babylon. There, I would be safe from the Levites and the jealously of David's women.* Immediately she reproached herself. *If I tried to do that, then I would not be fulfilling my destiny. The Goddess has decreed that I will end my life here in the Land of the Israelis.* She got up and entered the room that Nintu had so long ago arranged as a shrine. She approached and knelt before the statue of the Goddess. *I have spent all my life as a priestess and have never once questioned the decisions or ways of the Goddess. To run away would truly be blasphemy. Here I am at the age of twenty and one, I have known riches, power, glory and love. I have lived a full life. Soon I will rejoin my Goddess and be released from my physical body and truly become a spiritual being once more. Then I will not have to endure the pain for a love that was lost.*

When she felt ready, Ceelyha rose from her knees, thankful that the women had left her to her own thoughts. She called Nintu and Thu who both came running up the stairs. Ceelyha led them up to the roof and all three of them looked down at the twinkling lights of the houses on the hills below. Ceelyha breathed in the night air as she checked to see the exact phase of the rising moon. She then turned to her faithful servant. From the folds of her dress, she produced a parchment scroll. "Nintu, I want you to take this and hide it somewhere. It is a journal of my life with David. It holds his secrets and mine. If Nathan threatens to destroy the Temple or any of its occupants, then you must produce it. The information in here will save the rest of you."

Nintu began to weep uncontrollably. "My Lady, let us flee from this barbarian land. We can go back home or even to Egypt. Thu has already looked into our passage. Come this night and the three of us will go!"

Ceelyha smiled as one might when a small child does not understand. "No, my friend. I have already thought of that but that would mean instant death to those left at the Temple. I bargained my life for theirs." She reached out and stroked Nintu's face while looking directly at Thu. "Besides, I cannot undo what has already been decided. Surely, you both know that."

Thu sadly nodded her head in agreement then reached out to embrace her friend. With a shaky voice she said, "I have never known a bond of friendship as deep as ours. I know with all my soul that we shall meet in the afterlife and come back to this world together. As we have shared before, we will again. I will inform your mother of your circumstances. Actually, Nintu and I have been discussing what we will do when you are gone. We may go to Babylon then onto Egypt if that is agreeable with you."

Ceelyha smiled for the first time in days. "I would be so happy if you did that!" she cried with enthusiasm. Then her joy ended as she added, "I fear that the time for the Goddess worship in this land is over." She recalled her vision of the Temple crumbling and the fear and sorrow in the dweller's faces. Although she had no idea how far in the future that catastrophe might take place, at least she could save the priestesses currently residing there. Her tone was urgent, "You must go and take the others with you. Here," she removed and then her mother's necklace to Thu. "Take this and the amulet which David gave me. Sell them! Secure the passages for all the Temple daughters. I can now die in peace knowing that my responsibilities for the others and my friends are fulfilled."

She suddenly felt joy in her heart, as if a weight had been lifted. Her fears dissolved as a surge of love ran through her. The Goddess had descended, pleased with Ceelyha's acceptance. In the darkness of the night, she saw the faces of her friends glow with a beautiful radiance and knew she was being allowed the privilege of seeing their true selves. She silently thanked the Goddess as Her energy was released. "Come, Nintu, I want to be in my most dazzling robes when my time comes. Order the servants to bring hot water!"

In the early dawn, when the others had finally drifted into sleep, Ceelyha sat on a bench in the courtyard garden dressed in the royal blue garments of an Entu. She wore all her jewellery: the pewter snake armband, the sparking gold diadem, jewel encrusted sandals, the various gifts of rings, anklets and bracelets from her initial initiation rite in Babylon and the Goddess necklace that Thu had promised to take later. It had been a long night, one without sleep. David's face kept appearing each time she tried to close her eyes. His eyes were like dark pools of murky water, a strange combination of fear and regret. She had reached out to touch his face. His beard was as she always remembered, perfectly waxed and scented like the outdoors. She thought she heard his husky sensuous voice pleading over and over, "Forgive me my Golden One, and forgive me." Then other sounds interfered, the evil laugh of Macaab, the crying of Bathsheba, the foreign tongue of Nathan, the sarcasm of her father and the weeping of her mother. It had been a horrible past few hours. She prayed aloud in hopes of clearing her thoughts,

"Ishtar, Lady of Life, Mother of All Goddesses

Bestow Your gifts upon me.

Allow the morning sun to warm my shivering body and weary soul."

She sensed, rather than heard someone approaching. She anxiously clutched her mother's necklace, the Goddess's seal of protection. For reassurance of her priestess status, she deftly felt for the coiled serpent armband. These possessions seem to give her courage to deal with whatever was in store for her. She let out a sigh of relief as Nintu came around the corner of the house, her arms spread open to embrace.

"Oh, Lady Ceelyha. Here you are! I have been looking all over for you. I told you not to let me fall asleep!"

Nintu lowered herself onto the stone bench beside her mistress and folded Ceelyha into her embrace. Memories flooded the minds of both women- playing at the Temple, the festivals of Marduk, the sedan rides in the Land of Two Rivers, the caravan trip on camels across the desert, the slaughtering at the oasis, the Temple of Dor, the trip to Jerusalem, the love of their respective men and the loss of Nintu's child. This would be the last time in this lifetime that they would share together.

When Nintu finally released Ceelyha, she murmured through the mist of her tears, "Oh, Lady, won't you change your mind and flee with us? Or at least take a draught so you do not feel the pain of the stones as they hit you."

With a sad sigh and a voice devoid of emotion, Ceelyha answered, "Nintu, we have been over that before. I will face what has been preordained. You...."

Scuffling noises and voices came from the direction of the street. Horses neighed; a sleepy servant opened the gate. Two soldiers rushed in, upsetting the serenity and peacefulness of the courtyard. One yelled, "Beniah, there she is!'

Both women sat transfixed as the larger of the two approached with his drawn sword flashing in the rising light of the sun. Before Ceelyha could even react, she felt its cold iron pierce the skin of her throat. A pain struck like none ever she had experienced before. She could not breathe. Then a surge of power began to course through her, one that overcame the physical pain. She was aware of rivulets of blood pouring out over her neck, covering the Goddess's necklace, dripping between her fingers and saturating her gown. She thought that she heard what sounded like David's voice saying, " Forgive me, my Golden One. I could not save you

220

from death, but the least I could do was to rescue you from the humiliation of stoning. Forgive me, my Golden One. Forgive me."

The screams that surrounded her might have been of her own making or Nintu's. It did not matter as she sensed a luminous energy field, flowing and moving like a fountain of light separate her eternal soul from her body. She was no longer attached to the crumbled form that lay in a pool of red on the mosaic tiles! She had freedom of body and spirit with no ties to the world of form! She knew she should comfort a hysterical Nintu who was stooped over her lifeless form but she was being pulled away. The next thing she knew, she soared like a falcon, higher and higher over the aquamarine sea outside the Temple of Dor. The thought that the Goddess had indicated, so very long ago, that she would see this water again crossed her mind. The panoramic view ended as her essence sought out Dinah whom she found at the foot of the Asherah Pole saying, "Let the Goddess take you, let Her lead the way. Be thankful you are in Her hands."

Ceelyha's spirit swooped down and kissed the kind priestess on the cheek. She sensed her time was running out and quickly sought Shiroka. On her way, she willed herself to pass through the Sacred Passageway of the Ishtar Gates. She marveled at its lapis and gold designs of bulls and dragons before finding her mother in one of the gardens of the Marduk Temple. She was clutching her throat whiles tears streamed down her face. Ceelyha knew she had felt her death and quickly sent her the message, "I am not in pain. I will be waiting for you, my dearly loved mother, when your time comes." Then she was whisked away by an intense need to see David for one last time. He was in the hills outside of Gilead looking tired and disheveled, his face streaked with tears as he knelt in prayer. She noted his robe was rent in several places and intuited he had done that in respect for her death. He kept repeating over and over, "I am sorry, My Golden One."

Ceelyha knelt beside him and whispered, " Thank you for sparing me death by stoning. Be happy for what we had! Love is the closest possible feeling to divinity on this plane of existence. It aroused the mystical energies in both of us. We worked out what the Goddess wanted. It was meant to be, my beloved. We shall meet again." She wanted to linger but was distracted by a bridge of light, in brilliant sparkling unearthly hues, that magically appeared before her. As her spirit gravitated towards it, half way across, she could make out a figure beckoning her to approach. It was Bernice, glowing with the same radiant gold as the Goddess! She was waiting to guide her across to the other side! She immediately floated over to her and became bathed in a golden light of love. Further along, her father was approaching, shimmering with less intensity than Bernice, with his arms stretched out. She sensed a lightening of her soul as she forgave him for not being more of a father. Then others joined him; the woman from the desert who she tried to bring back to life, people from the past and people she did not recognize but somehow knew. Behind them was a light so sparkling and luminescent in its golden glow that she knew it could only be the Goddess. She felt her mind; emotions and soul alter with its frequencies; then an ageless, voice full of wisdom and unconditional love spoke, "Welcome home Ceelyha, my daughter of light. You have met your fate with your eyes wide open. You have fulfilled your destiny."

Also written by Catherine Bowman

Crystal Awareness - *Over 200,000 copies sold, printed in 12 languages*
ISBN 0-87452-058-3
This book gives you all the scientific and spiritual information you need in order to work with crystals for yourself and helping others. Scientifically, you'll learn what crystals are and how they are made. You'll learn the differences in their shapes and what causes some crystals to be colored or have inclusions. The book describes what happens when the energy fields of human and crystal interac

Crystal Ascension- Llewellyn Publications
This book teaches readers how to use the mineral kingdom to gently trigger the sleeping souls to release evergies into conscious expression through colour, sound and meditation.

Other Titles from
Soul Asylum Poetry and Publishing

Whispering Souls – An Anthology of
Soul Asylum Poetry
ISBN 978-09780087-1-0

Wandering Through Paradise
S.D. McDaniel
ISBN 0-9780087-3-1

A Bountiful Adventure
Charles David Lawton
ISBN 0-9780087-4-X

Cajun Moon - A Journey Through Life
Kenneth W. Cowle
ISBN 141207596-3

The Enchanted Doorway
Kathleen Zvetkoff
ISBN 978-0-9781338-4-9

Fairy Tales & Mermaids
Marne Sayre
ISBN 0-9780087-5-8

Harold Can't Stand to Be Alone
Kenneth Wm. Cowle/Andrew Dorland
ISBN 0-9781338-3-8

A Lyrical Journey Through Life
Charles Henry Grocock
ISBN 1-4120-8868-2

Dear One, Where Have You Been?
Emilia N. Young
ISBN 978-0-9781338-5-6

My Poetry Garden
Dee Anne Blades
ISBN 1-4120-8725-2

Magic of the Muse
D.M. Andre
ISBN 0-9781338-2-X

Ravens Way
Kerry L Marzock
ISBN# 0-9780087-6-6

When I Grow Up
Robert Hewett Sr.
ISBN 978-0-9781338-7-0

Patches of Life
Donna Lynn Tanner
ISBN# 978-0-9781338-6-3

LaVergne, TN USA
20 July 2010

190083LV00002B/8/A